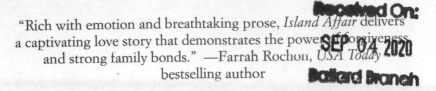

"Rich with emotion and breathtaking prose, *Island Affair* delivers a captivating love story that demonstrates the power of forgiveness and strong family bonds." —Farrah Rochon, *USA Today* bestselling author

"*Island Affair* is a perfect, romantic Caribbean escape. Much like a warm ocean breeze, Priscilla Oliveras's beautiful take on the beloved fake fiancé trope sweeps readers into a heartfelt story about two people who fall in love while helping each other overcome substantial personal obstacles. Don't miss this lovely beginning to Priscilla Oliveras's new series. Can't wait to take my next trip!" —Jamie Beck, *USA Today* bestselling author

"Priscilla Oliveras writes about families and love with warmth and charm. If you love nuanced characters and big emotions, read *Island Affair.*" —HelenKay Dimon, author of *The Secret She Keeps*

Praise for Priscilla Oliveras's Matched to Perfection series

"Moving familial relationships and splashes of Puerto Rican culture round out this splendid contemporary." —*Publishers Weekly*, STARRED REVIEW

"Oliveras takes all the right steps in this sweet romance . . . Packed with emotion, humor, and memorable characters." —*Booklist*, STARRED REVIEW

"Well written and full of fun, welcoming characters. Readers will laugh and cry and be uplifted." —*RT Book Reviews*, 4 Stars

Books by Priscilla Oliveras

His Perfect Partner
Her Perfect Affair
Their Perfect Melody
and
"Holiday Home Run" in *A Season to Celebrate*

Island Affair

Priscilla Oliveras

ZEBRA BOOKS
Kensington Publishing Corp.
www.kensingtonbooks.com

ZEBRA BOOKS are published by

Kensington Publishing Corp.
119 West 40th Street
New York, NY 10018

First Zebra Trade Printing: May 2020

ISBN-13: 978-1-4201-5017-9
ISBN-10: 1-4201-5017-0

ISBN-13: 978-1-4201-5018-6 (ebook)
ISBN-10: 1-4201-5018-9 (ebook)

10 9 8 7 6 5 4 3 2

Printed in the United States of America

Dedicated to *mi familia*,
those by blood and by choice,
whose boundless support fuels my desire
to create similar love-filled,
beautifully diverse
story worlds for readers.

Chapter 1

"Who the hell complains when their captain gives them time off? Oh, wait, you!"

"*Forced* time off," Luis Navarro grumbled. Not that his older brother gave a rip about the clarification.

Sure enough, Carlos responded with a caveman grunt as he shoveled more of their *mami*'s black beans and rice into his big mouth. Luis glared at his brother from his side of the black leather sofa squared off in front of the big-screen TV in the lounge area at the Key West airport fire station.

The only reason Luis had volunteered to bring his brother's lunch while Carlos pulled his shift with the county fire station was because Luis had expected the bonehead to commiserate with him. Not side with the damn Captain, who'd dropped his bomb earlier this morning. Right after Luis had finished his shift downtown with the city fire department.

¡Coño! Didn't anybody see that time away from the job and the distraction it offered was the last thing Luis needed right now? *Damn* wasn't nearly a strong enough word for his frustration.

"I should be so lucky that my boss made someone switch their Kelly day this month to give me a full week away from here," Carlos protested around a mouthful of food.

"Will you pipe down? I don't want people finding out about this." Luis shot a pointed look through the open archway, past the high-top table in the eating area, and into the kitchen where another firefighter stood in front of the microwave heating up his own lunch. The guy normally worked at Station 17 up the Keys, so Luis didn't know him well. No need for him to overhear Carlos and Luis's conversation and spread the news from the city up through the county fire stations.

As the microwave hummed, the spicy scent of refried beans, onions, and bell pepper from a frozen burrito heating up filled the air. Luis scowled at his brother. The fact that Carlos, the ingrate, would have been stuck eating the same processed, frozen concoction if Luis hadn't agreed to deliver their *mamá*'s freshly cooked meal upped the not-cool level of Carlos's lack of empathy.

"What's your problem?" Carlos complained.

Luis jutted his chin toward the dining-kitchen area where the sub had moved to the high-top table with his lunch. "I don't want you fanning the trash-talk flames through the houses farther up the Overseas Highway."

Carlos grunted again, though he reined in his caveman behavior by wiping his mouth with a paper towel instead of the back of his hand. "You think no one's yammering about this already?"

Luis frowned.

"Right," Carlos scoffed. "I guarantee you Soto's been blabbing about what went down. You know him. Soto likes to kiss ass, trying to weasel his way into a Driver Engineer spot. Hell, I'd be surprised if he's not telling people he and the Captain came up with the idea to swap your Kelly days. *Ese tipo siempre está hablando mierda.*"

Luis huffed a pissed-off breath. Carlos was right. Soto *was* always talking shit. Especially if it made him look better than someone else.

No doubt the little prick was spinning some tale about him being such a team player that he actually offered to switch his extra day off this month. 'Cuz he cared about helping his fellow firefighter decompress, "get his head on straight," as the Captain referred to it, after the accident Luis had worked several weeks ago.

An accident that was far too similar to and equally as senseless as the one that had altered Luis's life six years ago.

The idea of Soto using Luis's situation to paint himself in a good-guy color when the prick was anything but a team player at the station grated on Luis's already-stressed nerves.

His ire rising, Luis plopped back against the sofa cushion. He plunked his scruffy workbooks on the scarred wooden coffee table beside his brother's, tugging on his jeans leg to adjust himself. This damn situation kept getting rosier and rosier.

Thankfully it was a quiet day at Key West's small airport. A United flight had landed about fifteen minutes ago without incident. Another firefighter had ridden out to notch one of the five daily runway inspections, while another sat in the Watch Room listening to the control tower over the radio and keeping an eye on the runway. Carlos and the new guy rounded out the team of four manning this shift.

So far, Luis's visit hadn't panned out like he had anticipated. On top of Carlos brushing off the Captain's edict, the ungrateful jerk had barely mumbled his thanks when Luis showed up to deliver the glass container from their mom. Even though it meant Luis retracing his route this morning to make the ten-mile drive back down to Key West from Big Coppitt.

After his shift, he'd swung by his parents' house for the obligatory bi-weekly visual check-in, which under no uncertain circumstance could be lumped in with their weekly *familia* dinner. Luis had planned to make his morning visit short but sweet. Long enough to appease Mami's need to keep visual tabs on her kids, despite the fact that all four of them were adults.

Ever the dutiful son, he'd reached Big Coppitt Key and passed the turn to his house on Emerald Drive, where solitude and his boat, *Fired Up*, awaited in the canal out back. Instead, he made the next left onto Diamond Drive, heading to his childhood home. Praying he'd be in and out before news of his forced time off reached his parents.

The last place Luis wanted to be was sitting in his *mami*'s kitchen, her henpecking him for details about what was new in his life. Not that he ever had anything special to report or that he'd want to keep secret. Except for today.

His *mami* possessed a something's-wrong radar the likes of which the US government would kill to possess. If—more like when—she got wind that his captain had felt compelled to sideline him, her worry gene would kick into overdrive.

Even now, safe from her watchful eyes, Luis cringed at the thought. Few things were more intense than a Cuban *mami* hovering over her offspring, hell-bent on making things better for them. Whether they wanted her help or not. Case in point, the multiple ways she consistently worked in a plea for him to make true peace with his little brother, Enrique.

No matter how many candles his *mami* lit after mass at St. Mary's, praying for her middle and youngest sons to reach an understanding. That wasn't going to happen. There were some things a man couldn't get past. Not Luis anyway.

This morning, despite the ants-in-his pants sensation that had him as jittery as a rookie on his first call, Luis had tried to play things off, reassuring her with a casual, "*Estoy bien*," when she asked how he was doing.

One look at her arched brow, right fist planted on her plump hip, and he knew she wasn't buying his "I'm fine" routine. He'd realized right then and there, he needed to get out of her kitchen, outside her radar range, ASAP. Or he risked her interrogation.

Hell, he was too ramped up to discuss the reasons and potential ramifications of the Captain's decision.

Too frustrated.

Too . . .

The word *scared* filtered through Luis's head like the devil had perched on his shoulder and whispered in his ear. Luis shook the evil antagonist off, ignoring the obnoxious voice and turning his ire on his brother.

"*Coño, 'mano*, the only reason I volunteered to bring your sorry-butt lunch was 'cuz I thought you'd side with me. Not Turner. You can't possibly think the Captain's right!" Luis glared at Carlos, who stabbed a piece of *amarillo* with his fork, then shoved the sweet plantain in his mouth. "Would you quit stuffing your pie hole for a minute and help me figure out how to change Turner's mind?"

"Maybe," Carlos mumbled around his food. "I think—"

A Tone Out rang through the speakers, interrupting Carlos. The series of low- and high-pitched sounds signaling an emergency, distinct for each firehouse in the county and city, alerted those on duty in seconds which station should be on the move. Within a couple notes of the Tone Out, the firefighters were either continuing about their business, like Carlos and the others here, or racing for their vehicle.

The walkie-talkie hooked to Carlos's belt squawked a message from Dispatch relaying information from a 911 call. The rescue unit from Stock Island, the key located immediately before the entrance to Key West, was needed at a residence where someone was experiencing chest pain. Knowing how the Battalion Commander over there ran his station, Luis figured the truck would also head out in support of the ambulance.

Dispatch quieted down, but an uncomfortable sense of dread lingered over Luis. As it had after every Tone Out that had sounded over the past few weeks. Especially when the call from Dispatch involved a car accident. Just like—

Tension seized his chest. The knot in his gut, the need to lash out at someone, something, had him jittery and on edge. He clenched his jaw, burying the unwanted responses. This would pass. It always did. It had to.

Running a hand down his face, Luis wiped the sheen of sweat off his brow. A check of his watch told him he should get out of the way here. Carlos and the other three men would need to start their daily medical and fire training as well as the extra duties required by the FAA since they were located at the airport. Luis wasn't getting any sympathy over the unfairness of his current dilemma anyway.

"You know what? Forget I said anything," he grumbled. "I don't know why I thought you'd understand."

Lifting his feet off the coffee table, Luis pushed up to a stand. The weight of frustration pressed down on him, squashing his anger, leaving him irritatingly tired. Tired of people telling him how to cope. Tired of hearing that he should seek professional help or he'd never move on.

He didn't need to sit down with a grief counselor. Forget having another chat with the fire department's chaplain. The best therapy for him involved pulling shifts at the station. Losing himself in the rhythm of the day-to-day required duties and responsibilities. Fueling his body with the occasional adrenaline rush.

Carlos should understand. The adrenaline was a big part of what drew them all to the job. That whoosh of pulse-jumping excitement when you pealed out of the station, ready to help someone in need.

"*Oye*, come on. Don't leave all pissed off." Carlos set the glass container on the table as he stood. "I'm just saying, maybe some time out on your boat will do the trick. A little sun, fresh ocean air, dropping a line in the water. Yeah, that's it! Go catch some fresh fish for us." Carlos's lips spread in a silly grin, his straight teeth a white flash against his deeply tanned face.

Luis gave his brother the finger on his way through the eat-in kitchen, heading toward the front entrance. Carlos followed, their boot heels thumping on the linoleum floor.

The other firefighter waved at Luis but didn't look away from the baseball game on the small TV mounted on the wall above the table.

"Take the *Fired Up* out past the reef on the Atlantic. Troll for some mahi and bring home dinner," Carlos persisted.

"I hope you get indigestion from wolfing down Mami's food so damn fast," Luis said over his shoulder as he pushed open the main door. Hot, humid air blasted him in the face. Early May and already the intense summer sun beat down, threatening to bake tourists and locals alike.

"Bite your tongue," Carlos complained.

"Bite me!"

His brother barked out a laugh and jabbed Luis on the shoulder with a sharp punch. "Ohh, that mouth of yours. What would Mami say if she knew her quiet, saintly son talked like that."

"Whatever." Luis dodged Carlos's second jab and stepped onto the landing. His brother followed him outside, but while Luis continued to the top of the concrete stairs leading to the parking area below the fire station, Carlos stayed behind.

"Hey, I know this isn't what you want!" he called out. "*Pero...*"

Halfway down the stairs, Luis paused. "But what?"

He turned to find Carlos still on the landing, one hand wedged between the frame and the door so it wouldn't close all the way while allowing them a bit of privacy.

They squinted at each other for a few heavy seconds. Luis watched his older brother weighing his words. Carlos's jaw muscles worked as he chewed on whatever advice he contemplated offering. Advice Luis probably wouldn't want to take. His brother's easy grin from moments ago had been wiped away by the serious expression now blanketing his face. He stared back at Luis with the same pursed-lips scowl he used when his young sons misbehaved in a way that might cause harm.

"But maybe it's time you took a step back from helping everyone else and . . . and thought about helping yourself."

Across the tiny parking lot, on the other side of the chain-link security fence separating the public area from the runway and tarmac, the prop plane that shuttled tourists to the Dry Tortugas for snorkeling trips cranked its engine. The loud, sputtering noise mimicked the discord pounding through Luis's chest.

"There's no need to. I'm fine," he assured his brother. A refrain Luis had been repeating for years now. Whatever good it did. "I wish everyone else would get that through their heads."

To Luis's surprise, Carlos muttered an oath and moved to the top step. The fire station door clicked shut behind him. "Look, I get that you're pissed about the way the Captain handled things. But you've been simmering like Mami's old pressure cooker off and on for a while. That call a few weeks ago made it worse. I'm not saying you gotta fix things with Enrique, but—"

"Don't go there," Luis warned, an angry edge in his voice.

Carlos held up a hand, stalling Luis's argument. "I'm not. That's between you two. I *am* saying, you were dealt a raw deal back then. Sure, we handle things our own way. The thing is, as much as you'd like to think so, you can't save everyone. But shit, you're not even trying to save yourself."

His brother's plea slammed into Luis like a battering ram to the chest. It caught him by surprise, but not enough to shake his resolve.

"That's because I don't need saving."

He simply needed to keep his mind busy, distracted. That's what kept unwanted memories and thoughts at bay.

Carlos let out an exasperated huff as he rolled his eyes. "You've got a week off, use it to figure out how you can get out of your rut.

Hell, surprise us all by shaking things up a little. It'll do you good, my saintly brother."

Hands on his hips, Luis squinted up at Carlos, shocked by his unexpected, unsolicited advice.

Rut? What the hell?

"I have no idea where this unnecessary pep talk is coming from. Like I said, I'm fi—"

"Fine. Yeah, I heard you," Carlos interrupted. "I've been hearing you for years now. I'm just . . ."

Raising an arm to wave off his brother, Luis hurried down the last few stairs. "Okay, okay! I'm off to 'shake things up.' I'll catch you later. Don't pull a muscle climbing into your truck to inspect those runways. I know how demanding that can be on your old-man body!"

"Bite me!" Carlos yelled back, his typical laughter back in his voice. Seconds later, Luis heard the station door slam shut.

Chuckling at his brother's goodbye, he pulled his Ray-Bans from his T-shirt collar and slipped them on. He crossed the shaded area underneath the fire station to his dark blue Ford F-150 King Ranch pickup, parked in a spot next to the south end of the airport near the baggage claim area.

Shake things up. Get out of your rut.

Carlos's words taunted Luis with their infantile "I dare you" undertone. He blew out an irritated breath, then pushed the conversation aside when his attention was drawn to a group of rowdy college-aged kids piling into a taxi van nearby. Voices raised, they excitedly discussed barhopping plans while snapping selfies with their cell phones. Behind them, two middle-aged couples dressed in shorts and matching tropical button-ups awaited the next available taxi.

Luis fished his keys out of his front jeans pocket and watched passengers streaming out of the building. Some wearily dragging rolling suitcases. Most clutching cameras, island maps, sun hats, or some type of beach paraphernalia, their expressions bright with expectation.

So many people scrimped and saved for ages dreaming of visiting his hometown. They traveled for miles, vacationed for days, brought money to local businesses, then left. Poor souls.

He remained among the lucky ones who called Key West home. Always had. Always would. A Conch through and through.

The highs and lows of his life had taken place here, or somewhere within the stretch of Keys linked by the Overseas Highway. One of those lows, and the difficult aftermath it caused, had nearly pushed him to leave. Take a better-paying job at a firehouse on the mainland.

But no. His *familia* was here, had been for three generations. Even Enrique, the younger brother he now kept at a slight distance but would never shut out. *Familia* was *familia*. Good, bad, or indifferent. Their parents had tried to instill that loyalty in them. Unlike Enrique, if there was one thing Luis took seriously, it was his responsibilities.

Luis reached his truck at the same time a beat-up beach cruiser sedan pulled out of the passenger pickup lane. Its engine revved, then backfired. The shotgun sound startled Luis, along with several passengers who ducked for cover. His keys slid from his fingers, clanking onto the asphalt near the rear driver's side tire.

He bent down to pick them up, more of his brother's words echoing in his head. *It's time you took a step back from helping everyone else.*

Screw that. Helping was in Luis's DNA. It's what led him to graduate high school having already earned his EMT certification so he could immediately enroll in fire college in Ocala. Then straight onto a shift with the city.

No, what he needed was to find a way to kill the next seven days. If not, he'd go out of his mind, reliving the accident his truck had responded to several weeks ago. Consumed by the painful memories of another grim car crash the recent one had unearthed.

"What do you mean you're not coming? You promised!"

A woman's harried voice grew louder, her footsteps crunching in the gravel edging the airport sidewalk and the fire station parking lot. Crouched down behind his King Ranch pickup, Luis spotted a dainty pair of gold sandals and orange-painted toenails standing in front of his vehicle.

"Ric, you were supposed to be arriving thirty minutes from now." Several beats passed, punctuated by one sandaled foot tap-tap-tapping on the gravel. "Unbelievable. You can't possibly leave me stranded like this. My parents are expecting both of us, and you know things have been tough for my mother. I just don't see how you could . . . uh-uh, this has been on our calendars for . . . you gave your word, that's why I'm upset. How could you do this?"

The mounting agitation punctuating the end of the woman's question snagged Luis's attention, even if her apparent distress already hadn't. He moved to stand, let her know the privacy she'd probably sought by stepping away from the other passengers hadn't been achieved. His left knee creaked in protest, and he put a hand on his bumper for support.

Blond head ducked down, cell phone pressed to one ear and a finger plugging the other, the woman faced the building, her back to Luis. A pale peach tube dress draped her slim figure. Cinched at her waist, the material skimmed her slender hips, falling to play peekaboo with a set of shapely calves.

"I was counting on you this week. I've already admitted how uneasy it can be for me spending time with my family. They're expecting . . . I'm not prepared to do this without . . . because you promised, that's why."

Whatever she heard on the other end of the line apparently didn't make her happy. She shook her head vigorously, blond waves swaying along the top of her pale shoulders. Hopefully she'd packed plenty of sunscreen. If not, her fair skin would burn under the intense Key West sun.

Luis edged closer to the front of his truck, intent on getting her attention, stop her from inadvertently revealing more personal information. Maybe offer her some assistance or local information if needed.

"Save the excuses. They don't matter. This trip is supposed to help boost my mom's morale after her chemo. Not cause more stress. You can't . . . No, I just should have known better than to count on you," she told whoever it was who seemed to have stood her up. "Whatever, Ric! We're done! *¡Vete pa'l carajo!*"

She jabbed her thumb at the tiny screen to disconnect the call, frustration dripping from her throaty groan.

Surprised by the blunt "go to hell" spoken in flawless Spanish, Luis was caught off guard when the woman spun on her heel to face him.

"Oh!" she gasped, eyes wide as she stumbled back a couple steps.

"I didn't mean to scare you." He held up his hands, palms facing her to signal he meant no harm. "I was getting in my vehicle but couldn't help noticing your distress. You okay?"

Hands pressed to her chest, the woman bit her full lower lip and nodded. The worry pinching her brow and darkening her deep ocean-water-colored eyes told him differently. Her gaze dropped to the KWFD emblem on his gray T-shirt before coming back up to meet his. Straightening her shoulders, she dragged her rolling bag in between them, like the silver hard-sided suitcase was a buffer offering protection.

Not that she needed protection from him.

"My name's Luis. Luis Navarro. I'm with the Key West Fire Department." He held out his right hand to shake at the same time he jerked his left thumb over his shoulder at the elevated building behind him. "I was just visiting my brother, a firefighter with the county, here at the airport."

The woman leaned to the side and rose up on her toes. Chin jutting up in the air, she craned her slender neck to look over his shoulder in the direction he pointed. Her oversized reddish-brown leather tote slid down her arm until its strap snagged in the crook of her elbow.

"Fire department, huh?" she murmured.

"Yeah, with the city. Finished my shift this morning; now I'm off for a few days." Whether he wanted to be or not.

She lowered back onto her heels, eyeing him with guarded interest. One corner of her mouth hitched in a cute little half frown as she seemed to weigh her options.

Finally, she clasped his hand with her own. Strong, slender fingers wrapped around his in a firm shake. Her smooth palm nestled against his, cool and soft, and Luis found himself loath to let go.

"Hello, Luis Navarro, local firefighter. I'm Sara Vance, tourist."

"Nice to meet you, Sara Vance, tourist."

His teasing response earned him a husky chuckle paired with a full-blown grin that rounded Sara's cheeks and sucker-punched him in the gut. She slid her hand from his to heft her big purse back onto her shoulder.

"Wow, talk about impressive service. I haven't even called nine-one-one and a rescue squad has arrived. Not that I need saving or anything. Because I don't." Her confidence nearly convinced him, but he caught the flash of worry washing over her face before it whisked away like a tiny wave on the beach's shore.

"You sure about that?" he asked.

"Um, yeah. I just need to, uh . . ." The humid breeze blew her blond tresses against her cheek, and she tucked them behind her ear with a crooked finger. "Reevaluate a few things, I guess. Yeah, that's all."

Her voice trailed off uncertainly.

Luis cocked his head, thinking about the conversation she'd just had with some guy who, by all indications, seemed like an absolute loser if he was dumb enough to leave her high and dry in the Keys.

Sara glanced down at the phone clutched in her left fist. Her short, manicured nails, painted the same orange as her toes, were a stark contrast to the shiny black case. The name "Ric" flashed across the screen, signaling an incoming call. Lips pinched with anger, she pressed the side button to ignore the call, then dropped her cell in her shoulder bag.

Fascinated by her resolve to jettison this Ric guy when doing so seemed to put her in some kind of pickle, Luis waited for her next move.

Chin tucked into her chest, she rubbed at her forehead, as if the reevaluating she mentioned caused her pain.

When several moments ticked by without a word from her, he stepped backward toward his truck, his helping-hand instinct telling him to do the opposite. "Well then, if you're all good, I'll head out."

He turned away, craning his neck to catch one last glimpse of her slender figure over his shoulder. She gazed down at the gravel scattered at their feet, her brow puckered, her bottom lip caught between her teeth once again. Far too often he'd seen a similar look of devastation on a person's face when he responded to a call. Loss, uncertainty. Their mind scrambling to make sense of the situation.

"Good luck and welcome to the island," he called to her.

The soft click of his automatic door lock made her flinch. Her chin shot up.

"Wait!" Indecision and desperation swam in the depths of Sara's blue-green eyes. "I'm not. Not good, I mean. Actually, I'm more like..." Her voice drifted off as she jabbed her fingers through her hair in obvious frustration. "More like in a mess, actually."

She winced as if the admission hurt.

Intrigued, Luis lifted his sunglasses to the top of his head, meeting her gaze.

Sara swallowed, took another deep breath, then squared her shoulders, like a rookie set to answer her first alarm. "Everything's a wreck, and I'm about to disappoint my parents. Again. If your offer is serious, I could really use your help."

And just like that, Luis knew his first day of forced time off was definitely about to get interesting and maybe help him "shake things up."

Chapter 2

Sara Vance watched the firefighter's warm brown eyes closely. Hoping with all things good and right in the world—the likes of which the self-centered jerk Ricardo Montez was *not*—that she'd made the right move by blurting out her SOS.

Her sorority sisters would be throwing up red caution flags. Well, except for Wendy. She'd probably say it's about time Sara tried something wild and crazy. A column under which this idea definitely fell.

But right now, the clock on her parents' arrival was ticking. When it came to options, Luis Navarro might be her only viable one. She certainly couldn't think of anything else.

Her family was already in the air, somewhere between Phoenix and Key West. If she didn't find some way to pull herself out of the pit of quicksand she'd inadvertently created, before everyone else landed, this seven-day vacation with her parents, siblings, and their spouses was doomed before it even started. She refused to be the unwanted damper on the celebration of her mother's recent cancer-free diagnosis. Especially after her dad's rare edict demanding that they all clear their schedules and not cause any fuss.

"What's going on?" Luis asked. "You need a ride? Suggestions on a place to stay?"

Oh, if only it were that simple of a problem. "Probably the first, unless I take a cab. Got the second one covered. It's a little more involved than that."

Much more involved.

She speared a hand through her hair, despair threatening to override her nervousness. Along with her common sense.

Would Luis say yes to her outlandish idea? Did she really want him to?

Yet the alternative was to disappoint her mother, when the oncologist had ordered her to remove all stressors. Finding out that Sara may have fudged a little about how serious she and Ric had gotten wouldn't go over very well. Not at all.

Which was why Sara needed Luis to agree with her request. For her mother's peace of mind. As much as her own.

Cuidado con lo que pides.

Mamá Alicia's voice whispered in Sara's ear, as if her beloved nanny stood behind her, reminding Sara to be careful what she wished for. Mamá Alicia had always known the right answer, delivered in a mix of Spanish and English to ensure Sara learned both languages. She'd always given the best advice. Usually over hot chocolate and homemade *churros*.

Sara pictured the diminutive woman who'd once been a tiny but influential force in Sara's life. Jet-black hair in a tight bun high on her head, floral apron tied around her thin waist, stern yet compassionate expression as she wagged a finger and spouted sage counsel. Or a needed reprimand. No doubt Mamá Alicia stared down from heaven now doing the exact same thing.

"So, when you say everything's a mess, define *everything* for me," Luis said, pocketing his keys as he strolled toward her.

Crossing his arms, he leaned back against the shiny silver front bumper of what Sara could only think of as a he-man behemoth of a truck.

Scanning the guy's muscular biceps, broad shoulders, and wide chest, gloriously displayed thanks to the tight gray KWFD tee hugging his upper body, Sara figured the supersize-tired vehicle fit the man. All six foot plus of the raw power and masculinity he embodied should have been intimidating. Only, when she gazed into his friendly dark brown eyes she couldn't resist believing the open honesty softening the serious expression on his tanned face.

"You want the short or the long version?" she asked.

His lips twitched like they wanted to crack a smile. "I'm in no hurry."

Too bad she couldn't say the same.

"Oh-kay then." Clasping her hands to keep them from fidgeting, she rested them on her suitcase's extended handle. This pitch had to be as convincing as the one she'd given when she nabbed the initial sponsor for her lifestyles blog. "I'm the first of my family members to arrive for our celebratory vacation. My parents, two older siblings, and their spouses should be landing in a few hours. Only, they're expecting to meet me at our Airbnb with my boyfriend. Or, um, potential fiancé."

"Potential?"

"Not really," she rushed on, worried she might be botching things before they even got started. "But my mother may have been *slightly* led to think otherwise . . . by me." Luis's raised-brow surprise had her quickly adding, "Under duress. And with good intentions."

A low whistle blew through Luis's lips, doing nothing to assuage her guilt over not setting her mother straight when she had leapfrogged from Sara's *would it be okay for me to bring someone?* to her own *Sara's finally serious about settling down* interpretation.

Sara's therapist had had a field day with that one. It was classic approval-seeking behavior. Sara knew it. Only, she hadn't stopped it from happening.

"And this boyfriend-fiancé would be the Ric guy you were talking to when I walked up?" Luis asked.

"Yes."

"The same dude who, if I heard correctly, isn't planning to show."

"The one and only." Irritation hardened Sara's tone.

Luis bobbed his head slowly. The corners of his mouth tilted down in a frown at the same time a deep V wedged itself between his dark brows. "Sounds like he deserved more than the 'go to hell' you gave him."

"You heard that?"

An embarrassed blush heated Sara's cheeks at Luis's, "Sure did."

"Here's the thing," she explained, trying to lay the groundwork for her request. "No one in my family has met Ric. Or seen a picture of him. They all live back home in Phoenix. I'm the one who flew the coop, once I graduated university. Now I'm based out of New York. Ric and I met last December when I was in Miami for business, and we've been sort of dating long-distance since then. This trip was supposed to be his introduction to my family."

Along with his being a buffer for her if her mother or sister's pushy personalities risked setting off any of Sara's disorder triggers.

She paused, letting the information she'd shared sink in. Luis scratched the light scruff on his left cheek. His hand slid around to rub the back of his neck, eyes narrowed as if he were contemplating her story. Eventually he folded his arms again and leaned against his truck. All with only a mumbled *humph* as his response.

Apparently, he was the living, breathing version of the strong and silent type. That could actually work in their favor. *If* he agreed to her admittedly bizarre plan.

Uncomfortable, Sara toed the gray chunks of gravel with her right foot as she continued. "My family's . . . different from me. High achievers. Type A, to the extreme. All successful doctors busy saving lives. While I . . . I'm . . ."

Her ability to form words failed her as her old nemesis self-doubt poked its head out of the dark hole where she doggedly tried to keep it buried. Its beady eyes bore into her psyche like a mangy prairie dog refusing to stay underground.

Luis's dark gaze slowly traveled from her head, down to her toes, and back up again. Heat spread through her as if he'd physically touched her.

She was used to people watching her, taking pictures at conferences and speaking engagements. Some were looking to find fault. Plenty others were awed. In her line of work, she invited the interest. The more likes and shares and followers, the better.

And yet, with Luis, his perusal felt different. Personal.

Her request would make it even more so.

"While you, what?"

His deep, warm voice rumbled over her. It reminded Sara of lazy mornings snuggling in bed after a night that left the sheets tangled and bodies sated.

She shivered at the seductive image. Then quickly reminded herself she had no business entertaining such thoughts. Not when she was about to make him what she hoped to consider a business proposition.

Well, crap. *Proposition* wasn't quite the word she wanted to use. It sounded suggestive. Too lurid. Too—

Doubts screamed like banshees in her ears. Pressing a hand to her forehead, Sara squeezed her eyes shut, grasping for one of the tools she had learned in therapy when her mind threatened to spin out of control. Positives. Think about the positive angles here.

She ran a successful small business. Hired people for short-term contracts all the time. Granted, they were typically photographers or stylists, but the role of a fake boyfriend could potentially be considered along the same lines as an extra in a photo shoot. Couldn't it?

Oh my god, what the hell was she thinking?

"Sara, how are you different from your family?"

Luis's soft question broke into her mental downward spiral. The kind of spiral that had gotten her into trouble in the past.

Lowering her arm, she peeked at him through her lashes.

He'd crossed his jeans-clad legs and relaxed against his truck's front bumper. One dusty black work boot rested heel to toe on top of the other. A man with time on his hands, if what he'd said earlier was true.

In spite of her undoubtedly odd behavior, his whole demeanor remained calm, patient. It vibrated off him, weirdly quieting her misgivings.

"How am I different?" she repeated his question, keeping the *let me count the ways* to herself when he nodded.

For someone who projected confidence and poise to those who followed her career, it was uncanny how easily talk of her family could suck those traits right out of her. It didn't, however, mean she couldn't fake them when needed. She'd had plenty of practice with that over the years.

Tossing her head so the humid breeze would comb her hair out of her eyes, Sara answered, "Let's just say, unlike my family, the closest I ever came to being a doctor was the Halloween I dressed up as a sexy physician for a sorority social my sophomore year at Arizona State."

After a stunned second, Luis threw back his head and laughed. The deep, throaty sound startled a white and gray pigeon pecking the ground nearby. The bird flew off, wings flapping as it soared over the cream stucco building.

A nervous giggle pushed up Sara's throat. She pressed her fingers to her mouth as if that would stop the awkward sound from escaping. Luis's laughter slowed to a deep chuckle. His dark eyes sparked with amusement. The crow's-feet crinkling their corners merely added to his rugged charm.

"I'm sorry." He knuckled the moisture from one of his eyes. "Really. I'm not laughing at you. I just did not expect you to say that."

"Believe me, my highly respectable parents, one of whom is Chief Pediatric Surgeon on medical leave and the other Chief Cardiothoracic Surgeon, both at Phoenix General, did not find the pictures too amusing."

Luis tucked his thumbs in his front pockets, one dark brow quirked at an angle she found oh, so sexy. "I'm betting you looked pretty hot in that outfit, though."

"Damn straight. It won me best dressed at the party."

His answering chuckle loosened the knot of stress tightening her chest. If all else failed, she could thank Luis for the momentary distraction that had quieted the negativity in her head.

Angling her body to the side, she stared off in the distance, past the parking garage in front of the tiny airport. Across an expansive grassy area, a small redbrick fortress lush with vegetation sat on the edge of the main road that butted up against the open ocean. A sailboat floated on the water, a lone figure standing near the mast. The white sail billowed in the breeze as the ocean wind pushed the boat farther away.

The idea of sailing off into the sunset, not facing her parents'... really, her mom's... disappointment and guilt held intense appeal. She was so tired of chasing her mother's approval. Angry at the unhealthy decisions that chase had led her to make. And yet, the long-ing for that approval remained. Needing that validation was what had first driven her to start—

No!

Shaking her head, Sara halted thoughts of her disorder and the circumstances that led her to think those decisions were the an-swer. They no longer held sway over her. Sure, she may have back-slid a little while her mom was going through chemo. Fear of losing her, of never having another chance to make her proud, had trig-gered the beginnings of a spiral. But no one other than Sara's ther-apist knew about the slipup. She planned to keep it that way.

"So, your medically-inclined family is about to descend and your boyfriend—"

"*Ex*-boyfriend," she emphasized, swiveling her head to face Luis again.

He met her gaze, his features set in that serious, calm expression she was coming to associate with him.

"Your *ex*-boyfriend"—he added the same emphasis she had— "is a no-show for the fun. Not sure I'm seeing the gravity of the sit-uation. Sounds like the guy needed to be cut loose anyway."

"That he did. Only, I'd been hoping he'd stick around until after this trip to appease my family. Assist with covering up a minor lie of omission I may, or may not, have slipped my mom."

The sting of guilt had Sara making a quick sign of the cross. Her practice of the faith Mamá Alicia had instilled in her, another area that set her apart in the Vance scientifically minded household.

"The plot thickens," Luis mused. "Tell me, are we still on the short version of your story, or have we moved into the longer one?"

Sara shot him a playful *are you kidding me?* glare.

The grin he flashed transformed his angular face from ruggedly handsome to boyishly charming.

Oooh, he was dangerous, this one. Far more attractive and ap-pealing than she should be getting involved with right now. What she had in mind was temporary. A few days. Maybe a week, tops, if they didn't pretend he had to leave early on business.

If anything, this mess with Ric was a sign she should sideline her dating life and focus on her career. A big change was around the corner if she could get everything to fall into place. And she would.

First, she needed to get through this week, without upsetting her mother, which would annoy Sara's older sister, inevitably disappointing her father, and basically ruining everyone's vacation. Making Sara feel like persona non grata within her family. Again.

Off to her right, a large passenger airplane rumbled down the runway, a glaring reminder that she had less than three hours to figure something out.

The ticking clock forced her hand, precipitating her bold plan.

"Long story short. Or longer," she said, once the plane had lifted off and the jet engine noise faded. "In my family's eyes I've never really been thought of as capable of living up to the Vance potential. Things that came easily to my siblings were harder for me, academically speaking. In my mother's words, sometimes expectations have to be lowered. You know, to avoid disillusion."

She waited for the telltale disquiet to flare. The burning deep in her belly that usually spurred panic clawing at her chest, sucking the breath out of her. Pushing her to make those bad decisions.

Only, the burning didn't appear. A dull ache pressed on her heart. Painful, but manageable. She sucked in a cleansing breath like she'd been taught. Finally able to subdue the trigger.

It had taken her a long time to reach a place where she could talk, even think, about the memories and behaviors that had originally spawned her symptoms without fearing the unhealthy repercussions she brought on herself. Kudos to her therapists, and Sara's own hard work, for her ability to speak so frankly with Luis now.

"That's gotta hurt," he said. "I mean, no kid, even an adult one, gets feel-good vibes from a loved one who's busy drawing attention to their shortcomings rather than their talents."

She nodded.

Luis rolled his lips together, compassion evident in his gentle expression.

"They don't mean it in a hateful way," Sara explained, knowing she wasn't supposed to make excuses for others, but also aware of her own role in their messed-up family dynamics. "I know my family loves me. They just don't 'get' me and what I do. Happens with a lot of people." Elbows bent, she spread her palms up and gave a self-deprecating shrug. "I mean, I'm not a physician, but I'm supporting myself with a successful small business. One I'm working on expanding in the near future. So, it's all good."

"What exactly is this non-potential-reaching career of yours?"

"I'm a social media influencer."

A confused frown wedged Luis's brows together. His head tilted like he was trying to make sense of something, and she practically heard his unspoken *huh?*

"I have a fashion, beauty, and lifestyle blog that's tied to my own YouTube channel and Instagram," she clarified. "We hit over five hundred thousand followers earlier this year."

He blinked, but his lack of recognition remained obvious.

Interesting.

Sara tucked her hair behind her ear, considering Luis in a new light.

With most people, at this point they'd start peppering her with questions, often asking for tips on taking selfies. If they followed her, there was typically a favorite post, product, or location they wanted to know more about. Of course, there were also those angling to see how her name recognition could help them in some way. She'd learned the hard way to steer clear of them.

The idea that Luis didn't fall into any of those categories added another notch in his favor. A small measure of relief for her nervous qualms over the request she sought.

"I guess tough-guy firefighters with monster trucks aren't really my target demographic," she admitted. "So, it's doubtful you would have seen my Insta ads or promo come across your feed."

He shook his head. "Naw, I don't have a feed. I'm not really into social media. Too much hype and oversharing."

"Great," she muttered. "You'll get along marvelously with my family then."

"Meaning."

"In their eyes, my career lacks stability." She waved a hand nonchalantly, as if their disregard didn't matter. She knew better. "They think it's time I settled down. Found a partner with a more reliable career. Preferably someone who meets with my parents' approval, who they think can take care of me. Which I don't need but does lead to my current predicament. And you."

She tipped her head toward him.

Luis squinted up at her. The strong and silent bit she'd found appealing earlier now had her anxious and uncertain. The man's even-keeled demeanor made it very difficult to tell what he thought about the gross amount of oversharing she'd practically word vomited at his feet.

Rolling her suitcase off to the side, Sara stepped closer to him, desperation pushing her to up her persuasive game. "Here's the bottom line. My invincible mom has been battling a nearly invincible foe for a while now. But she finished her chemo and was recently declared 'cancer-free.' Her doctors have ordered rest and relaxation. Two things she's not the best at doing. Ever. For some reason this health scare has made her up the pressure on me to find someone steady and reliable. Someone I would invite to a family vacation celebrating my mom's good news. Someone, maybe like—"

She broke off, her bravery suddenly failing her.

Instead, she pleaded with her eyes, her gaze locked with his. Praying the good-guy vibes Luis Navarro emitted were for real.

Over in the secure area of the airport, voices called out. Two airport employees sauntered past on the other side of the chain-link fence. Sara followed them until they moved out of sight, mainly because she was losing her nerve here.

The gravel crunched under Luis's boots, his long shadow stretching across the ground as he rose to his full height. Even at five foot nine she had to tilt her chin to meet his gaze.

"You can't possibly be thinking what I think you're thinking. Are you?" Disbelief colored his tone, stamped his angular features.

Sara stared back at him, resolute in her bid for him to say yes. "I need a pretend boyfriend for the next seven days. Maybe less if we invent some business trip you suddenly have to take. This will keep my family off my back, and allow my mom to have the relaxing, stress-free vacation she deserves and needs. The one my dad, who is never the heavy when it comes to my parents, practically threatened the rest of us to attend. At the end, they'll all fly home to their busy lives in Phoenix." She flung out her arm, emphasizing her point. "And I'll head back to New York. After a few weeks, I'll simply tell them things didn't work out with Ric and me."

Luis scrubbed a hand over his closely cropped hair, the muscles in his arm rippling with the motion. "Wow, you're actually serious."

"Yes, I am." Seriously tired of being the bane of her family's expectations.

"*No puedo creer esto,*" he murmured.

That made two of them. She was having a hard time believing she'd concocted this crazy plan herself.

Luis shook his head. She hoped more in disbelief than in rejection of her idea. "This is like something out of a movie my kid sister would watch."

Probably *The Wedding Date*. Sara had seen the rom-com multiple times. Only, her real-life version didn't involve a male escort and a huge family wedding, thank God. And she certainly wasn't counting on the Hollywood-style romantic comedy ending.

"What if we think of this more as a business transaction?" she suggested, rushing on before he could flat out reject her. "I hire local photographers and stylists all the time when I'm traveling. This could be the same. A simple contract job, and I'll pay y—"

"Eh-eh-eh!" Luis swiped a hand in the air between them, effectively stopping the flood of words pouring out of her mouth like a hose without a spigot on the end. "I have never been paid to spend time with a woman in my life. And I do *not* plan to start now."

Sara blanched, embarrassed by the crassness of her offer when he put it like that. "I'm sorry. I didn't mean to offend you."

His mouth a grim line, Luis stared at her for several heart-stopping seconds before turning to gaze out at the strip of runway visible between the fire station and airport on either side of them. The muscle in his square jaw tightened, and Sara cursed the nervousness that had made her blurt everything out so rashly.

God, she needed him to say yes.

She could not spend the next seven days feeling as if once again she'd brought worry and discord into her family circle. It was one thing to be the person who didn't fit in. The surprise baby born thirteen years later who sometimes wondered if the stork had dropped her on the wrong front porch. The child raised and mothered by a nanny because of her parents' time-consuming jobs and her siblings off at college before she even hit kindergarten. But it was quite another to be the adult child stressing her parents out because of her eating disorder. The one who, even now, after years of therapy, still couldn't seem to get her personal life on track.

She might not make it through this vacation without backsliding under the pressure of not measuring up, and that was simply not an option for her. No, she'd do whatever it took to convince Luis to say yes.

"You already mentioned that you have a few days off," she said, working to keep a measure of calm. A little less *the sky is falling* doom in her voice. "I'm not sure how many that is or if you have other plans. But, as crazy as this sounds, and I will admit that it does, I'm asking. I *have* to ask. Would you consider pretending we're a couple? Just while I'm in town."

The intense, squinty-eyed look Luis slid her way had probably caused men twice her size to cower. Not her. She didn't have the luxury of backing down.

"If you're not comfortable with me paying you for your time, how about if I make a donation to a fund the fire station supports? Or something along those lines? I know I'm asking a lot. So, I'm willing to do something in good faith as a thank-you. That's only fair."

He shook his head, and Sara's heart sank. Without thinking she grasped his forearm, anxious to reach him. "Luis, please," she whispered. "I wouldn't ask this if I wasn't desperate for your help. Please, don't say no."

Something flared in his eyes at her ragged plea. Something dark and intense. Conflicted. The muscles in his arm flexed under her fingers as he clenched his fist.

"I'm not saying no to you," he finally answered. "More like to the sane voice in my head telling me there are a hundred reasons why this is a terrible idea, and only one that makes it right."

For the first time since Ricardo had bailed on her, the sinking sensation in the pit of Sara's stomach changed course and buoyed.

"And that one reason is?" she asked, hesitant. Hopeful.

Luis covered her hand with his, sandwiching it between his callused palm and muscular forearm. Strangely, the warmth of his skin soothed her rattled nerves.

"While I may not be my *familia*'s wild child—that role is easily filled by my idiot younger brother—I understand the pressure and guilt that comes with disappointing your parents. Even when it's someone else's fault or beyond your control," he said. "You're asking for seven days, and it just so happens that's exactly how much time off I have."

Elation shot through her like the starting pistol at her last half marathon.

"Are you for real? You'll do it?" she asked, her heart racing.

He dipped his head in answer. "You need help, and I need some way to fill the empty days off ahead. Sounds like a win-win if you ask me."

Yes! He said yes!

Euphoria fireworked inside her, brightening the dark sky that had loomed over her family's vacation. Sara squeezed Luis's forearm with gratitude, a rush of thank-yous tripping off her tongue.

Mamá Alicia's voice wormed its way through Sara's head, a stern warning dampening her glee. *Cuidado con lo que pides.*

Sí, Mamá Alicia, Sara silently promised, she'd be careful what she wished for. But this was a prayer answered. No way could she be anything but thankful that she'd crossed paths with Luis Navarro.

Granted, convincing her family wasn't going to be easy. Especially given that she and Luis had so little time to learn everything they possibly could about each other.

It was no small feat. But something about her hunky, serious but sweet lifesaver told her they'd be fine.

"Okay then," she told Luis, "let's do this."

Chapter 3

Luis turned right onto South Roosevelt Boulevard to exit the airport, a little shell-shocked at his current situation.

Beside him, perched nervously on the edge of the black leather passenger seat in his truck, sat an intriguing woman he'd known less than thirty minutes. Yet he'd just agreed to lie to her parents—no, her entire family—about a make-believe relationship. A harebrained idea that could only end in a mess.

Resting his left elbow on the driver's side windowsill, he massaged his temple in a failed attempt at easing the headache threatening.

¿Qué carajo estás haciendo?

That's exactly what Carlos would ask. Part of Luis wondered the same thing. What the hell was he doing saying yes to this kind of crazy?

One lesson he'd learned firsthand, lying to your *familia*, even when you believed you had good reason, never worked out.

Ask his baby brother.

Their relationship hadn't been the same since Enrique's lie of omission.

Maybe Sara's wasn't as grave.

Yeah, right, that was lame rationalization. Who was Luis to judge what her family would think was grave or not?

Big lie or small one didn't matter. Years of Catholic school and his *mami*'s occasional smack upside the head had drummed into him the folly of even the smallest fib. Adding to the promised fires of hell, he hadn't missed Sara's quick sign of the cross when she admitted that lying to her mom in the first place is what had gotten her into this mess. If her parents were anything like his, instilling their faith in their kids from the cradle, Sara had to know this charade would blow up sooner or later. With no good to come of it.

Then again, shared faith or not, her mom and dad seemed different from his. Luis couldn't remember a time his parents had ever made him feel less than or lacking. In any way.

The fact that hers did was pretty messed up. It made her bid for an ally this week even more irresistible.

"Oh, I could get used to this view. It's so beautiful."

The awe in Sara's words mimicked her wide-eyed expression. She leaned forward to peer out the front windshield at Smathers Beach on their left. Luis pressed back against his seat so she could look out his window, too.

A few food trucks and water sports equipment rental vendors lined the road and sidewalk along the public beach. Tall palm trees held watch over the creamy sandy shore and patchwork color of towels, chairs, and blankets. Swimmers dotted the shimmering water. Some splashed out by the sandbar while others floated on tubes and rafts soaking up the sun's rays. Along the water's edge, a few couples strolled hand in hand.

"Never gets old," he answered, shooting an appreciative glance at one of his childhood playgrounds. More often now, it was an inspiring stretch during a run.

"I bet. Have you lived here long?"

"Born and raised. Only left for fire school up in Ocala."

"So, you're what they call a Conch, right?"

"Uh-huh, second generation. My *abuelos* moved here before my *papi* was born, so he was the first. Mami came as a young girl. They met in seventh grade. Started dating in high school and have been together ever since."

"How romantic." Dreamy wonder tinged her voice, a common reaction his parents' story often elicited.

"They're the real deal," Luis said, the words true in many ways when it came to his parents. "Now my older brother, Carlos, and his wife are following their example."

"And you?"

"What about me?"

"No high school sweetheart?"

"Uh, no." His sweetheart had come later, with disastrous results.

Not one to usually bare his soul, Luis drummed his thumbs uncomfortably on the steering wheel.

"Me neither. Still, I can't imagine how amazing it must have been growing up here. Oh look, someone's parasailing!" Sara ducked toward the windshield again as she tried to follow the bright yellow parachute floating high in the clear sky, a long line tying it to a boat out on the water.

Luis slowed the vehicle so she could watch a little longer before the road curved onto Bertha Street and they left Smathers behind. "If that's something you're interested in, we can stop and ask about making a reservation."

"Maybe another day." Sara settled into her seat with a sigh, adjusting her safety belt strap across her chest and bare shoulder as she did. "We have a lot to figure out and not much time before everyone arrives."

She smoothed a hand down the peachy material covering her lap, then shot him a hesitant smile. The way she switched back and forth from Nervous Nellie to friendly ease fascinated him. The nerves seemed to take hold whenever her family came up. Which didn't bode well for this little charade she'd talked him into playing. If she couldn't relax, no amount of preparation would matter. They'd blow their cover five seconds into him meeting her parents.

"How about, instead of eating at the diner, we get our food from the Sandy's counter down the street and eat at the beach?" he asked.

The location change would 100 percent relax him. Maybe it'd do the same for her.

"You don't mind?"

He glanced at Sara as he slowed the truck at the stoplight on the corner of Bertha and Flagler. "One thing you should know about me, I wouldn't offer if I didn't mean it."

She bent over to dig in the tote at her feet, her blond waves falling to cover her face. When she straightened, she held a pink ballpoint pen and a leather-bound notebook. "That's good to know. Let me start jotting info down."

"You're gonna take notes?"

"Yeah. I'm a visual and tactile learner. It took a while for my tutor and me to figure that out, but if I write something down and then read over it, I'm more apt to remember. It's the only way I made it through college." She tucked her hair behind her ear, nonplussed. Like they were discussing studying for some kind of test. Not preparing to try to pull a fast one over her family.

"How about I ask you some basic questions to get us started while you drive?" she suggested.

The pen clicked under her thumb; then she spread the notebook open on her lap. He watched her write his name at the top of the page in a neat script, following it up with a definitive line underneath.

The sane part of him that had been thinking maybe she'd reevaluate her offer over lunch and together they'd come up with a Plan B shriveled up like the potted plant his *mami* had saved off his back porch last week. He'd been ready to toss the plant in the trash, but his mom had balked. Something about it needing water, food, and conversation. Silly him, he'd thought he'd bought a fern, not a metaphor for a date.

Forget the fact that in recent years his dating life had the same mortality rate as any fern, ivy—hell, even the aloe—he brought home.

A car honked behind them, alerting Luis that the light had changed. He eased his foot from the brake to the gas pedal and turned left onto Flagler. The farther they got from the airport, the higher his reservations mounted. But he'd made a commitment.

"One small problem," Sara said, tapping the top of the pen against her chin.

"There's only one?"

Her *give me a break* glare had him chuckling. He liked the fact she felt comfortable teasing him, which made their banter more fun.

"Thinks he has a sense of humor," she mumbled, writing the words in her book.

"Hey now, don't knock my jokes. They grow on you. You'll see."

"Uh-huh, I can only hope." The playful twist of her lips softened her dry tone.

He grinned, something he found himself doing often around her. Despite their bizarre situation, Luis realized he'd laughed more with her in their short time together than with anyone else in ages.

Edging his truck around an older couple pedaling a tandem bike, he snuck another glance at Sara.

Her plump lower lip caught between her teeth, she scribbled in her notebook. Sweetly studious. The type of study partner that had a guy imagining all kinds of non-scholastic shenanigans in the library.

Yeah, there were quite a few things about Sara Vance he found appealing. And he wanted to know more.

"Any chance your middle name is Ric, or some derivative?"

"Excuse me?" Luis did a double take at her question. "Why?"

One of her slender shoulders lifted in a casual shrug. "Thankfully, I've learned to share very little about my dating life with my parents, so they don't know much about Ric. Except his name"—she counted the list on her fingers—"that he's in community development, and we met in Miami."

Luis digested the info, thinking of ways they might tweak it to suit his life. "The closer to the truth we can keep this, the better. Less chance we'll slip."

"Ooh, smart. We definitely don't want any slipping." She pointed the pen at him, nervous energy humming off her again.

"That's something else you should write down about me. I'm smart."

Her eyes narrowed, but her pink glossy lips twitched before stretching into a smile that chased away her reservations. Good. Nervous meant mistakes. Something every rookie had to learn on the job.

"Time to hit pause on your note taking. But you've already got some stellar-boyfriend-material facts about me." He flipped his blinker, signaling his intent to wait for a car pulling out of a space on White Street. Ahead on the left, Sandy's red and white awning welcomed customers.

"You know, for someone all serious and stern, it's interesting how much of a comedian you think you are."

"Serious and stern?" Was that how she saw him?

Damn, that made him sound more like his *papi* when he or his brothers or sister crossed the line. Those were not the words a guy wanted an attractive woman who snagged his interest to use when describing him. Talk about ego deflating.

"What makes you say that?" he asked, relieved he kept *the hell* out of his question.

"Oh please." Fingers splayed, Sara swished her open palm through the air from his head down to the seat as if encompassing all of him. "Don't try and tell me you have no idea about this whole Vin Diesel tough-guy vibe you've got going on."

Luis's foot nearly slipped off the brake at his surprise. "My what?"

"Hunky, muscular man of few words showing up to save the day? Classic action film superhero."

Vin Diesel?

Him?

Okay, *now* she was talking.

While the other car took its time pulling out of the parking spot, Luis considered Sara's description. "So, you think I'm hunky, huh?" He waggled his brows playfully.

She laugh-snorted and rolled her eyes. "Like you didn't already know you are."

"Yeah, well, if you ask me, this Ric guy is an idiot for giving up a week with you," he said, enjoying the pink blush that rose up her cheeks as she murmured a thank-you.

Years of driving the fire truck had Luis deftly parallel parking his vehicle. Turning toward her, he draped his left arm over the steering wheel. "If we're about to start a study session, we need sustenance. You good if I hop out and order us a couple Cuban mix sandwiches? Or do you prefer to order for yourself?"

"A Cuban mix sounds delicious. With a water, please? Here"—

she bent down to dip her hand into her purse again—"let me give you some cash."

"I got it. It's your first meal on my turf. My treat," he added when she tucked her chin as if she were about to argue.

She hesitated a beat before dropping her wallet back into her tote. "Fine. This time. But we're gonna discuss logistics moving forward. As soon as you come back with our food. I'm too hungry to argue."

"Whatever you say." Though he wouldn't be comfortable having her pay for him, especially in front of her family.

Blame it on a streak of machismo he wasn't sure he'd ever be able to completely erase. His sister complained about double standards in their culture and within the firefighting community all the time. On the job, he worked hard to be fair, understanding the importance of treating every firefighter with the same respect and value. They all pulled their weight. Off duty, if a date wanted to split the bill, he didn't mind. But outright taking care of the bill, without it being a special occasion? It went against the manners ingrained by his parents.

Leaving his truck running, Luis jogged diagonally across the street to Sandy's. As always, the popular counter location attached to a coin-operated laundromat was packed with people eating, ordering, or waiting.

"¿Oye, Luis, cómo estás, 'mano?"

Luis clasped hands and leaned in for a one-armed hug with an old high school buddy standing on the crowded sidewalk. "Hey, Franco, long time no see, brother. I'm doing good. What's new?"

"You know how it is, working hard when I'd rather be hardly working. Así es la vida en Cayo Hueso," Franco joked.

He had it right. That was life for many locals in Key West, trying to stay on the island as the cost of living rose. If you asked Luis, the juggle was worth it.

They swapped stories about work and familia, pausing when it came time for Luis to place his order.

"Eating for two?" Franco teased. "What, you lifting heavy weights or something?"

"Picking up food for me and a...a friend in town for the week." Luis eyed his truck, the cab visible over the little sports car parked in front. Sara's head was bent, probably over her notebook, her blond waves bright against the black seat leather.

"Anyone I know?"

Luis turned to find that Franco had followed his gaze and noticed Sara waiting for him. His mind froze for a blip at the potential glitch he hadn't considered.

Crap. No way they could avoid running into people who would inevitably ask about Sara if they were together.

People who knew him as Luis, not Ric. A definite problem if they bumped into another Conch while with her family. Many of the locals knew each other, and gossip flew around their tiny island faster than a speedboat racing. No doubt he'd be seen with Sara's family at some point over the next week. If someone got wind of his "relationship" with her, his family would find out in minutes.

And if they confronted him about keeping a girlfriend a secret, no way he'd lie.

Not after the raking over the beach bonfire coals he'd given his brother Enrique for lying to him.

Time to improvise and start playing Sara's game before he wound up having to deal with damage control.

"You don't know her," Luis said, stepping up to the counter to grab a handful of napkins. "She's not from here. We met while I was in Miami a while ago."

As he expected, Franco followed, his back now to the street, and Sara. "She's vacationing here with her family, and I volunteered to play tour guide while I'm off."

"There you go, always doing something nice for somebody. San Navarro at it again."

The old man behind the counter shouted Franco's name and shook a brown paper bag in their direction. Franco smacked Luis's shoulder in a good-bye, then headed off with his food.

Usually Luis would have snapped a comeback at the stupid nickname he'd picked up in high school. One good deed at a church retreat his mom had made him and his older brother attend, one nun who sang his praises as an example for the rest of the teens, and a guy couldn't outrun an annoying moniker like Saint Navarro.

Today he didn't want to. Let Franco think he was doing a friend a favor. Racking up good guy points. Anything to keep the local chatter quiet. It was pretty much the truth anyway.

Sure, Sara needed his help in a bizarre sort of way, but it kept him occupied rather than spinning his wheels at home.

Moments later, Luis climbed back into his cab. The scent of roast pork, ham, and Swiss cheese tucked inside freshly baked Cuban bread, hot from the grill press, wafted from the brown paper bag he carried.

"Smells scrumptious!" Sara took the bag from his outstretched hand so he could set two bottles of water in the center console cupholders.

"Tasting one of these was on my Key West bucket list," she added, her entire face alight with a pleasure that teased an answering delight from him. "I'll snap a photo when we get settled at a picnic table. Then swing by later to take one of Sandy's awning so I can whip up a graphic with both."

"Or you could just eat it and enjoy the good food," he suggested.

He never understood the compulsion to send someone a photograph of your plate. It's not like they could taste it. Seemed more like a, *Ha, look what I'm enjoying that you're not.*

Sara's smile dimmed.

Damn, maybe his bluntness had offended her. Remorse prickled his conscience. "I didn't mean—"

"Oh, don't worry. I'll definitely be eating my sandwich, too. That's part of the fun with my job. Having new experiences and sharing them with others. Although our arrangement is a little outside my norm, and I certainly don't plan on mentioning it on my blog." Sara closed her notebook and set their paper bag on top with a flourish. "My followers know I'm on vacation, and though I didn't say where for privacy reasons, I promised to share highlights and recommendations after. While I'm here, I've scheduled a few posts to go up and my assistant will cover the other days. That way it's only a matter of replying to comments and adding some live posts to stories. I'm compiling pics and notes for a future travel blog. Plus, I'll be doing some recon for an expansion deal that's in the works in Miami."

Luis tried to keep up with the flurry of activities she rattled off.

But for a guy whose life revolved around the fire station, occasional charted dive tours on his boat, *familia* and friends, workouts, and sleep, all her social media talk about posts and going live and commenting made his head spin. She might as well have been speaking a different language.

Give him a lazy afternoon on *Fired Up*. A cooler full of food and cold drinks. His cell off. A fishing line in the water. That all made for a great day.

"Seems like this is more of a working vacation for you," he noted, buckling his seat belt.

"Honestly, there's always something I can be doing for my business. I don't mind because I love what I do. *Although . . .*" Her dull emphasis on the word had Luis cutting a look her way as he put his truck in gear. One corner of her mouth hitched up, drawing his attention to her glossy lips. "Thanks to Ric, the vacation part of this trip is what's shaping up to be stressful."

"Speaking of Ric, or me stepping into his shoes." Luis made a U-turn to head toward White Street Pier and Higgs Beach. "I ran into a buddy of mine from high school in line. He saw you waiting for me and asked about you."

"Does that happen often?

"All the time. Island life and the close-knit local network can be a blessing, unless you're pretending to be someone else. With a different name."

"Oh no!" Sara's eyes widened with surprise, dismay swimming in their depths. "I didn't think about that."

"Yeah, me neither." Luis rolled his shoulders, pushing off his lingering misgivings over the lie now set in motion. "I hedged a bit. Said you were a friend from Miami. We'll have to be careful and stick with that if we run into any other locals. It's probably inevitable that word about us being seen together will get back to my family."

"I totally understand. If we see someone you know, I'll follow your lead. Listen—" Swiveling in her seat to face him, she placed her cool fingers on his arm below the edge of his T-shirt sleeve. Luis's skin tingled at her gentle touch.

"I know this is a lot to ask," she said. "More than a lot. That's

why I'm serious about donating to whatever nonprofit you'd prefer. Just, please, don't back out on me."

Luis kept his gaze on the road ahead as he turned onto Atlantic
Boulevard, then pulled into an empty parking space in front of the
picnic tables on the beach side of the road.

Without even looking at Sara, he could already picture the entreaty in her blue-green eyes. The earnest plea puckering her
smooth brow and blanketing her classic features. Back at the airport he hadn't been able to say no to her. Fat chance of him doing
so now. Not with her light citrusy scent teasing him. Urging him to
lean closer and drag in a deep whiff of whatever she'd spritzed on
her creamy skin.

"I'm not backing out," he assured her. "Like I said, once I give
my word, you can depend on it. On me."

He cut the truck's engine.

"Thank you." Sara's fingertips lightly brushed his biceps, the
soft caress strangely both soothing and tempting. Then she reached
down to grab her purse, and he found himself missing her touch.

"Look, I know we're both worried about keeping things straight.
Hence, my notebook." She tapped her pink pen on the edge of the
leather-bound book before dropping both items inside her bag.

"At least Franco bought the idea of me playing tour guide for
your family when he noticed you waiting. Me helping out a friend
isn't too farfetched."

"Somehow that doesn't surprise me." Her droll tone had chagrin warming his neck.

"Unfortunately, while the tour guide story might be enough to
cover things on your end," she said, back to business, "we'll have
our work cut out for us convincing my family. We really need to get
started on our meet-cute story."

"Our what?"

Pushing open the passenger door, she slid out onto the asphalt,
banging her elbow when she lost her footing as she landed. "Wow,
I didn't realize that would be such a far drop."

"Try using the running board to step down next time," he suggested. "And for the record, I don't normally *do* cute."

"*Meet*-cute, tough guy. It's a rom-com term," she explained.

Like that made any sense to him. "You know, when the hero and
heroine meet for the first time. Sparks fly. Attraction shimmers in
the air. But there's some problem getting in their way."

Hell, if you asked him, they could check all those boxes.

Each time she touched him sparks flew.

Her lush lips had him craving a sweet sample like an infatuated
teen, definitely attraction.

As for a problem, the big fat lie they were gearing up to tell
everyone certainly qualified.

But in the short time he'd spent with Sara, her engaging smile,
palpable frustration with her family, the joy on her face when she
talked about her career . . . who was he kidding? The whole package that made up Sara Vance was one he'd like to keep unwrapping
to discover what other surprises lay hidden inside.

If nothing else, spending time getting to know her sure beat
moping around his place feeling sorry for himself. Dodging memories he didn't want to face. Ignoring a truth that stung worse than
snorkeling through a school of jellyfish.

It just might knock him out of the rut Carlos had baldly accused
him of living in. Not that Luis would admit his brother was right. It
wasn't a rut, more like a slight hitch. There'd be no living with Carlos and his crowing if Luis allowed him even an inkling of an "I told
you so."

Bottom line, Sara might think he was doing her a favor. In reality, she was saving him from himself.

"Come on, Vinny D., you and I have some homework to get
done if you plan to help me save the day." With a playful wink, Sara
pushed the door closed, then traipsed through the sandy ground
toward the concrete picnic table under a nearby cabana.

Vinny D. to the rescue sounded a hell of a lot better than Saint
Navarro. Especially since Luis found himself entertaining more
than a few unsaintly thoughts when it came to Sara.

Oh, he might have reservations about this zany plan, but he
couldn't think of a single reservation about spending more time in
Sara's company.

Chapter 4

Sara pulled the supersize sandwiches from the brown paper bag and set them on the cement table. Good Lord, everything about Luis Navarro seemed extra large—his truck, his muscles, his nice-guy streak. Even the sandwiches he'd bought them for lunch.

She snuck a quick look at the handsome firefighter from under her lashes.

Luis sat across from her, patiently waiting while she opened her sandwich and smoothed out the butcher paper wrapping for a makeshift place setting. If he felt any of the same anticipation zinging inside her over their plan, he hid it well under his steely, calm façade.

Behind him, the sandy beach and wide-open ocean created an inspiring backdrop. Sunlight glistened across the water in wavy ribbons. Off to the right, an old wooden walking pier jutted out into the water, and a friendly coed sand volleyball match was in full swing nearby. Shouts of victory accompanied the smack of hands punching the ball through the air.

Luis twisted the cap to break the seal on her water bottle but didn't remove it.

"There you go," he said, setting the drink closer to her. "You good?"

When he sat back on his bench, his unwrapped sandwich dwarfed in his big hands, she realized he was making sure she was ready to enjoy her meal before he started on his own.

"You are a wonderfully considerate person, you know that?" she told him.

The serious expression she was quickly coming to know as his default morphed into a confused frown. "That's a bad thing?"

"Not at all. Simply an observation. And a compliment."

His thick shoulders rose and fell in an easygoing shrug. "Any good manners or behavior on my part stems from my parents' strict rules, and my mom's *chancleta*."

Sara chuckled as Luis mimicked the age-old threat of Hispanic *mamás* everywhere—a slipper clutched in hand, waving it in the air, ready to fling at the perpetuator of mischief if needed.

"My Mamá Alicia had a *chancla*, too," she shared. "Granted, I never experienced a *chancletazo* from her, but I was around when that slipper found its mark if one of her sons misbehaved."

Luis raised his brows and nodded as he took a bite, in obvious commiseration.

"And Mamá Alicia is?" he asked, once he'd swallowed.

"My nanny growing up. Well, more like a second mom, really."

A wistful sigh blew through Sara's lips as she recalled the woman who'd been there for pretty much every important moment. Especially the most life-changing ones.

"She was an incredible person," Sara murmured.

"Was?"

"She passed several years ago. A brain aneurysm." Sara ducked her head, blinking away the tears that still formed when she thought about that call from Pedro, Mamá Alicia's youngest son. The mental battle Sara had gone through, working to not let the subsequent grief become another trigger. Something her mother had worried about as well.

Luis's warm hand covered hers on the table, startling Sara out of her sad memories.

"It's never easy when a loved one dies. I'm sorry for your loss."

His earnest tone was a balm easing her sorrow. Quieting the rush of loss cresting through her. More than likely this was a skill or gift he relied upon to calm victims when responding to emergencies at work. Now his tender, sympathetic nature soothed her.

"I bet you're great at your job," she blurted out. "Like firefighter of the month all the time, right?"

He pulled his hand back, a grimace chasing away the kindness from his tanned face. Silly, but now that it was gone, she realized she liked the comforting weight of his hand over hers. The light brush of his thumb across her skin.

"I'm not sure my captain always agrees. What makes you think that?" he asked.

"For being such a tough guy, you've got a compassionate, protective nature. It's nice."

An embarrassed flush climbed his cheeks. His gaze shifted away, tracking a car that passed behind her.

That small vulnerability, his honest humility, made him all the more likable.

Not for the first time, Sara considered herself lucky for running into Luis Navarro. After her string of crappy dating experiences in recent years, Luis was a refreshing reminder that there were still some good fish in the proverbial sea.

Useful info for when, more like *if*, she decided to eventually dip a fishing pole in the water again. After this debacle with Ric, concentrating on work seemed like a safer bet.

On that thought, Sara picked up half of her Cuban mix and angled it against the other half to better show off the ingredients inside. Melted Swiss cheese blended with rows of dark roast pork and lighter ham. Green dill pickles and a slathering of yellow mustard added a dash of color in between the doughy white Cuban bread. Leaning away from the table, she ducked down, eyeing her food. At the same time, she reached for her cell and thumbed the screen to activate the camera app.

"You're missing out on a tasty meal," Luis said, before taking another he-man-sized bite.

Sara cut her gaze over to him, marveling at the fact that in just a few bites nearly a quarter of his sandwich was already gone.

"I'm taking my time," she answered. "The better to savor it. Unlike someone else I know."

A full-mouthed *humph* answered her.

The typical tough guy grunt had her smiling. Pleasantly surprised at the sense of ease she'd found with him.

There'd been a moment, back in his truck, when he chided her about eating her food, that had sent a trickle of unease dribbling down her spine. Just as quickly, she realized his focus was on simply enjoying the moment, not her actual lack of food consumption. There was no need to let her personal issues color his words.

Even before Ric had dropped his no-show bombshell, she'd been feeling the stress of a week with her family. Second-guessing her decision to introduce Ric to everyone. The two of them hadn't been clicking for a while. Probably because she had ignored the fact that he was more her parents' type than hers. More suitable as part of a power couple, rather than capable of making a real, honest connection with someone.

Her flight had landed in Key West with Sara waffling between dread and blind hope. Ric's no-show move had tipped the scales toward dread.

Then Luis arrived on the scene. All white knight–ish. With his monster truck and heart-palpitating hunkiness. And in spite of the charade they were preparing to play, Sara found herself enjoying his company.

Maybe it was the magic of the island air. Maybe it was this generous man who'd agreed to help her, a woman who was a total stranger. Albeit one with a public following many in her line of business worked hard to achieve.

More than likely, it was a combination of both.

Either way, the weight she'd been carrying like extra baggage she couldn't check on her flight had been chucked aside. Thanks to him.

Squinting at the image on her cell screen, Sara concentrated on snapping a good pic for her followers. She moved the camera around her sandwich, mindful of her subject, noting the details framing her shot in the blurry background. The rough, grainy concrete table edging the opaque butcher paper, a flash of dark brown and green from a baby palm tree, the corner of an orange beach towel tossed haphazardly on the sand.

Click. Adjust the angle. Click. Tap the screen to refocus. Click.

Satisfied with the mix of photos, she slid her cell into her purse, swapping it for her notebook and pen.

"How about we stick with the basics. Enough to get us by without tripping ourselves up," she said, opening the book to the page she'd marked with his name earlier. "Age, birthday, family details. Favorites. Non-negotiables."

"Hm, I like that last one."

"Non-negotiables are key." She wiggled her pen at him, emphasizing her point. "Like, scary movies? Hard pass. My stomach in knots, spending most of the time covering my eyes or burying my face in my date's shoulder because I can't look. Not my jam. You?"

"I can take or leave 'em. I'm more of a documentary or action flick viewer. Let's see, my hard pass would be . . ." Luis wiped his mouth with a paper napkin, eyes squinting at something in the distance as he considered his answer. Seconds later, his pensive frown brightened. "Got it! Karaoke. Definitely not for me."

"No way?!"

"Yes way."

"Come on, karaoke's so fun." Using her pink pen like a pseudo-mic, she pantomimed a singer. "I figured you and I'd be signing up for a duet. Maybe 'Summer Nights' from *Grease*."

The horrified expression on his rugged face was so meme worthy Sara threw back her head and laughed. Add a *WTH?* caption and it'd easily go viral.

"*Nonnegotiable.*" Luis enunciated the word clearly, his *hell no* tone softened by the laughter tilting his full lips and flashing in his dark eyes. He dipped his head toward their table. "Eat up. We have work to do."

"Fiiiine." She scrunched her nose in protest but picked up her sandwich and took a hefty bite. "Mmmmm."

Her eyelids drifted closed as the mix of spices tempered by Swiss cheese with the added tang of mustard and pickles teased her taste buds. The explosion of flavor had her mouth watering. Swallowing, she opened her eyes to sample more.

Her gaze connected with Luis's across the table. She froze, spellbound by the intensity tightening his angular features. Sara licked at a trace of mustard on her bottom lip, her pulse blipping when his heated gaze followed the motion.

A different kind of hunger, swift and unexpected, swooped deep at her core. An electric charge sizzled through her, leaving tingles of desire in its churning wake.

Suddenly a bird's squawk pierced the air. A seagull glided into their cabana to land on the end of their picnic table.

Luis blinked, breaking their silent connection. He shooed the bird away, then gathered his trash into a ball with one fist.

"Worth the wait?" he asked, indicating her sandwich.

Sara nodded, still reeling from the startling awareness arcing between them.

"Uh-huh. It's, um, delicious." Clearing her throat, she picked up her drink and worked to get her thoughts back on track. "I can see why Sandy's made Key West's Top Five Cuban Mixes list. Definitely a must-try recommendation for my followers."

"Told you so."

"Gloating is not nice. Don't make me break out my *chancleta*," she threatened.

His raspy chuckle sent a delicious shiver across her shoulders.

Dangerous.

Thrilling.

Completely inappropriate for the friendly agreement they had made.

"Okay," she said on a deep, *get your head in the game* breath. "Time to start Twenty Questions Fake Relationship Edition."

"Yay!" Luis lifted his fists in triumph, his expression alight with mock excitement. "My favorite game!"

"Wise guy," she grumbled, fighting her answering smile.

She clicked her pen with her thumb, then tossed the first barrage of questions at him.

Over an hour later, Sara had filled two pages with notes. Luis, having seen the wisdom of her ways, had decided to start his own study guide, so she'd torn a piece of paper from her book and dug out an extra pen from her purse.

In between questions and devising their story of how they'd met, Luis had finished off the last half of her Cuban mix after she cried "full." Him, volunteering to "take one for the team" to avoid letting good food go to waste. Her, failing to use that opening in their conversation to divulge her personal struggle with an eating disorder.

It wasn't necessarily something she kept secret. In recent years, her struggle with the disease had actually come up in a few interviews. The journalists had all been respectful. Each granted her request that the disorder not be the focus of an article about her business. She recognized the importance of sharing her story, how it might help others, so she didn't shy away from the topic. And yet she wasn't ready for the change that would inevitably occur if Luis knew. As it had with her family.

The pointed interest in what she ate. Or didn't eat. The covert glances at her figure checking for noticeable weight loss. Cataloging her actions. The questions. The pity. The disappointment and guilt.

Luis would only be around for a week. Less if the situation nose-dived and they had to invent a reason for "Ric" to bug out early. More proof why Luis didn't even need to know.

"We've covered quite a bit," Luis said.

"I agree. The trick is in remembering it all."

"Well"—holding his paper up at one corner, Luis waved it back and forth—"thanks to my handy dandy cheat sheet, I think I'll be okay."

"You're quite welcome."

"Now who's gloating?"

"You know I'm right, though," she singsonged.

Luis responded with a mature eyeroll that had them both grinning.

Seated under the cabana's shade, the humid ocean breeze keeping the May heat at bay, they quietly mulled over each other's answers on their respective papers.

By now she'd discovered he was the second child of four kids, with only one sister born immediately after him. He didn't admit it, but Sara sensed some kind of distance between Luis and his baby brother. When Enrique's name came up, the light that brightened Luis's mahogany eyes when he talked about his sister and older brother dulled. The smile that curved his lips, showing off his straight teeth, as he shared stories about his *mami* and *papi*, vanished.

And yet he hadn't volunteered any reason why.

Apparently, she wasn't the only one here keeping secrets.

Still, the way his face softened when he talked about his family—or *familia*, the word he often used—sent a pang of yearning through Sara's chest. Nostalgia, bittersweet and strong, filled her. The Navarro home sounded a lot like Mamá Alicia's, Sara's favorite place to hang out when her parents were out of town or hung up at the hospital.

The comfortable, homey ambiance born of shoes and backpacks scattered by the front door. The delicious scent of bell peppers, garlic, and tomatoes simmering in a pot on the stove. Voices raised in laughter, disagreement, or praise, but always tinged with love. *Familia* and friends coming and going as if the kitchen had a revolving door. One that was always open, welcoming all.

So different from the stark perfection and sterility of the Vance house.

Behind her, a group of tourists riding mopeds puttered by, drawing Sara's attention. Dressed in bathing suits and flip-flops, they were obviously more interested in catching rays than safety on the road. One driver called out to the others, motioning for them to turn onto the large fishing pier nearby. En masse, they made a right turn, moving out of her view.

When she swiveled back on her bench, she found Luis tracing a finger down his chicken scratch handwriting. His blunt fingertip stopped, as if he were committing something he'd written down to memory.

Wondering what had nabbed his interest, she leaned forward, the rough concrete digging into her elbows. He had already known she was a surprise baby for her parents. She'd dropped that info back at the airport, during her initial plea for help. But, like her, he'd made a point of keeping track of her family members' names and occupations.

Only, while he had easily answered her questions about his siblings' favorite fun-time activities—coaching his young sons' baseball team for Carlos, working her personal trainer side hustle for Anamaría, and some kind of art for Enrique—she'd drawn a blank with her brother and sister. Jonathan and Robin were so much older. They'd already been off adulting and starting their medical careers by the time she reached adolescence. Sara had never really connected with them.

"Looks like we have a mission this week. If you're up for it." Luis arched a brow in a challenge. His finger tapped whatever piece of info on his sheet had stopped him moments ago.

"I'm listening."

"By the time you board your plane to leave next Friday, let's see if we can answer this question about Robin and Jonathan, your parents, too, with something more personal than reading medical journals or fundraising for some hospital-driven charity you can't name. I mean, I know the title of your Mamá Alicia's favorite telenovela, the pan dulce she always ordered from the *panadería* even after her doctor recommended she cut back on the sweet breads. And that she made sure you learned Spanish. Though no doubt your grasp of curse words came courtesy of her boys."

"Yeah, she was not too happy about that discovery." Sara pursed her lips, remembering Mamá Alicia's threat to wash her mouth out with soap.

"The thing is, and correct me if I'm wrong." Luis placed one hand over his heart, the other splayed out toward her. "I get the idea you'd like to know a little more about your brother and sister. So you don't feel like such an outsider. Maybe this week, we can work on that for you, together. What do you say?"

Shocked by his perception, Sara fell back onto the picnic bench with a thud. In this short time, Luis had picked up on her deepseated desire to connect with her loved ones. Share meaningful conversation without feeling like everyone else talked around or over, rarely *with*, her. For them to view her more as an equal and less like someone who needed to be taken care of.

Which was why she absolutely had to walk into their rental home with a partner. Not as the baby sister who'd been dumped or duped by another loser boyfriend.

Luis's use of "we" and "together," as if the two of them were a team . . . as if she wasn't going into this potentially stressful vacation with her family alone . . . as if somehow he understood her secret need to feel a connection.

She wasn't sure what kind of mission she had expected him to suggest. But she never would have guessed this.

Tears pricked Sara's eyes. Relief, warm and comforting, seeped over her, rising to clog her throat as she stared back at him with awe and gratitude.

"Mission accepted," she answered softly.

"Yes." He hissed the word in triumph, his outstretched hand slapping the table between them. "So, if we start to feel the heat from their questions about us, we'll turn the hoses on them."

"Oh my goodness," Sara groaned good-naturedly. "Again with the firefighter analogies."

He gave her a playful wink that should not have curled her toes or spurred the butterflies in her belly as easily as it did.

To quote Mamá Alicia's most frequent exclamation . . . *¡Ay Dios mío!*

Sara gulped down her dismay. Oh my god indeed. Like her favorite summer linen skirt if she'd been seated too long, her zany scheme suddenly developed a new wrinkle. A big wrinkle she needed to steam-iron out immediately, or she'd risk making another mistake in her personal life.

Luis Navarro would be oh, so easy to fall for if she wasn't careful. But jumping into another long-distance relationship, with a guy she'd offered to pay to spend time with her, was most definitely a no. Totally nonnegotiable.

Her relationship with Ric had started fast and furious and for all the wrong reasons. Namely, to please her parents. Exactly like her current situation with Luis.

Sara refused to confuse his friendly assistance with anything more serious. Doing so could only end badly.

From inside her purse, Sara's cell phone vibrated. She reached for it without thinking, immediately sucking in a sharp breath when she saw the text notification from her mother.

Landed and picked up our car. Will meet you and Ric at the rental house shortly.

"What's wrong?"

Luis's sharp question cut through the whirr of doubts suddenly buzzing in her ears.

What if this didn't work?

This *had* to work.

But what if they crash and burned?

Heart in her throat, second-guesses scrambling through her brain like invaders intent on demolishing the getting-to-know-you bridge she and Luis had built between them, she met his inquisitive gaze. "My parents landed and are on their way to our rental. In your jargon, the fire alarm just rang. Looks like we're up."

Luis stretched his arm across the concrete picnic table, palm up. "If you're sure this is what you want to do, I'm with you, Sara. We got this."

Her gaze dropped to his open palm. An invitation. A belief in her. A commitment the likes of which she'd wanted from a loved one for years. Only, this commitment was temporary. An illusion.

"Sara? What do you want to do?" Luis asked, his voice calm, certain. Devoid of even the slightest hint of pressure or doubt.

Exactly how she yearned to feel when surrounded by her family. Maybe, just maybe, Luis could help her achieve that.

Sara let her eyes drift closed as she sent a plea for extra good luck prayers from Mamá Alicia above. Then, her heart pounding, she placed her hand in his, hoping that, together, she and Luis could pull off this convoluted plan she had concocted.

Chapter 5

The closer they got to the rental house in downtown Key West, the tighter Sara's death grip strangled her leather purse strap. The faster her left leg bobbed up and down on the ball of her foot, evidence of the jitters she was doing a terrible job of hiding.

While Luis wasn't too keen on lying to her family, he was even less inclinded to mess this up for Sara. Based on her current state, he'd have to figure out how to help her get over her nerves. Fast.

Luis made a left onto Eaton, then had to wind up and down a few of the Old Town streets, keeping his eyes peeled for an open spot big enough for his truck. All the while he remained aware of Sara, shoulders stiff and her face pale. If she wasn't careful, the nervous bite she had on her full lower lip would draw blood.

Finally, a gray van pulled out about a block away from the rental house, and Luis parallel parked under the shade of a sprawling poinciana tree. The tiny bright orange-red flowers that gave the tree its Spanish name, *flamboyán,* thanks to its fiery, flamboyant colors, popped against the pale blue sky background. A dusting of the flame-colored petals and green fern-like leaves coated the cracked sidewalk in front of a two-story wooden Conch house under renovation.

Leaving the engine running so the AC would cool the cab, Luis laid a hand on Sara's shoulder, hoping to calm her.

The harried look she gave him was at odds with the relaxed, quick-witted woman who'd peppered him with Twenty Questions and awed him with the story of how she'd grown her business, going from a college coed killing time posting pictures online to a full-blown social media entrepreneur.

"Hey, everything's going to be okay," he assured her.

Gently, he squeezed her shoulder. An *I got you* squeeze meant to reassure. Instead, she stiffened. Her brows furrowed, wrinkling her forehead, telegraphing that she felt anything but "okay."

Concerned, Luis swiveled to face her, releasing her shoulder to drape his forearm across the back of her bucket seat. "Sara, what's going on?"

"I just . . . I need this to work." Knuckles white, her fists tightened on her purse strap as she stared out the front windshield. "I need to not be the cause of more worry and stress for my parents. Especially my mom."

"More? What do you mean?"

Her slim shoulders rose and fell on a heavy sigh. "It's nothing. Never mind."

Luis ducked down, trying to catch her gaze. "You sure?"

"Yeah. I mean, um, it's nothing you need to be bothered with."

Whatever Sara was keeping from him didn't seem like it was *nothing*. Not based on the way she hedged, refusing to look him in the eye.

Coño. The word shot through his head like a warning flare, its red flame lighting the sky. Several other choice expletives, much stronger than *damn*, followed it.

Fifteen years on the job dealing with victims hiding info for one reason or another. Growing up with a younger brother who'd skirted the line of deviant behavior as a teen. They'd taught Luis the signs pointing out evasion of the truth. But he had also learned that pushing wasn't always the best option.

"We're on the same side here, remember?" he told her, purposefully keeping his voice low, his tone measured.

She fell back against her bucket seat, chin tilted up at the roof. Her slender neck exposed, Luis noticed the rapid beat of her pulse.

"Whatever it is, you tell me when you're ready. No pressure." Gently he combed her blond tresses behind her ear, marveling at the silky softness.

He didn't stop to question this strong compulsion to soothe her. Even though it made no sense.

Hell, they barely knew each other. He rarely let people outside his immediate circle get close to him. And yet, in only a few short hours with Sara, he found himself captivated by her. Trusting her more than he trusted most people outside his immediate *familia*.

Carlos would tell him to get his head out of his ass. Stop finding ways to avoid his own problems by focusing on someone else's.

Stubbornly, Luis ignored his older brother's imaginary advice.

The seat leather groaned its protest as Luis shifted toward Sara. "If your goal is to put your mom at ease, convince her that you've found the most amazing man to be with, I can totally help with that. This'll be a walk in the park 'cuz, well, I'm pretty amazing."

She lolled her head to her left, shooting him a raised-brow, are-you-kidding-me glare.

He winked, and a few seconds later a corner of her lush mouth twitched before slowly stretching into her sweet smile.

"A real *papi chulo,* huh?" she teased.

"Damn straight." He tapped his chest with his other palm. "Hot-guy material. That's me."

Her low chuckle sent a shiver of awareness shimmying over him. Lust pooled low in his body. The urge to kiss her, to turn that sexy chuckle into a groan of desire, hit him, hard and fast.

"I don't know how the three of us manage to fit in your truck," she mused.

He frowned, his thoughts stuck on the delectable idea of sampling her lips. "Three?"

"You, me, and your ego." She flashed a cheeky grin.

"Funny," he groused, actually, relieved to see her spunk reviving.

"I'll be here all week. Maybe you can catch my show."

"Ha, I'm *in* your show, sweetheart. All the . . . What did you call me? Oh yeah, all the hunky parts. I got those covered." He gave a lock of her hair a playful tug. Inadvertently the back of his hand brushed her bare shoulder, heightening his desire to touch more of her soft skin.

Sara cupped his elbow.

Luis figured she meant it as a request for him to back off. Immediately he moved to withdraw his hand, but her grip tightened, holding him still.

"I'm nervous," she whispered. The raw sincerity blanketing her beautiful face gutted him.

"Truth?" he asked.

Lips pressed together, she nodded.

"If we're confessing here," he admitted, staring intently into her eyes. "I'm a bit nervous myself. But I'm also really looking forward to spending the week with you."

Desire turned her blue-green irises into tumultuous waves, echoing the lust that blew through him with hurricane-force winds. When she glanced down at his mouth, then tugged her bottom lip between her teeth, Luis nearly groaned out loud.

She shifted toward him. The smallest, most infinitesimal of movements. Her gaze slid up to ensnare his and he found himself drowning. In her. In this intense need to feel her lips against his.

Unable to resist her pull, Luis leaned in. Slowly. Careful to watch for any hint that he was misreading her signs.

Instead, Sara met him halfway.

The air thickened around them. Hot. Heavy. Humid with their mingled breath. Tangy with her citrusy scent.

It was crazy. This attraction, swift and strong, arcing between them.

Her eyes drifted closed. Luis's gaze traced a thin blue vein faintly crisscrossing one of her pale eyelids. The slight flush tinting her high cheeks. It was inevitable, his need to taste her sweetness. Undeniable in a way he'd never experienced before.

Featherlight, his lips brushed against hers. Once. Twice. The cool scent of the breath mint she had popped in her mouth earlier teased him with the urge to taste it on her tongue.

She pressed a hand against his chest, her eyelids fluttering open, and he stilled. Ready to back off. Her fingers curled, gathering his shirt in her fist as if she wanted to drag him closer. Desire surged, pushing him dangerously close to the edge of reason, and he cautioned himself to take it slow, when all he really wanted was to dive right into the pleasure he felt certain they'd discover together.

The *chi-ching chi-ching* of a bicycle's metallic bell chimed outside the truck window. Luis and Sara started at the intrusion, inadvertently knocking foreheads.

"Oooh!"

"Ow!" Luis jerked back, smacking his left elbow on the steering wheel.

Beside him, Sara peered out at the street as she massaged the area above her left brow.

An old man wearing a ratty T-shirt and shorts, a beat-up straw hat shoved low on his head blissfully pedaled by on a rusty beach cruiser. Luis followed the guy until he turned left on Eaton, probably headed a few blocks over to check out the action on Duval.

Coño, talk about rude interruptions.

"I guess we don't have to bother making up our first-kiss story," Sara murmured on a shaky laugh. An embarrassed blush bloomed on her face. "Not that I expect anyone in my family will ask."

"That'd be my *familia* who wouldn't mind butting in with unwanted personal questions. Which, *gracias a Dios*, we don't have to worry about."

Sara didn't respond, and an awkward silence filled the cab.

Luis tracked a flurry of *flamboyán* petals the breeze chased across the truck's hood. Their fiery color mimicked the heated passion Sara had ignited in him with nothing more than the feel of her soft skin against the back of his hand. The soft brush of her lips against his.

This was supposed to be pretend, he reminded himself. Their zany circumstances seemed to have skewed his sense of right and wrong. But he'd do well to remember that she'd asked him for help as a friendly favor. He had agreed mainly to fill the void of time off and assist someone in need. No sense mucking up their plan by allowing hormones to get in the way of common sense. Even if his hormones had never gone haywire like this before.

Outside, a young couple stopped while their goldendoodle puppy sniffed the ground where the sidewalk butted up against a white picket fence in front of a neighboring Conch house. Probably a normal everyday activity for them.

But for Luis, this entire afternoon was way outside his norm. Since Mirna's death six years ago and the subsequent fallout with his younger brother, Luis hadn't let himself get involved with anyone. He went about his job, pulling extra shifts as often as possible. Concentrated on building up his dive and snorkel side hustle with his boat. Answered the call for help from *familia* and friends.

Sure, he had the occasional hookup. That wasn't out of the ordinary.

Real intimacy, though? What he thought he'd had with Mirna until the truth of her duplicity had been revealed after her accident? *No gracias.* Getting played for a fool by love once was enough.

And yet here he was getting himself embroiled in another situation involving a lie and a woman he thought he could save.

Helping Sara was one thing.

Confusing her gratitude for interest was a mistake he didn't need to make. If he'd learned anything from Mirna, it was that gratitude or, even worse, hero worship was no substitute for real love.

Sara was in the midst of an emotional, stressful situation. She felt thankful for his assistance. That's it. He'd do well to remember that.

Which meant he needed to pull the extinguisher trigger and put out the remnants of the flash fire smoldering inside him. If not, her plan and his bid to help were doomed.

"Are you—"

"About that—"

They spoke in unison, each quickly breaking off.

"Ladies first." Palm up, Luis gestured toward her.

Sara dipped her head in thanks. "I'm the one who instigated all of this." She motioned back and forth between them. "This whole charade idea, infringing on your time off. And, while it's probably a good thing that we're, uh, you know." She stopped, swallowed nervously. Rubbed at the tiny worry lines wedged between her light brown brows.

"That we're, what?" he prodded.

Sara huffed out a rush of air on what sounded like an embarrassed laugh.

"God, it's like I've time warped back to high school," she muttered under her breath. Twisting completely around to face him, she hiked up the material of her peach dress, treating him to a flash of her shapely calf as she crooked her knee over the cupholders in the center console. "Look, you're an attractive guy. And I'm, well, I like to consider myself a reasonably attractive woman—"

His snort of disbelief had Sara stopping to give him the stink eye.

"That was totally meant as a 'hell yeah,'" he clarified, swiping a hand through the air to underline his point.

Lips pursed in a cute pout, she hummed an "uh-huh" weighty with snark. "As I was saying, it's only natural that we might be, you know, attracted to each other."

She paused, brows raised like she expected some kind of answer from him.

After her less-than-thrilled response to his reaction moments ago, Luis played it safe and nodded.

"I mean, I guess our, um, attraction might make us more convincing, you know? Make our relationship more believable? Though we should be clear. This is simply you doing me a huge favor, and me in turn making an anonymous donation to the fire station's upcoming fundraiser for local schools. We are starting and ending this whole affair as friends. Nothing more. Right?"

He couldn't tell who she was trying to convince, herself or him, but her logic seemed—

Hell, who was he kidding, logic had absolutely nothing to do with this plan of theirs.

Sara waited, her brow creased with anxious expectation. Her hands wringing impatiently on top of her knee.

Logical or not. He was all in.

Luis turned the key to cut the truck's engine. "I'm ready if you are."

A relieved smile spread across Sara's mouth. And damn if that didn't make him start thinking about kissing her all over again.

Her cheeks plumped when she grinned. Her eyes flashed with the excited glimmer that made him want to do whatever it took to keep her feeling that way.

Madre de Dios, he was in over his head here. Talk about shaking things up? This was earthquake, Richter-scale worthy.

Thing was, for the first time in a long, *long* time, Luis didn't care. Maybe this nutty idea of a one-week pretend affair with this quick-witted, intriguing woman who discombobulated his regimented, mostly solitary life was just what the doctor or, in his case, the Captain had ordered.

The thought had Luis's body responding as if a station Tone Out had sounded inside his cab. Adrenaline raced through him. His pulse ramped up. Every cell inside him tingled, invigorated and alive.

In a flash of clarity, he realized Carlos had been right. In recent weeks—hell, even longer than that—Luis hadn't felt this high, this thrill, on the job. Not like he used to. Definitely not since the car accident that had taken the life of a young college student several weeks ago. Dragging him back to a different accident. One with more casualties than the life it had taken.

One that had left him basically treading water. Fighting against a current teeming with a barrage of painful, unwelcome memories. But this entire afternoon with Sara, he hadn't thought about any of it.

Any doubts he may have harbored were instantly quelled. Instinct reassured him that here, enjoying this welcome reprieve Sara unwittingly offered, was exactly where he was supposed to be.

Now to make sure they made her family believe that, too.

Chapter 6

The rattle of Sara's suitcase wheels quieted as she and Luis drew to a stop in front of a stately two-story Conch house.

Luis let out a low whistle she took as a sign of his approval.

Like many other restored historic homes in Old Town, this butter yellow beauty beckoned weary travelers with an expansive wraparound verandah on the first floor and matching balcony on the second. Traditional white wooden railings edged their perimeters, while dainty gingerbread latticework accessorized the high corners of each banister.

Vastly different from the stark lines, minimalist structure, and neutral colors of her childhood home, the rental's warm welcome continued at the top of the five or so white stairs leading to the verandah where it waited with open arms stretching out on either side of the front door painted to match the seafoam green shutters. Off to the left, a pair of rattan rocking chairs and a small, round end table in the same seafoam green, their plump seat cushions covered in a tropical print, created a perfect spot for relaxing. On the right, a matching ottoman and hanging bench swing invited visitors to settle in and get comfy. Potted ferns and gerbera daisies in a bright mix of colors dotted the lower space, while hanging baskets teeming with lush ferns and vines decorated the upstairs balcony.

This home spoke of family gatherings and special memories made, not secrets kept and young spirits wounded by overheard words and unbridged differences.

A deep longing for the former seared Sara's chest.

"She is a beauty," Luis noted. "I've always been fascinated by these old homes. How renovators take a crumbling structural shell, bring it up to code, and transform it into something like this." He waved a hand to encompass the stunning building.

"Apparently, my mom fell in love with the idea of staying in an authentic Conch house. She did all kinds of research on their architectural history. Then scoured several rental sites to find the perfect one."

"This looks about perfect to me. Your mom's got great taste." Luis reached around Sara to grasp the metal handle on the white picket fence gate.

"That she does." Her mom excelled at practically anything she put her mind to. Unfortunately, hands-on parenting hadn't been a top priority. Sara pressed a hand to her belly, willing the nerves buzzing inside like fireflies caught in a glass jar to calm. "I'm told she also devised a detailed itinerary of all the local tourist spots she plans for us to visit while we're here."

He pushed open the gate but stepped aside for her to lead the way up the bricked pathway. "Are you telling me I'm going to have to arm-wrestle her for main tour guide designation?"

Sara chuckled, angling her head to look up at him as she passed by. Buoyed by his presence. "Now that I'd like to see."

Luis placed his hand on her lower back and fell into step beside her. Warmth from his touch seeped through the thin material of her dress. She started to move away, aware of the temptation he presented but that could only complicate their situation.

"There you are."

The sound of her mother's cultured voice had Sara stumbling a step. Luis's hand slid from her waist to her hip, tugging her against his side to steady her. Instinctively her right arm looped around his waist for support.

Casually dressed in navy capris and a light blue blouse, her dirty-blond hair styled in a cropped pixie cut now that it had finally started growing back, Sara's mom stepped through the open front door. Despite her diminutive stature, her strong personality loomed large in Sara's mind.

"It's wonderful to see you two," her mom greeted, hands spread in welcome. "I was beginning to worry you'd gotten lost trying to find your way here."

"Hi, Mom, how was the flight down? Not too rough for you, I hope?" Sara asked.

Her mom had been prone to airsickness before chemo. Since starting her treatment, the nausea had gotten worse whenever she traveled.

"Oh, I've been better. But I've also been worse. Nothing a little reading or morning yoga in the gorgeous sanctuary out back won't cure." Her mother's easy quip, so unlike her usual staid personality, had Sara slowing her steps with caution.

She and Luis reached the end of the brick pathway, and he deftly lowered the handle to carry her suitcase up the stairs.

Sara's mom stared at him, her oval face, still thin from the weight loss during her treatment, alight with interest. The tiredness that had weighed down the corners of her light gray eyes had mostly lifted since Sara's last visit to Phoenix over the Christmas holidays. Now a strange softness, vastly different from the usual keen determination, loomed in their depths.

"Mom, this is Ric Luis." Sara rattled off the double name they had agreed on, looping her arm around Luis's waist again as they climbed the steps together. "Sweetie, I'd like you to meet the best pediatric surgeon in the state of Arizona, if not the entire West, my mom, Dr. Ruth Vance."

Luis held out his hand when they reached the verandah. "It's a pleasure, Dr. Vance. I was just telling Sara, you selected a beauty as your Key West home away from home."

"That I did. But please, call me Ruth." Sara's mom clasped Luis's large hand between both of hers, the typical reservation with which she had met Sara's previous boyfriends curiously absent. "It is such a joy to meet you, Ric."

"Uh, likewise." Luis shot Sara a glance she interpreted as *here we go.* "Actually, with family and close friends I usually go by 'Luis.' It's nice to welcome you to my childhood home, Ruth."

"Oh, I hadn't realized . . ." The tiny lines crossing her forehead deepened as her brows rose in obvious surprise.

"I look forward to showing you and the rest of Sara's family what makes the island so special to us locals," Luis finished.

"Sara, why didn't you mention Ric, or"—Ruth's eyes crinkled with a smile she sent his way—"Luis, was from Key West?"

"I thought I did, didn't I?" Heart pounding with unease at the fib, Sara leaned in to press her cheek against her mom's cool one for an air kiss. "It probably slipped my mind in all the trip preparations."

Once again, her mom surprised Sara by reaching her slender arms around Sara for a hug. After a stunned second, Sara stiffly reciprocated the gesture. The bony shoulder blades along her mother's back were a stark reminder of Ruth's frailty. Despite whatever happy front she was putting on for Luis, she was still regaining her strength. The stamina that had driven her for hours at the operating table not quite what it used to be.

Her mom's frailty reminded Sara that this trip was meant to be a rejuvenating, mood-lifting vacation. No matter how nervous Sara felt about lying by pretending with Luis, her mother's peace of mind held more importance.

Leaning back from their hug, Sara gently grasped her mother's shoulders. "You're looking great, Mom. I think a little island sun and balmy weather will do you good."

"Yes, well, this humidity will probably turn my hair into a frizzy football helmet. But at least it'll be a full helmet now." She palmed several spots around her head where, until recently, the hair had only grown in patches.

Angling toward the lush front yard with its thick green grass, dark pink bougainvillea vines trailing across the picket fence, and stately palms, Ruth sucked in a chest-lifting deep breath. "There's something about the ocean air, isn't there? I'm anxious to dig my toes in some sand and stare out at the vastness of the open water. It has such a calming, Zen-like effect. We don't get this in Phoenix, do we?"

Sara stared in disbelief at the woman whom she favored in coloring and facial features but who stood a good three inches shorter
in stature while towering over her in strength of character. Who
was this introspective woman? Dr. Ruth Vance didn't talk about
calming effects and Zen anything. She was more interested in learning about cutting-edge procedures and medical devices. Pushing
herself to the limits if it meant saving another patient.

Rest and relaxation? That was for the weak.

"Ruth, are you out here?" Sara's dad poked his head around the
door, his brow wrinkling as the blue-green eyes his DNA had given
her widened with joy when he spotted her. "Sar-bear, you made it!"

He opened his arms for a hug, and Sara scooted around her
mother, happy as always to oblige him. "Hi, Dad, it's great to see you."

"Thank you for making the effort to come," he whispered in her
ear. "This is important to me. To her."

"I wouldn't have missed it for the world."

Her dad squeezed her tighter, something he'd been doing more
of the last few times she'd visited. "You've been feeling okay? No,
you know, urges or triggers?"

Sliding out of his embrace, she gave a brisk shake of her head.
"I'm good. You don't have to worry."

And she wanted to keep it that way. Her strong, dependable
dad had been devastated by her mom's breast cancer diagnosis.
Battling the disease as patient and caregiver rather than physicians
had changed them both. In ways Sara was still getting used to herself.

"Charles, meet Sara's partner, Luis." Her mom grasped Luis's
elbow, ushering him closer.

"Hel—excuse me? I thought it was 'Ric'?" Her dad stared at
the three of them, one graying brow quirked, hands deep in the
pockets of his khaki slacks. His infamous penetrating gaze had intimidated many an intern and resident over the years.

"Ric Luis," Sara clarified.

She plastered on her camera-ready smile, hiding her inward
cringe. *Por favor, Mamá Alicia*, she prayed, let her parents buy this
first of many threads to the story she and Luis had concocted.

"Luis to close friends and family. Hello, Dr. Vance." Calm and collected as always . . . well, as he'd been the entire afternoon . . . Luis dipped his head in greeting. "I've heard quite a bit about you, sir."

"That makes one of us. Though rest assured, I intend to learn quite a bit about you during our stay here."

Hands clasped, the two men eyed one another. Her father blatantly sizing Luis up. Luis doing his Vin Diesel impression, all measured calm and tough guy–ish and, God help her, sexy as hell. If she wasn't so freaking nervous, she would have laughed at the male posturing.

"Charles, don't intimidate our guest," Sara's mother admonished. "Let me show them to their room; then we can all meet around the pool to get acquainted."

Sara's stomach bottomed out at her mom's words. Crap! How had she not thought about sleeping arrangements? About the fact that Luis didn't have a—

"Did you leave a suitcase in your car?" her dad asked. "Isn't this one yours, Sar-bear?"

She met Luis's gaze, her mind spinning with possible responses. If the same *oh crap* thoughts clamoring in her head also clamored in his, it didn't show. His composure remained unruffled.

"I thought you might appreciate some privacy all together," he said, and Sara found herself bobbing her head in agreement. "It's not a problem for me to stay with family this week."

"Nonsense. We're looking forward to getting to know you." Sara's mom linked her arm through Luis's. Another friendly gesture atypical for the woman who used to work harder than she played and rarely loosened up unless it involved charming hospital benefactors.

Until she'd faced, and beaten, cancer.

"Obviously, we don't want to take you away from visiting with your loved ones. I understand how important that is," Sara's mom went on. "But it would mean a lot for you to join us as often as you can. Right, Charles?"

The speculative frown on her father's lined face eased into a caring smile for her mom. "Whatever makes you happy, dear."

Whether he intended the subtext or not, Sara understood her dad's meaning. She and her siblings had been given their directives:

ensure their mother relaxed, rested, and enjoyed their time to-gether.

While her parents made goo-goo eyes at each other—another unexpected, if endearing behavior—Sara mentally telegraphed a message to Luis. *Please, go along with me here.*

Luis's jaw muscles flexed. His nostrils flared on a deep breath that Sara didn't think was as soul cleansing as her mother had im-plied earlier. Finally, blessedly, he gave Sara the tiniest of nods.

She sagged with relief.

Without a doubt, she owed him for this. Big-time.

"I appreciate your hospitality," Luis said, his amiable tone hid-ing the misgivings she felt certain he was uncomfortable with. "If you're sure, I'll see about bringing my bag with me in the morning to join you."

"We're sure. Anyone who's special to our Sara is special to us. I am delighted you're here." Her mom patted Luis's forearm affec-tionately. "Perhaps you'd like to invite your family to join us one—"

"No!"

Sara's outburst startled her parents and had her dad, once again, giving her and Luis his formidable stare-down.

Trepidation marched like a row of army ants across her shoul-ders. She and Luis hadn't even made it through the front door and her father already suspected something. This did not bode well.

"I mean, the last thing we want is for Mom to feel like she needs to entertain," Sara hedged. She swallowed nervously. "Let's just play that part by ear, okay?"

God help her, if her parents insisted on meeting Luis's, this plan was doomed. With a capital *D*! Luis had already made it clear that he refused to lie to them. He'd been adamant about that point.

While she, on the other hand, fully anticipated lightning to strike her down in retaliation for all the bad energy she was putting out in the world thanks to the whopping lies she planned to feed her loved ones.

Self-confidence personified, Luis eased over the awkwardness by leaning toward her mother to mock-whisper near her ear, "Our super-secret plan is to pamper you, Ruth. Make sure that when you leave Key West next Friday, you'll feel rejuvenated, already plan-ning a return trip."

"I like the way that sounds," she said, a rich chuckle Sara couldn't remember hearing before underlining her words.

Sara shook her head, feeling like somehow her mother had morphed into the mom she had always longed for. Warm, accepting. Ready to greet her with open arms. Only, now it was Sara whose actions might force a rift between them.

"This week is shaping up rather nicely." Her mom leaned into Luis as if they were old friends.

"That's our master plan." He winked, and Sara swore her mother sighed like a schoolgirl. Not that she blamed her.

Damn, he was good. From the sexy little half smile that gentled his strong features and chiseled jaw to the enticing mix of sincerity and strength in his deep voice. It all had Sara wishing he'd lean over and whisper something in her ear. Or maybe nibble on it.

"Shall we?" Gesturing toward the front door, her mom continued her Martha Stewart impersonation, ushering Luis arm in arm into their home.

"Ruth, Sara tells me you've been busy researching the island and planning your itinerary." Luis continued laying on the charm. "What do you say we go over everything together, see how I can best serve as your guide?"

"We'll be along in a minute," her dad said to them.

Her mom nodded over her shoulder; then the door slid closed behind her and Luis.

Once they were alone, Sara's dad stepped to the edge of the verandah, where he rested a hip against the wooden railing. Behind him, the same couple who'd been walking their puppy earlier strolled by again, hand in hand. By now the puppy had slowed, having lost some of his stamina after their long walk.

Staring down at his open palm, Sara's father rubbed his thumb over his gold wedding band. "Your mother seems quite taken with your young man," he mused.

"Luis tends to have that effect on most people."

Herself included.

"That's good to hear. Sara, I know this week away, rearranging your schedule, is a lot to ask—"

"No, it's not," Sara rushed to assure him. "Having us all here, supporting mom, is important." Though stressful.

Moving to join him, she pressed her stomach against the railing and leaned over the edge. The hard wood bit into her hip bones, the sharp pain grounding her in the reality of the turbulent outcome if this ruse she'd set in motion was exposed.

Out on the street, a beat-up sedan rumbled past at a leisurely island-life pace. Salsa music played through the open windows, carrying on the humid breeze. The rapid beat matched the pounding in her chest. The desperation over her desire to be seen as an equal and connect with her siblings and parents. A desire Luis had easily pinpointed.

"I'm glad we're here," she said. "We haven't done something like this in . . ."

She trailed off, realizing they had actually never taken more than a long weekend away all together. Usually Robin or Jonathan or one of her parents were unable to break away from the hospital for longer. Or didn't want to. Once, everyone else had attended a medical conference in Mexico, but Sara had signed a contract with a sponsor and the shoot date hadn't been flexible.

Even their family holidays were a mash-up with someone on call or covering for a colleague. Christmas and Thanksgiving dinner often became lunch or brunch, sometimes a day early or late.

This week . . . everyone under one roof . . . it set a precedence that could prove monumental for them all. She'd do anything to ensure it did so in a positive way.

"We've missed quite a bit," her father mused, melancholy weighing his words.

Regret pinched his wide brow and broad cheekbones when he angled his head to gaze down at her. He'd aged over the course of her mother's illness. The grooves along either side of his generous mouth were more pronounced, his hair now more salt than pepper.

Sara's gut clenched with an answering sadness.

"Focusing on our careers. Not enough on each other, or you kids. When we found out about your disorder"—his gaze slid back to his palm, where his thumb continued worrying his ring—"I knew I had failed you. In the previous years, in that moment. And since."

"Dad, no."

Aching at the sight of the pain rounding his proud shoulders,

Sara covered his hands with one of hers. She curled her fingers around his palm tightly.

Her father's blue-green eyes glistened, the crow's-feet at their edges deepening with his grimace. "I know this will always be a struggle for you and I could be, should be, doing more. Your mother's sickness . . . it overwhelmed me in a way I never expected. And . . . and I haven't been there for you. Helping you find your way to recovery. Making sure you stay healthy. Mentally and physically."

"I'm a big girl, Dad. As much as you might still think of me as your little Sar-bear who climbed on your lap to snuggle when you finally made it home after long shifts at the hospital. Or the sorority girl who knew something was wrong but was too afraid to verbalize it until Mamá Alicia confronted me."

His eyes squeezed shut as if he sought to block out the past. Sara wrapped her other arm around him, willing him to feel her love. Her newly found strength.

"I'm not any of those anymore. I mean, I won't lie, you're right, it hasn't been easy. And it was really hard when Mamá Alicia died, then Mom's diagnosis hit us all. But I work at it every day. My therapist helps. As do the tools I've learned. I'm okay, dad. I'm gonna stay okay."

The vow was an affirmation to herself, as well as him.

"And Luis, he's good for you?" Her dad gazed down at her, hope mingling with a father's conviction. "He supports and cares for you, like you deserve?"

The question pierced her chest with a poison dart that sent guilt burning through her. Unable to look her dad in the face, she pressed her cheek against his shoulder.

"Luis is a good man," she told him, certain it was the truth. "Right now, what we have works for me. That's what I'm focusing on."

Her dad was silent for a few moments. Then he pressed a kiss to the top of her head like he'd done when she was a child. Her heart warmed.

"Okay then," he murmured. "If you're happy, then I'm happy."

Content in this rare father-daughter moment, Sara sincerely believed that Ric Montez showing his true colors today by standing her up had been an act of divine intervention.

In the end, she'd swapped one ruse for another but come out for the better.

With Ric, she'd been kidding *herself*. On paper, they may have seemed like a match. But other than their desire to do well in their careers and traveling in the same social networking circles in Miami, they had very little in common on a personal level. She would have spent the next week pretending his braggadocious manner wasn't a drag. That the self-confidence that had appealed to her in the beginning stages of their long-distance relationship hadn't mutated into an egotistical arrogance that often rubbed her wrong.

And yet the guy could schmooze like the best of them. The skill served him well in commercial development. No doubt he would have been at his most masterful with her parents and siblings, maneuvering conversations to his benefit while bowling them over. In truth, though, she found being around him for too long draining.

On the other hand, there was no pretending about wanting to spend time with Luis.

This afternoon, hanging out at the beach, trading serious and silly questions, laughing with each other, being herself. No watchful eyes assessing her. The kiss that hadn't been anything more than the whisper of his lips against hers, but had still made her pulse race and her insides quiver with anticipation.

Only, taking things further with him could prove disastrous.

Luis was here as a favor. Seven days from now she'd fly back to New York, nose to the grindstone, determined to close the deal with Foster Designs. Bringing her one step closer to collaborating on a new line of clothing with her own brand. One step closer to finally making her mother, her entire family, proud of her accomplishments. Gaining their confidence that she could indeed take care of herself.

When this was all over, at best she and Luis might wind up as friends who stay in touch. Maybe reconnect should their paths cross. She hoped so anyway. But allowing herself to fall for her own charade would be foolish.

"I guess we should head inside before they come searching for us." Her father pushed off the railing, and Sara dropped her arms from around him.

She turned to take a last look out at the front yard, teeming with rich foliage and vibrant color. Rising onto her toes, she lifted her face to the sky and soaked up the sun's rays as they warmed her skin.

If you're happy, then I'm happy.

Her dad's words rang in her head. Words she hadn't heard often growing up. Especially from her mother. The fight against cancer and her mom's recent good news had shifted the dynamics of their relationships. Sara hadn't quite figured out exactly how yet, but if they were fortunate enough, this week could help them reach a new place with each other.

"You coming, Sar-bear?"

She swiveled on her heel to find her dad holding the brightly painted door open for her. The warmth on his face reminded her of Luis. The gentle giant of a man who, so far, was setting the bar pretty high for when Sara decided to get back in the dating game.

First, she had to concentrate on doing her best to make it through the next seven days without blowing their cover. All while not falling for the lie she had fabricated.

Easier said than done when right now inside, Luis was probably winning over her family with his unique mix of calm, easygoing assurance. The same way he'd done with her.

As Sara slipped through the door, she made a quick sign of the cross, ending with a kiss of her fingertips and a roll of her eyes to Mamá Alicia in heaven. She had a feeling she'd need all the assistance, divine and otherwise, she could get this week.

Chapter 7

"I don't mind dropping everyone off at Mallory Square, then hoofing it back to catch up with you if we can't find parking," Luis offered after Sara's family had decided to catch sunset on the pier along with dinner and music at El Meson de Pepe. Two activities that topped many tourist Must Do lists while visiting his island.

"Nonsense, after that long plane ride, it'll be nice to stretch our legs," Ruth answered. "A body can only take so much lounging, even in paradise."

She waved an arm Vanna White–style to indicate the backyard oasis.

"I don't know, Mother; this place makes even the non-loafer feel like loafing around!" Sara's sister, Robin, called out.

Tall and slender like Sara, Robin wore her blond hair cut short in a wash-and-wear style. She and her husband, Edward, sat at the shallow end of the pool nearby. Robin's tan sandals and Edward's boat shoes had been shucked and neatly set aside. Now their bare feet rested on the wide first step leading into the water.

Luis ran through the facts he knew about them one more time. Not that there were many. Sara hadn't provided much during their cram session. Robin was a cardiothoracic surgeon like their father. Edward punched his time clock as an orthodontist. No kids. Both career driven. Robin's decisive personality balanced by her husband's somewhat nerdy, yet equally intelligent, one.

During their conversation, Luis had already discovered a new piece of information for his and Sara's sibling fact-finding mission. Apparently the couple enjoyed hiking in the mountains around Arizona. According to them, it allowed for requisite mind and body rejuvenation.

While he might prefer the open ocean to the mountains, Luis had to admit Robin was right about this backyard.

The rental homeowners had spared little expense in designing and landscaping the courtyard. Although Key West had much to offer in the way of history, nature, arts, and entertainment, the soft splash of the rock waterfall cascading into the deep end of the rectangular saltwater pool, along with the thick palm trees, potted ferns, and splashes of vivid color in the birds-of-paradise, yellow and red hibiscus, and fuchsia geiger tree blossoms, created the perfect ambiance for relaxation.

It definitely gave visitors a luxurious welcome to Key West.

Barring an emergency call, Luis rarely visited a place this upscale. His crowd hung in the older homes located in Midtown and up the Keys. Enrique had moved into an apartment off Duval after fire college in Ocala, but Luis could count on one hand the number of times he'd been there.

Sitting back against the sunset red cushion plumping his deck chair, he propped his work boots on the matching footstool and admired the view from the raised porch.

Along the main house and master bedroom wing, the shady porch with wide plank wood flooring made an expansive L shape, its white support beams and eaves tangled with flowering vines. Several dark gray rattan loungers and the chair set he and Sara occupied were situated down the length of the master bedroom side. A distressed-wood table allowed for casual dining in the area that opened off the living-dining room and kitchen.

A few stairs led down to the redbrick pool deck where two more loungers called to sunbathers. Near the pool's far end, by the waterfall, Sara's brother, Jonathan, an ER doc, and his wife, Carolyn, a stay-at-home mom, sat together on some kind of newfangled ottoman with a collapsible shelter cover. The design of the opaque, sun-reflecting material reminded Luis of a convertible car's top providing shade from the intense mid-May rays. Still pretty strong as the sun made its late afternoon descent.

Jonathan and Carolyn huddled, heads close together, on a video call with their two young children named . . . *coño*, Luis mentally fumbled through the info on his cheat sheet, trying to recall Sara's notes.

"William and Susan have specifically requested videos and pictures while we're on the Conch Tour Train," Jonathan alerted everyone, inadvertently answering Luis's question. "Susan's hoping for a picture of Grandmother holding a starfish at the aquarium."

"I can probably arrange that," Ruth answered from where she lay in one of the rattan loungers by the master bedroom.

"And William wants it to be known that he is bummed, his word," Carolyn added, hunkering closer to the cell screen to make a silly face for her kids, "that he's missing a day out on Luis's motorboat."

"We'll take him next time." The offer slipped out before Luis could stop it.

Sara choked on her water. Leaning forward in her deck chair, she covered her hacking cough with a fist.

"But I'm sure you'll get away to another beach location as a family sometime, and he'll have a chance at a boat ride then," Luis amended. He rubbed a hand on Sara's spasming back until her coughing quieted.

Chin to her chest, she tilted her head his way. Eyes wide, she sent him a clear are-you-kidding-me glower. Luis hitched a shoulder in a tiny shrug. The offer was a natural reaction for him. Obviously, he'd have to be more careful. There wasn't going to be a next time visit to Key West for the Vance family that involved him.

Thankfully, Jonathan and his wife didn't catch anything amiss and they went back to their video call, promising to bring home a surprise for each kid before hanging up.

Over on her lounger, several feet down from Luis and Sara, Ruth took another sip of the pukey purple protein and vitamin smoothie Charles had whipped up for her.

"You don't know what you're missing," she told everyone, tapping the side of her glass. "Best eight ounces of energy-packing punch."

Luis had passed up her invitation to join her for a glass earlier, saying yes instead to the bottle of Stella Sara's brother-in-law had held out to him.

"And we're saving it all for you, dear." Charles, who sat on the end of Ruth's chaise with her feet in his lap, stretched his arm to clink his beer bottle with her glass.

"I smelled that concoction, Mom, no thanks!" Jonathan called out. "If I drank that, Carolyn might not want to kiss me. And, at the risk of over-sharing with you people, let me say, we are kid-free this week, so I'm hoping to get lucky."

His cheeky announcement earned him a swat on the arm from his wife and a laugh from the rest of the group. Even Robin and her husband, who hadn't contributed much to the fun and games conversation thus far, cracked smiles.

It was strange really. The atmosphere among Sara's family was different from what she had described. He'd expected stuffy, even snotty doctors filled with that inevitable God complex he'd run up against dropping patients at the hospital.

Earlier, after stowing Sara's suitcase in one of the upstairs bedrooms, Luis had followed Ruth out back where the rest of the family had already settled. Robin and Edward had greeted him with the polite hellos and pleasure-to-meet-yous Luis expected based on his notes. Jonathan and his wife, on the other hand, came across as more approachable, a little more down-to-earth.

For the past hour or so they'd all shot furtive, and not-so-furtive, glances Luis and Sara's way. He figured they were reserving their judgment on the interloper in their private family vacation.

He completely understood. Let his sister, Anamaría, try bringing a stranger home for dinner without expecting the Cuban Inquisition from the rest of the *familia*. Odds were better his *mami* would serve hot dogs and mac 'n' cheese, a meal he doubted she had ever cooked, instead of her go-to picadillo, black beans, and rice that Anamaría's date would leave unscathed.

Still, the reticence Luis felt like heat waves in the air around them wasn't just about her family sizing him up.

Even when Sara and her father had joined the group, the siblings' reunion had been subdued. Sara had shared an awkward hug with her sister, one less awkward with Jonathan, who ruffled her hair playfully and called her kid. Then Sara had seemed to crawl into a shell of the outgoing, vivacious woman she'd been with him at the beach.

Ruth's cheeriness, comfortable and genuine when Luis had arrived, felt a little unnatural with the others. As if she were trying a new dress on for size. Except for with her husband, who doted on her and more easily navigated around their kids.

Sara had mentioned having a closer relationship with her dad growing up. Luis figured as much based on their private welcome home when he'd come inside with Ruth. Evidently Charles was the connector between them all.

Luis sipped his beer, thinking of the difference when he showed up at his parents' house. Inside, there'd be several conversations going on at once. Music, food, and kinship held court. Disagreements inevitably cropped up, but never got in the way of *familia* time. Even long-standing ones like his and Enrique's.

When it was time to leave, there was always the inevitable round of hugs and cheek kisses with everyone. People often joked about the need to start saying your good-byes at least fifteen minutes before you actually had to hit the road. If not, by the time you made the rounds you were late.

His mom had been known to stand at the door and yell at him to come back inside and hug a *tía* he'd skipped. God forbid he be seen as disrespectful to his aunt.

As it was, his mom had texted twice in the few hours since Luis had left his brother at the fire station. If he didn't get back to her soon, the next message from her would be a lament about his lack of regard for the woman who'd given him the gift of life.

"Sara mentioned you're in community development." Robin scooted around on the edge of the pool to face Luis. "I'm wondering how a real estate developer from Miami meets a social media butterfly from New York."

Out of the corner of his eye, Luis noticed Sara's fingers tightening their grip on the edge of her armrest. Thus far they had managed to keep the conversation on local vacation hot spots and the itinerary Ruth had planned for them. Easy topics with no need for him to worry about mixing up their story.

Looked like the time clock on their reprieve had expired.

"Mutual friends in Miami were hosting a cocktail party. Lucky for me I was in town that weekend," Luis answered. He reached across the small end table in between their chairs to cover Sara's hand with his.

Sara's blue-green gaze slid his way. Hesitant. Worried.

He rubbed his thumb along her delicate wrist bone, hoping to calm her worries. "I knew right away she was someone I wanted to get to know better."

Stick as close to the truth as possible.

The last part of his story was certainly the truth. From the moment she'd spun around and bumped into him at the airport, he'd been charmed.

At his wink, the tension in Sara's shoulders eased. She twisted her hand so they were palm to palm, then linked her fingers with his.

"You travel for work a lot?" This from Jonathan, still sprawled on the double ottoman, beside his wife.

"Not like Sara does. Though I spend as much time here in the Keys as I can."

"Mom mentioned you have family in the area, right?" Jonathan asked.

Sara's hand squeezed his in a death grip.

"Yeah, I do. Three siblings, my *abuelos* on my mom's side, and some extended *familia*. My parents actually live up the Keys a little ways."

"Are any of them firefighters?" Robin asked.

Sara's soft gasp drew his attention. He continued his gentle caress with his thumb along the side of her hand, then turned back to her sister. Robin pointed at him, and it took Luis a few seconds to realize she indicated the KWFD logo on his T-shirt.

"Oh yes, they are." He focused on remaining calm in this first test of threading the truth into his fake backstory. Knowing Sara counted on him. "It's pretty safe to say that firefighting is our family business. Ever since I was a kid, there's pretty much been a"— he barely caught himself before saying *Navarro*—"been one of us on shift practically every day in the city or county."

Dios, he didn't know how people did this. People like his ex, Mirna, straddling the line between truth and lie. Sweat beaded his brow. The knot in his gut twisted uncomfortably. The running list of details he and Sara had conjured up made his head throb.

So much for enjoying the relaxing atmosphere.

"I guess you and Sara have that in common then."

Luis figured his frown matched the one puckering Sara's brow at her sister's strange statement.

"Bucking the family business. Going off to do your own thing. Not that dealing with the real estate market has much similarity to being some kind of internet sensation." Robin's foot swirled through the pool, lifting to send a splash across the water's surface. "I'm still scratching my head at the idea that social media influencer is actually a viable career."

Sara jerked back as if her sister had slapped her.

"Robin!" Charles's and Ruth's sharp cries signaled a parental warning.

"What?" she complained. "It's the truth in this millennial-driven society."

At the other end of the pool, Jonathan vaulted to a seated position. Carolyn put a hand on his forearm, her lips moving as she murmured something in his ear. He glared at his older sister, lips pressed together in a pissed-off line.

From the branches of a lush geiger tree in the corner of the yard, a warbler trilled in the tense silence. The bird's sweet, high-pitched whistle was answered by another, and a tag-team harmony ensued.

Robin swished her foot in the pool water, clearly nonplussed by her blunt jab.

Hell-bent on supporting Sara, his tag-team partner in this oddly dysfunctional dynamic, Luis lifted their joined hands to press a kiss against her knuckles. "Sometimes you have to go out on your own to find your way. Find yourself. And if you're lucky, the road home is easy to traverse. No roadblocks or danger ahead warning signs making a return more tricky."

Sara's wobbly smile tugged at something in his chest. At the same time, the sting of his own hypocrisy lanced his side like a sharp blade.

Shortly after Mirna's death, when his own brother had finally decided to give up his dreams of being an artist and go to fire college instead, Luis had hoped he'd stay away. Take a job in Miami, where Enrique had friends from art school. Instead, Enrique signed on with the city of Key West. Luis had to admit, if he could have hammered a Road Closed sign where US 1 entered the Keys the day Enrique was scheduled to drive back home, he would have.

Instead, Luis forced himself to make peace with the fact that he and his brother would never be as close as they'd once been. Not after Enrique's betrayal.

But Sara?

Unless their Twenty Questions game had been cut short too soon and she had left out an important detail when it came to her relationship with her sister, Sara had done nothing he was aware of to warrant Robin's taunt.

"As for her business, Sara's pretty much killing it, if you ask me. I mean, she's easily up . . . What is it now, babe, close to five hundred thousand followers?" He tilted his head toward her in question, knowing full well the answer but wanting her to own it.

"Over," she said, that spark of sass that drew him flickering in her ocean-water eyes. It heated him up in ways a simple look never had before.

"She may have *over* five hundred thousand followers," Luis stressed the word, keeping his gaze locked with hers. "But I'm her number one fan."

"Oh my goodness!" Sara rolled her eyes, her pale shoulders shaking with her laugh. "That is so cheesy!"

Maybe. But it wiped away the hurt clouding her expressive eyes.

He kissed her knuckles again, waggling his brows at her.

Shaking her head, she turned away, but Luis caught the pink blush climbing her cheeks.

"Suck-up!" Jonathan yelled out. Carolyn swatted his shoulder playfully.

Luis raised his beer bottle in salute. When Jonathan did the same, Luis figured he might have found an ally.

The fact that he liked that idea subdued his good mood. This was temporary, he reminded himself. Nothing more.

"You'll have to get in line behind us for that number one fan moniker," Ruth warned.

The older woman swung her thin legs off her lounger and set her empty smoothie glass on the low end table. Angling her head, she shot her husband a secretive smile. Charles stroked his wife's slender back, his expression attentive and loving as he nodded at whatever question he read in her gaze.

"Your father and I recently came to a decision," Ruth announced. "We plan to be more focused on each other, on our children and their partners." Her gaze slid pointedly to Sara and Luis, then Robin and Edward still seated at the shallow end of the pool, then on to Jonathan and Carolyn. "And our grandchildren. Life's too short. We have missed out on far too much. That stops right now." She tapped her knee, emphasizing her point. "With us spending more quality time together, starting this week. Really getting to know one another better."

Beside Luis, Sara stiffened. She shot him a sharp, slightly panicked look out of the corner of her eye.

If he guessed right, the last thing she wanted was her parents poking into their sham relationship.

He sandwiched her hand tightly with both of his, hoping she understood his we-got-this signal.

"You may want to rethink some of that togetherness when you have to sit through Susan's dance recital. Twice!" Jonathan's playful warning had his wife and parents chuckling.

Luis liked the guy's sense of humor. Plus the fact that he'd started to come to Sara's defense when their older sister bared her fangs.

"Says the man who was mouthing the steps to his daughter's routine from his seat in the auditorium," Carolyn threw in. "I thought he was about to volunteer to dance in the wings with their instructor, helping preschoolers struggling to remember the next step."

Jonathan shrugged good-naturedly. "What can I say, my little girl has me wrapped around her pinkie. I could have easily filled in for the teacher."

"Now that I would have liked to see. I'm sorry I wasn't feeling well that day," Ruth said, sliding her feet into her black sandals. "Next year, I'll do my best to be there."

"Me too," Charles chimed in. He and Ruth exchanged another secretive nod before he continued. "Robin, you've done such a fine job covering for me while I cared for your mother. While we're here, I'd like us to discuss keeping this division of duties permanent. If you agree, we'll talk with the hospital when we get back."

Surprise widened Robin's gray eyes at her father's announcement. Her jaw dropped, leaving her mouth a shocked *oh* that smoothed the rough edges of her caustic personality.

Beside her, Edward clumsily patted her thigh, his mouth tilted in a crooked smile his orthodontist skills might not be able to straighten but that showed his pride for his wife.

"Dad, are you sure?" Robin asked, her abrasive tone tempered with awe and uncertainty. "Stepping back, permanently, that means—"

"That means more cases for you. More responsibility and leadership expectations. You'll be the Dr. Vance that's paged first for difficult consultations, not me. If you're ready for it."

"Yes! Of course, yes!" Pulling her feet out of the water, Robin hurried toward the shaded porch. A trail of darkened wet footprints marked her steps across the bricked deck. Charles rose from his seat on Ruth's lounger to wrap his oldest in a bear hug.

"This is what you've worked for, and I'm happy to hand over the reins to you. Just like—" Charles pulled back to grasp Robin's shoulders. He peered down at her, the same authoritative expression he'd aimed at Luis and Sara when they'd first arrived. "Just like I'm happy for each new follower person or sponsor opportunity Sara garners. Or each patient you and your brother save. And especially any dance recital moves Jonathan teaches us this week."

"Which could possibly happen tonight, if we all hurry and freshen up." Ruth checked the dainty gold watch encircling her left wrist, then rose to stand beside them. "It's nearly five thirty. If we plan to eat before sunset at eight, we'll need to get a move on."

Jonathan and Carolyn strolled over to join the rest of the group. Luis stayed in his deck chair, waiting to take his cue from Sara. While their banter had eased her discomfort earlier, she didn't appear in a hurry to congratulate her sister. Instead, she gazed at her family standing in a huddle, without her.

The longing on her face made Luis want to wrap his arm around her, make their own circle of trust, and reassure her that everything would be okay.

He was used to being the voice of calm and reason with many victims on the job. Only, this pulse-racing urge to hold and comfort Sara wasn't something he ever felt for the random strangers, even the locals he knew, who relied on him for aid. Not by a long shot.

"This is an unexpected move, Dad. But a good one," Jonathan said.

Father and son shook hands; then Jonathan one-arm hugged his mom, cautiously tucking her slender body against his side with care.

Luis wished he'd known Ruth before her body had been weakened by cancer. Then again, it seemed the weakness of body may have precipitated a strength in spirit in a whole new way. One her family was only getting used to. Her children anyway. She and her husband appeared to be on the same new page.

"And you," Jonathan told his older sister, nudging his chin at her over Ruth's head. "I'd tell you to make sure you do the Vance name proud. But you're so damn hard on yourself, I figure you're already mentally giving yourself a tougher speech than I would."

Hands clasped at her waist, excitement contained and her reserved demeanor reestablished, Robin gave her brother a brisk nod. "You are correct."

"Let's be clear, though," Jonathan said. "Two Vances will continue practicing at Phoenix General. So, it could very well be *my* Dr. Vance page you hear."

"I'll keep that in mind the next time you call from the ER, needing *my* expertise." Robin's haughty reply was tempered by a smug smirk that had her brother barking out a laugh.

Throughout the exchange Sara remained apart from the others. Brows knitted with a frown, silently watching her family in their tight circle. One she had admitted she didn't quite fit into.

Still, Luis had trouble reconciling the information Sara had given him back at Higgs Beach with what he'd learned after spending time in the company of her parents and siblings.

It was a little strange studying the Vances all together. They spanned nearly three separate generations between parents, oldest siblings, then Sara. It was understandable that she might feel like the odd man out with the others paired off in age groups. And clearly Robin's bluntness may not always be easy to deal with.

But it was more than generational differences. Luis sensed a stronger undercurrent of disconnect going on here. At the same time, Sara's parents were pretty clear they wanted to steer their family boat in a new direction. One with warmer waters between them.

Unfortunately, when it came to family dynamics and making up for past mistakes Luis knew firsthand it was easier said than done.

For Sara's sake, he hoped she could find her way across whatever impasses lay between her and the individual members of her family. So she no longer felt stranded on one side, alone.

Once again, Luis made a mental promise to do whatever he could this week to make that happen.

"Okay, everyone, the clock is ticking," Ruth announced. "Twenty-minute warning. You'll get another with ten to go."

Like well-trained firefighters following their captain's orders, the rest of Sara's family marched inside. She pushed slowly up from her rattan deck chair, releasing her grip on Luis's hand to fall quietly in line behind the others.

"Oh, Luis, there's a basket with toothbrushes and basic toiletry items in your and Sara's bathroom," Ruth told him. "Feel free to use anything, since you haven't brought your suitcase over yet."

The implication being that he was eventually bringing his suitcase to stay overnight with them. Problem was, at home he slept in his own king-sized bed, mostly to make up for the nights spent cramped in a single at the station. However, that little queen mattress upstairs meant he and Sara would be getting a hell of a lot cozier than either one of them had anticipated.

His mind instantly flashed back to the brush of their lips in his truck. The almost kiss that teased him with the sweet sample of her mouth against his. The warmth of her smooth skin along the back of his hand when he playfully tugged her hair. The anticipation and awareness of wanting more. Much more.

As he followed Sara to the stairs at the front of the house, he reminded himself that this was only pretend. They were helping each other get through this week and the personal challenges it presented for them both. Though Sara had no idea about his, and Luis intended to keep it that way.

Sure, he might admire the gentle sway of her hips as she took each step. Or think about running his palm up the soft skin along the calves the peach hem of her dress played with. Stopping her at the second floor landing so he could lean in, breathe deeply of her light citrusy scent, press slow, lazy kisses up the smooth column of her throat.

Sí, he might think about doing all those delicious things with her. But he wouldn't. Couldn't.

Sara had made it clear, when this charade was over, she hoped they'd wind up as friends.

No matter that the attraction luring him to her like the age-old siren's call that lured fishermen to certain ruin the world over felt all too real.

Chapter 8

"I am so sorry about all that." Sara rounded on Luis as soon as he closed the bedroom door behind them. This was much more complicated than she had anticipated.

Luis did a quick double-take shake of his head. "Uh, I'm not sure what you're apologizing for. I thought we did okay."

She waved off his words, turning and crossing the small space to plop on the queen bed with its coral-reef-inspired comforter.

"You were great, thanks. But my family." Sara heaved a sigh laden with *what the hell is going on?* doubts. It was like she'd walked into a *Twilight Zone* episode where some things were the same but others weirdly off in a delayed answered prayers kind of way.

Pressing her fingers to her temples, she massaged at the stress headache threatening. "Everyone's acting weird. Especially my mom. I mean, Robin's . . . well, Robin. Always blunt and opinionated. With no qualms about sharing hers. And, annoyingly, she's usually right. In a crisis, she's the one you want around. But her bedside manner, sheesh, leaves much to be desired."

"Well, let's hope we don't encounter a crisis. If we do, I'm pretty good in a pinch if I do say so myself. Should I need a wingman's assistance, I'll know Robin is the one to rely on," Luis answered, not sounding even the slightest bit annoyed by Robin's rudeness. "Jonathan seems like a good guy to depend on, too."

His big frame dwarfing the already-small room, Luis crossed to the light-stained wood plank extending along the length of the outside wall, where the ceiling angled down. The plank served as a makeshift desk in the center, with two white drawers holding up either end. Dragging out the wicker desk chair, he swiveled it around on one leg to straddle it, then draped his tanned forearms along the backrest.

"Outside of that, you can count on me to help you volley back anything she lobs your way. Though I couldn't help but notice you didn't seem inclined to do that yourself. Any particular reason why?"

The keen, sincere interest in his dark brown eyes made it difficult for Sara to dodge his question. Even if admitting the ineptitude she always experienced around her accomplished sister wasn't high on her favorite things list.

Late afternoon sun shone through the large skylight on the angled ceiling behind Luis, brightening their room. She squinted at him, considering how much to divulge while also distracted by the man himself. His dark closely cropped hair, sharp angular features, and bronze skin were a contrast to the wispy clouds and light blue sky framed behind him. Her real-life Vin Diesel, playing the role of an avenging angel, come to help save the day.

Only, the muscles rippling in his strong arms as he crossed them and the rakish tilt of his mouth gave rise to unangelic ideas involving him and her and the comfy bed she currently occupied.

Something about Luis Navarro compelled her to trust him. And yet she'd been bit by bad decisions with guys in the past. Ric and his self-centered personality. Before him there'd been Chris, the photographer, who it turned out was more interested in her connections. In college there'd been Thomas, the frat boy who'd been her plus-one to countless sorority socials but who couldn't get away fast enough once her eating disorder had been diagnosed.

Gun-shy about letting someone else get too close. Already on shaky emotional ground thanks to her parents'—really her mother's—mind-boggling new life philosophy, Sara skirted Luis's question about her inability to call Robin on her bitchiness. Sidestepping uncomfortable conversations was a maneuver Sara had perfected over the years, until her first therapist had called bullshit.

"Arguing with Robin isn't worth upsetting my mother." Sara lifted a shoulder, letting it fall in a practiced blasé shrug. "I'm still trying to figure out what's going on with my parents and their new Brady Bunch routine. It's a little bizarre."

If bizarre meant exactly what she had always wanted as a kid.

"But?"

"What makes you think there's a but?" she hedged.

Luis huffed out a breath that screamed, *Yeah, right.*

She blinked innocently at him. He stared back, not buying her act.

"What?"

"I'm just saying," Luis pressed. "Based on what you told me, you've always wanted your parents to play a more active role in your life." The half smile of his that had her belly and other parts aflutter made an appearance. "While I'd prefer that happen *after* this week . . ."

"Exactly!" Sara jumped on the easy answer to why her parents' sudden interest worried her, instead of admitting her deep-seated self-doubt and fear that maybe her parents had been right about her all these years. Giving credence to Robin's digs. "If they're all keen on getting chummy, you and I'll have to up our game. Case in point, this!"

She spread her arms in front of her to indicate the room that had gone from hers to theirs in one express train guilt trip from her mom.

She watched Luis's gaze make a tour around the room, from the queen bed facing the door and wardrobe, across the few feet of walking space to the small bathroom on the far side opposite the plank desk along the outer wall. Definitely close quarters.

"I'll search around for some extra blankets to make myself a pallet," she offered.

"I'll take the floor."

"Nonsense, I'm the one who master-planned this. You get the bed." Sara stood up, jerking her thumb at the item in question.

"No can do. The floor's probably as hard as the mattress at the station. I'm used to it."

"Luis . . ."

When he rose, his handsome face set in that implacable, I-mean-business mask, then deftly swung the flimsy chair out of his way and stepped toward her, Sara held her breath.

This was their first disagreement. She didn't know what to expect. A continuation of their debate. A he-man put-his-foot-down declaration that enough was enough, which would annoy the hell out of her. Certainly not a simple, *Okay, you win.*

"How about we share?"

His easy-going, unexpected response stalled her rambling thoughts.

Instantly her gaze darted to the queen-sized mattress. The vision of Luis's big frame sprawling across the jellyfish, coral, and other sea creatures swimming merrily across the comforter had her mind jumping to all sorts of intimate what-ifs.

"Friends, right?" he asked, drawing her fervent mind away from the two of them tangling in the sheets together.

Thumbs hooked on his front jeans pockets, he seemed completely at ease, totally fine with the idea of them sleeping together.

As friends.

A friend she found herself lusting after in a definitively unfriendly manner. Despite the fact they'd only met today. And, she had unequivocally decided that jumping into anything for the wrong or misguided reasons was off limits.

"Well? What do you say?" he prodded.

This was not a good idea.

The smart thing to do was—Sara nodded dumbly.

Luis's sexy grin flashed. Like the flick of a match, desire burned through her. Quick and hot.

Holy hell, what had she gotten herself into?

Cuidado con lo que pides. Yet again, Mamá Alicia's warning whispered in Sara's ear. Be careful what you wish for indeed.

A cell phone vibrating sounded seconds before her father's voice boomed up the stairs.

"Ten-minute warning!"

Luis pulled his phone from his back pocket. He checked the screen, then motioned with his cell toward the bathroom door.

"How about you freshen up first? I need to answer this text from my mom."

Thankful for a reason to escape, Sara grabbed her suitcase and ducked into the bathroom.

With the clock ticking, she vetoed a change of clothes, instead snagging her toiletry and makeup bags and setting them on the black granite counter. She brushed her teeth, dabbed the oil from her face with a sheet of blotting paper, and touched up her makeup. All the while, that *Twilight Zone* sensation shimmered around her. Thoughts of Luis, waiting on the other side of the door for her, heightened the strangeness of her situation.

A friend who wasn't a real friend. A lover who wasn't a real lover.

But in the eyes of her family, he was both.

And in the crazy musings of a woman jilted by her unworthy boyfriend, stressed by her mother's illness and the need to be worthy of her praise, he *felt* like he could be both.

Only, she had drawn a line in the sand at Higgs Beach earlier. For smart, protective reasons.

"Friends," she mumbled at her reflection as she ran a wide-toothed comb through her hair.

"Friends." Repeated under her breath as she tugged open the bathroom door.

"Okay, it's all—"

She broke off as she spotted Luis, shirtless, his broad back to her as he faced the skylight, cell phone pressed to his ear.

"*Mami, por favor, estoy bien.* Don't worry." The slope and planes of his muscular back rippled with the roll of his shoulders, as if he was trying to shrug off his discomfort at the same time he reassured his mom he was fine. "No, don't save me a plate. I'm grabbing dinner with friends... Not tonight, it'll be late when I head back to Big Coppitt. I'll swing by in the morning."

He reached up to massage the back of his neck, and had they been more comfortable with each other, if they were really friends, Sara would have hurried over to rub his neck and shoulders herself. A small thank-you in appreciation for him being such a good sport in all this madness.

Instead, she cleared her throat to alert him of her presence.

Luis spun around, and Sara barely kept her mouth from falling open at the sight of his incredibly hot, spectacularly well-defined abs and pecs.

Hello, *Men's Health* magazine, meet your new cover model!

An apology furrowed his brow as he held up a finger indicating for her to give him a minute.

Sara couldn't be sure, but she thought she nodded.

She did not, however, have any luck convincing herself to stop ogling his wide shoulders, broad chest, and the light dusting of dark hair that tapered down to his washboard abs. His light wash jeans hung low on his trim hips, and she had the insane urge to hook her fingers through his belt loops, tugging his body closer.

He shook his head at whatever his mother said . . . good Lord, Sara felt the tiniest trickle of guilt that he was on the phone with his mother while Sara stood here contemplating the successful odds of tackling him to the mattress and seeing just how friendly they could get in the next ten minutes.

"*Sí*, tomorrow. *Te quiero, mami. Adios.*"

The earnest note in his voice as he told his mom, "I love you," warmed Sara's heart. He really was such a good guy.

She sagged against the doorframe, totally smitten with the complete package that was Luis Navarro.

Luis tapped his cell screen, then slid the phone into his pocket. "Sorry about that. Something went down at the fire station earlier today and my parents heard about it. She texted a few times earlier, asking for details, but we were already here, so I hadn't answered. I'll wash up fast. We don't wanna keep your family waiting."

He strode toward her, stopping less than a foot away when she didn't move.

"Everything okay?" he asked, lightly grasping her shoulders.

The heat of his hands on her bare skin curled wantonly through her. Without thinking, she grabbed on to his waistband. Her fingers instinctively curled into his belt loops, turning her earlier musings into blessed reality.

She sucked in a breath, dragging in his musky scent, slightly sweat tinged from their afternoon together in the humid tropical outdoors.

His fingers flexed, their tips pressing into her flesh. She traced the supple skin above the edge of his waistband with her thumbs, marveling at his rock-hard obliques. The pupils in his dark eyes flared.

"Sara?" Rough and gravelly, his voice stoked her desire.

She edged infinitesimally closer. Testing. Tempting. Wanting.

The tips of her gold sandals bumped up against his black work boots.

His gaze lowered to her chest, less than another deep breath away from brushing against his. His eyelids fluttered closed, his long lashes shadowing his tanned skin. He swallowed, and the longing to hitch onto her toes to press a kiss against his throat, lick his tangy skin, overwhelmed her. Surprising her with its intensity.

"Sara." Her name on his lips was a heady mix of gruff warning and lusty plea.

"Yes," she whispered, desperate to quench this raging need to kiss him. Maybe if they did it already, sated the attraction simmering between them, it would ease.

Luis bent closer. Sara licked her bottom lip, anticipating his taste on her tongue.

Instead, he pressed his warm forehead to hers and dragged in a ragged breath. Her gut clenched at the innocent gesture that left her wanting to do less-than-innocent things with him.

Desire crested through her like a wave crashing onto one of the island's coral reefs, strong and dangerous.

"We probably shouldn't do this," he said, his breath warm on her lips.

"I figured you were going to say that."

He grinned, sexy and sure, and her entire body quivered with hunger. "I'm trying hard to remind myself why."

"Same here," she admitted.

Heart pounding, she stared intently into his eyes. That damn line in the sand she'd etched between them taunted her. She edged closer to it, her toes temptingly close to crossing over.

"Maybe we could—"

"Two minutes!" Jonathan's cry from the hallway interrupted her.

A sharp double knock on their bedroom door had Sara and Luis breaking apart.

"Damn," she muttered, sagging back against the bathroom door-frame. "Older brothers can be such a pain in the neck."

A corner of Luis's mouth hitched up in a wry grimace. "Duty calls."

He dropped a chaste kiss on her forehead, then stepped around her into the bathroom without another word.

Her body tingling with almost, Sara hurried across the room.

"Hey, squirt, everyone else is downstairs," Jonathan greeted her when she tugged open the door. He'd changed into a tropical button-up shirt and had either showered or washed up in the sink, because his blond hair was dark with water.

"First, I'm long past the squirt phase," she complained.

"Yeah, but I wasn't around much to tease you when you were younger, so I'm making up for lost time."

Sara rolled her eyes. Fatherhood and marriage to his down-to-earth wife had mellowed her brother. Usually that would be considered a positive, but this older-brother teasing had started last Thanksgiving, much to Sara's chagrin. Good news for him, his goofy grin proved contagious.

"Fine, goofball," she quipped. "We're going to need a few minutes. Luis had to take a call, but he'll be fast."

Jonathan gave her a thumbs-up, then headed to the stairs.

Once she closed the door, Sara leaned back against it, her mind racing. She wasn't sure where she'd felt less confused. Outside with her family and their changing dynamics or inside here with her sexy, good-hearted fake boyfriend.

The sink water shut off in the bathroom. Luis would be out shortly. She gulped, her shoulders shimmying with a little thrill.

He'd been right to put the brakes on things. The friend rule had been set when she'd been a little more clearheaded.

Luis lived here. Her life was in New York. Potentially part-time in Miami, *if* the deal came to fruition.

Jumping into something with Luis based on the false sense of intimacy wrought by her plea for help could only lead to confusion and hurt feelings in the end.

She didn't want that. Not for Luis or for herself.

Disappointment warred with practicality. Then, the bathroom door opened, and lust jumped into the skirmish.

The man of the hour ... or more like the week ... strode out.
With his shirt on, thank God for small blessings.

Time to get back on a friendly footing.

"You ready, Vinny?" she asked.

The dark flush that slowly crawled up his cheeks threatened to
blow her level-headed thinking to smithereens. She winked, liking
the fact that she'd gotten under his skin.

"You sure you wanna go there?" he challenged.

"If the nickname fits."

"Fine, let's go, blondie. We're already three minutes behind."

"Punctual. I like that."

"In my line of work, three minutes can save a life."

A lifesaver. The description certainly fit the man.

Luis strode toward her and damn if she didn't want to stay right
where she was. Door closed. Just the two of them. Learning a
whole lot more about each other.

Fortunately, sanity prevailed. She twisted the doorknob at her
side, then slipped into the hallway and headed toward the stairs.

"Another one of your many virtues," she teased. In reality, she
was awed by the ease with which he spoke about the high stakes in
his job.

"Oh yeah, I'm the real deal. Isn't that already on your cheat
sheet of notes?"

"Sounds like someone needs a little ego check."

"Yeah, we better help your sister with that," Luis countered.

Sara threw back her head with a laugh, accidentally bumping
into him on the step above her.

Luis grabbed ahold of her when she pitched forward. His big
palms spanned her hips. His fingertips pressed low on her belly. Instinctively she leaned back against him. With his arms wrapped
around her, the warmth of his chest seeped into her bare shoulders,
eliciting a deep yearning that careened straight to her core.

Her laughter quieted as the attraction simmering underneath
their banter bubbled to the surface.

Jonathan poked his head around the banister at the bottom of
the stairs. "Hey, lovebirds, let's go. I'm starving."

A breath she hadn't even realized she'd been holding gushed
from between her lips.

Luis's right hand patted her hip. He released her, and Sara continued down the stairs.

Apparently, her brother had developed another fine trait to match his teasing—terrible timing.

Or maybe, without even realizing it, he was saving her from making a mistake.

Right or wrong, she looked forward to the night ahead in Luis's company, even if they'd have to be on their toes in case they ran into someone he knew.

Mallory Square bustled with an energy and excitement that infused the ocean air and had Sara feeling invigorated.

With the nightly sunset celebration in full swing, the pier was packed with revelers of the local and tourist variety. All seeking a good spot to view the next performer or haggle a deal from a vendor or jockey for their position to marvel at the majestic ball of fire spreading its kaleidoscope of rich colors across the sky and rippling water.

Up ahead, Robin and Edward peered around others gathered to watch a sword-swallower wow them with his talents. Sara's parents had wandered off, called as if by the Pied Piper in the guise of an older gentleman dressed in Scottish regalia, his thick thighs flexing under his kilt as he moved to the beat of the bagpipes he played. Enamored by a vendor's seashell jewelry display, Carolyn had dragged Jonathan over to help select a gift for little Susan. The three-year-old was on a Little Mermaid kick at the moment, dreadfully sad about missing a beach vacation that might potentially include meeting a "real-live mermaid."

They'd arrived downtown an hour ago and found the wait for a table at El Meson de Pepe would have them eating right as the fiery ball heated the waters during its nightly bath. With the scent of freshly fried conch fritters wafting from one of the vendors nearby, Luis had sent the rest of the group to hunt down the appetizer while he chatted with the restaurant manager, another schoolmate of his. By the time he'd caught up with the group, everyone else in Sara's family cradled paper boats of fritters in their hands. She had eyed the brown paper napkins mottled with dark spots from the hot grease dripping off the fried balls of breading, conch meat, and spices, then passed on ordering.

Sara nibbled a fritter her parents had nagged her to sample, but did snap a photo of the booth and smiling salesman, promising to tag him in her post-vacation blog next week.

Now she and Luis strolled on the fringes of the revelry so she could take it all in. Whenever the crowd swelled near a performer, Luis put a hand on the small of her back and tucked her closer to his side. Ever the protector, he blocked errant elbows and body shoves from those pushing their way through the masses.

Rising on her toes, Sara craned her neck to see around a tall, gangly teen standing at the back curve of a horse-shoe-shaped crowd oohing and aahing. Inside the half ring, a juggler in ratty sneakers, ripped jeans, and a white tank proclaiming "All's Better in the Keys" balanced on a unicycle. The bike's seat and pedals sat about ten feet high. At the top, the juggler jerked the bike forward and backward with his feet, fighting for balance while tossing bowling pins in the air with ease.

"This is a popular place," she mused.

"You should see it during tourist season, around mid-December to late March or April. Northerners we call snowbirds flock to the Keys to escape the cold. People are packed in here like sardines." Luis leaned in so she could hear him over the competing music, continual ware hawking, and general conversation.

Her shoulder brushed against his chest and she ordered those butterflies in her belly to hunker down. No use wasting their energy. Absolutely no good would come of their efforts to get her all fluttery over Luis.

During the short drive to Mallory Square, with Jonathan and Carolyn in the truck's backseat, Sara's brother peppering Luis with questions about growing up in Key West and wrongly assuming she had visited her boyfriend here before, the gravity of this ruse sank in even more. The compounding lies. Even the ones left unspoken but that allowed her family to believe an untruth she didn't, couldn't, correct.

She'd hopped out of the truck with the fleeting idea of admitting everything. Taking Luis off the hot seat. Facing the firing squad of questions her family would barrage her with.

Then, while Luis helped Carolyn climb down from the backseat on the driver's side, Jonathan had shut the passenger door on their side and skewered Sara's intent to come clean by revealing, "He seems like a nice guy. I get why Mother's smitten with him. Seeing you with someone like Luis has her relieved. It's good."

With another annoying ruffle of her hair, her brother had saun-tered off to catch up with his wife and Luis.

And Sara had been left with no choice but to swallow the truth ready to spring out of her.

That did not, however, give her permission to join her mom on the smitten cruise ship. Not at all.

Instead, Sara vowed to keep a clear head. Avoid as many lies as possible while reminding herself she could not, would not, fall for them herself.

Her therapist would caution her about jumping into something too quickly, remaining cognizant of her need to feel connected to others. How that need manifested in good ways and bad. It's part of why she excelled as a social media influencer. A benefit in busi-ness; a curse when it came to her personal life.

The unicycling juggler finished his act in a flurry of flying bowl-ing balls that had a few onlookers nearby ducking. After a re-minder that he earned his keep via their generous tips, he posed for selfies and pictures and called thanks to those who dropped bills into a floppy straw beach hat marked "Donations."

As she and Luis followed the crowd toward another act farther along the pier, a male voice called out, "¡Oye, Santo!"

Luis stiffened beside her. He quickly shifted direction, sliding his big hand along her lower back and guiding her toward the sun-set. Away from the row of booths now behind them.

"¡San Navarro, ven pa'ca!"

The pressure on her lower back increased.

Sara glanced over her shoulder, then slowed her steps when her gaze collided with a guy in his mid-thirties looking right at her and Luis. "Um, I think someone's calling you back there."

"Ignore it," Luis said, his voice a low growl.

"Did he say, 'Saint Navarro'?"

Luis nodded. His scowl told her he wasn't a fan of the nick-name.

Sara bit back a smile. The moniker actually seemed to fit him almost as well as the one she'd given him already.

"Santo, don't be like that! Come here!" the man yelled again.

Muttering a curse, Luis stopped in the middle of the crowd. Several people bumped into them from behind, but like a huge boulder parting a running brook, he remained immovable, forcing others to step around him.

Slowly turning, Luis's chin jutted a greeting at the guy who stood several booths away. Geometric-shaped pieces of wood with painted tropical scenes decorated the sides and counter of his stall. He was dressed in the typical Key West attire of comfy shorts and a tee, and the guy's darkly tanned skin and curly black hair were a foil for the slash of white teeth at his huge grin.

The vendor raised an arm in the air to wave them over.

Luis cut a sharp look at Sara, then shook his head.

Undeterred, the man motioned again, this time with more gusto.

"*Coño*," Luis muttered, angling himself to block Sara from the other guy's view.

"What's wrong?" she asked, catching Luis's pinched expression in the waning sunlight.

"Freddie grew up around the corner from us in Big Coppitt. Graduated with my older brother, Carlos."

Sara immediately ducked down like that would help her hide from Luis's friend. "Damn" was right. The last thing she wanted was to make things more difficult for Luis by running into someone close to his family. It'd only compound the lie fest she had initiated.

"I can't blow him off or I'll risk hearing about it later." Luis's pained expression intensified. "Our moms attend weekday mass together every Monday, Wednesday, and Friday."

"Omigosh, you should go!" Sara splayed her hands on his chest to give him a little push. Fat lot of good it did. The man was like a brick wall. "Go! I'll be fine."

"Are you sure?"

"Yes, go!" she assured him. Seeing him with a family friend would be a vivid reminder that he belonged here. While her stay was only temporary. "I'll poke around, see if there's anything I might want to buy, while you chat."

"This should only take a few minutes. I don't want you to miss your first sunset."

Sara shooed him off, then ducked her head for cover as she moseyed over to the booth next to Luis's friend's. Once there, she picked up a shell necklace, pretending to read the tiny price tag. Her gaze flicked back to Luis nearby.

He clasped hands with Freddie, both men leaning in for a one-armed hug that was more like a thump on the back. Luis dwarfed his friend by at least thirty pounds and several inches, vertically and horizontally. Sara heard Freddie slip into Spanish, either for privacy or out of habit. Probably a little of both.

Luis shrugged off a question about who he was with, turning the tables by asking Freddie about his mom. All the while, Luis's posture remained stiff, hands deep in his front jeans pocket. The relaxed, yet guarded, calm she'd come to expect from him had vanished like the day's heat.

Behind Freddie's booth, another man stepped out of the shadows cast by a stately palm tree and the streetlight above it. He moved toward the tiny walkway separating the two booths, his black tee and jeans easily camouflaging him in the dark. The humid breeze fluttered the palm fronds and the shadows undulated, the yellow streetlight illuminating the man's face.

Sara started. A younger, slimmer, but equally as tall version of Luis stared back at her. His dark eyes peered at her with interest, assessing. He shared the same angular jaw, straight nose, and olive-toned skin. Yet his loose-hipped walk and confident, definitely cocky smirk gave him a kiss-my-ass swagger that reminded her of the type of men her girlfriends complained about scrolling through on those dating apps she was reluctant to try—the players.

His smirk broadened when Luis took a step in their direction.

"Hey, it's almost like a family reunion with two Navarros swinging by tonight!" Freddie crowed.

Neither Navarro brother looked as thrilled by the situation as their friend. If anything, based on the tic of his jaw muscle and the thundercloud frown creasing his forehead, Sara'd guess Luis was inwardly freaking out about having to introduce her to a member of his family.

"*¿Oye, Enrique, me traíste mas pedazos pa' vender?*" Freddie asked.

Even if their friend hadn't mentioned his name, based on the question of whether or not Luis's brother had brought more pieces of art to sell, Sara would have guessed this was Enrique. One of the few bits of information Luis had shared about his younger brother was that he'd gone to art school before joining the city's fire department. Now Enrique made a little money on the side selling his artwork through a few local spots.

Besides, based on what she had gathered earlier today, if this had been Carlos she was fairly certain the handshake, back-thumping greeting would have been exchanged between the two brothers. Not the tight-jawed head dip Luis gave his younger sibling now.

What Luis hadn't mentioned was the friction between them that practically zapped everyone in a five-foot radius of the brothers' unplanned gathering.

Not wanting to add more tension to the situation, Sara edged away. Unfortunately, an older couple sidled up to the shell jewelry booth at the same time, inadvertently sandwiching her between them and Enrique.

"I sat a box of those heart-shaped pieces with beach scenes you asked me for on your lawn chair," Enrique answered Freddie's question, his curious gaze sliding from Sara to Luis.

"Sweet! Lemme check 'em out." Their friend scampered back behind his booth leaving Enrique and Luis facing off, with Sara wishing she could melt into the group of shoppers nearby.

"Didn't expect to run into you here. This isn't your typical scene," Enrique said.

"Just enjoying the nice weather before summer temperatures descend," Luis answered.

"'Cuz all of a sudden the downtown crowds beat the privacy of the sunset view from your boat?"

Tension vibrated off Luis as he folded his arms across his chest, his fists clenched. The universally understood defensive, back-off pose. Sara cursed herself for following him over here and putting him in this predicament in the first place.

"I see you're still trivializing your talent rather than capitalizing on it with a real showing," Luis shot back.

"Maybe I'll reconsider my choices when you start doing the same."

Whatever Enrique's jab meant, it must have hit home. Luis's nostrils flared on a deep breath. His chest rose and fell, his mouth thinning as if he fought to hold back a retort.

Feeling like an interloper, despite the crowded pier, Sara edged closer to the older couple next to her. Thankfully, they moved on, making room for her to follow suit.

"And this is . . . ?" Enrique turned to ensnare her with his question.

Shocked, Sara's gaze flew to Luis's.

In the shadows of the waning sunlight, she caught his indecision. He hadn't wanted his family involved with their deception.

Guilt climbed her throat to choke her, and she prayed he read the apology in her eyes.

Earlier today, Luis had carried the conversational ball like a Super Bowl champ. Chiming in when she'd clammed up in the backyard. Time for Sara to do the same for him.

Whipping out her best camera-ready smile and video blog upbeat attitude, she stuck out her hand toward Enrique. "Hi, I'm Sara. A friend of Luis's."

"A friend?" Enrique's large hand engulfed hers, innuendo and disbelief dripping from his words.

Funny, despite his sexy, bad-boy vibe, lanky athletic frame, and heavy-lidded bedroom eyes, she didn't get the same tingling sensation of attraction as when Luis simply looked her way.

"Yep," she answered, gamely stepping into her role. "I'm in town playing tourist with my family. They're scattered about this marvelously eclectic celebration. You have some beautiful pieces for sale over there."

She gestured toward their friend's booth behind them, all the while reminding herself of Luis's advice.

Stick with the truth. Change the direction of the conversation toward someone else.

Now she added another trick: Get the hell out of the situation ASAP.

"Pick one you like. It's on me."

Enrique flashed a suave, come-hither smile Sara imagined had worked on many a charmed individual. Not her. Not when smoldering tough guy with a soft heart stood behind door number two.

"Thanks. It's my first night here, so I'm waiting to take everything in before I decide what I absolutely can't leave without. I'm limited to my carry-on bag. I appreciate the offer, though."

"No problem. If you've got my saintly brother showing you the sights and making sure you're taken care of while you're here, you'll be set. Right or wrong, he's helpful that way."

Again with the dig she didn't quite understand. Enrique's cryptic words had Luis straightening his spine. His scowl grew more fierce.

"*Oye*, play nice over there. Don't you two go squaring off and frightening the paying customers away," Freddie ordered from behind his booth.

For several tense seconds, the brothers held a grim-faced staring contest.

Then, with a muttered, "Whatever," Enrique spun around. "Hold on to my cut of the sales, Freddie. I'll settle up with you on Sunday."

Without a good-bye for his brother or Sara, Enrique strode off toward the shadowy parking lot.

Luis remained where he stood. Shoulders straight. Jaw muscle tight. Anger emanated off him, and yet Sara sensed an aura of sadness lingering in the humid air.

The need to reassure him, as he'd done for her when Robin had pounced earlier, guided Sara closer to gently caress his back. He stared in the direction his brother had disappeared, lost in whatever memory or thoughts Enrique had stirred up.

Sara remained at Luis's side, her palm warming as she rubbed soothing circles along his lower back and higher. His shoulders slowly relaxed, releasing their tension.

He blinked, then glanced down at her. The streetlight reflected in tiny gold circles in the black irises of his eyes. Surprise flashed in their depths as he seemed to come back from wherever he'd gone after his brother's jab.

"Shall we go?" she softly asked.

Uncrossing his arms, Luis motioned for Sara to lead the way.

"I'll see you around, Freddie!" Luis called out as he fell into step beside her.

The sprinkling of soft hair on his forearm tickled hers as their arms brushed. Their hands met, and Sara linked her fingers with his.

Without a word, they moved toward the mass of people standing along the pier, gazing at the sun, already halfway into its nightly dunk in the ocean. Streams of golden red and deep orange arced across the water's glossy midnight blue surface.

Around them people murmured their awe. Cell phones were held high and fancy camera shutters whirred as tourists tried to capture nature's beauty to take home with them.

Next to her, Luis remained silent. Once again the broody man of few words. The hunch she'd gotten during their game of Twenty Questions had been confirmed. Beneath his calm, unflappable exterior lay much more than a nice guy who went out of his way for others. Something darker, painful, lay deep within him. Separated him from someone he loved. Because she didn't doubt he loved his younger brother; his pain made that obvious.

In that moment, awed by the last fingers of the day's light clinging to the water, Sara came to a realization. Much like Luis had offered to help her bridge the gap with her family this week, she vowed to somehow help him do the same. He deserved to have that.

Instinctively her hand squeezed his. In her peripheral vision, she caught Luis looking at her.

Afraid what he might see, the rising attraction and admiration for him she might reveal, Sara kept her eyes trained on the curved sliver of sun barely noticeable on the horizon.

Instead, she rested her head against Luis's strong shoulder. Maybe she couldn't allow herself to fall for him, but she could damn well do her best to make sure her firefighter in shining armor found a little bit of peace in his part of this beautiful paradise he called home.

Chapter 9

Luis wasn't sure why, but for some reason, running into his bone-head younger brother had done something to Sara.

And it wasn't the swooning falling at Enrique's feet that happened with most women. Even the ones who claimed they loved someone else.

Ever since Enrique had stormed off in a snit (what else was new) Sara had remained quiet. Introspective. Close by Luis's side.

Not that he was complaining. He liked the feel of her smaller hand in his. Maybe a little too much. The tender smile she sent his way made his chest tighten. His breath a little harder to catch. Probably not the wisest reaction to have with someone he was intent on keeping in the friend zone.

Now the whole Vance clan sat at a long table on the outdoor patio of El Meson de Pepe. Sara had snagged a chair at the end of the table's left side. The brick wall behind her, she faced the makeshift stage set up across the bricked walkway that led to Mallory Square in one direction and the street in the other. Soon the large walkway in front of the outdoor bar would become a dance floor, inviting patrons at their tables and those passing by who stopped to appreciate the live band.

While the trio of musicians set up, Sara's family enjoyed the savory Cuban food that made the restaurant a crowd favorite.

"Here, taste this." Jonathan scooped up a bite of *ropa vieja*, then held out his fork for Carolyn to sample the shredded skirt steak with red and green peppers.

Carolyn's eyes closed as she chewed the food, her review of his dish humming from her mouth before she'd even swallowed. "Mmmm, that's delicious."

"Are you sure you don't want to try it?" Jonathan lifted his plate, extending it across the table toward Sara, who sat in front of him.

"No, I'm good, thanks," she answered.

"What about my pork roast?" Charles asked from the other end of the table. "How do you say it in Spanish again?"

"*Lechón.*"

"*Lechón.*"

Luis and Sara answered in unison, each cutting off the last syllable on a grin. Sara's faded quickly when her dad repeated his invitation for her to try his meal.

"That's okay, Dad; I got enough to eat. Honestly." She poked her fork at the remains of the two appetizers she had ordered.

Half of a *tostón relleno* leaned on its side, the *ropa vieja* stuffing from inside the fried green plantain mini-bowl spilling onto the cream plate. She'd eaten one and pawned off the other on Luis. A lonely ham *croqueta* had been sliced in half, then pushed aside after Sara had eaten the others in the appetizer trio.

Luis hadn't missed the way her family kept an eye on what Sara ordered, offering to share one meal or another with her when she balked at getting her own entrée. She brushed off their suggestions. Later, when their meals arrived, a few tried sending a small plate of their dish down to her. Which she promptly sent back, along with a pointed shake of her head.

At first Luis took the banter as a sign of their close connection. Everyone wanting to taste a little of everything. It didn't take him long to notice the attention was solely directed at Sara, whose polite "no thank yous" slowly bled into irritation.

"Are you sure you don't want—"

"Mother, I said I'm good." Sara's steely, back-off tone silenced everyone at the table.

Robin, who'd been deep in conversation with Edward about the artwork and flora they anticipated viewing during a tour of the Audubon House and Tropical Gardens, broke off mid-sentence. She plunked her fork on her plate's edge and leaned forward to glare at Sara. "There's no need to speak to her that way."

"Robin, it's okay." Ruth held up her hands as if to calm them all down.

"No, she's right," Sara acquiesced. Head bowed, she stared down at her plate. Yet again a muted version of the vibrant woman who teased and charmed Luis when she wasn't around her family.

"I realize some of you are looking out for me. And I appreciate that. I do."

Jonathan reached across the table to cover one of Sara's hands with his, stopping her fingers from worrying a hole in the fabric napkin she clutched.

Luis remained quiet. Assessing the situation for clues to the cause of the strange tension that had cropped up moments after the others had opened their menus. His mind ran through the information Sara had revealed earlier. It didn't help. He continued drawing a blank as to what everyone seemed to be tiptoeing around here.

With him feeling like he was missing an oar, there was no way he could steer Sara out of whatever tempestuous waters she and her family navigated. Instead, he felt like he'd been left behind on the shore. With no idea how to defuse the situation.

"I'm doing okay. I promise." Sara directed her words at her mom and dad, both of whom wore the pained expression of a worried parent. "This week is about celebrating Mom. So please, can we keep the focus on her and trust that there's absolutely nothing to worry about with me."

"*Uno, dos, tres.* Testing one, two, three," the band's lead singer said into his microphone.

Cradling his guitar, he nodded at the keyboardist, then turned to the bongo drummer, who gave a thumbs-up.

"Excuse me, I'm going to run to the ladies' room before the music starts." Sara slid from her seat and fast-walked to the door leading inside the restaurant. The material of her peach dress clung to her shapely hips, accentuating their exaggerated shake as she hustled away.

The sound of a chair scraping against the brick floor brought Luis's attention back to the table. Down at the opposite end, Ruth half stood. Charles's hand on her shoulder kept her from rising completely.

"Let her be. Pushing her won't help," Charles cautioned.

Ruth's thin face crumpled at her husband's words. She opened her mouth to respond, but the bandleader's voice drowned her out.

The older gentleman in olive dress slacks and a cream guayabera shirt welcomed everyone and introduced the opening song, a well-known bachata. The first strains of the slow song brought several couples out of their seats to gravitate toward the band.

"C'mon, Mom. They're playing our song." Jonathan slid his chair away from the table, then moved to cup his mother's elbow.

Ruth hesitated. Her troubled gaze bounced between the restaurant's back entrance where Sara had disappeared and Jonathan.

"Time for me to wow you with my dance moves like I promised." Jonathan attempted a box step but wound up tripping over his own foot.

"Son, I've seen them before. Wow's usually appropriate, but not in the way you'd want to brag about."

The others chuckled at her quip and Ruth's worry eased.

"Honestly, Mother, you really know how to make a guy feel special." He winked and led her away.

Luis mumbled a quick "excuse me" to the others, then beelined to follow Sara. Whatever was going on, he needed to be clued in.

Inside, he strode through the cigar store, the air pungent with the rich scent of tobacco mixed with those of the spices and meats from the steaming dishes waiters balanced on serving trays held high above their heads. The gift shop was packed with shoppers searching for the perfect memento to take home. Some would venture over to Mi Abuela's bodega, where they'd find shelves lined with dry and canned ingredients. Perfect for those eager to try their hand at cooking the Cuban and Caribbean dishes that made the restaurant famous.

Luis wove through the tourists, ignoring the pictures and paintings that told the history of the Cubans who'd left their island and made Key West their home centuries ago. Eventually the crowd thinned as he reached the open path leading to the indoor restaurant space at the front of the building.

He drew to a halt when he spotted Sara eyeing one of the brightly colored murals and 3-D artworks decorating the walls. One hand pressed to her stomach, she gazed at a scene depicting three men in a Cuban barbershop.

"Makes me wish I wouldn't have left my phone back at the table," she told him when he reached her side. "I'll have to come back later to snap a picture."

"You want to use mine?"

She shook her head.

"You feeling okay?" Luis dropped his gaze to her flat belly where her hand still rested.

Sara turned away and strolled farther along the walkway. The waves of her blond hair swayed along her bare shoulders, teasing him with the urge to brush the tresses away and drop a kiss on her pale skin.

"You care to tell me what that was about back there?" he asked.

"God, I love all these colors. They're so vibrant and rich. Soulful." She ran her fingertips lightly over the thin wood cutouts of a chicken surrounded by different variations of flowers local to the Keys.

A flicker of annoyance flared through him at her obvious avoidance. He couldn't help if he didn't know what they were dealing with. "Ignoring me isn't going to work, you know."

She sucked her teeth and flicked an exasperated glance his way. The same mature response she'd given her brother when he tried convincing her to share his *ropa vieja* entrée.

The door to the women's restroom opened a few feet away, and two middle-aged women exited. Luis waited until they had passed by before pressing Sara again.

"We're supposed to be on the same team here. That's not going to work if I'm kept in the dark. What's going on?"

"Nothing. Like I told the others. I'm fine. I can handle it on my own." Sorrow traced across her beautiful face, etching strained grooves between her brows, telegraphing that she was the opposite of "fine."

"Hey." Driven by the compulsion to soothe her, Luis stepped closer, stopping just inside her personal space. "We may be lying to everyone else right now, but things will tank if we start lying to each other. C'mon, talk to me."

Unable to resist the temptation to touch her, he gently tucked her hair behind her ear. Allowed his fingers the treat of softly trailing along her jawline. Her eyes drifted closed, her lips trembling with vulnerability. A strange flutter tickled his gut, shimmering lower in his body.

Had they been somewhere more private, he would have bent to kiss her, offer her comfort in his arms. To hell with pretending he was fine keeping things between them platonic.

Just as he'd convinced himself to go for it anyway, her eyes opened, mesmerizing him with the mix of determination and pain filling her blue-green gaze.

"If I share a secret, then you have to do the same," she challenged.

"I don't have any." *Mierda.*

"Bullshit."

Luis kept his surprise in check when she repeated the curse that had immediately sprung through his head after his bald lie at her challenge.

"Liar, liar, pants on fire," she chanted softly.

Elbows bent, she set her forearms on his chest and leaned into him. Her right hand patted the KWFD emblem on his T-shirt above his left pec. "Everyone has secrets. Things from the past that shape our present. Even our future, if we let them fester."

Coño, an alarm clanged in his ears as he sensed her edging closer to a question he should have known was coming after their run-in with his brother before sunset.

"What's going on between you and Enrique?" Sara asked.

Instantly, the same wall he put up between himself and those who dared to raise the subject of the bad blood with his brother loomed between him and Sara. He stepped back, distancing himself out of habit. Her arms slid from his chest to fall at her sides.

At least he had the presence of mind not to tell her to piss off, his usual response with everyone except his mother—he knew better than to disrespect the matriarch of their *familia*. Instead, Luis dodged and deflected. Two tactics in which he excelled out of practice. And necessity. That's what happened when you were part of a nosy, busybody *familia* with the best of intentions. Most of them anyway.

"This is about you, not me," he told Sara, jamming his hands in his back pockets.

She crossed her arms, inadvertently pushing her cleavage higher up the edge of her strapless dress. Luis ignored the urge to dip his gaze to appreciate the enticing view. Instead he kept his gaze locked with hers. Refusing to give in on this important issue.

"About you wanting to get closer with your family this week. Let's keep mine out of it like we agreed and focus on whatever yours was tossing around like a hot potato out there. I can't avert disaster if I'm not sure what's coming at me. You're setting us up for failure."

Sara opened her mouth but snapped it closed without uttering a word. Based on the scowl twisting her lips, he probably wouldn't have liked what she was thinking anyway. She eyed him for several tense seconds. Her pupils tiny black islands in the middle of turbulent seas.

The door down by the cigar shop leading to the patio bar and salsa band must have pushed open, because the strains of a classic tune known to bring his *mami* and *papi* out onto the dance floor, or the middle of their living room, whispered on the air.

Luis waited. Determined, implacable. Sara narrowed her eyes. But this was a game of chicken he refused to lose. Not if it compromised his ability to help her.

Several tense beats later, Sara spun away, frustration evident in her out-flung arms and low groan. "Okaaaay. Here's all you need to know."

After a step, she swiveled to face him, resignation dripping from her words. "I had . . . will probably always have to deal with . . . a health . . . situation. But I've got it under control now. They're all hypersensitive in one way or another. Well, Robin's more protective of our mother and how stressing about me affects Mom's health. But like I said already, I am fine. They don't have anything to worry about. And you, for this one week, certainly don't either. Okay? Are we good?"

Uh, no. Not by a freaking long shot.

His paramedic training instantly kicked in. Typical health assessment questions flipped through his head like the cards in that old Rolodex his *papi* used to keep on his desk at the fire station.

What kind of "health situation" did she mean?

Was she on some type of medication he should be aware of in case of an emergency?

Could being on vacation, off her regular routine and diet, adversely affect whatever vague *situation* she was dealing with?

What should he be doing to better protect this driven, intelligent, temptingly gorgeous woman he was coming to care about more that was probably wise? The one who'd so easily convinced him to step outside his comfort zone?

Way outside.

Luis pulled his thoughts up short. That last question was more personal than he tended to get on the job. But he wasn't on the job here. And this was not a typical situation. There was absolutely nothing typical about Sara.

Which gave him all the more reason for wanting solid answers. Now.

One look at her tight-jawed, don't-push-me expression had the questions melting on the tip of his tongue like the cotton candy he'd bought his nephews at Children's Day in Bayview Park last October.

Coño, she'd give his sister a run for her money when it came to hardheadedness.

But he . . . Well, he was a patient man.

He intended to get to know her better. Find out exactly what she meant by having it "under control." Whatever *it* was. To ultimately convince her that she could trust him to do everything in his power to make sure she truly was "fine."

"Well?" she insisted.

Right hip cocked in a jaunty angle, she tapped the toe of her gold sandal against the brick floor, telegraphing her irritation. Now why wasn't she this pushy when her sister threw out one of her blunt jabs?

Another question Luis planned on answering.

Not that she would appreciate hearing so, but she actually

looked kind of cute when she let her anger loose. Blue-green eyes flashing. Lips pursed in a kiss-my-ass pout that had him thinking about kissing several other parts of her sexy body.

He'd known her less than a day. Yet somehow, he felt certain there'd come a time when he'd count it among the best days he'd ever had.

"Here's another tidbit for that 'Why He's So Hot' list you're compiling about me." Tucking a hand in the arms she still kept folded across her chest, he gave a little tug that had her stumbling forward a step while he backpedaled.

"More like my 'Why He's So Annoying' list?" she countered.

Again with the sass. He liked the color it brought to her cheeks.

"If you don't want to find me, or pretty much anyone in my *familia*, on the dance floor, don't start the music. C'mon, they're playing one of my favorites."

He watched the playful grin dawn on her face. Slowly. Hesitantly. Then in all its full glory, like the sun peeking its hello across the sky when he was out for an early morning run. It transformed her classic features, rounding her cheeks and crinkling the corners of her eyes. Invigorating him at the idea that his words had brought her this much pleasure.

"Is that a promise or a threat?" she teased.

Luis halted, and Sara bumped into his chest with an "oof!" He palmed her hips, holding her soft curves firmly against him.

"*Cariño*, with me, either one could get you into trouble."

The endearment felt natural when it came to her. If him calling her sweetheart bothered Sara, she didn't show it. Instead, she tipped her head back on a husky laugh that had lust tightening his jeans.

And damn if he didn't feel like a red snapper caught on the end of her fishing pole. Only, fool that he might be, he wasn't squirming to be released.

Sara sighed in full-on swoony appreciation.

There was something seductive about studying a man who looked at home on a dance floor. His hips fluidly moving to the beat of a quick-tempoed salsa or merengue. Swaying to the sultry rhythm of a bachata.

She watched as Luis guided her mother in another spin around the open area between the outdoor bar at El Meson de Pepe and the small stage where the band played. Enclosed on three sides and raised a couple feet high in the air, the stage provided shelter from inclement weather. Although the thin walls also kept out the breeze wafting in from the ocean. That's probably why the three men had recently returned from their first set break, refreshing drinks in hand.

"Your mother appears quite taken with your young man."

Sara turned to her left to find her father standing next to the wooden pillar she leaned against. A warm, heartfelt smile deepened the wrinkles around his eyes and mouth.

She followed his gaze back to where Luis and her mother stood, facing each other, in front of the band.

"She certainly does," Sara murmured.

Under the glow of the streetlamps dotting the area and the hanging lights over the patio bar, Luis held her mother's hands in each of his while patiently demonstrating, once again, the one-two-three-four count footwork for the bachata. "Loose-hipped" would never be a description used for Ruth. Still, she seemed hell-bent on trying to add the little hip hitch on the four and eight beats that came so naturally to Luis. Like so many other moves he made.

Yes, Sara had definitely taken note of how deftly he mastered the dance floor, even in well-worn work boots and loose-fitting jeans that hung low on his trim hips. As had a group of middle-aged women seated at a nearby table openly ogling the handsome firefighter.

She and Luis had danced a salsa and bachata together earlier. Then, with Sara's pulse still racing after the floor-sweeping dip he'd shocked her with at the end of a salsa, they'd swapped partners. He'd gently swept her mom up in his strong arms, then followed up with Carolyn. Much to their delight.

Despite Jonathan's good-natured cry of, "Show-off," to Luis, Sara's brother had rallied long enough to trounce on her toes a few times before she cried uncle.

Ultimately, Luis's contagious pleasure on the dance floor coupled with the lively music had diffused any sign of her family's earlier discord. After taking the time to teach them a few basic steps, he was the hit of the evening with pretty much everyone. Even sour-faced Robin had been convinced to join him for an easy merengue.

Sara knew she should be thankful. She hadn't seen her mom so full of life and laughter in . . . well, ever probably. Luis was single-handedly winning over them all. Just like she'd wanted.

If only she could stop her imagination from four-counting the two of them off the dance floor and into a different, decidedly more private space. Specifically, the bedroom they would share for the next week.

The smooth hardwood flooring at the rental house would prove a much better dancing surface than the bricked walkway here. And if that surface happened to lead to a softer, more giving one . . . namely the queen-sized bed . . .

Ooh, the thought of a private bachata lesson with Luis sent a delicious shiver through her. Body aflame from her sensual musings, Sara fanned herself with the paper To-Go menu she'd snagged from the hostess stand earlier.

"This humidity is something else, isn't it?" her father asked. He wiped the sweat glistening on his brow with a handkerchief.

Sara lifted her hair up with one hand to fan the back of her neck. "We're not in Arizona's dry heat anymore, Toto."

Her father chuckled.

"You know we mean well, right, princess?" Leaning his shoulder on the curved wooden support beam, her dad peered around it. A garish green streaked across his forehead from the neon beer sign above the bar behind her.

"Most of you anyway," she murmured.

"*All* of us."

Biting back a sigh, Sara nodded. She didn't want to get into it with him, not here. Not this week. Not anymore, really.

The fact was, unlike with her and Jonathan, the emotional distance between her and Robin hadn't diminished when Sara reached adulthood. After their mom had been diagnosed, that distance only lengthened.

"We're different." Hands loosely clasped, Sara lifted them toward her sister and Edward. Both born with two left feet, they'd given up trying to master the steps and now rocked back and forth in a slow circle together. "Always have been. Always will be."

"Yes, but different doesn't have to be a bad thing. Look at your brother and Carolyn. Her easy-going manner has mellowed him. In a wonderful way."

Watching her brother and his wife bumbling through a partner turn and swing that looked more like the jitterbug than the bachata had Sara grinning.

"Their relationship has been a welcome example for your mother and me."

"She's good for him," Sara answered. "He seems more relaxed. More content."

"Exactly. And based on what I've seen of him today, I'd say Luis is good for you, too. It brings me comfort to know you've found someone who'll take care of you."

Guilt and disillusion partnered in a quick merengue beat that hammered in Sara's chest. She ducked her head. Ashamed by her lie. Yet angry at her dad's inability to understand that she wanted someone to care *for* her, not take care *of* her.

"Come on."

She glanced up at her dad's words. He tapped the tip of her nose lightly with his finger, a playful gesture he hadn't done since she was a little girl.

"Let's go rescue Luis from your mother's lack of rhythm."

Before she could respond, her father scooted around a nearby couple, sidestepping another as he made his way to her mom and Luis. Sara wanted to call him back, reassure him that she had learned to take care of herself. But her whole life they'd assumed otherwise. First counting on Mamá Alicia to fill in for them. Later assuming her sorority sisters would bolster her. Missing the boat on what she really craved from her family.

Swiveling along the pillar's curve, Sara rested the back of her head against the wood surface and faced Mallory Square. She stared at the area that had been teeming with activity a couple of hours ago. Now it lay quiet and empty. Dark shadows and patches of light from streetlamps and the half-moon's glow chased each other across the brick and cement surface. If you weren't careful, especially near the pier's edge, danger loomed in the shadowy recesses. Much like her psyche before she'd sought treatment.

When she'd been diagnosed with Other Specified Feeding or

Eating Disorder her sophomore year of college, her family threw themselves into information overload mode, researching and educating themselves on every aspect involving OSFED. Suddenly she became a patient case for them to study and heal.

Mostly, Sara believed her parents and siblings were shocked that they hadn't been the ones to recognize her struggles. It didn't matter that her symptoms intermingled binge eating disorder and bulimia, which made OSFED more difficult to detect or diagnose. Or that it lay outside their respective areas of expertise. Sara became the focus of her parents' attention based on their sense of responsibility. Too bad what she'd actually wanted was their attention borne of love.

As it turned out, Mamá Alicia, the one person Sara had always been able to count on, a person with no formal medical training but armed with a loved one's intuition, had picked up on the behaviors Sara had hidden for years. Knowing something was wrong. Part of her desperate to stop the destructive behavior. Unable to figure out how.

"Mallory Square looks different at this hour, doesn't it?" Luis asked as he sidled over to her.

"Almost spooky, in a Gothic romance kind of way."

"I'll have to take your word on that. I'm more of a murder mystery reader myself." He stopped a hair's breadth from her shoulder, apparently comfortable invading her personal space. Not that she minded. "Are you feeling tired, or can I charm you into one last dance?"

Squinting down at her under the bright patio lights, his supersize physique a heady mix of power and strength and grace that set parts of her aflutter, this man could probably charm her into doing almost anything. If she wasn't careful.

"Who said anything about being tired?" she balked.

"It's been a stressful day for you. On multiple levels."

"The fun would barely be getting started in New York and Miami." Though she rarely lingered out late into the night, even for influencer events.

"I don't want you to overdo it."

Sara's heart sank with unease at his concern. This was exactly why she had avoided mentioning her OSFED. All day he'd seen her as an average girl, not someone who needed to be treated with kid gloves. If he knew, he'd wind up behaving like the others. Analyzing her food intake. Noting her trips to the bathroom or her amount of exercise. Peppering her with questions.

She wanted him to be interested in her, Sara. Not the patient with the eating disorder or the sought-after social media influencer. Just plain Sara.

"Actually, I've been standing here considering the idea of getting a tattoo across my forehead that says: 'I'm fine.' What do you think?"

Her belly flip-flopped at the sexy grin hitching up a corner of his mouth.

"Where? Right here?" He traced a faint line across the center of her forehead with his fingertip.

Sara held her breath. Savoring the tingles of awareness his light touch evoked.

"I guess it might be a good conversation starter at all your cocktail parties."

He winked and she found herself free-falling through the air like a novice base jumper. Anxiously flailing for the ripcord to release her parachute before she hit the brick walkway with a splat.

"Whatever has this little worry line marring your beautiful face"— Luis gently rubbed the space between her brows with his thumb pad, and her eyelids fluttered, longing coursing through her—"I've been told I'm a good listener. If you want to talk about it."

Part of her wanted to be up-front, confide in him her fears of inadequacy.

But she wasn't ready for him to look at her differently. As crazy as it might sound considering she'd known Luis for such a short time, she'd truly come to value their relationship. She didn't want him to see her as less than. Not like her own family did.

"One more before we take another short set break," the lead singer announced over the microphone. "An oldie but goodie whether sung in English or Spanish."

The opening notes of "Unchained Melody" strummed from the guitar, a swoony bachata rhythm infusing the classic love song.

Sara pushed off the pillar, its rough wood scraping her shoulder blade. "Oh, I love this one."

"That's my cue."

Luis held out his hand, palm up. Sara laid her fingers over his, electricity charging through her when he tugged her gently into his open arms. She landed flush against his hard body, one of his muscular legs wedged between hers. His left hand cradled her right one over his heart. His right palm on the small of her back held her in place, its soft pressure nudging her to follow his lead. She went willingly.

This time he barely moved his feet in the one-two-three-four count. Instead, his hips cajoled hers into joining him for a sexier, sultrier version of the dance. He looped their clasped hands around his waist, pressing them to his lower back where his T-shirt tucked into his jeans before releasing hers to wrap his arm around her in an intimate embrace.

His left hand splayed in the center of her back, firm, insistent, as he spun them in a tight circle. She pressed her cheek to his shoulder, lost in the swirl of light and dark as they twirled. Closing her eyes, she breathed in his musky scent, marveling at the muscles rippling across his back as she clung to him. He bent his knees, lowering her with him to the beat. She rode his thigh, lust and desire bubbling to a boil inside her.

Her hips moved in tandem with his, wantonly mimicking the moves her body craved. Secretly seeking his touch in her most intimate of places.

They dipped, swayed, spun as one. Sara trusting him to lead, allowing herself to let go and simply feel the rhythm. The sensual beat. Him.

All too soon the love song drew to an end. Around them patrons clapped their praise for the band, but Sara wasn't ready to let Luis go.

His arms tightened around her. Ducking his head, he nuzzled her cheek with his nose. Pressed a warm kiss on her temple, the scruff of his jaw scratching her sensitive skin. Tendrils of desire curled through her. Sara fisted his shirt in her hands, her knees buckling under the onslaught of lust he ignited.

"You are so damn sexy." His gruff whisper had her body quivering with need.

Heart racing, her brain screamed for her to back away. She was playing with dangerous fire here.

But her feet refused to listen. Her body, relishing the rush of emotions, urged her to fan the flames higher. With his back to the well-lit patio bar, his angular features fell into shadow, his eyes pools of deep mahogany, rich with intensity.

"You really know how to show a girl a good time on the dance floor," she murmured, hoping to lighten the mood before she combusted in his arms.

His right palm slid down her lower back to cradle her butt. "That's not the only place, *cariño*."

Sara melted into him. Far too eager to investigate the "places" where he excelled.

Someone roughly bumped into Luis, jarring them aside.

"That's my little sister you're manhandling, bud. You better watch it!" Jonathan's teasing leer lightened his threat.

His interruption pulled Sara out of her lust-induced stupor, and she realized the crowd had dissipated.

"Leave them alone," Carolyn chided. She shot Sara an *I'm sorry* grimace as she pulled Jonathan back to their table.

Luis's hands roamed up Sara's spine, settling in a more public-appropriate spot, her shoulders.

Sara dropped her forehead to his chest, embarrassed by her brother's antics.

"All my life I missed having a big brother around. Lately, I'm realizing how obnoxious big-brother teasing can actually be."

She felt Luis's chuckle rumbling through him.

"That's nothing," he said. "Wait till you see my brothers, sister, and me go at each other."

The unexpected—unwise—thrill she experienced at the thought of meeting Luis's *familia* signaled the folly of her behavior. Abruptly Sara stepped back, out of his arms. Putting the physical distance she should have been keeping between them.

"I'm sorry I won't get to see that."

Luis tilted his head in confusion, then understanding dawned in his dark eyes. "Yeah, me too. But it's better not to muddy the water with more lies."

Muddy the water.

His words hung in the humid air between them as they stared at each other. Bar patrons and tourists strolling by, the canned music playing over the speakers, the skateboarder cruising the sidewalk on the street behind them ... everything faded into the background as Sara stared up at Luis.

What if it wasn't lies? What if this could be the start of something special? Something—"

Stop it!

She pulled the mental emergency brake on her careening thoughts.

Holy crap! How had she let this happen?

Somehow, her simple plan to hire a fake boyfriend had turned into something bigger. Something scarier. Especially for a woman with a terrible dating track record and an unhealthy need to prove herself worthy.

In short, a woman who had no business falling for a sexy firefighter with a savior complex and his own secret family issue, even if he wouldn't admit it.

Not that she was having any luck stopping that from happening.

Chapter 10

"Mami, *por favor*, I'm fine." Luis wrapped his arms around his mother's plump figure, giving her a tight hug as she rinsed out the moka pot from their *café con leche* Saturday morning.

It wasn't lost on him that Sara had said the same words to her family and him last night at dinner. But this was different.

Sara had been, maybe still was, dealing with some mystery health issue that had them all worried. Perhaps with good reason. He needed to find out for sure.

He, on the other hand, really *was* fine.

"I worry about you," his *mami* said. "All of you. Have you talked to your sister and brothers today?"

Translation, had he talked to his younger brother. Tried to make amends. Something she prayed for every day.

Anger and disillusion slithered through Luis's chest, a two-headed viper he couldn't seem to slay.

Why should he be expected to extend the olive branch?

Enrique was the one who had lied. Withheld the fact that Luis's fiancée had propositioned him during a group beach party at Bahia Honda. Or that he and Mirna had hooked up once in Miami. Supposedly before Enrique knew Mirna and Luis were an item. Convenient excuse.

That made Enrique the one with a problem. Along with Mirna, who had only confessed her unfaithfulness as she lay in a hospital bed barely clinging to life. After fighting with Enrique at the beach party, she'd made the ill-fated decision to get behind the wheel intoxicated. Luis's brother had done nothing to stop her.

Another strike against him.

"Your silence answers my question about your younger brother. As for you, I know my son. Fine? *Por favor, no me mientas,*" his *mami* scolded.

"I'm not lying." Hunching over, Luis propped his chin on top of her head, dodging the tight bun that held her shoulder-length hair out of her round face. "It's all good."

"How? It is not good being forced to change your Kelly day, ordered not to come around the station for the whole week. *¿Verdad?*"

Yeah, she was right, a move like this would look bad if it went on his record. But his captain had stipulated this time off as an alternative to some type of official measure. Something they both wanted to avoid.

Heaving a sigh, Luis reached over to pump the clear plastic soap dispenser when his *mami* lifted her rubber-gloved hand under the spout. The green liquid pooled to the size of a dime on the yellow scrubbing sponge.

He hadn't liked it yesterday when the Captain laid down his edict. But today . . .

Strange how a guy's outlook could change in the span of twenty-four hours.

Since the Captain's move freed Luis up to spend time with Sara, he now viewed the forced time off as a serendipitous twist of fate.

Not that he planned on sharing his change of perspective with his mom. Or Carlos, who apparently had dialed the Mami 911 line after Luis had stormed out of the airport fire station yesterday. The bigmouth claimed he wanted to warn their *mami* that Luis was pissed and might need some distracting this coming week.

Oh, he'd found a way to distract himself all right.

More like someone.

A charismatic, sexy-as-hell woman with a sense of humor that sparked his own laughter and a secret he was determined to un-root. If only to make sure she was safe on his watch.

A woman who'd kept him awake late into the night after he dropped her, Jonathan, and Carolyn back at the rental and drove the ten miles up the Keys to his place in Big Coppitt.

When he'd finally fallen asleep, Sara had invaded his dreams like a sexy marauder on the high seas. Enticing him with her infectious smile. Drugging him with the citrusy scent that clung to her soft skin. Driving him crazy with her sweet lips he ached to sample.

"*¿Qué vas a hacer?*" his mother asked, dashing the montage of Sara-themed images that had his pulse pounding.

"What am I going to do about what?"

"About work? Will you go talk to the Captain or the Watch Commander?"

"I'm not going to do anything."

Pressing a kiss to his *mami*'s temple, he felt the sheen of perspiration glistening on her skin and moistening her hairline. Between the steam rising from the dishwater and the hot flashes she complained about, the poor woman looked like she'd just finished one of those crazy hot yoga classes his sister raved about.

"What is it you always tell me?" he continued. "What's done is done. I can't fight the Captain over this. And honestly, I don't want to."

"*¿De veras?*"

"Yeah, it's the truth." He drew the sign of a cross over his heart.

"*¿Por qué?*" His *mami*'s all-knowing narrow-eyed stare, the one feared by neighborhood kids and her own in particular, underlined her sharp "why?"

He hated lying, but no way could he share the truth with her. Like a Florida crawfish scurrying back in its hole to avoid capture, Luis spun away to snag the dish towel hanging on the refrigerator door, avoiding her wily gaze.

Lydia Quintana de Navarro possessed a sixth sense when it came to her kids. Little got by her unnoticed. Good luck if you were trying to pull a fast one on her. No question, she'd catch you. Growing up, Carlos and Enrique had faced countless *chancletazos* to prove it.

Equally as powerful, her devout prayers seemed to have a direct connection to heaven. Or maybe it was the number of candles she lit each week after mass that made such a huge smoke signal, no way could the good Lord ignore her. What really mattered was if Luis's *mami* added you to her daily prayer list, you couldn't help but feel you had a fighting chance.

When he worked his shifts at the station, Luis counted on those prayers. But today, with the secret he withheld from her, that keen parental radar of his *mami*'s had him on red alert.

Turning his back on her penetrating gaze, Luis strode to the round breakfast table by the window overlooking their backyard and canal. Outside, his *papi* bent over a boat engine propped up on a sawhorse where the edge of the green lawn met their property's concrete seawall on the canal. The engine cover had been removed to leave the motor exposed for repairs.

Always tinkering on something, that man. As a kid Luis had followed in his *papi*'s footsteps. Asking questions, serving as an extra pair of hands for whatever his *papi* needed. Learning everything about boating and fishing and living a life on the ocean from the man who'd always been his hero. On the job and off.

Papi had been quiet over breakfast. But Luis knew, if asked for advice, his old man wouldn't sugar coat his thoughts. At the same time, he'd let Luis, all the Navarro kids, make their own decisions.

Pushing one of the old wooden chairs closer to the table, Luis answered his *mami*'s question. Carefully sticking to the truth as much as possible. "I'm not going to fight the time off because the more I dig in, arguing that there's nothing wrong with my state of mind since we responded to that car accident last month, the more Captain Turner pushes back. If I have to go along with this to convince him I'm fit to pull my weight on the team, so be it."

"And are you?"

"Am I what?"

"Fit, mentally, with everything."

His knee jerk reaction was to answer in the affirmative.

Since Carlos's kick-in-the-ass pep talk yesterday, then meeting Sara and getting swept up in something he had to admit had become bigger than simply helping someone, Luis wasn't as sure anymore.

Through the window, he watched his *papi* rotating a spark plug wrench with his left hand. He paused to wipe a dirty rag over the engine part, then rotated the wrench again. A normal task Luis had watched and participated in countless times over the years. Only, today, he didn't feel like his normal self. He felt both off-kilter and energized, uncertain if that was good or not. Unwilling to question it.

Behind him, the kitchen faucet shut off. A cabinet door creaked open, then clattered closed. That would be his *mami* putting her rubber gloves in the plastic basket under the sink.

A quick check of his sports watch told him he should be leaving in less than five if he planned to make the twenty-minute drive to Sara's place and arrive by nine thirty. Last night her family had decided to ride the Conch Tour Train today. The seventy-five-minute loop winding through the island streets treated patrons to the highlights of Key West history and lore courtesy of the drivers running monologue. Even though he'd grown up on the island, Luis had actually never ridden the tourist train or the trolley. He was actually looking forward to the activity.

Who was he kidding? The chance to spend the day with Sara was what had him jumping out of bed like his nephews on Christmas morning. Not some historical ride around the three-by-five-mile island in a yellow and black open-air train on wheels.

His *mami*'s Kino sandals slapped against the mottled cream tile, signaling her approach.

"I worry about you, *mijo*." She covered his hand with hers on the chair's curved backrest. "Anamaría and your *papi* walked me through that call. How you tried to calm the poor girl's fears while she was trapped inside her car. Talking with her as the others struggled with the Jaws of Life."

Her hand tightened over his and a stinging, sinking sensation in the pit of his stomach warned him what was coming.

"Having her die in your arms must have been horrible. I know you, *mijo*. I see the way you've always taken on another's pain."

Luis closed his eyes, trying in vain to erase the image of the college student's mangled car. The front windshield shattered by the aluminum ladder that had poked out of the truck bed and wound up inside her front seat after she rear-ended the other vehicle. Her straight, black hair sticky with blood. The trickle oozing from her left nostril, dark red against her pale skin. Her hazel eyes pleading with him for help. Her wheezy gasps of breath as she brokenly begged him to call her parents.

"Every single one of us who answered that call was affected by her death," he rasped. "It was senseless and stupid. Avoidable."

"Just like Mirna's."

"Don't!" Pulling his hand from under his mother's, Luis reared back, bumping into the windowsill behind him. The cream curtains with their smattering of brown and green palm trees flapped around him. "Don't even bring that up. It's in the past. It's done."

"It will not be done until you make peace with your *hermano*," his mom warned, her face pinched with maternal worry and caution.

Coño, her refrain was a recording stuck on a never-ending loop, repeating her insistence that he clear the air with his brother. Too bad that would never happen. Luis could never forgive Enrique's betrayal. Or the role he had played in not stopping Mirna from driving away that day.

Spinning on his sneaker, Luis stomped toward the sliding glass door leading to the back porch.

"*Necesitas hablar con alguien*," his mom insisted.

Luis paused, his fingers crooked around the metal handle. No, he didn't need to talk to anyone or rehash the past. He needed to forget. Keep himself busy. Help the next person in need.

"If not me. If not Father Miguel at St. Mary's. If not a grief counselor. Then with your *papi*. He understands loss, on the job and off."

Head bowed, Luis nodded. She made a good point. As always.

"Think about it. Now come give your *mamá* a kiss good-bye. You know better than to leave without one."

Like the dutiful son he tried hard to be, Luis trudged back to his mom. Her plump face, its wrinkles a sign of a life well lived as she liked to say, softened with her benevolent smile. She angled her head for him to kiss her cheek.

"*Dios te bendiga, mi vida*," she told him.

As he pushed the sliding glass door open to say good-bye to his father, Luis found comfort in the farewell his mother had said to them all for as long as he could remember.

God bless you, my life.

As screwed up as his personal and work life might be at the moment, he could always count on his parents' love and support. Something Sara had unfortunately missed out on growing up.

It seemed as if her parents wanted to change that now, and if he could facilitate the process, help someone else's family situation when he couldn't help his own, that would make this forced time off work worth it.

Anxious to see Sara again, Luis hurried down the back steps. He gave his dad a quick hug and kiss on the cheek, then double-timed it to his truck.

He had plans with his enticing fake girlfriend, and they made the week ahead loom brighter.

Luis pulled into the parking space behind the Vances' blue rental SUV to find Ruth, dressed in a navy and white short-sleeved dress, pacing back and forth along the verandah. She paused mid-step, her gaze peering intently through his front windshield. Seconds later, her thin shoulders slumped, and she returned his wave with a feeble one of her own.

Unease skittered down Luis's spine.

His cell phone nested in the console cupholder, so he knew he hadn't missed a warning call or text from Sara. But based on Ruth's sentinel-guarding-the-door routine, he'd guess something was wrong in the Vance household this morning.

Grabbing his duffel bag off the front passenger seat, he hopped out of his truck. By the time his sneakers hit the grass, his mind shifted into problem-solving mode, his eyes assessing the premises as if he were arriving on the scene of a call.

"Good morning!" he said, shifting into the upbeat tone he used when visiting elementary schools or speaking with children about life as a firefighter. "Weather looks great for a day of island sightseeing."

Ruth didn't take his bait. Instead, she waited for him at the top of the stairs, her hello smile shaky, her gray eyes stormy.

"Have you heard from Sara?" she asked.

Halfway up the steps, Luis paused, suddenly leery. Was their ruse up?

"Uh, no," he answered, ping-ponging between disappointment

and unease. Trying not to let either show. "But I wasn't expecting to. When I left last night, we arranged for me to be here at nine thirty after I met my parents for breakfast. Do you need something?"

Ruth shook her head and pivoted, crossing the wooden flooring to perch on the end of one of the rattan rockers. She rubbed her palms up and down her thighs, a nervous gesture that stretched, then bunched the navy and white wavy-patterned material of her short-sleeved sundress.

Figuring he would have been given the boot had their fake relationship been exposed, Luis dropped his bag by the front door, then crossed to sit in the rocker beside hers.

"She left the house at seven thirty to go for a short run." Ruth crooked her elbow to check the time on the gold watch circling her tiny wrist. Her lips thinned. Her brows angled even closer as her frown deepened.

"The island's beautiful in the morning," he mused. "Sun rising over the ocean. Quiet early AM sounds like our famous stray roosters crowing. Less hustle and bustle of tourists clogging the streets. Maybe she decided to extend her run."

"That's what I'm afraid of. Aren't you?"

He drew a blank on how to respond to Ruth's question. Personally, he enjoyed a long morning run around the island when he finished a shift.

"I've tried calling, but her phone goes direct to voice mail. Doesn't that worry you?" Ruth's concerned, slightly accusatory, gaze pierced him.

It was obvious Sara's mom thought him privy to some kind of info Sara herself hadn't felt the need to divulge. The only answer he could guess was the mystery sickness she was supposedly recuperating from.

"Sara has assured me, all of us"—he placed his hand on Ruth's forearm, stalling her agitated motion up and down her thighs—"that she's feeling fine."

There was that damn word again.

"Yes, she has. But recovery can be so precarious. I'm sure with your paramedic training you're aware of the dangers. How easily someone can slide back into obsessive habits."

The words *recovery* and *obsessive habits* in reference to Sara caught Luis so completely off guard, he blinked at Ruth in surprise.

Case studies from his training and real-life experiences on the job filed through his mind, with him quickly cataloging and searching for similar signs he may have missed in Sara. With each symptom or side effect he recalled, Luis came up short. The only hard facts he had to go on were her family's odd behavior at dinner last night, the mysterious "health situation" Sara had alluded to but didn't care to discuss, and now Ruth's comments.

It wasn't nearly enough information, and his bid for answers came up frustratingly empty.

Luis stared back at Ruth, her high cheekbones and pert nose so like Sara's etched with pain. The older woman's fear was a needle pricking his skin, jabbing at his innate need to soothe another's discomfort.

"I promise you that I'll do whatever it takes to make sure Sara's safe." As soon as he uttered the words, he winced with regret.

It was an empty promise at best. One he wished he could snatch out of the air like a pesky mosquito. Life had taught him the inevitability of shit happening. Of his inability to stop others from making a wrong decision or duping him by keeping something illicit or painful hidden.

Just like Mirna had. And his brother.

Annoyed he'd let them color his thoughts, Luis swiped the memories away. Sara wasn't his ex. They were completely different people who shared no similarities.

Other than a disconnect with their families.

A secret they withheld. Deeply rooted issues he wasn't fully aware of.

And him thinking he could ride in on a white horse, or his white dive boat, to save them.

¡Coño! Luis bit back the curse. First his mom, now Sara's, stirring up memories and doubts he preferred to bury.

Ruth sucked in a shaky breath. Her eyes drifted shut as she patted his hand where it lay on her forearm, leaving him uncertain whom she sought to comfort. Herself or him.

A tiny warbler glided out of the poinciana tree branches spanning from the neighbor's yard into theirs, the tree's green leaves adorned by the delicate flaming red flowers. The little bird's wings flapped, his spindly legs stretching out to catch him as he landed on the white verandah railing with a stutter step. The bird trilled a high-pitched, musical hello.

"I'm so happy you joined us this week." Ruth's voice, thick with emotion, drew Luis's attention. She offered him a shaky smile, and he was relieved to find the turbulent storm in her gray eyes had quieted.

"One of the lessons I learned over the course of my battle with cancer was the importance of having a loved one by your side," she told him. "Seeing you with Sara, knowing she has someone else in her corner, brings me a wealth of relief and hope."

The repercussions of his and Sara's duplicity taunted him in the face of Ruth's genuine sincerity. Guilt soured the saliva in his mouth, and Luis struggled to swallow it along with the truth he owed it to Sara to not reveal.

"I'm happy to spend this week with you," he finally answered, speaking from the heart.

As for what came after, Luis could only hope that, by then, Sara would have repaired the unraveled threads that bound her and her family. Doing so would make the guilt and their lies worth it.

"I'm sure Sara has a perfectly good reason for being gone a little longer. If it makes you feel better, I'll try reaching her when I take my bag upstairs," Luis offered.

"Thank you," Ruth murmured, her faint smile tinged with sorrow. "Maybe my daughter will answer your call. She tends to avoid mine sometimes. Actually, often. Probably retribution for my neglect when she was younger."

Before Luis could come up with a suitable response, the front door swung open, chasing away the warbler with his song.

"Mom, are you out here?" Robin stepped onto the verandah. She drew to a halt when she spotted him. "Oh, hi, Luis."

Her gaze zeroed in on Ruth's hands, still clasped with his on her lap. The corners of Robin's mouth curved downward, and she shot an annoyed glare out at the street.

"Mother, you didn't eat your oatmeal and fruit. You need something in your stomach with your vitamins and meds."

Ruth leaned toward Luis, her brows raised, lips tilted in a conspiratorial grin. "She talks to me like I'm her patient. Not the well-trained physician I am."

"I hate to break it to you, Ruth, but doctors are often the worst patients," Luis mock-whispered to her.

Sara's mom *tsk*ed at his assertion, then chuckled when he tilted his head and shrugged as if to say, "You know it's true."

"Exactly," Robin asserted. "Come on, Mom, you have to eat something. Let Luis pick up the Sara worry stick for a while."

With a pointed look at him, Robin hovered at her mom's side.

Luis rose from his rocker. Ruth followed his example, like he'd hoped.

"I'll give Sara a call," he said, as the three of them made their way into the house and the refreshing air conditioning.

"Please let me know if you reach her," Ruth asked.

Luis nodded, then took the stairs to the second floor by twos. The door to Jonathan and Carolyn's room had been left ajar, neither one in sight. Luis figured the couple was downstairs with the rest of the family.

Trying not to worry about Sara, he pushed open the door to her room—technically their room now—and came to a halt.

The subtle citrusy scent he'd come to associate with her lingered in the air, teasing him with each breath. The gold strappy sandals she'd worn yesterday rested side by side in front of the white-painted wardrobe on his right. A pale yellow sundress with skinny straps hung from one of the wardrobe's wooden knobs. The short length was a sure sign he'd be treated to the sight of her shapely long legs once she slipped on the dress.

Her silver rolling suitcase sat in the corner between the wardrobe and long shelf desk that ran the length of the far outside wall, bolstered by the two drawers on either end. The sun's rays streamed through the skylight cut into the sloping ceiling, brightening the small space that would be home for the rest of the week.

Uncharacteristic doubt raised its shrill voice. Luis shushed it, hoping like hell this hadn't been a mistake.

He crossed to the double drawers under the right side of the plank desk where he dropped his bag on the hardwood floor, then dug his phone out of his back pocket and dialed Sara's cell. Immediately it went to voice mail. Either her phone was off or she'd run out of battery. Neither option would assuage Ruth's worries. Or his, the more time passed without word from Sara.

He wasn't typically a worrier, but he was working with unknowns here, and he didn't like it.

His thumb tapped the darkened cell screen as he considered his next move. Unpack quickly, then go for a spin around the downtown area if Sara hadn't arrived by the time he was done.

It didn't take long to add his shorts, tees, exercise clothes, and boxers to an empty drawer. He shook out the wrinkles from a red button-down shirt and hung it, along with one navy and one olive polo shirt, a pair of jeans, and a pair of khaki slacks, in the wardrobe. His plain, nondescript clothes lined up next to Sara's brightly colored, frilly designer tops and dresses were a vivid reminder of their differences.

That didn't stop him from running his fingertips lightly over the gauzy coral material of a flowy top with multicolored ruffled sleeves.

Vibrant. Delicate. Fun.

Basically, Sara.

He rubbed the material between his fingers. Pictured doing the same while she actually wore the flimsy blouse. Imagined her soft gasp as he traced her skin along the top's scooped neckline. Caught the heat in her seawater eyes as she gazed up at him. Just like when he'd held her in his arms as they danced last night.

The sound of Ruth's and Robin's raised voices carried up the stairs, jolting Luis out of the silly clothing fetish stupor he'd fallen into.

Downstairs, the front door opened, then closed with a slam that reverberated through the walls.

Time for him to get a move on it.

Snagging his duffel bag off the low shelf desk, Luis strode into the adjoining bath to unpack his toiletries. His blue toothbrush and tube of Crest toothpaste were dropped into a white ceramic glass alongside Sara's red one. A bottle of dandruff shampoo went in the shower. He was elbow deep in his bag, reaching for his razor and shaving cream, when the front door opened and slammed again. Raised voices made him pause. He strained to make out what was said, but as quickly as they'd risen, the voices lowered.

Hurrying to finish, Luis pulled open the medicine cabinet door, moving aside random bottles of ibuprofen, acetaminophen, and heartburn relief to make room for his shaving items.

"You too, Jonathan? How could you snoop like this!"

Luis spun around at Sara's impassioned cry.

She stormed into the bathroom, her face a mutinous scowl. The instant she saw him, she drew to an abrupt halt. Her eyes widened with shock and surprise. "Oh! It's you."

Dressed in a pair of black formfitting leggings and a neon yellow tank, a light sheen of perspiration shining on her chest and face, blond hair pulled back in a high ponytail with sweat-darkened curls clinging to her slender neck, she looked like a sexy post-workout magazine ad come to life.

Her gaze darted from the open medicine cabinet to his empty duffel and back. Suspicion narrowed her eyes as her gaze met his. "What are you looking for?"

"Just putting my stuff away," he answered, purposefully keeping his tone casual. "You have a nice run?"

Sara's throat moved with her swallow. Fear, indecision, and distrust chased each other across her face. She took a hesitant step backward. "I, uh, I thought you were Jonathan. Sorry. Didn't mean to barge in on you like this."

"What would your brother be snooping for?"

"N-nothing." She shook her head and backed up another step.

Luis followed, unwilling to let her keep shutting him out.

Her sneakers squeaked in protest against the hardwood floor as she spun away from him.

"Sara, wait! Don't keep pushing me away. We can't work together if you do."

His softly spoken words must have reached her, because instead of walking out, she reached the open door and stopped. Her left hand squeezed and released the brass doorknob indecisively.

"You can trust me," he promised, praying she believed him.

Several tension-filled seconds passed before she softly closed the door, then rested her forehead against it. Relief seeped through him like an afternoon rain shower washing away the sun's heat. Her slender back rose and fell on a sigh so weighty he felt the heaviness himself.

Silently Luis moved to sit on the foot of the bed.

"I don't want you to look at me differently," Sara finally said, her back still to him. Her forehead still pressed against the door.

"I won't. I couldn't."

Her fists clenched at her side, she swiveled to face him. Resolve stamped her classic features. "I thought you were Jonathan, ransacking the bathroom looking for a hidden stash of laxatives."

Hidden stash of laxatives?

What the hell? That didn't make sense. Why would she be hiding—The question dissipated as quickly as it had formed as Luis sifted through moments of their time together.

The weird food-sharing dance her family had done over dinner last night. Her mom's fears about Sara extending her morning run. The use of words such as "recovery" and "obsessive behavior." The belief that her brother might be combing through her belongings in search of laxatives or purgatives.

Each clue clicked into place, the puzzle finally starting to make sense as the pieces aligned to show a clearer picture. Sara suffered from—

"I have an ED. An eating disorder," she clarified. Though Luis understood the acronym.

Chin high, shoulders stiff and straight, she stared back at him. Almost daring him to prove himself wrong. Change the way he thought or felt about her based on whatever incorrect label her disorder might lead others to brand her with.

Luis had studied the basics about EDs as a paramedic. His sister, Anamaría, a firefighter paramedic and a physical fitness trainer–nutritionist herself, knew a hell of a lot more about the disorder. What he did remember was that while recovery was a healthy stage for Sara to have reached, individuals suffering from an eating disorder benefitted when they had support and encouragement from their loved ones and those within their close inner circle. He also knew without a doubt that he wanted to belong in Sara's inner circle.

"Thank you," he told her.

"For what?" Her brow furrowed with confusion.

"For trusting me. I'm sure it wasn't easy."

Her slender shoulder hitched, an apathetic shrug from the woman he knew hurt more than she wanted to admit. Also one he believed was stronger than she recognized.

He held his hand out to her.

Sara dropped her hesitant gaze to his open palm. Her fists curled again, then slowly relaxed at her sides. An innate certainty told Luis that this was the moment. Right here. Right now. In this small upstairs bedroom with the Key West sun streaming through the skylight turning Sara's high ponytail a burnished gold. They tiptoed on the edge of a precipice in their crazy, swift-moving, no-longer-only-made-up relationship.

The need for her to take that leap, to truly trust him, roared in his ears. It squeezed his chest like a vice, tightening with each second that ticked by without her answering. He waited, patience personified on the outside, while on the inside his gut clenched with his need for her to let him all the way in.

He didn't stop to ask himself why this was so important. For now, he simply accepted that it was.

Her gaze slowly traveled up his arm, rising to meet his, and Luis found himself drowning in the hope he saw churning in the sea green depths of her expressive eyes.

She edged a baby step forward to place her cool hand in his. Her fingers trembled. The proof of her vulnerability humbled him, and Luis curled his fingers softly around hers. The corners of her mouth tipped up the tiniest bit, and in that instant he knew he was lost.

"Come, sit with me for a sec, will you?" he asked, relieved when she nodded and joined him.

Chapter 11

Sara plopped onto the queen-sized bed next to Luis, hyperaware of her sweaty workout clothes and ripe post-run smell. Especially when the scent of his musky aftershave drifted over her like an aphrodisiac.

She wanted nothing more than to skip the soul-baring conversation and, instead, bury her face in his neck and breathe in his deliciousness. Allow the warmth from his bronze skin to seep into her, melting the cold dread in her chest.

Thanks to her therapists, she'd come a long way from the high school girl disillusioned and hurt by her lack of parental love and support. Or the college kid desperately trying to find her place in the world, convinced she'd never be good enough to follow in her parents' and siblings' footsteps. Lack of self-confidence coupled with the need to feel a sense of control over something, anything, had nudged, then pushed, then fueled her down a path that quickly spiraled into an uncontrollable addiction.

"It's not really a secret," she started, her gaze trained on her gold sandals paired off in front of the wardrobe a couple feet away.

Beside her, Luis remained silent, their hands lightly clasped.

"I mean, I've talked about it in a few interviews. I just don't, you know, advertise my struggles with OSFED."

"That's your official diagnosis?" he asked, his tone low. Devoid of recrimination or, worse, pity.

"Yeah. Other Specified Feeding or Eating Disorder. I've suffered from a mix of bulimia and binge eating, with a propensity for over-exercising. Although this morning had nothing to do with that," she rushed on, anxious to assuage any concerns. "I stopped to talk with the owner of a small clothing boutique I came across during my cooldown walk. I didn't even realize my phone had died."

He rolled his lips in and slowly nodded. "Makes sense now."

"What does?"

"Your mom's worry when I arrived, and you were still out."

He traced the knuckles of her hand, absently running a finger lightly up and down the back of hers. Tingles danced up her arm at his faint touch.

"I suggested that you'd probably just extended your run around the island to enjoy the early morning peace and cooler weather," he continued, slowly shaking his head. "She was *not* happy. I guess she figured I knew a long run might not be the best idea for you. She seemed a little annoyed that it didn't bother me."

Sara winced. "Sorry. I should have been up-front with you from the beginning."

"No, don't apologize."

Luis scooted around to face her. His left knee bent between them on the bed, partially covering a green and dark gray octopus floating among waving seaweed leaves on the underwater-themed bedspread. "You don't have to do or say or be anything you don't want. Not with me. Not with anyone."

She ducked her head, swiveling to crook a leg next to his. Her gaze locked on the curve of his calf muscle, the light dusting of dark hair on his shin, the contrast of his tan skin juxtaposed with her paleness. Their clasped hands rested on his knee, their fingers entwined.

"It's taken me a long time to understand that," she admitted. "And I don't always remember. Especially when it comes to my family. But thank you for saying so. For understanding."

"It's the truth. And when, or if, you're ready to talk to me about your OSFED, I'm here for you. No matter what, anything you need."

Tears burned her eyes at his easy understanding, and she blinked rapidly trying to dry the moisture before it spilled down her cheeks.

Luis continued to surprise her in marvelous, unexpected ways she wasn't certain she deserved considering the monumental favor she had asked of him. But she knew she owed him the truth. At the very least, the basic details her family would expect him to be familiar with. It was selfish of her to keep him floundering in the dark simply to avoid altering his perception of her.

Swallowing her discomfort, Sara channeled her fledgling confidence, along with her pride in how far she'd come in her recovery process, and clung to the faith that she could trust Luis with what had once been her biggest secret.

"It started in, um, in high school." She paused. Cleared the discomfort from her throat. "After I overheard my mom's conversation about college and lowering her expectations for me."

Luis's lips parted as if he wanted to say something. When he didn't, she rushed on with her story, anxious to finally have it out in the open.

College life, the binge eating in her dorm room aided by her unlimited meal pass. The unhealthy "body cleanses" she regularly put herself through. The hours she'd spent running through campus and along Tempe Town Lake pushing her body, convinced she could leave her fears and shame behind her. Hiding the truth from roommates, sorority sisters, her parents, and siblings. Even Mamá Alicia, until the wise woman who'd changed her diapers, soothed her scrapes and bruises, and scolded with an eagle-eyed stare eventually caught on to Sara's ways.

"She saved me from my worst self," Sara admitted softly, feeling tired and exposed. Yet oddly relieved.

"And in doing so, she also helped you get back on track to finding your best self."

Luis's words brought a lightness washing over her, like the sun's rays reaching through the skylight above them. Oh, how she ached with wanting him to still see her that way—her best self.

"Yes, she did," Sara agreed. "Though it took me a while to get there. To get here." She traced a finger along the wavy edges of a seaweed leaf on the comforter, memories of those difficult, scary days assailing her. "I checked into a rehab facility the summer between my sophomore and junior years. Inpatient therapy was followed by cognitive behavioral therapy. Now I maintain regular outpatient visits with my therapist in New York. There's been the occasional backward slide. But also leaps and bounds of forward progress. And I'm making it."

Outside, the clouds shifted and a sunbeam streamed through the skylight, cutting a swath across the bed. It reminded her that there was light at the end of that dark tunnel of self-doubt and recrimination. She had found it. Stumbled, trudged, crawled, and reached it. Yes, she would always have to take precautions. Stay mindful of healthy habits and dangers. But she was succeeding.

Luis's fingers curled around her nape, their slight pressure drawing her gaze to his. Certainty shone in his dark eyes. "When I look at you, the woman I see is strong, resilient, sometimes scared because we all are, but equally determined. Full of love for her family and passion for her career. Beautiful, inside and out."

A heated blush crept up Sara's neck at his moving description of her.

"Thank you," she murmured, relief and awe over his uncanny ability to know exactly what she needed to hear clogging her throat. With Luis she felt whole and worthy. Seen in a way no one else ever had before.

"It's the truth." He dipped his head as if to emphasize his point.

The warmth of his palm along her neck seeped into her, spreading into her chest. His thumb brushed her jawline, pleasure humming through her at his tender touch.

"I appreciate you sharing this with me. Trusting me enough to tell me," he said, his voice a deep rasp that at once both soothed and excited her.

"I do," she answered, moved by his sincerity. Grateful it was him by her side here. "You're a good man, Luis Navarro."

Overcome by a rush of emotions, Sara leaned forward to press a kiss on his cheek. His fingers flexed along her nape and she found herself nuzzling his cheek with hers. Unwilling to break their contact.

"I have my moments," he teased, a puff of his breath tickling her ear. "But if there's anything I ever do that exacerbates a trigger." Luis leaned back, his dark eyes intently on hers. "If something or someone else does, don't hesitate to tell me. Don't hold back. I want to help any way I can while you're here."

His words were like a splash of cold water, startling her awake from a dream-filled slumber on the back patio.

What was she doing?

They were alone upstairs. There was no need to pretend she and Luis were a couple behind closed doors. It was foolish to let herself get caught up in thinking they could be a real one. Her life was centered in New York, making calculated moves to expand her business interests and proving to her family that she could be successful in her own right.

Luis's caring, empathetic concern was an innate part of what made him such an amazing person. He'd treat anyone else the same. She'd do well to remember that they could not allow the forced proximity of their situation to cloud their better judgement.

He was here as a favor. She, despite needing his help, was here to prove that she didn't need saving. Not by her family. Not by a long-distance boyfriend she had dated for the wrong reasons. And not by the nice guy she had sweet-talked into being her partner in crime, for a brief period of time.

"Th-thank you," she mumbled. Untangling their fingers, she slid backward until she reached the corner of the mattress. Purposefully distancing herself from unrealistic expectations she couldn't, wouldn't, allow herself to entertain.

"I've got it under control," she assured Luis. "Though I'm sorry if you felt ambushed by my mother this morning."

Confusion clouded his dark eyes and wedged between his brows. "Not ambushed. Just a little out of my depth. But it's all good. I'm serious, if you need—"

"Right now, what I need is to get ready for the day and figure out how to deal with my parents."

Pushing herself off the bed, she crossed to the left side drawers, intent on retrieving a bra and panties so she could escape to the bathroom. Sure, this was classic avoidance of a problem, but maybe a cold shower would clear her head.

"This Brady Bunch style of parenting can't last long," she complained. "I'm sure they'll go back to their old ways soon and won't be hovering like they are right now."

"I thought you wanted them actively involved in your life?"

"Not like this!" Anger surged through her, and she slammed the drawer shut. "I don't want them checking up on me out of guilt. Or responsibility. Because I was so emotionally screwed up that I turned to bingeing and purging. I'm not a patient or a charity case. That's not what I want from them. Or you."

"Wait a minute!" Luis shot off the bed, his broad shoulders and full height dwarfing the room. His affronted scowl menacing. "I doubt they see you that way. I certainly don't."

Sara huffed out an exasperated breath. Aware she was behaving irrationally, yet too overcome with doubts and desires and the inevitability of their situation that she couldn't contain herself. She cupped her forehead in one hand, as if doing would calm the scattered, scared thoughts running a hamster race through her mind. In reality she wasn't sure whom she was frustrated with the most.

Her parents, for realizing too late her need to be accepted by them?

Luis, for making her feel and want in ways that would only hurt when the time came for her to leave?

Herself, for craving the sense of belonging she found with him, despite the inevitable heartbreak if he came to view her as someone who simply needed saving? Forget his beautiful words moments ago, he'd simply meant to boost her. Not woo her.

Suddenly overwhelmed with self-doubt, Sara hurried to the wardrobe, where she snatched her sundress off the round doorknob. The clear plastic hanger clattered against the wood.

"Look, I felt you deserved the truth since you agreed to this farce. But I don't expect you to be a therapist or another medical professional assessing me. I have enough of those already."

Jaw tight, hands stuffed deep in the pockets of his khaki walking shorts, Luis eyed her stoically.

"I've gotta get in the shower; everyone's already downstairs," she said, her voice stiff and uncomfortable. Nervous that by sharing, she'd changed the course of their friendship. Afraid that, as had happened with others, her disorder might wind up causing a rift in their budding relationship.

Without waiting for his response, Sara brushed past him, her shoulder grazing his muscular arm.

"It's not within me to ignore someone who needs my help, Sara."

Luis's softly spoken entreaty held an undercurrent of conviction and promise she couldn't ignore. Not when his white knight tendency was what had drawn her to him in the first place.

She paused in the bathroom doorway. Staring at their reflections in the medicine cabinet mirror, she met his gaze. Honest, steadfast.

"I know," she told him, her heart yearning for something she couldn't quite put her finger on. Afraid to even try. "I wouldn't ask that of you. It's just . . . Isn't there some way we can go back to yesterday afternoon? When we were simply a girl and a guy agreeing to be a pretend couple in order to hoodwink her family. You know, normal vacation fun?"

A corner of his mouth curved up in that sexy half grin she found way too enticing for her own good.

"That's what you want? The Key West sun and fun experience tourists write home about?" he asked.

She nodded, hoping he'd go along with her bid to move on from their argument.

"That I can definitely give you," he promised.

A promise she found herself excited to help him keep.

After wrapping up a short call with her assistant early Saturday evening, Sara strolled into the open kitchen area at the rental house. There she found Jonathan with his cell phone propped up on the granite counter as he video chatted with Susan and William.

"Here's the mermaid magnet we bought for you at the aquarium today after we rode the train." Jonathan held up the glittery clay memento along with another one shaped like a pirate ship. "And here's one for you, buddy."

Catching her brother's cheek-splitting grin and the matching openmouthed "ooohs" from her cute niece and nephew whose sweet faces filled the entire phone screen, Sara grinned back. Her father was right; parenthood and marriage to Carolyn had softened her once solely career-focused brother. Oh, he still loved his job, but he now *lived* for his family. No more jumping at the chance to pull a double shift and potentially get in on an interesting case that came into the hospital's ER. This was the man who could perform his three-year-old's ballet routine. Proudly.

This last trait endeared him to Sara even more. It had her thinking maybe it was time she quit distancing herself to avoid being hurt by Jonathan's old propensity to give her the brush-off. They weren't the same people anymore. At least, she and Jonathan weren't. Robin might be a different story.

"Hi, guys," Sara singsonged, swooping in to press her face next to her brother's. The image of their matching blond heads, high cheekbones, and blue-green eyes in the smaller box at the top of the screen drew her gaze. Her smile widened.

"Aunt Sara!" William cried, squirming his little body with so much excitement he fell onto his side and rolled out of the picture for a few seconds.

"Aunt Sar-bear!"

Sara's grin softened at little Susan's use of the silly nickname her father had gifted her with years ago when she was about Susan's age. Silly, yet it never failed to warm her heart.

"Are you two staying out of trouble? Not giving your other grandparents a hard time?" she teased.

"Yup!" William crawled back into view, his shaggy hair, the same dark brown as his mom's, mussed from his antics.

"I'm aw-ways a good girl. Cwoss my heart." Susan's tiny finger drew a cross in the center of her chest, a little off from the exact location of her heart, which, had Robin been here, she might have corrected.

"Yes, you are, sweetie," Sara confirmed. "And William, I know you're being the best big brother. That's why I keep telling your dad he has to bring you both home lots of presents."

"Yay!" Cheers rose from both kids, who clapped their approval.

"Ease up there, Sister," Jonathan complained, elbowing her in the ribs.

She nudged him aside with a laugh, then stuck out her tongue at him playfully and backed away, waving to her sweet niece and nephew. Feeling lighthearted around her brother in a way she rarely had in the past.

After the misunderstanding this morning with her mom and Robin over Sara's absence, and the emotional toll of sharing the history of her disorder with Luis, the day had actually gone really well. In large part thanks to Luis and his calm, reassuring presence.

He'd charmed her mother, buddied up with Jonathan, and handled Robin's rapid-fire questions about the island without batting an eye. To Sara's immense relief, he wasn't treating her any differently than before their heart-to-heart.

Despite having grown up here, Luis seemed to enjoy playing tourist with them, adding commentary from a local Conch's perspective during their train ride. When they'd hopped off the bright yellow cab with its black rooftop to explore Ernest Hemingway's house and the historic Key West Lighthouse, he even accepted her challenge to march up all eighty-eight steps of the lighthouse after admitting he'd never been to the top.

Later, at the aquarium, he'd filled in as their tour guide, providing info on the animals in the touch tank. Robin had peppered him with questions about the conchs, sea urchins, sea stars, and other animals they had the chance to hold. Even Sara's brainiac sister had been impressed with the conservation facts Luis had provided for many of the other area fish and wildlife.

Sara's family genuinely liked him. Maybe a little too much. That would make it harder when the time came to announce their breakup. For now though, she refused to think about that.

While her brother continued regaling the kids with stories about their day, Sara tugged open the fridge in search of some sparkling water. Over the conversation inside, she heard a rumbling clatter, like the tumble of clay pieces clashing against each other.

Following the sound, she stepped to the large window alcove that opened to the outdoor patio dining area. Seated at the wooden table, Luis, her parents, and Edward were selecting dominoes from a pile spread between them. During the rare times her family was all together, they usually played cards or Trivial Pursuit. Robin always chose the latter because she kicked butt at it. If Jonathan's kids had been here, Pretty Pretty Princess or Candyland would have been on the game menu, too.

"Once you've picked your seven pieces," Luis explained, "whoever has the double six starts the game, then play moves to their left."

He continued with the instructions, explaining that partners sat across from each other. This meant Luis teamed up with Sara's mother, while Edward and her dad were a pair. Ruth grinned like the cat who ate the last of the delicious sautéed shrimp dinner they'd enjoyed earlier, thanks to a local restaurant's delivery service.

"Honey, you should come listen to the rules," Edward called to Robin, who along with Carolyn lay reading a book in one of the loungers next to the pool. "I think the counting and strategizing will appeal to you."

Sara bit back a smirk. Of course, the mental agility aspect would draw her sister over, not necessarily the camaraderie.

"So, you grew up playing dominoes then?" her mom asked Luis.

He nodded, his big hands deftly situating his pieces, resting them on their long side facing him. "It's how my brothers, sister, and I first learned addition. At every family gathering, there's at least one domino table set up. My *abuela* was a champion. As a kid, my younger brother avoided partnering with her because she used to get upset if he wound up distracted by the TV and missed a key move. She was a fierce competitor, and pretty amazing person all-around."

The love he felt for his *abuela* rang in his deep voice. It was evident in the soft smile curving his lips and the faraway look in his eyes as he stared at the dominoes, lost in his memories.

Sara noticed his use of *was* and she wanted to ask him about his grandmother. He hadn't shared much more about his family other than basic details to help with their charade. Not even a family photo. She'd only met his younger brother. By mistake. There was no reason why she'd meet any of the others. No reason other than her keen interest in all things Luis Navarro related. And the *familia* that reminded her of Mamá Alicia's.

The image of her beloved nanny flashed in Sara's mind. Diminutive yet firm when a reprimand was needed, which hadn't been often. Watchful dark eyes and jet-black, later gray-streaked, hair she wore in her signature sleek bun. The lilt of her Mexican heritage dancing through her Spanish, heavily accenting her English.

Sara liked to think Mamá Alicia and Luis's *abuela* were probably looking down on them all right now. If so, Sara figured the two older women would be shaking their heads at Luis and Sara's ruse. Although, after her family's fun-filled day and the sun-kissed color on her mother's thin face, Sara had a hard time seeing the error of her ways.

Twisting the cap off her bottle of sparkling water, Sara strolled out to the back patio, feeling oddly at peace around her family. Mostly thanks to Luis, whose calm demeanor seemed to rub off on all of them. Including her.

Robin and Carolyn left their lounge chairs to join everyone at the table. Her sister-in-law stepped around one of the citronella candles dangling on a hook at the top of a waist-high metal stake stuck into the soil near her lounger. Several others dotted the perimeter of the raised porch, while two more candles burned in the sitting area. Orange flames flickered inside the dark glass orbs cradling the candles.

A light breeze blew away the heat and humidity of the day. While the sun's last rays poked through the tree branches, splaying wispy shadows and light across the backyard oasis.

"Is Jonathan still talking to the kids?" Carolyn asked, motioning with her head toward the kitchen alcove. "I don't know which one of us feels worse about not bringing them along. But couple time is hard to come by these days."

Sara's brother appeared in the large window, holding the phone out toward them. "Say bye to everyone!"

Good-byes and talk-to-you-soons and a "Mommy loves you" from Carolyn chimed in a raucous farewell to the little ones; then Jonathan hung up.

"Anyone need another drink?" he asked.

By the time Jonathan made it to the table carrying several dark green beer bottles for the other guys, Luis had kicked off the domino game by slapping down the double six. Sara's mom's triumphant "yes!" coupled with her wide leer drew a rumbly chuckle from him.

"I have to warn you," Sara told Luis as she moved to stand behind him. "Game night can get pretty cutthroat in our house."

Resting her hands on his shoulders, she bent down to peer at his dominoes. Luis turned to look at her, his handsome face inches from hers. The corners of his eyes crinkled with the easy smile she had quickly grown fond of seeing. He surprised her with a peck on her jaw that sent tingles tap-dancing their way down her body.

"We'll go easy on him, Sar-bear. Don't worry," her father promised, sending her mom a satisfied smile. Ruth patted his hand on the edge of the table, punctuating some secret between the two of them.

Sara wasn't sure whether to be relieved they'd fallen for her ruse with Luis. Or worried about what they might be scheming themselves.

"Oh, I can hold my own," Luis assured them. "I'm not easily intimidated. Though what I've got in front of me should scare you two." He pointed at Edward and her dad, seated to his left and right.

"That's what I like to hear," her mom crowed.

Sara rolled her eyes. Apparently, no one was holding back when it came to trash talk. Not even Luis.

"Do you have a good . . . is it called a hand in dominoes?" she asked him.

"Yeah, 'hand' is the right terminology. Same as with cards." Luis rearranged his dominoes matching ones with the same numbers of black dots on one half or the other. "Does anyone want me to talk us through this first game, provide some options they could choose from based on their or their partner's dominoes?"

"I'm already Googling domino strategy," Robin said, tapping away at her cell phone screen. She dragged another chair closer to Edward, her serious game face already in place. "No need for a practice round. We'll pick this up quickly."

Jonathan snagged the sixth dining table chair and set it between their parents. As soon as he sat down, Carolyn sank onto his lap, one arm casually draped over his shoulder.

"We'll watch and learn," he said, before taking a swig of his beer.

"Here, join me." Luis scooted his chair back a little, opening his arms for Sara to sit with him.

It all seemed so cozy. A little surreal. An average family snapshot she'd always dreamed of. Her entire family together with her not feeling like an outsider, either too young or too different or too emotionally weak to be an equal.

Time had eroded the age gap once she'd reached adulthood. Regular therapy had helped with the other two.

But somehow, having Luis here with her, partnered with someone she respected and cared for like her parents and siblings were, gave her a sense of belonging she had always craved.

She recognized that this wasn't real, but for now, she allowed herself to believe it.

Stepping between the artfully scarred wooden table and Luis, Sara squatted tentatively on his left knee.

"You can't possibly be comfortable like that. Come here." His large hands grasped her hips, easily sliding her toward him until her bottom rested snug in the crook of his lap. The motion pulled the hem of his shorts up a few inches, leaving the warmth of his thigh cushioning her legs.

He rested his chin on her bare shoulder, the day's growth of scruff rough against her skin. Earlier, while they'd waited for dinner to arrive and she responded to emails and social media comments in the first-floor office, he had showered and changed. Now his earthy scent mixed with a clean soapy smell luring her closer.

Instinctively she melted against him, barely curbing the urge to burrow into the sanctuary of his muscular arms and chest.

Luis's hands tightened on her hips for the briefest moment, before releasing her to fiddle with his domino pieces. He picked up one, set it back in the same place. Moved another to the end of his tiny row, only to put it back in its original spot. A pointer finger tap-tap-tapped the top of another piece but didn't change its position. As if he were . . . nervous. Or distracted. By her, maybe?

Did he feel the same drugging pull? A similar impulse to bag the game and head up to their room to explore where their pent-up attraction might lead?

"Okay, so I'm next," Edward announced, thwarting Sara's ill-advised musings as he plunked down a domino.

The play continued around the table, with Luis sometimes stopping one of the others from making a move that might potentially block their partner. Occasionally the game slowed as someone counted the pieces, trying to ensure they didn't "lock" the game, as

Luis called it, by placing the last domino with a certain number on one end of the train while the same number remained at the other end. In essence, leaving no one with the ability to make another move.

"How do you say that in Spanish again?" Robin asked.

"*Tran-car,*" Luis repeated, enunciating the syllables. "To lock, or to get stuck, basically."

Robin repeated the word in her heavily English-accented Spanish. "I have taken medical terminology Spanish to help communicate with patients, but my tongue simply cannot master the rolled r," she told him. "Of course, I didn't have the added benefit of a nanny who spoke the language to teach me from a young age like some of us did."

Sara flinched at the blunt accusation in her sister's tone.

"No, you had your nonfluent mother setting aside her career until Jonathan and you started school," Ruth countered.

She shot a sharp look at Robin and reached for her vitamin smoothie. Lips pursed around her metal reusable straw, Sara's mom swallowed the rest of her usual reprimand, though her disappointment etched her thin face.

The age-old mother-daughter disagreement and the way Robin dragged Sara into it scraped down Sara's spine like sharp fingernails. It used to draw blood, send her tiptoeing away to avoid the fray. The years her mother had stayed home with her first two children, putting her blossoming career on hold, later choosing not to do the same after Sara was born, were a thorn in all three Vance women's sides. For completely different reasons.

While Sara had been working hard to figure out how to let go of the abandonment she felt, every once in a while, Robin poked at the sore spot.

"And thus began the merry-go-round of college student nannies, many of whom required babysitters of their own." Robin's lips twisted with sarcasm. "Remember the one who needed my help with her algebra when I was in seventh grade?"

"Oh god, how about the girl who mixed up the sugar and salt when she tried to bake us chocolate chip cookies? Twice!" Jonathan threw in, his scrunched face mimicking his mouthed "gross."

A chorus of moans greeted his addition to the bumpy trip down memory lane. Sara heard Luis's muttered "yuck" and glanced over her shoulder to find his expression matched her brother's.

Robin laughed, her sour mood thankfully lifting. "Yeah, chemistry was definitely not her best class. However, silver lining, mother, tutoring her and several others actually aided me with my own studies."

Ruth dipped her head, accepting Robin's attempt to smooth over their rough patch.

"Now that I think about it, many of them must have been one of those undecided, cakewalk Humanities majors like art or basket-weaving."

Sara cringed inside, recalling her first two years as an Exploratory Humanities, Fine Arts and Design major until she settled on her general BA in the Arts degree. One of those often belittled "cakewalk majors" Robin so easily denigrated.

Her father's gaze slid to Sara's. He winked, understanding how her sister's inadvertent dig might chafe. In years past, comments like this had burrowed under her skin. Festering. Contributing to the self-doubt that drove her OSFED.

With therapy, she'd learned to separate her sister's perspective from her own. Focus on the positives about herself rather than the perceived shortcomings.

"Cakewalk or not," Sara answered, "humanities majors make successful social media influencers. From my experience anyway."

"Touché." Jonathan tipped his bottle toward her.

Luis reached out to tap his beer with her brother's, the show of solidarity lightening the weight of Robin's dismissal.

"So, where'd you go to school?" Robin asked Luis, at the same time she tapped a domino to indicate Edward should play it. "University of Miami?"

Nestled in his lap, Sara felt Luis stiffen. She realized, they'd gone over details like this about her family because the Vances prided themselves on their academic pedigree, especially med school. But Luis hadn't mentioned whether or not he'd gone on to earn a bachelor's degree after getting his EMT and paramedic certifications and joining the fire department.

Sara pretended to fiddle with one of Luis's dominoes; then she laid her hand over his on the table in a silent show of support. Luis twisted his wrist to thread his fingers with hers in a move that felt completely natural.

"I started here at Florida Keys Community College," he told Robin. "It saved money, and I was able to keep working, leading dive and snorkel tours. After that, I finished up online."

"The blue-collar route to improving your opportunities," Robin said. "Nothing to be ashamed of."

Sara gritted her teeth, annoyed by her sister's condescending tone. Even though Robin probably didn't intend to be.

Jonathan started to say something, but Carolyn tightened her arms around his shoulders with a playful jostle. He gave her a squinty-eyed glare, but it quickly dissolved into a sheepish grin that ended with them giving each other a quick kiss.

Sara marveled at her mild-mannered sister-in-law's ability to distract her brother in a bid to keep the peace among the siblings.

"I think it shows initiative. Not to mention sound financial decision-making," Sara's dad noted. "I admire that. Especially in the person dating my youngest."

Luis shifted in his seat. When she teetered on his lap, he wrapped his arm around her waist, securing her comfortably against him.

"As the son of a local firefighter and stay-at-home mom, I learned early on to appreciate what we had," Luis explained. "My parents taught me the value of hard work, faith, and service to others."

"Important values," Sara's mother said. "If your siblings are anything like you, your parents must be as proud as I am of my three."

Robin, of course, preened under their mother's praise. Sara focused on appreciating her mother's compliment instead of questioning it, remembering her therapist's advice to not add unwarranted subtext to others' statements.

Jonathan, the smart aleck, leaned toward their mother with a sly smirk. "Yeah, Mom, but we all know *I'm* your favorite."

Ruth shushed out a breathy laugh and pushed him away with a hand splayed across his face.

Robin rolled her eyes with a muttered, "Whatever."

"Son, I hate to disappoint you, but it's a known fact that *I'm* her favorite." Their dad bent across the corner of the table toward his wife, who met him halfway, her lips puckered for a mushy smooch.

Sara watched, love for her parents mingling with disbelief. They were rarely demonstrative. At least, until her mom's sickness they'd never been that way. This type of behavior—kisses and hugs and romantic declarations—had lately become the norm.

It was a sweet, welcome change, if you asked Sara. One that had her hoping maybe this really could be their new normal. Maybe she could reach an understanding with her mother, perhaps even Robin. Someday.

"Okay, you two, you're holding up the game. Mother, it's your move," Robin interrupted, waving a hand over the domino train winding its way across the table.

"Life is short, my fastidious, analytical child," Ruth admonished as she settled herself into her rattan chair.

"Yes, that's why Edward, Dad, and I plan to beat the three of you quickly and mercilessly." Robin's quip earned her a belly laugh from their dad and a disbelieving shake of her head from their mother.

"Luis, please tell me your family isn't as cutthroat as this bunch!" Ruth cried. Resting a forearm on the edge of the table, she stretched out to place a domino on the far end of the train in front of him.

"Oh, it can get bad in our house, too. But there's no doubt I'm my *mami*'s favorite."

"And Sara's," Ruth said, her satisfied smile spreading wider when Luis placed a chaste kiss on Sara's temple.

He wrapped their clasped hands around her waist, her torso now crisscrossed in his tight embrace. As much as she reminded herself this was all pretend, the thrill she felt enveloped in his co-coon of sexy masculinity was undeniably real. Dangerous, but she let herself continue to enjoy it.

"She's definitely mine," Luis murmured, his lips brushing her temple in another heated caress.

"Hey, cut that out. You're making the rest of us men look bad here," Jonathan teased.

"Sweetie, I think you should be taking notes instead of arguing with the man," Carolyn countered.

Even staid Edward chuckled at Carolyn's quip.

"It's your move, Charles," Sara's mom prodded.

Her dad scanned the pieces already played, strategizing his next move.

With only one domino left, Luis laid it facedown, then flicked his wrist to set the piece spinning. The white rectangle blurred, the stone clattering against the wooden tabletop.

"Speaking of teams winning quickly and mercilessly." He stopped the spinning piece with a blunt fingertip. "This is the domino that'll give Ruth, Sara, and me the first round."

Call her catty, but Sara couldn't squelch her grin at her sister's irritated game face. Robin hated losing.

"Let me see," Sara murmured.

She covered Luis's hand with hers and together they tilted up the piece for her to count the black dots—three on one half, none on the other. Glancing at the train, she saw a three on one end and a blank on the other. Luis was right. No matter which end her father played off, Luis would close out.

"Speaking of families, are you sure you don't want to at least invite your parents to join us for dinner or lunch? I'd love to have them over," Ruth offered.

Sara and Luis's domino clattered onto the tabletop. Panic rushed up to choke her, and she abruptly sat up, out of the false security of Luis's arms.

"Uh, no. That wouldn't be . . . it's not . . . I mean, th-thank you for asking, Mother. But, um—" She twisted around to face Luis. Once again, praying he interpreted her what-the-hell-do-we-do expression. "Didn't you say they were busy this week?"

He rubbed her side, his calmness reassuring her as he nodded. "Actually, my *tía*—my mom's sister—is in town from the Fort Lauderdale area. They've got sister-bonding plans, as my *papi* calls it."

"That sounds lovely. Will you get a chance to see your *tía* while she's here?" Ruth asked.

"I'm meeting up with most of my family for mass tomorrow morning while you're having brunch."

As soon as Luis mentioned mass, Sara winced, anticipating her mother's next words.

"Well then, I should change our reservation to a table for four.

Sara, you mentioned attending an early morning service when we were trip planning. I'm assuming you're going with Luis to meet with his parents instead of joining us, correct?"

Horror flashed in his dark brown eyes. He gave an almost imperceptible shake of his head. Sara knew the response he expected from her. Only, she couldn't give him what he wanted.

If she told her mother no, her family would wonder why. She'd been attending mass since first grade, when she'd told Mamá Alicia she wanted to make her First Communion alongside Pedro, Mamá Alicia's youngest son. And yet, if she went to mass with Luis, her presence would inevitably raise questions from his family. Questions he did not want to deal with.

She'd simply have to make sure not to put him in a position requiring him to do so. She owed him that much.

"Yes, I'm going to mass tomorrow. I meant to tell you that earlier, Mother." Swiveling around to face her mom, Sara sank back against Luis. Trying not to miss the warmth of his arm, no longer holding her securely to him. "It slipped my mind when I got that call from my assistant confirming my upcoming guest posts and shoot dates."

Lacing her fingers with Luis's on the table again, she gave his hand a squeeze. *Trust me.*

"I was hoping you wouldn't mind us skipping brunch and golf so we could spend time with his family."

Luis stiffened.

Regret nipped at Sara's conscience, and she brought their joined hands to her chest. She cradled them against her racing heart and silently pledged to make things right.

Her mom's expression brightened. A breeze blew her short pixie cut bangs off her forehead, a reminder for Sara that not even a year ago her mom had still worn a head wrap to cover her patchy hair. This ruse was meant to ensure nothing marred her vacation. That remained Sara's main priority.

"I think it's a marvelous idea for you to spend the day with Luis's family," Ruth said, her smile widening.

Sara offered a wobbly smile in response. Well, at least one of them thought so.

Chapter 12

"Like I said, just drop me off at a coffee shop while you go to mass. I'll hang out there," Sara repeated.

Luis shook his head. No way was he going along with her idea.

"Why not?" she asked, heaving a disgruntled sigh as she leaned against the bathroom doorjamb.

The bathroom's overhead light streaming behind her and the soft glow of the bedside lamp turned her blond waves a burnished gold and cast her face in soft shadow. There was no mistaking the hint of frustration in her hushed voice.

"Not an option," he reiterated. The same answer he'd given her the first two times she'd outlined her idea for how they'd convince her family Sara had gone to mass without the complication of involving his in the increasingly tangled web the two of them wove.

He turned away to grab a T-shirt out of his drawer, then shrugged it on, momentarily blocking her from his view. *Gracias a Dios* for small favors. At least she'd slipped on a pair of black shorts under the silky spaghetti-strapped mini pajama dress barely covering her shapely ass.

He was finding it hard to concentrate on his rationale for refusing to go along with her latest scheme.

When she'd stepped out of the bathroom earlier wearing the

pale blue nightie Luis had nearly swallowed his tongue. One look at the low-cut design, the slope of her perky breasts on marvelous display, and the front of his shorts had instantly tightened.

She'd scurried to her side of the drawers, grabbed the shorts, and hightailed it back to the bathroom. Her cheeks flushed as she mumbled a, "Sorry, I forgot something," and shut the door.

His body's instant reaction to her sexy nightclothes solidified his decision to *not* share the bed with her. Sara's "just friends" mantra taunting him.

Ha! In his life rulebook, friends didn't lust after each other this badly. Didn't daydream about sliding the other's pajama straps off her delicate shoulders, trailing kisses down her elegant neck, filling their palms with the other's luscious curves.

What he wanted to do with her would take them definitively out of the friend zone.

He was a short fuse away from marching across the bedroom, swooping Sara into his arms, and carrying her to the queen-sized bed where they'd both learn how amazing they would be together. Because make no mistake, based on the chemistry sizzling between them, he was absolutely certain the sex would be mind-blowing.

Instead, he grabbed a pillow off the bed and dropped it on the hardwood floor in front of the white nightstand. He'd have to find an extra blanket. A comforter or duvet would be a better option. Sleeping on the floor didn't bother him, but his back would appreciate something with a little cushion between him and the hardwood. If all else failed, he could grab the shaggy sky blue rug from their bathroom and drape a sheet over it.

"What are you doing?" Sara asked as he strode to the wardrobe and tugged on the knobs to fling both doors open wide.

"Looking for something I can use to make a pallet," he grunted. "I figure the bed's kinda small, maybe sharing isn't the best idea after all."

Not with the horny impulses he harbored.

Pushing aside their hanging clothes, he checked behind them for extra linens. No luck. The gauzy multicolored material of one of her sundresses caught on his thumb. The image of her wearing the outfit seared his brain. Followed quickly with one of him peeling it off.

Not helping!

He shook his hand trying to dislodge the distracting dress. The plastic hanger clattered against the top of the wardrobe as it swung violently on the metal pole.

Okay, so he was a little amped up. Dipping his big toe into the freaked-out pool he rarely swam in. Basically, doing a piss-poor job of hiding it or dealing with it now that Sara's family wasn't around and he didn't have to pretend.

But *coño*! The situation was snowballing out of control, and this Conch who'd never even seen snow was wide-eyed by the avalanche of repercussions that had been tumbling their way all day.

This was why he never *shook things up*, like Carlos had recommended. It only led to messes and confusion and problems. Case in point, his current situation.

First, there'd been his and Sara's heart-to-heart this morning, which had him fighting not to slide deeper into the comfortable saver-of-all role. As if he wasn't in deep enough already with her.

Then, spending the day with Sara and her family, even prickly Robin, who Luis would bet a dive trip's gas money often snarked from a place of hidden pain similar to Sara's. Today had chased away a loneliness Luis had refused to acknowledge for years. Until his captain's edict and his brother's ass chewing. No, until he'd met Sara.

Not that he was ready to do something monumental to change the situation. Like walk into St. Mary's with Sara at his side, basically inviting the Cuban Inquisition from his mom. If she rallied his *tías* to join the interrogation, he didn't stand a chance.

Yet, what was the alternative?

No way was he dumping Sara at some café on her own, making her miss mass. Talk about an even worse sin in his *mami*'s eyes. Not that she'd ever find out. But the Catholic guilt would inevitably weigh on him.

San Navarro.

That damn nickname Carlos had given him after the church retreat in high school heckled Luis like an adolescent teen in sex ed class. Eight years of private school at St. Mary's and a lifetime of rosaries, rituals, and Holy Days of Obligation under his *mami*'s and *abuela*'s watchful eyes had him mastering Catholic guilt as well as a monk housed on a high mountaintop monastery.

If Sara regularly attended mass like her mom had implied, no way was she skipping because of him.

Sara pushed off the doorjamb. Her blue nightie flirted with her upper thighs as she strolled toward him, giving rise to un-saint-like cravings that thrummed in his body.

"I thought we settled this yesterday?" She crossed behind him to snatch up the pillow and throw it back on the bed. "But, if anyone has to sleep on the floor, it'll be me."

"No way, you will not—"

"Which I don't plan to do either," she interrupted, hands fisted on her trim hips. "This is a perfectly good bed that should fit the two of us just fine. Unless you're a bed hog."

She arched her brows in challenge.

Luis scratched his head, then dropped his hand to hinge on the back of his neck. He could already feel the ache in his back muscles he'd wake up with if he slept on the hard floor. The idea held little appeal.

If she didn't have a problem sharing a bed, why should he?

One of her thin straps slid off Sara's slender shoulder. She pushed it back up with her index finger. He imagined sliding it down again. Trailing kisses along its delectable path.

Dios lo ayude, por favor.

Yeah, he was definitely in need of divine help here. His thoughts were careening dangerously out of control. He hadn't felt this tied up over a woman since—

Luis stomped the brakes on the memories revving in his head. The ones he avoided, knowing they'd burn rubber on his psyche— worse, his heart—if he unleashed them.

His gaze moved to the queen-sized bed, then back to Sara, her hands still fisted on her waist. Brows still arched, daring him. Her kissable lips now pursed with impatience.

A litany of curses pricked the tip of his tongue. Curses directed at himself.

He'd been acting like a moody, hormone-raging teen from the moment they'd entered the privacy of their room. Not the calm, self-possessed man he prided himself on being, both on and off the job.

Sara deserved better than this from him.

"Fine." He closed the wardrobe doors. The tinny magnetic click when they latched was a reminder to keep a lock on his lust-driven imagination, as well as old memories and emotions that tended to color his present.

"Fine?"

"Yeah, I'm good with sharing. As long as you're not a sleep kicker." He turned to face her in time to catch her puzzled frown.

"A what?" One fist slipped down her hip, leaving her arm dangling at her side. And there went that loose strap, sliding down her shoulder again.

"You know. A mover-sleeper. Playing soccer in your dreams. Only, it's not a soccer ball you wind up kicking. Enrique was notorious for taking potshots in his sleep if we had to share a bed on family trips."

Sara's perplexed expression relaxed into a grin. "I only played soccer one season in middle school. Wasn't that coordinated but loved the running. The next year I went out for cross-country."

Luis couldn't help himself. His gaze scanned her long legs, admiring the smooth dips and curves of her adductors and quads, the rise and slope of her calves. Definitely runner's legs. Legs his hands itched to trace.

"So, we're good here." Sara pulled back the ocean reef–inspired comforter on her side, then crawled onto the mattress. The front of her silky pj's gaped when she leaned forward to adjust the sheet, giving him an enticing glimpse of her breasts.

Luis swallowed and looked away. Not fast enough, though. Not before the flash of those pale mounds was emblazoned on his brain.

He walked stiffly to the other side of the bed, absently rubbing a palm over the center of his chest. His heart pounded like he was a horny teen on his first date with the hottest girl in school.

Cálmate, chico, he ordered himself.

It had been an eventful day. Alternating between pretending to be her attentive partner and squashing his desire to be her real one. The stress from learning about her recovery and the mental calisthenics trying to stay on guard, mindful of potential triggers. Then Ruth's assumption that Sara would attend mass with him in the morning.

He should be mentally spent. Feeling like one of the limp dead-weight simulation mannequins they used for practice drills at the fire station.

Knowing his body would benefit from rejuvenating sleep, certain he'd get very little tonight, Luis swiped a hand along the inside bathroom wall to flip the light switch. When he turned back around, the low-wattage bulb in the bedside lamp, its glass bowl filled with seashells, bathed Sara in a soft, inviting glow.

She lay in their bed, the covers tucked primly under her arms, her blue-green eyes watching him intently. "I'm sure there's a Starbucks or breakfast café near the church where I can wait."

Luis climbed in beside her. Painstakingly careful to stay on his half of the far-too-small mattress. "You can't miss mass on account of me. Or my *familia*."

"I don't want to cause a problem. So, if—"

"How 'bout we drive together and walk in separately. My parents like to stay and enjoy fellowship over donuts and coffee after mass. I'll do a quick round of hello-good-byes, then meet up with you at my truck. We'll clear out of the parking lot before anyone sees us."

It was doable. The weekly catch-up that his parents, *tías, tíos*, extended relatives, and friends engaged in following mass often turned into a lengthy gabfest. *Chisme* flying between groups. Even the men were known to gossip, though his *papi* would never admit it.

As kids, Luis and his siblings wound up drifting over to the elementary school playground to run off the donut and red fruit punch sugar high. As teens, they'd lived for the day Carlos turned sixteen and bought his first car. That beat-up old Hornet with its rusty patches, faded blue paint, and threadbare seat cushions had seen better days, but to them it meant freedom.

Sara worried her lower lip as she considered his idea. "You think that'll work?"

Luis slid underneath the cool sheets. "Yeah," he answered, more confidently than he actually felt. Pulling a fast one on his *mami* was not an easy feat.

The worried furrow between Sara's brows eased. Though it didn't completely smooth away. "If you're sure, I'd like to go. I haven't been to mass here, and I have a tradition when I visit a new location."

Chin tucked, she poked at the dark green embroidered design swirling along the top few inches of the sheet. He waited, expecting her to elaborate. Instead, Sara propped herself on her left elbow to reach up and switch off the lamp.

Luis had a tantalizing glimpse of the length of her slim figure hugged by her silky pj's before the room plunged into muted darkness. Overhead, the skylight offered a picture-framed view of the starry midnight sky. Moonbeams streamed in, stretching across the bed like a lazy lover.

Lying on his back, Luis folded his hands on top of the sheets and stared up at the ceiling. He wanted to ask about her tradition. What it was. What it meant to her. How it started.

Hell, he wanted to know everything about her. That increasing need, the fear of it taking off in a blazing fire he couldn't contain, made him keep those questions to himself.

Sara shifted beside him. Her arm brushed against his, and Luis immediately tensed. Hyperaware of her nearness.

"Sorry," she murmured. The sheets tugged as she slid away.

An awkward silence joined them, another unwanted bedmate.

Luis forced himself to lie still. Measuring his breathing. Ignoring the faint citrusy scent that perpetually lingered on her skin. Sleep eluded him. For the second night in a row, he accepted the fact that, thanks to the enticing woman lying only a few inches away, he wouldn't get much rest.

"Thank you," she whispered.

"For what?"

"Everything."

He shrugged, then realized she probably couldn't see his reaction in the dark. "No problem."

Sara's soft chuckle sounded in the quiet; then she rolled onto her side to face him. Luis swiveled his head to find her watching him, her right arm bent at the elbow, tucked between her head and the pillow.

Her beautiful face with its classic features was a pencil artist's study of light and dark. The moonlight reflected in her eyes, tiny bright squares in the shadowed pools. The corners of her mouth curved in a teasing, impish grin.

"What?" he asked.

"No problem? Seriously?"

He shrugged again, uncomfortable under her teasing scrutiny. Secretly admitting that being with her had quickly become a *big* problem, only not in the way she probably thought. Finding it more and more difficult to maintain the emotional detachment that enabled him to excel at his job. Or not blow up what remained of his tentative relationship with his younger brother.

More important, it kept him from making the same mistake of falling for the wrong woman again. Someone who took his trust and love and twisted them into grotesque weapons used to deeply wound him.

"You've put up with my sister's bluntness and, call a spade a spade, her snobbery," Sara continued. "You've buddied up with my brother. Bowled over my parents, especially my mother. And survived our hypercompetitive family game night. Most men would have hopped in a speedboat and gunned the engine to get away."

"I'm not most men."

Her grin widened, the flash of her straight white teeth drawing his attention to her mouth, her kissable lips.

"No, you're definitely *not* like most men. And for that, I'm immensely grateful."

"Yeah?" Despite his better judgment, Luis found himself rolling onto his side to face her. Mimicking her position, he tucked his left arm under his head.

They weren't touching. In fact, a good six inches separated them. And yet the quiet of a house tucked away for the night, the moonlight bathing them in soft shadows, and their hushed conversation created an air of intimacy that pulled at Luis. It drew him to her like a fishing hook ensnared in his chest, slowly reeling him in.

"Yeah," she murmured. A lock of her golden tresses slipped across her cheek when she nodded.

Luis reached out to gently comb her hair away, tucking it behind her ear.

Sara's lids drifted closed and it took all his willpower for him not to lean in, sample her sweet lips. A good-night treat he hungered for.

Reluctantly he pulled his hand away, leaving it in a tight fist in the space between them on the bed.

Eyes downcast, Sara feathered her fingertips over the back of his hand. Once. Twice.

Luis held his breath. Wanting more. Craving all of her. But firm in his conviction that he not make a move unless she made it clear she wanted him to. The moment she did—

The warmth of her soft sigh filled the small space separating them. She set her hand next to his. Her thumb caressed the side of his pinkie finger and damn if it wasn't both the sweetest and sexiest sensation. Blood pooled low in his body, urging him to throw caution to the high-seas wind. Let her know he was interested in taking this pretend relationship to a very real, very satisfying place.

"So, let me clarify. Thank you, for being such a stand-up guy," she said softly.

He nearly groaned in frustration. Talk about a splash of ice water on his libido and the un-stand-up-guy impulses he barely held in check.

"I'll stay in the back pew at mass in the morning," she continued. "Your family won't have a clue about me. I promise. There won't be any problems with them for you when this is all over."

Because—mood buster—it would eventually be over.

He'd do well to remember that. Along with his vow to never give another woman the power to hurt him by abusing his trust and compassion.

That hadn't happened with Sara. Yet. He needed to keep it that way.

Without another word, he rolled onto his back and stared at the patch of inky black sky. A faint star winked in the distance, like it was in on some cosmic joke unknown to him.

After a short while Sara's breathing evened out, and he sensed that she had fallen asleep.

Luis lay awake long into the night thinking about the last time he'd been convinced he could save a woman deeply wounded by her broken family situation by showering her with love and his commitment to building a happy life with her. Only to have it all blow up in his face. Him left reeling at the truth, dealing with the irreversible damage.

If he made the same error with Sara, nothing would pull him out of the deep abyss—screw trying to call it a rut—that mistake would leave him in. Not even if his brother gave him another ass chewing.

He'd simply have to stay on guard. And pray the walls of St. Mary's didn't tremble in protest when his lying butt walked through the doors tomorrow morning.

Chapter 13

"*¿ Qué te pasa?*"

At his *mami*'s harsh whisper Luis swiveled his head around to face the front of the church so fast pain seared the left side of his neck.

"Nothing's wrong; why?"

Seated beside him in the third row, she frowned, her worried mother hen impersonation in perfect form. On the other side of her, wearing a freshly pressed gray guayabera with black slacks, his father shot Luis a questioning frown of his own.

Up on the altar, Father Miguel continued with his homily. Thank goodness for the reprieve. His mother was a stickler for no chitchat during mass. Each of her kids had received the surreptitious swat of her fan or a swift elbow jab in the ribs enough times growing up to know that much.

"*¿A quién buscas?*" his mom rasped.

With Father Miguel still in the midst of explaining the value of the day's readings, Luis's *mami* breaking her silence rule to ask him who he was looking for was so surprising, he nearly answered her truthfully. Seconds before Sara's name slipped off his tongue, Luis clamped his mouth shut.

He ducked his head in deference to the crucifix and eye-catching stained-glass image of Stella Maris, the church's namesake, centered high in the altar's pale blue back wall. With a mental sign of the cross for the half-truth, he whispered back, "I thought I saw someone I knew when I came in."

His mother's brow furrow deepened, a sure sign she wasn't convinced. Keeping his gaze straight ahead, Luis rubbed the pain still warming the side of his neck after his whiplash move moments ago.

Father Miguel wrapped up his teaching with his customary "And the church says . . ."

The congregation answered, "Amen," as they all stood to recite the Apostles' Creed. The rustle of feet shifting rippled through the open nave, ricocheting off the vaulted ceiling decorated with pressed-metal panels.

Luis stopped himself from angling sideways to peer through the crowd again, searching for Sara. He figured her multicolored sundress would be easy to spot. But since they had parted ways in the far back corner of the parking lot before mass, he hadn't spotted her.

This morning, when his cell phone alarm had chimed at seven forty-five, he'd woken to the warmth of her snuggled up to his side. Her head pillowed on his shoulder. His palm cradling her hip.

It was the best good morning greeting he'd had in years.

Based on the way she had scrambled off the bed with a mortified, "I am so sorry!", Sara obviously hadn't felt the same. She politely offered to head downstairs for coffee first, giving him some privacy to shower and change. Then she'd hurried from the room like they were in the midst of a fire drill.

Luis had gotten ready in record time. Afterward, he'd sipped a cup of coffee on the back patio alongside her dad, leaving her alone in the room to get ready and Luis stuck trying not to remember the welcome warmth of her body cuddled with his.

By the time they climbed into his truck for the short drive to St. Mary's, Sara's earlier jumpiness had passed. Good thing, too, because, as they neared a potential run-in between his *familia* and Sara, his agitation mushroomed.

Sara tried making small talk. Until his monosyllabic responses quieted her. At St. Mary's, before leaving the sanctuary of his truck cab, she had tried reassuring him that everything would work out. His *familia* would never know she'd been there.

Strangely, her assertion didn't sit well with him. Though he didn't have the time to ask himself why that would be.

Then she had disappeared in the sea of parishioners heading into mass.

The clap of cushioned kneelers hitting the stone floor signaled the time for the consecration, and Luis knelt with everyone, his gaze straying to his right through the open shutter door leading to the grounds. Sara had mentioned visiting the well-known Grotto of Our Lady of Lourdes while she waited for him after mass. Apparently, the Grotto reminded her of an outdoor rosary garden at Mamá Alicia's old church. Sara planned to pray a decade of the rosary in honor of her beloved nanny. Forgoing donuts and fellowship with his *familia* to join Sara held more appeal than was wise.

He refused to ponder that truth. Instead, Luis closed his eyes in search of the peace he sought here.

With the wide doors spaced every few feet along both sides of the building open, the muted sound of passing cars and mopeds drifted in, occasionally mixing with the choir voices and organ music. Every so often the ocean breeze blew through, providing much-appreciated cross ventilation.

For someone like Luis, who often itched to be outside, the openness of St. Mary's spoke to him. The nave and sanctuary's neutral ivory and white walls, the round arches and thin columns separating the pews from the side aisles, and the natural light illuminating the stained-glass windows above each door generated an aura that blended the outdoors with the tranquility found within.

Carlos and his family sat in the pew in front of Luis, his parents, and Enrique. At ages seven and five, Carlos's boys reminded Luis of when he and his brothers had snickered at each other's silly antics during mass. Similar to Luis and his siblings, José and Ramón had both parents and their *abuelos* keeping them in line. With extra help from the occasional Spanish fan tap on the head from their *abuela* and *mami* if necessary.

This church had witnessed many rites of passage for Luis's *familia*, starting with his parents' wedding, then, years later, Carlos and Gina's. Every Navarro kid in Luis's and the younger generation had been baptized on that altar, by Father Miguel.

First Communions, confirmations, funerals.

Every spot Luis's gaze fell upon in St. Mary's and the lush grounds outside evoked one memory or another. Mostly good ones. Some that may have sucked at the time but made him smile when the Navarros reminisced.

Like the time some punk had teased Anamaría about the crooked bangs she'd cut herself that morning. Luis had found her out in the Grotto, crying. At age six, she'd had the bright idea to play beauty shop before Sunday mass, even though Mami had said she would give her a trim that afternoon.

To teach her impatient daughter a lesson, Mami had made Anamaría attend mass with her bangs sheared in a crooked line halfway up her forehead. She looked like one of the Three Stooges, which made Anamaría a prime target for teasing. After mass, Luis had found her in the Grotto, crying. Her face smeared with tears and powdered donut sugar. Needless to say, all three Navarro boys had taught the obnoxious brat who'd hurt their sister's feelings a lesson of his own. Luis had drawn the line at anything physical—they *were* on church grounds—but when the Navarro brothers surrounded you, a kid tended to take the warning to heart.

Luis snickered at the memory, earning him another *qué pasa?* frown from his *mami*.

On the other side of their *papi*, Enrique leaned forward to catch Luis's eye. Luis made a cutting motion with his pointer and middle fingers. His younger brother flashed the cocky grin that had always made young girls and grown women swoon and the Navarros' *mami* make a swift sign of the cross because it meant Enrique was probably up to no good.

For a moment it felt like they were back to their old selves. His younger brother cooking up some scheme that Carlos perfected, with Anamaría and Luis playing devil's advocate but ultimately agreeing to participate. The four of them had always been close. Until Enrique had broken Luis's trust.

Their *mami*'s advice whispered through Luis's head, imploring him to make peace with Enrique. But she wasn't privy to everything Enrique had kept to himself.

Dark memories, the information Luis had learned after the fact, swooped in like fallen angels, dragging Luis away from the olive branch his brother's grin extended.

How Enrique and Mirna had secretly messed around in high school, but Enrique had broken things off, preferring to play the field. How Mirna hadn't gotten over him, inviting him to meet up with her and some friends one weekend during his last year of art school in Miami. The weekend when they wound up sleeping together. Even though Mirna and Luis had been dating for a couple months. Of course Enrique claimed he hadn't known.

That had been Enrique's first mistake. Keeping his tryst with Mirna a secret once he found out she was dating his brother.

Flash forward about a year and a half later. Enrique had finished art school and unexpectedly moved back home, giving up his artistic dreams for a reason he refused to elaborate on. Drunk at a beach party in Bahia Honda, Mirna propositioned him again. Ignore the fact that by then she wore Luis's engagement ring.

That's when Enrique threatened to rat her out if she didn't come clean with Luis herself.

A threat that precipitated Mirna's foolhardy decision to flee the party and drive back to Key West.

She never made it home.

Lying in her hospital bed, Luis by her side, she finally admitted her duplicity. The next afternoon she passed.

That day, Luis lost his fiancé and his brother. He hadn't been the same since.

His *mami* nudged him, and he joined everyone moving into the center aisle. Lining up for communion in front of the altar, Luis did what he did every Sunday that he and his brother were both off shift; attending mass with the *familia*, he prayed for absolution. For his soul to heal, allowing him to find some way to breach this divide and make his *mami* happy.

So far, his prayers remained unanswered.

Back in their pew moments later, he knelt on the padded knee rest, the organ music and choral voices swelling with the notes and lyrics of "The Prayer of St. Francis."

The irony of the hymn's lyrics wasn't lost on Luis. A prayer asking to be a channel of peace. Someone who consoles others, who brings hope and light to dispel despair and darkness. As a firefighter paramedic, he did his best to epitomize those words at the station and on every call. He took pride in excelling at his job, helping others.

And yet, with his own brother, he couldn't let go of the past.

Staring blindly up at the large stained-glass rendition of Saint Mary centered high in the altar's back wall, Luis steeled himself for the onslaught of remorse, pain, and disillusion he'd battled the past six years.

Battled, and continuously lost.

He looked at his younger brother, once the prankster who'd almost never failed to egg a laugh from Luis, the serious, follow-the-rules middle child.

A flash of color in the line of people along the front of the altar caught Luis's attention.

Hands pressed together in prayer, Sara sang along with the choir. She turned the corner to proceed up the walkway between the rows of pews and the exterior wall with its tall shutter doors ajar. Her gaze met his, and her pink lips curved in the sweetest of smiles. For him.

Instantly, the warmth of peace filled his chest.

It felt right. Seeing her here, in this place that held deep meaning for his family's traditions and values, a place he came to seeking solace.

In that moment, whatever had been off-kilter inside him shifted, falling back into place. With sudden clarity he knew what he wanted.

He wanted to spend the rest of the day with her as they'd done Friday afternoon when they first met. Just the two of them, swapping stories and laughing together.

He wanted to follow her to her own pew, let the church empty of everyone else, and share the tales of the antics that he, his siblings, and their cousins had pulled here. Like the time Carlos hid Luis's black dress shoes when they stayed over a friend's house one Saturday night. To Mami's horror, Sunday morning Luis had been stuck wearing his red Spider-Man sneakers with his altar boy frock.

Or the morning of Anamaría's First Communion, when she decided to paint her nails pink, accidentally smearing some of the polish on her waist because the crinoline underneath was itchy. She'd burst into his and Carlos's room, scrubbing at the stain but only spreading the bright pink blob bigger. Her big eyes had pooled with tears. Luis ran outside to cut one of Mami's white roses from the bushes lining the sunny side of the yard. A couple strategic safety pins later, the rose hid the pink stain from view. Anamaría dubbed him her savior. Until the next time they butted heads and she challenged him to a wrestling match.

Now, eyes locked with Sara's, Luis followed her until she reached the end of their pew, where his gaze collided with Enrique's. Busted!

Tilting his head toward Sara, Enrique arched an inquisitive brow.

¡Coño! Too late, Luis remembered his brother meeting her Friday night at Mallory Square.

Ignoring Enrique's unspoken but clear what's-up-*hermano* smirk, Luis faced the front of the church without a word.

Moments later, Father Miguel trailed the end-of-mass procession down the center aisle. The rest of the congregation followed, some more anxious than others. Free donuts, coffee, and punch awaited in the Fellowship Hall.

A retired firefighter who used to work with Carlos stepped into their pew. The two men struck up a conversation and Luis's *papi* joined. While Mami chatted with Gina and reminded Luis's nephews to walk, not run, he moved to the open side door facing the Grotto. Hands deep in the pockets of his dress pants, he leaned a shoulder against the shutter door and waited.

Parishioners of all ages strolled by. Señor and Señora Hernández, longtime friends of his parents, waved hello. A friend from high school, his arms filled with a crying toddler, sent a chin jut greeting Luis's way. Finally, Sara stepped into view.

She walked through the grass to the Grotto's entrance, where she smiled a greeting to an older lady whose shoulders stooped with age. A black lace mantilla covered the woman's curled bob of white hair and she clutched a string of rosary beads in her wrinkled hands. They exchanged words; then Sara grasped the other woman's right elbow and helped her to one of the concrete benches, gently lowering the elderly woman to her seat.

"Isn't that your blonde from Friday night?"

Luis ignored Enrique's question.

Enrique didn't take the hint or deliberately chose to be a pain in the ass, because he brushed past Luis to stand on the sidewalk outside. He followed Luis's gaze to the Grotto, where Sara stood, head bowed as if in prayer.

"She seemed pretty friendly. Someone you might bring to *familia* dinner anytime soon, or is it not like that?"

"Drop it," Luis grumbled.

He didn't want to talk about Sara with his brother. Not when the last woman they'd discussed had ripped Luis's heart out. With Enrique's silent help.

"*Oye, estúpido*, I'm trying here," Enrique groused. He swatted at Luis's shoulder with a sharp punch. "Give me a damn break!"

"Ooooh, Tío Enrique said the word *stuuu-pid*!" seven-year-old José singsonged as he and Luis's younger nephew burst through the opening.

"Don't let Abuela hear you," little Ramón cautioned. "She'll give you the *chancleta*!"

The two boys howled with laughter at the thought of their *abuela* swatting their brawny uncle with her slipper.

"Hey, we're gonna have a donut-eating contest before our *mami* shows up. Wanna join us?" José asked, hopping from one foot to the other like he was already hyped up on sugar.

"I'm in," Enrique said. He shot Luis a *whatever* scowl, then trailed behind their nephews, who were already racing toward the sweets in the adjacent building.

So much for their *abuela*'s walk-don't-run reminder.

Blowing off his brother's sour disposition, Luis remained by the door. He scanned the open area between the church and school, his gaze continually drawn back to Sara. Eventually the rest of his *familia* scooped him up in their chattering midst, ushering him along to the Fellowship Hall.

By the time they arrived, five-year-old Ramón was complaining of a stomachache and Luis's sister-in-law, Gina, rushed him to the bathroom.

Luis made the rounds among his relatives—some by blood, others by choice. Asking about grandkids, fist-bumping a teen cousin who had finally worked up the courage to ask a girl out, high-fiving others excited about end-of-the-school-year events, and commiserating with a high school buddy over a lost job. You name it, very little was kept secret when it came to their community. Including the news about his mandated time away from the station and the concerns for how he was handling the mental and emotional stress after the horrific car accident.

Some people promised to pray for him. Others doled out advice. Señora Gomez even offered to set him up with a niece from Tampa who was "perfect" for him. Like a blind date would solve the problems he'd been running from for the last few weeks. For the past six years if he was honest with himself.

By the time Luis made it back to the foldable gray picnic table where his parents, Carlos, Gina, and the boys sat, his jaw ached from the tight grip he kept on the mind-your-own-business response ready to spring from his mouth. His smile had grown forced. His usual patience with the nosiness of island life worn thin.

Feeling like a caged shark, he dragged a metal folding chair away from the table, noting that Enrique had already managed to give the place the slip. Smart move.

"*Mijo,* you haven't been by the house since yesterday morning," his mother complained. "*¿Estás bien?*"

She sipped her *café con leche,* her dark brown eyes assessing him over the rim of her Styrofoam cup. Everyone at the table understood the prying subtext in her question. Luis should have been on shift today, like Anamaría. This type of departmental reprimand, a step shy of going on his record, had never been handed down to a Navarro. Not in all the decades one of them had served on the KWFD. Not even to Enrique, who craved the adrenaline high of pushing himself, along with his captain's patience, to the limit.

"I'm good," he grumbled, chafing at the question he'd fielded multiple times already this morning.

"How are you planning to fill your free time? You know there's always help needed around St. Mary's," she noted.

"I told him to make himself useful and take the *Fired Up* out on the Atlantic. Catch us all some fresh mahi," Carlos chimed in from the other end of the table. "*Pero* he hasn't listened to me yet."

Because he'd taken Carlos's other advice. The one his older brother was smart enough not to mention in front of their conservative, worry-prone mother. No way she would approve her firstborn son's "shake things up" mantra.

"Ohh! I wanna go fishing! Can we go today, Tío Luis?" José clambered off his chair, running to throw himself at Luis's side. "¡Por favor!"

Luis ruffled the seven-year-old's hair. "I'm sorry, *papito*. Not today. I'm busy."

"*¿Haciendo qué?*"

Everyone at the table zeroed in on his answer to his *mami*'s sharp question. Luis shifted uncomfortably on the cold metal seat.

"I'm helping a friend who's in town. Showing their family around a bit," he hedged, anxious to punch his time card here, then clock out, like Enrique.

"That's very *nice* of you," his *mami* said, layering the word *nice* with enough innuendo it became a synonym for *interesting*. "Is she someone we know?"

Ha! He hadn't said the friend was female.

Luis caught Carlos's sly grin. They both knew their *mami*'s parental radar must be pinging. Alerting her that something was up with one of her kids. If only Carlos knew.

It was ironic. The one brother Luis normally confided in had no idea about Sara. Yet, the one he had lost faith in, had already met her.

Luis's skin itched with unease. He didn't want to talk about the station or the accident. He was tired of unsolicited advice about his supposed lack of healthy coping skills, and no way was he interested in answering pointed questions about whomever he chose to spend time with.

What he needed was an excuse to split. If not, his *mami*'s probing questions would continue.

"*Bueno, mijo*, who is she?" His *mami*'s intuitive gaze still glued on Luis, she absently slid a glass of watered-down fruit punch out of the way before one of his nephews knocked it with his elbow.

"It's not anyone you know—"

His cell phone vibrated in his pants pocket, interrupting him. Luis slid the device out to find a text from Enrique lighting up the screen: *Warning, Blondie's hanging out by your truck.*

Surprised, Luis reread the message. After their squabble earlier, he wouldn't have expected Enrique to give him a heads-up about what he probably thought might be potential female trouble.

Decent move on his brother's part.

After sending a cryptic *gracias* in reply—a little more personal than the plain thumbs-up emoji; two could play the let's-be-nice game—Luis pushed away from the table. The hard rubber grip on the bottom of the chair legs screeched against the linoleum floor.

"*Perdóname,* Mami, I need to get going."

"Sorry? *Pero* you just sat down," she complained, her round face crumpled with dismay. Under her dark floral blouse, his *mami*'s shoulders lowered with disappointment. "First Enrique. Now you. What is going on with *mis hijos*?"

"Your sons have busy lives. But we love you." Luis bent to kiss her forehead, then quickly made his way around the table doling out cheek kisses and hugs good-bye, adding a shoulder punch for Carlos, who shot him a what's-up glare. Circling back to his mom, Luis gave her another hug.

"*Dios te bendiga, mi vida,*" she called to him.

He sent her a wink in reply to her habitual blessing.

No amount of time with her beloved children was ever enough for Lydia Quintana de Navarro. When they were teens, anxious to spread their wings, her mother-henning used to drive them up the wall. By now he had learned to take it in stride. Most of the time he appeased her. Hung out a little longer. Stopped by the house a second time on his day off.

Today, though, there was somewhere else he wanted to be.

With someone else he *really* wanted to be with.

Someone who didn't care about his past. Or his inability to let bygones be bygones. Or the fact that since Mirna, he'd never allowed himself to have faith in another woman. Until now.

Around Sara, he felt alive again, in all the right ways.

Since he only had one week with her before she flew back to New York and her real life, he planned to make the most of it.

Chapter 14

Sara pressed the back of her hand to her forehead and upper lip, dabbing the sweat droplets forming courtesy of the midmorning sun and humidity. Even with her standing under the shade of the expansive palm trees at the back of the church parking lot, the day's heat wrapped her in its clammy arms as she waited for Luis.

A few minutes ago she had ducked behind the tree's prickly trunk when she spotted his younger brother striding her way. A sigh of relief shuddered through her when he zig-zagged around another car, then stopped at a black SUV a few spots down from Luis's truck.

The last thing she needed was to draw Enrique's attention.

She leaned against the truck's mammoth tailgate, hoping Luis would make it back here before she turned into a puddle of perspiration. A dip in the backyard oasis pool sounded more and more like a great idea.

"Hey, sorry it took so long."

She spun around at the sound of Luis's deep voice.

Regret creased a line between his brows as he jogged closer, then rounded the truck's hood to meet her by the front passenger door. He dug a hand into the left front pocket of his dress pants, and Sara heard the click of the vehicle doors unlocking.

"No worries," she assured him. "I enjoyed exploring the grounds after visiting the Grotto. I haven't been waiting long."

"Long enough. The sun's brutal today. You'll have to remember to put on extra sunscreen so you don't burn."

Luis brushed the back of his fingers gently along her shoulder. Desire swooped through her, a homing pigeon heading straight to her core.

They stared at each other, Sara trying but failing to read the storm of emotions in his dark eyes. This morning, they'd been awkward with each other. Her, embarrassed to find herself sprawled all over him as if he were her body pillow when she woke up. Him, stressed about his family potentially meeting her by accident.

Luis turned to open her door, and Sara stepped up on the running board to climb onto the seat. Rather than close the door, Luis remained standing beside her, filling the tiny space with his broad shoulders. The deep red material of his polo shirt complemented his bronze skin, the short sleeves taut over his muscular biceps. Her dashing he-man with a savior complex that she'd given thanks for during mass.

"You okay?" she asked, swiveling on the leather seat to face him.

"I'm sorry I was a jerk on the way over here," he said, his gruff voice softened with sincerity.

Touched by his unexpected apology, she placed her hands on his shoulders, seeking a connection with him.

"Well, you *were* a little more dark and broody than normal," she teased. A lot more, actually. With his cloud of doom and gloom increasing each mile closer to the church. "I tend to prefer that sexy little half smile you flash when you're laughing on the inside, but trying to appear all tough guy-ish on the outside."

A determined glint flashed in his dark eyes. "Sexy, huh?"

She gave him a playful swat and rolled her eyes. "Whatever."

"How about we forget role-playing around others for a little while, and spend some time just you and me," Luis suggested. "Maybe a bike ride around the island while your parents and the others golf?"

"You don't have plans with your family?"

For some reason she had assumed he would drop her off at the rental home now that everyone else was at brunch and she'd be on her own this afternoon while he did some regular Navarro Sunday activity.

He shook his head. "I'm all yours."

Whether he meant it or not, the double entendre had Sara imagining all the delicious things they could do together if he really was "all hers."

As if he read her wicked thoughts, Luis's lips spread in a mischievous grin. He edged closer, wedging himself between her knees. His large hands settled on her hips, sending furls of desire spiraling into her belly.

"What do you think?" he asked.

What she couldn't *stop* thinking about was how badly she ached to slide to the edge of the leather seat, wrap her legs around his waist, and invite him even closer. But this was a church parking lot, with parishioners trickling out after fellowship time. And she'd already had a close call nearly running into one of his family members.

"So, you're offering me a personal island bike tour?" she asked, excitement rising to brighten what had been shaping up to be a dull afternoon ahead.

"Yup."

"Just the two of us?"

Luis nodded.

"No complaints when I stop for a ton of pictures?"

"Nope."

"Or ask you to play photographer for me?"

"Add me to your list of devoted paparazzi."

Her heart melted at his silly answer. The idea of spending more time with Luis, alone, without the guise of their fake relationship hanging over them, sounded absolutely perfect.

"Heck yes, I'm in!" she blurted.

Luis leaned into the truck to press a far-too-quick but oh, so delicious kiss on her lips. Before she could react, he backed away to shut the door, then hurry around to his side of the vehicle. In seconds they were pulling out of the parking lot and making a left off the side road onto Truman Avenue.

In the passenger rearview mirror, Sara spotted a black SUV similar to the one Enrique had driven make the turn with them. The

SUV followed for a bit, but Luis made a right onto a narrow street and the car continued straight.

Back at the rental home, she headed upstairs to quick-change out of church clothes into her bathing suit along with a running skirt and racerback tank top while Luis hunted down the white binder filled with helpful details and notes the homeowners had prepared. He saved the combination for the bike locks on his phone, then changed his clothes while she grabbed bottles of water from the fridge and added them to the shoulder bag filled with their beach towels and sunscreen.

Out on the back lawn near the storage shed, Luis held out a faded red ball cap. She took it, running her pointer finger over the gray and white *KW* embroidered on the front.

"What's this for?" she asked.

"To shield your face from the sun. I wasn't kidding, it's brutal."

She turned the hat over in her hands, the bill curved from what looked like years of use. Inside, she found the initials *LN* with *#21* in black permanent marker.

"Is this your number?" she asked, swiping her thumb over the handwriting.

"Yeah. That's my old baseball cap from when I played in high school."

"Aww, and you trust me with it? I'm touched." She swatted the hat at him, secretly feeling like a high schooler, beguiled by the hunky team captain inviting her to wear his letter jacket.

"It's a classic, so don't lose it," he warned, playfully. "Here, let me adjust it."

He took the cap, deftly tightened the headband, then looped it over her head. His fingers carefully tugged her ponytail through the opening at the back.

"How's that feel?"

Perfect.

"Good," she answered.

"Now I won't worry about your beautiful face getting fried. I doubt your followers would be happy about that."

"I could always write a post about the importance of sunscreen, pairing it with an approved product sponsor."

"Always thinking, aren't you?" He tapped the tip of her nose and winked, making her swoon like a smitten teen again.

Soon they were pedaling down Eaton Street headed toward the main drag where they came to a stop at the red light.

"There's too much traffic to bike down Duval," Luis told her, his eyes hidden behind a pair of black Ray-Bans. "Let's make a left on Whitehead and bike toward the Southernmost Point. Less bobbing and weaving around tourists rubbernecking the sights and not paying attention to where they're going."

"Hey, I resemble that tourist remark," she complained.

He shot her a grin that softened the hard planes of his face with an appealing boyish charm.

A blue sedan crossed in front of them, heading down Duval. The driver honked the car's horn, and the older couple inside waved at Luis as they passed. His smile faltered, but he returned the greeting.

"Everything okay?" she asked, watching the sedan make its slow crawl down the busy street. It stopped for a group of teens jaywalking, cell phones high in the air recording their antics.

"Uh, sure. That was Señor and Señora Lopez. Friends of my parents." The light changed, and Luis pushed off with his foot. "Let's go."

As they pedaled, he pointed out buildings and interesting sights along the way. Filling in personal stories of him and his siblings and cousins growing up.

She enjoyed hearing about him as a kid. Always the voice of reason in the group, or so his stories told.

On Whitehead, they stopped for Sara to take the requisite tourist photo at Mile Marker 0, the end of US 1. Or, as Luis referred to it, the Overseas Highway.

She snapped a selfie, tapping her cell screen to focus on the green and white mile marker and black and white highway signs, blurring her own image.

"Have you ever thought about starting here and driving all the way up US One until it reaches Maine?" she asked.

Her mind jumped to the travel blogs she could write featuring the different people and interesting local sights. The sponsors who might be interested in the advertising. "Imagine the various changes in landscape and scenery, especially if you made the trip during fall foliage up north."

"Fall might be nice. Definitely not winter," Luis answered once they'd hopped back on their bikes. "I've never even seen snow, much less driven in it."

"Really?" Sara swerved around a pair of chickens pecking at the ground near a cracked street curb.

She'd already snapped a picture of a few of the stray chickens known to wander the island when she and Luis stopped to admire the huge kapok tree in front of the courthouse. He'd taken a photograph of her dwarfed by the towering tree with its unique trunk. Farther down the road, she'd marveled at an expansive banyan tree, its aboveground roots like thick gnarled fingers stretching up toward its branches.

"Not much chance of seeing snow when you live here," Luis said.

"Winter in the city can get pretty bleak," she admitted. "The snow's beautiful when it first falls, but with the dirt and grime, eventually the pristine white fluff turns to black mush. Which I affectionally call snirt."

He snorted a laugh and kept pedaling alongside her, his thigh muscles flexing. "Cute, but you're not really selling city living to me. I'll take the open water view of a blue horizon and the moped pace of island life any day."

"Have you ever thought about living anywhere else?"

They reached another intersection and Sara pulled her blue beach cruiser to a stop next to Luis's. One of the local Conch Tour Trolleys, seats packed with tourists, made the left turn onto Whitehead Street. A teen with her phone pointed out her window waved to them. Sara returned it with a friendly smile.

"No, not really." He drove a hand through his closely cropped hair. Mouth curved down, he seemed to give her question some consideration.

Not for the first time since he'd changed into a black tank with a pair of gray board shorts and sneakers, Sara found herself admiring the natural ripple of his shoulder, upper back, and arm muscles whenever he moved.

"What about you? Are you a New Yorker for good now?" The light changed and Luis pushed into the intersection, glancing over his shoulder at her.

"I don't know," she admitted once she'd caught up to him. "The city vibe is energizing. Though admittedly, it can be tiring at times. If this deal works out with the investors and boutique in Miami, I may relocate."

Luis gave her a double take, his bike swerving dangerously close to the curb before he corrected it. "For good?"

"For a little while at least. It might help with inspiration for the clothing line."

He seemed to consider her admission, and she wondered if, like her, he contemplated the potential of them seeing each other again. Miami was only a three hour drive up US 1.

Her family thought it's where she and Luis had met. Who's to say they couldn't meet up in Miami for real?

She'd love to. Would he? Or was he fine using this interlude to fill his time off and he'd wave good-bye at the end without wanting more?

The what-ifs tumbled in her head as they rode past the Ernest Hemingway Home and Museum, one of their stops on the Conch Tour Train yesterday. The two-story cream house with avocado-colored shutters and a walk-around porch on the second level already had a line of people waiting to enter. A high privacy wall kept the house and property mostly hidden from view, but passersby caught a glimpse of the famous writer's Key West residence through the open gates and ticket booth.

"Since you like the outdoors, I bet you'd love skiing in Vermont or New Hampshire." She veered closer to Luis as a pair of mopeds zoomed by. "The snow-covered mountains and ski slopes are a different view than the open ocean, but equally majestic."

"Actually, one of my sister's personal-training clients lives in Vermont and snowbirds here in the winter."

"Great skiing there. Does your sister work with her clients year-round or only when they're local?"

He nodded. "Anamaría trains several online and is trying to grow her business. She's actually planning to meet a group of them for a triathlon up north this fall. Threatened to drag me along just to get me off the island."

Eyeing the way his big frame dwarfed the bicycle, Sara couldn't imagine anyone dragging Luis anywhere. Though she could think of a few places she'd like to try.

Luis slowed as they neared the busy curve at the end of White-head Street where the red, yellow, white, and black painted monument marking the famous Southernmost Point of the United States sat. Tourists lined up for pictures. Some stood on the seawall staring across the ocean, straining their eyes to catch a glimpse of Cuba a mere ninety miles away. Others sampled fresh coconut water from a vendor or perused artwork and memorabilia for sale at another pop-up booth.

"Wanna take a picture?" Luis propped his sunglasses on top of his head and squinted at Sara.

"That's okay." With the swarm of people, the wait would be long, and she'd had a photo taken with her family yesterday. A rare group picture she would treasure.

"How about lunch?" he asked.

"I'm good, unless you need to stop."

"You're not hungry?"

She shook her head.

"There wasn't much time for breakfast before mass, did you grab a snack back at the house?"

"I'm fine," she assured him, her mood sinking with his line of questioning.

Luis started to say something else, but instead he clamped his mouth shut and slid his Ray-Bans in place to shield his eyes again. The lazy smile that had spread his lips throughout their bike ride wilted like the poinciana flower petals scattered along the road's hot surface.

"The Southernmost Beach Resort is up ahead." Luis maneuvered his bike through the crowd, tossing the words over his shoulder as she followed. "It's a public beach, so we can stop there and cool off. Maybe grab a bite at the resort café."

Disappointment tightened Sara's chest. Given one guess, she knew what lay at his desire to stop at a beach with a convenient café.

Once clear of the crowd, they pedaled off, heading toward the majestic Southernmost House at the end of the block. As she'd done yesterday, Sara marveled at the Victorian bed-and-breakfast with its round turret, intricate two-story balconies, and peach and pastel colors offset by the brick red roofing. Elegant gables added a dollhouse appeal and lush tropical grounds beckoned travelers seeking a respite in paradise. It was also, as Sara had emailed her agent about last night, the perfect spot for a photo shoot featuring the new line of tropical chic clothes she hoped to design with the investors from Miami. If—no, *when*—her agent finagled the final terms of the contract.

She and Luis pulled to a stop as Duval Street dead-ended with the Southernmost House on the right and a public beach with an open-air restaurant on the left. His expression grim, Luis walked his black beach cruiser to the bike stand, then waited for Sara to park hers alongside it. Working in silence, he looped the u-shaped steel lock through their bikes, securing them together.

Sara eased away from him and the issue she knew he wanted to push—what she had or hadn't eaten today.

Rather than argue, she strolled to the sidewalk's edge, where she kicked off her flip-flops to dig her toes in the sand. Turning to admire the open ocean, she remembered her mother's remark about the calming, Zen-like effects of breathing in the sea air. The meditative aspect of staring out at the vastness as you imagined the world and all its infinite possibilities ahead of you.

Anxious about Luis's need to take care of something she already had under control, Sara focused on their beautiful surroundings. Hoping to soak up some of the ocean's calming power.

In the distance, a pair of catamarans floated idly by, white sails filled with humidity-laden wind. Several couples strolled hand in hand along the dock that extended about a hundred yards out. Midway down, two teen girls sat, dangling their feet into the clear green water. Blue beach loungers and white umbrellas dotted the sandy area between the restaurant and the water's edge.

"I'll go see about renting chairs and an umbrella so you can get out of the sun," Luis said, still in gruff protector mode.

"I brought a spare sheet to spread out. If you're okay, I'm fine without a lounger. Shade is a good idea, though."

"That works. I'll grab a menu while I'm over there. Just in case."

He jogged off without waiting for her response.

Sara bit her lip, barely stopping herself from yelling that he should ask about renting a better mood while he was at it.

Instead, she swallowed the smart-aleck jab. He meant well. She believed that. But if he started hovering like her family, it would put a pall on the rest of their afternoon. She refused to let that happen.

Like she often did with her parents, she'd have to set him straight. Make it clear he could stop worrying about her eating habits.

Hefting their woven beach bag on her shoulder, she scoped out an empty spot. Then, with the refreshing breeze's billowing help, she spread the white sheet on the sand, securing two ends with one of her flip-flops and a third with their bag of supplies. By the time she was done, Luis had appeared with a young man wearing a navy polo and white shorts. The attendant quickly hammered a pole into the thick sand, then set up their umbrella before heading off to assist another customer.

Sara plopped down on her half of the blanket, waiting until Luis followed suit. As soon as he started removing his sneakers and socks, she bit the bullet.

"There's no need for you to be concerned about whether or not I'm eating." She pitched her voice low to avoid someone nearby overhearing their conversation. "If I'm exercising too much or downing laxatives."

Luis's fingers stilled on his left shoelaces.

He angled his head to look at her, his chiseled face serious. His gaze scanned hers for several tense seconds; she stared back at him, refusing to concede. Eventually he heaved a disgruntled sigh and got back to work unlacing his shoes.

After stuffing his socks in his black and red sneakers, he stretched across the sheet to place the shoes on the corner behind him, securing it from the stiff breeze.

"I noticed your reaction when you asked if I was hungry," Sara pressed, refusing to back down from the issue. She'd hidden her OSFED for too long. Now she dealt with it head-on. Successfully. "Look, I appreciate your concern. Believe me, I understand where it's coming from. You can ask, but not badger. What I really need is your trust and belief in me."

Her feet buried in the sand, Sara looped her clasped hands around her knees and hugged them to her chest. A shield protecting her should his faith in her prove too fragile to withstand her plea. Nervously, she scrunched and opened her toes, the sand shifting around them.

Beside her, Luis propped his forearms on his raised knees, his big hands dangling between his legs. He faced the water, lips set in that damn grim line.

Sara's heart raced. Her pulse pounded in her ears.

If he couldn't do this, if their budding relationship changed because of her OSFED, it wouldn't be the end of the world.

It'd be a hard blow. But she'd handle it. Therapy and positive self-talk assured her she could cope with anything and do so in a healthy way.

Better she knew where Luis stood now, before she got in deeper. Before she cared more for him than she already did.

Keeping her gaze trained on a young mother slathering sunscreen on a squirmy toddler, the cutie's round belly stretching a Little Mermaid one-piece suit, Sara stood her ground. "Like I already told you, I see my therapist regularly. I rely on learned cognitive behavior therapy skills. And Dr. Evans is on speed dial if I'm struggling with a trigger."

Luis shifted beside her. Not wanting him to interrupt her, Sara rushed on, needing to get this out before she second-guessed herself.

"Which hasn't happened in a while now. Not since my mom finished chemo and we got our first good news. My family hovers. Robin gets annoyed or aggravated or, whatever, for whatever reason. But you—"

She turned to face him, the sheet twisting beneath her crooked knees. Sand spilled onto the material, marring the white surface like the topic of her disorder had done to their carefree afternoon.

"You look at me differently than them, than a lot of others. Like I'm normal, whatever that really means. And I, I need for that to continue. For this, us, not to change."

Suddenly, like a kettle left too long on the stove, she ran out of steam. Agitated, Sara tugged off the ball cap, gripping the bill tightly in her hands. The wind cooled her heated brow, blowing loose tendrils across her cheek.

"You *are* normal." Luis twisted to splay his right hand on the sheet, leaning on his straightened arm for support. "I mean, we're all dealing with something we don't want to in our lives. In one way or another."

"Like whatever happened between you and Enrique."

He drew back at his brother's name.

"C'mon, if I can share my deep dark secrets, you can, too." Sara poked his shoulder with her knuckle. He didn't even budge.

With his dark sunglasses in place, she couldn't read his eyes. The rest of his face was set in a stoic, don't-mess-with-me expression that probably worked with recalcitrant individuals when he responded to a call. It wouldn't work with her.

Had they not spent the past few days together, basically fast-tracking their relationship, she might have backed off. Worried about overstepping some unspoken but definitive boundary.

Not now. Not when she'd picked at the scabs covering the painful scrapes in her personal life and revealed them to him.

"I know from experience, talking a situation out with someone actually helps."

His "humph" in response told her exactly how thrilled he was by her suggestion.

Sara refused to be deterred. This . . . relationship had to be a two-way street. He wanted to help her; she was determined to do the same for him.

"Here's the deal." Scrambling on the sheet to sit tailor-style, she straightened her shoulders and spread her hands palms up on her knees. "I'm going into the water to cool off. Join me. Talk with me. Be *honest* with me. Like I've been with you." She leaned toward him, her gaze boring into his, stressing her point for several weighty seconds. "Or stay here and pout on the beach."

It was either a brave or foolish move. This edict she laid out for him.

That little voice inside of her, the one she often thought of as Mamá Alicia whispering encouragement in her ear when self-doubt dodged her steps, cheered her mettle.

"I don't pout," Luis grumbled.

An ember of hope lit in her chest. She plopped back down on her butt, fighting a grin.

Above his glasses his brows angled down in a fierce scowl. His mouth pursed in what she would most certainly call a pout.

"Don't look now, but this"—she tapped his lips with her finger, then pushed to her feet—"is definitely a pouty face."

She shimmied her running skirt down her hips, folded the garment, then set it near one of her flip-flops. Her orange Lululemon racerback tank followed.

Despite the cover of his sunglasses, she felt the heat of Luis's gaze when she stood before him in nothing but her fuchsia string bikini. Reveled in the knowledge that she had his full attention.

Fists on her hips, she squinted down at him, the noon sun hot on her skin.

But the heat building on her inside . . .

Those flames were fanning to a blaze because of the mouthwateringly gorgeous, if sometimes frustratingly hardheaded, hunk eyeing her from behind his darkened lenses.

"The decision is yours," she challenged, imagining her hardwon self-confidence like a superhero's cloak, flapping in the breeze behind her. "Me? I'll be making like a saltwater fish cavorting in the surf. If you're lucky, you might catch me."

With an impish wiggle-fingered wave, she pranced toward the water, knowing full well that, thanks to a *healthy* diet and exercise, she rocked her bikini even better than a *Sports Illustrated* swimsuit model.

Despite her confidence in her figure, she acknowledged the deep-seated desire that more than just the extra shake of her hips would entice Luis to loosen his guarded reserve and meet her halfway.

Would he accept her conditions and join her in the water? She sure as hell hoped so.

Chapter 15

Damn if this woman didn't push all his buttons. Even the ones his *familia* knew were clearly marked "Don't Touch."

Luis wanted to be annoyed, like he was when Mami or Carlos or Anamaría pressed him to open up. Forgive. Move on. With Mami, he backed away from an argument. With his siblings, he grumbled at *them* to back the hell up.

Pero con Sara . . . He shook his head, unable to ignore the truth.

But with Sara something was different. He *felt* different.

Luis watched her confidently striding into the calm water, her trim body and sleek curves drawing the attention of others sunbathing and relaxing along the shore. Including some dude foolish enough to sport a man bun and a skimpy orange Speedo. The fumes from his fake orange spray tan must have killed a few brain cells if the guy was actually considering his chances of getting lucky with Sara.

No way. No how.

A curly-haired toddler in a pink princess bathing suit and with a round tummy that rivaled his old baseball coach's beer belly ambled toward the water near Sara. Giggling with glee, arms flapping at her sides to steady her wobbly gait, the cutie looked back over her tiny shoulder at her mother, who gave chase.

Sara grinned, bending at the waist with her arms open wide to keep the child from running in too far. Her throaty laughter caught on the breeze. Lust, dark and rich, pooled low in Luis's body. *Coño*, he'd be hearing that sound in his head, in his dreams, long after she flew out of his life, back to her big dreams in the big city.

Shin-deep in the water, the little girl tripped, yelping with fear as she threatened to go in face first. Surprise widened Sara's eyes, but she quickly hunkered down to catch the child with a muffled, "I've got you."

With Sara down on one knee, the child's slippery weight knocked her to the side. She landed on her butt, water splashing around them. The girl's pudgy arms wrapped around Sara's neck in a choke-hold.

The frazzled mom reached them, greeting Sara with a gasped, "I am so sorry!"

"I running," the child told the adults in her sweet, high-pitched voice.

"You sure were," Sara answered.

"Frannie, you cannot go into the water alone!" the mom cried. "You have to wait for Mommy!"

"But Ise wiff my new fwend." The cutie maintained her death grip on Sara with one hand while she open-palmed dark curls out of her face with the other.

Sara's grin widened and she waved off the mom's exasperated apologies.

Luis had no idea if Sara had spent much time around her niece and nephew. Based on the tentative banter she shared with her brother and his quiet wife, and Sara's admission that she wanted to get to know her siblings better, he'd guess probably not. And yet her ease with the friendly daredevil here on the beach suggested she wasn't a novice. Or maybe she was simply a natural.

The thought tugged at a dream he hadn't allowed himself to even consider since Mirna's death. One he'd be foolish to entertain now.

From the moment Carlos and Gina's oldest had been born seven years ago, Luis had happily changed José's dirty diapers and handled feeding time. He had even walked the floor in the middle of the night when the little guy suffered with colic and Carlos was on shift, but Gina needed some sleep. He also babysat so the couple could sneak out for the all-important occasional date night. It's what *familia* did for each other.

Like the weekend he and Enrique had tag-teamed baby duty so Carlos and Gina could check into a local Airbnb. She'd refused to go out of town. Worried about being too far away and the baby needing her.

Memories of the longest forty-eight hours of his years as a doting uncle rushed in on Luis.

Rock-paper-scissors battles between him and Enrique over who'd get to choose night feedings over poop diaper changes. Discovering José's dislike for strained peas and how far the seven-month-old could spit a mouthful of green mush. The number of shirt changes Luis had made thanks to José's projectile vomit, eventually giving up on wearing a shirt at all to avoid more dirty laundry.

By the time Sunday rolled around, Enrique had touted their nanny stint as the best form of birth control ever invented. Cementing his status as the consummate bachelor.

Luis had volunteered for regular bi-weekly date night duty. And decided to ask Mirna to marry him.

Six months later, she died from the injuries of her car accident, after revealing the truth of her deception.

Luis dug his fingers in the hot sand, betrayal bitter on his tongue. Picking up a fistful, he watched the grains fall at his side, the wind carrying some to fan across the sheet.

Life and love could be equally as fleeting. Whisked away by a force beyond your control.

Another bitter fact he'd learned on the job, surrounded by tragedy and loss, was the importance of cherishing life's blessings. Appreciating what you had. Because it could be gone in an instant. He'd seen enough tragedies, comforted enough survivors, to know this as a certainty.

Maybe finding out about Mirna's deception had been a blessing. One he'd been too hurt, too shell-shocked, to understand.

"*¿Oye, vienes o no?*"

Sara's question, spoken in a Spanish accent that would impress his *mami*, had Luis's gaze shooting up to meet hers.

She stood, knee-deep in the ocean. Head cocked to the side,

one hand fisted on her jutted hip. A challenge sparked in her blue-green eyes. Her string bikini begging for him to untie the scraps of material and show her exactly what happened when she challenged him with an "Are you coming or not?"

If only.

Brushing his hands on his board shorts, Luis rose to his feet and ducked under the umbrella's edge.

When an enticing mermaid beckoned with her sexy siren call, even he wasn't strong enough to resist.

Luis shed his tank, dropping it in a black pool on their sheet and sending Sara's pulse into overdrive.

He strode purposefully across the sand toward her. His eyes still shielded by those damn Ray-Bans, a smug grin spreading his lips.

Her stomach clenched, lust tingling in private places at the sight of his gorgeous body. She knew he kept himself in amazing shape. He had to for his demanding job. But good Lord, the man was sin and sex and so many things Mamá Alicia had warned her about when Sara first hit puberty.

No way Sara planned to heed that warning now.

She gulped. Trying to act cool and composed. Intent on not ogling him.

Totally failing.

The glorious slopes of his pecs rivaled the ridges and curves of his six-pack abs for her attention. The wide breadth of his magnificent shoulders tapered to a slim waist, dragging her gaze to his obliques and the tease of his board shorts low on his hips.

Luis's feet hit the shore and she stood paralyzed with desire. In four strides he reached her. His hands cupped her hips, his thumbs hooking on the strip of material.

"I caught you," he said, his voice a low rumble.

She arched her neck to gaze up at him, her heart tripping, stuttering, then heading off to the races again.

"Maybe. Maybe not." Looping her hands around his waist, Sara walked backward, leading him deeper into the water. "Maybe I wanted you to."

His cocky grin broadened to Cheshire cat level.

The cool ocean lapped against her lower back and she sucked in a quick breath. Caught in the swirl of hot lust. In danger of being sucked into the staggering undertow being in Luis's arms elicited.

His fingers tightened around her hips and she drew to a stop.

Luis took another step, closing the gap between them. His wet skin, slippery with sunscreen, hot from the sun, pressed against her stomach. Her breasts brushed his chest, their sensitive tips straining against her flimsy top, desperate for his touch.

She ran a finger along the edge of the waistband at his back, dipping her fingertip inside. His erection stirred against her pelvis and she savored his reaction. Reveled in the knowledge that her attraction, the desire consuming her, was mutual.

"We're playing with fire here," he warned.

"Good thing I know a hunky firefighter with a big—"

He ducked down to capture her lips in a searing kiss silencing her smartass comeback.

She opened for him, kissing him with equal fervor. Their tongues brushed. Sweeping, savoring, tangling in a swirl of hunger.

The intensity of emotion buckled her knees. Luis's strong arms wrapped her in his tight embrace and together they sank lower in the salty water. The cold caught her by surprise and she gasped. His lips tore from hers, tracing a delicious trail of hot kisses up her jaw, to the sensitive spot under her ear.

"*Bella sirena*," he whispered, his heated breath raising goose bumps on her flesh.

"This beautiful mermaid's caught herself a hunky sailor," she murmured.

A raspy chuckle shook his chest, rubbing her nipples through her suit top. Like a fiery line of lit gasoline, lust shot straight down to the spot she yearned for him to touch.

As if he sensed her need to be closer, to feel him in her most intimate place, Luis cupped her butt and lifted her off her feet, encouraging her to wrap her legs around his waist. She willingly obliged. Beneath the water, their bodies melded, her hips cradled in his lap. His erection prodded at her core through her suit bottom. Firm, insistent.

It wasn't enough. She bucked her hips against him, and he groaned, tightening his hold on her.

"Ah, *dios*, you're driving me crazy," he murmured.

His teeth nibbled on her earlobe; then he laved the tender spot with his tongue.

"Crazy in a good way?"

"The best way."

Their lips met in another salty-sweet kiss that had her heart soaring like the seagulls overhead. Elbows bent, she pressed her forearms up his back, her hands cradling his shoulder blades as she hugged him tightly. He suckled her lower lip, then sealed his mouth over hers for a deep, toe-curling kiss.

Another beachgoer splashed by. Laughter and chatter from others filtered through Sara's desire-hazed senses, reminding her of their very public location. She broke their kiss and dropped a chaste peck to the corner of his mouth, his chin.

"This is not what I had in mind when I invited you to come in the water with me," she said.

Betraying her own words, she licked the scruff on his chin, the saltwater tangy on her tongue. His hands tightened on her butt, his erection straining into her.

"Talking's overrated." He ducked his head to nuzzle his nose along her ear with a lusty grumble.

"Mmmm," she murmured. "I'd love to take this further, but my offer involved something a little different."

He paused, his mouth at her temple. "You drive a hard bargain."

"That's not all that's hard. But . . . I digress."

His chuckle tickled her ear. Made her fall a little deeper.

Luis leaned back a little to look down at her, his hold on her butt still secure. His smile faded at her seriousness.

Afraid he'd pull away from her, put up that emotional wall he was adept at erecting, Sara reached up to slide his sunglasses on top of his head.

"Hey—!"

"I wanna look in your eyes. Nothing hidden between us. Truth," she told him, staring in the mahogany depths of his eyes.

His throat worked. But he didn't argue. Didn't look away.

Progress.

The ocean lapped at their shoulders, a piece of leafy seaweed floating by on the surface. She pushed it away, then cupped Luis's cheek with her palm. "As long as we allow the past to negatively affect our present, it's impossible to build a positive future."

He rolled his lips together as if trapping a response in his mouth.

Gently she brushed her thumb over his mouth. "It's not easy facing our fears."

He shifted uncomfortably, turning his head to stare at the dock off to his right. Either because of the noon sun or the memories she was asking him to confront, he squinted at the distance. His jaw muscle tightened, evidence of an inner battle she had fought in the past herself. To reveal her most sacred secrets, trust another person with information that could wound her. Or remain silent, alone, hurting.

"Look, I'm not a therapist." She paused, frowning at her ineptitude, desperately wanting to say the right thing.

"But you did dress up as one for another Halloween party?"

Her lips quirked at his lame joke. "No, you dork." She swatted him with water, succeeding in splashing some in her own face.

Laughing at the situation could be a good sign. Or a deflection.

The faint smile curving the edges of his mouth calmed her unease. This was an important conversation for the two of them. Without it, they'd never get to a place of true intimacy. Even if this could only be a one-week interlude that served to help them smooth past hurts. She'd take it.

Seeking to soothe his obvious discomfort, she rubbed her palms over his shoulders, slowly drawing her hands up to support his neck. "No, I'm not a clinician. But I've had plenty of experience with therapists, and both in- and outpatient therapy."

His face sobered.

"So talk to me, please."

A heavy sigh pushed through his lips. He closed his eyes for several dull heartbeats before meeting her gaze, resignation haunting his face. "I was engaged once. About six years ago."

The admission took Sara by surprise. Not wanting any reaction from her to make him shut down, she worked to school her face into an open expression.

"Not for long, though we dated for almost two years before I proposed. We actually knew each other as kids. She graduated high school a few years after me, with Enrique. Who—"

He broke off. Frowned. Cleared his throat as he shook his head and looked away again.

Sara stroked her fingers at his nape, giving him the silent space to take his time, along with the reassurance that she was listening.

"Who it turns out was the brother she really wanted."

Sara's fingers stilled. Shock at the idea of some woman not recognizing her good fortune in possessing Luis's love and devotion knocked rational thought away.

In the next moment, despair and anger surged in Sara's chest, blocking her throat with tight-fisted empathy. She knew what it felt like to be compared to a sibling and come out the loser. To know you weren't considered good enough.

Above them, the sun slipped behind a cloud, casting a dull shadow across the water's surface. A breeze skittered over her wet shoulders, and Sara shivered. Luis dipped them lower into the warmth of the water, thinking of her comfort even in the midst of his difficult admission.

She hugged him, their cheeks pressed together for the sweetest of moments. When she pulled back to offer him an encouraging nod, his frown deepened to a scowl that hinted more at confusion than anger.

"I was too focused on being her savior," he continued. "Convinced I could show her that she was more than the troubled teen from a broken family who'd grown up to become a woman unaware of her potential, deserving of good things. But really, she'd said yes to our first date out of curiosity, thinking it'd make Enrique jealous. Then stuck around because . . ."

He scoffed with such harsh self-derision Sara's heart broke for him.

"Because I made her feel good when my brother wouldn't give her the time of day. Enrique knew she wanted him. Hell, they slept together after she and I first started dating."

"What?"

The outraged question slipped out before Sara could stop it.

"I'm sorry," she offered, not wanting to influence him in any way, especially if it would stop him from sharing. "It's not my place to judge."

"Why not? I have." Luis's mouth twisted with contempt. "Enrique was in Miami for art school at the time. I'm not sure if he knew we were an item. But he didn't confess once he found out. After he graduated and moved back home, then decided to go to fire college, she propositioned him again. Even though we were engaged by then. When he finally manned up and threatened to out her, she freaked. Left a beach party up at Bahia Honda in no condition to be driving."

Despair and disillusion clouded his dark eyes. The sad emotions painted the angles of his handsome face and Sara wanted to rail at the other woman for her stupidity. And his brother, for the hand he'd played in hurting this wonderfully generous man.

"Mirna survived a couple days after her car accident. Long enough to make peace with her erratic mom, say good-bye to the *abuela* who raised her. And admit the truth to me. She wanted absolution. As hard as that was for me. As betrayed as I felt, I had to . . ."

His lips trembled and he pinched them together. Sara gently cupped his jaw, willing him to sense her empathy, maybe find inner strength from it.

"I gave it to her because she needed it," he murmured, his tone a heartrending mix of disgust and defeat. "She needed peace before she passed. But my brother? He didn't even bother to come to the hospital. Then he showed up for the funeral and tried to bug out five minutes into the wake. Told me she didn't deserve to be mourned." Luis's jaw muscle ticced, his pain palpable. "Our fight on Mirna's *abuela*'s front lawn was not my finest moment. The little shit didn't even fight back when I tackled him. I got two solid punches in before Carlos and Anamaría pulled me off him. I didn't see Enrique until *familia* dinner a week later, but the shiner I gave him didn't look half-bad."

He reached up to grab his Ray-Bans, then dipped his head backward in the ocean, as if to wash away the painful memories in the salty water.

Rivulets ran down his temples and Sara wiped them away with her thumbs to keep them from stinging his eyes. His mouth curved in a sad semblance of the half grin that made her belly flip-flop and her chest tighten.

"And that is the end of my mood-killing sob story. Satisfied?" He squinted down at her before slipping his glasses back into place. The move shielded his eyes from her, hiding the windows into his soul that she longed to peek into.

Satisfied? Not by a long shot.

He'd talked about what had caused his rift with Enrique. Not why it continued. Six years later.

But he *had* opened up to her, so it was enough. For now.

Tapping her chin with a finger, she frowned up at the sky, pretending to search for an answer.

"I don't know?" she said, drawing out the words. "Satisfied can take on so many different forms. You know what I mean?"

Above his glasses, his right brow quirked. His arms tightened around her hips, pulling her pelvis closer to his. Desire curled wicked tendrils inside her, sensuous and rich.

Cradling his face in her palms, she stretched up to brush her lips against his. Featherlight. Teasing herself with the need to taste him. Show him how much she trusted him. With her secrets, her body. Maybe even, if she divested herself of all her reservations and fears, her soul.

"Thank you." She whispered the words a breath away from his mouth before sealing her lips over his.

He groaned, deepening their kiss.

His tongue brushed hers. Once. Twice. A tangle and caress ripe with the heady taste of saltwater and him that made her head woozy, her body pounding for more than kisses and underwater caresses.

She gasped, overwhelmed by the rush of desire. Luis dragged his mouth down her jaw, her neck. She tilted her head to the side, murmuring her pleasure.

"*Coño*, I want you so bad," he rasped.

He licked that sensitive spot behind her ear, and she bucked into him again.

"What if we skipped the rest of the bike tour?" she murmured.

Luis froze, his breath warm on her ear.

Arching back, she glanced up at him. Her pulse pounded in her ears, a bass drum throbbing an insistent, carnal beat.

He removed his sunglasses, holding them loosely on the water's surface. They bumped against her shoulder where his thumb brushed tiny circles on her suddenly hypersensitive skin. He stared at her, his serious gaze boring into hers.

"We have the house to ourselves for a few more hours," she went on, making her intent clear.

"Are you sure that's what you want?"

The fact that he would ask, even after her invitation, was further evidence of the height he reached on her good-guy meter.

Unhooking her legs from around his waist, she stood on wobbly legs. Her feet sank in the ocean's sandy bottom. She caught his hands in hers. Threaded their fingers together and tugged him toward the shore.

"This mermaid is ready for land. And a bed. And some privacy. With *you*."

Luis's dark eyes sparked with hunger, and a promise of the delectable afternoon ahead.

Chapter 16

Hot and sweaty after their Tour de France pace from the beach at one end of Duval to the rental house on the other, and with a different, more exhilarating activity on their minds, Luis and Sara didn't bother storing their bikes when they arrived home. Instead, they parked them in the grass in front of the pygmy date palm trees and flowering bushes hiding the corner storage unit from view in the backyard oasis.

Luis sucked in a deep breath, trying but failing to slow the pulse hammering in his chest.

His body thrummed with anticipation and . . . hell, flat-out eye-crossing lust. Things had gotten so freaking hot and heavy in the water, he'd barely made the walk from the shore to the bike rack without giving bystanders a peep show of his hard-on.

Coño, had he and Sara been alone, at one of the secluded areas around the tiny islands and sandbars out in the Gulf, they wouldn't have waited for niceties like a bed, clean sheets, or a shower.

The image of Sara standing under the chrome rain showerhead in their upstairs bathroom, water cascading down her body, now a captivating rosy gold after her time under the Key West sun, had Luis growing hard.

She hurried up the porch steps ahead of him, the cheeky grin she sent over her shoulder inducing him to pick up his own pace. She tapped the key code into the pad on the bath-laundry room door, then pushed it open.

The alarm beeped, alerting anyone inside that a door or window had opened. Thankfully, the house was empty.

Halfway through their race home she'd received a text from her mother. The golfers were starting the tenth hole, with the intention of arriving home by midafternoon. That meant Sara and Luis had the house to themselves for at least a couple hours.

And Luis knew exactly, and how deliciously, he wanted to fill them.

Once inside, Sara dropped the beach bag with their sheet and wet towels on top of the washer, then turned to face him. Her blue-green eyes swam with excitement as she held out her hand. A silent invitation from the sexy siren who had enticed him into the ocean.

Forget waiting for the bed! Luis grasped her tiny waist, lifting her to sit on top of the washer.

"Oh!" she yelped, eyes wide with surprise.

He stepped in between her spread knees, counting himself lucky when she leaned forward to meet his kiss. The minty taste of her gum and the coconut scent of the sunscreen he'd insisted she reapply before they hopped on their bikes again heightened his senses. Greedily he suckled her lower lip, nipped it gently with his teeth. Her tongue sought his. Twisting, exploring, taking everything he gave her and giving back in return.

His fingers found the hem of her Lycra tank, sneaking under to caress her trim stomach.

She moaned into his mouth, then hooked her legs around his back. Sliding to the edge of the washer, she brought her lower body flush against him.

His hands strayed higher, seeking the mounds of flesh he'd been dying to taste since he'd felt her nipples pebbling under the thin bathing suit material back at the beach. Only the threat of the two of them getting arrested for indecent exposure had kept him from peeling her top down so he could suckle her right there. Christening South Beach as his favorite make-out spot on the island.

Now, he cupped her pert breasts with his palms, rubbing the

pads of his thumbs over her firm nipples until she gasped. Her breath shuddered, the force rippling from her chest through her slender torso. Her sensual reaction urged him on, and he lifted her tank up to her armpits, revealing the fuchsia bathing suit triangles covering her from his hungry gaze.

Hands splayed on the washer for support, she leaned back, offering herself to him.

Luis growled with impatient lust, blood surging to his erection. He tugged aside the thin material on her right breast, then bent to take her into his mouth. Dried salt from the ocean water melded with her sweetness on his tongue.

She moaned again, deep and throaty. The heady sound of her pleasure encouraged him and he trailed his tongue down her cleavage intent on giving equal attention to both beautiful breasts.

Sara rocked her hips, pressing against his torso. Her body, like his, desperate to sate the innate need to be one in the most elemental way.

"If we don't . . . if we don't slow down . . ." she murmured, her palm on his nape encouraging rather than dissuading him from making love to her breasts. "I'm gonna orgasm on top of this washer like . . . like a teen sneaking a quickie, while her parents are busy."

Dios, her sense of humor slayed him. In the midst of some of the hottest foreplay he could remember, he found himself laughing. Feeling carefree. Something he'd never felt.

Not until her.

He peeked through his lashes to find her staring down at him, her lids heavy, skin flushed with desire. Wickedly, he lapped at her breast, then gently blew on her moist skin. Her blue-green eyes rolled. Her head dropped back as if too heavy for her slender neck to carry, only to bang against the cabinet behind her.

"Ow!" She ducked her head and swung her arm up to rub at the sore spot, accidentally knocking their beach bag to the white tile floor.

"That was not what I was thinking when I brought up slowing down," she said on a groan.

Under his exploring hands, her stomach muscles tightened with her laughter.

He pressed a kiss on her flat belly, then slid his hands under her ass to heft her in his arms.

"Let's get you upstairs," he said, striding down the hall toward the front of the house. "The only thing I want you thinking about is how amazing you feel. If you're even thinking at all."

"I heartily approve of that plan."

He approved of anything that put that satisfied smirk on her delicious mouth.

Sara buried her face in his neck where she placed a moist kiss over his pulse point. Flyaway tendrils from her blond ponytail tickled the underside of his jaw as she nuzzled her nose over his skin in a tantalizingly soft caress.

"You always smell so delicious," she murmured.

The erotic sound of her humming with pleasure as she inhaled deeply sent a spurt of lust arcing through him. His erection strained against his board shorts, anxious for release. At the same time, a need that had nothing to do with sex and was more about cherishing this precious woman who challenged and uplifted him pierced Luis's heart.

Dios mío, he had it bad for her.

The thought scared the hell out of him. He'd kept part of himself locked away for so long, refusing to risk the type of pain and rejection he'd experienced with Mirna's betrayal.

At least with Sara he was going in eyes wide open. They both were. This was temporary. Amazing and exhilarating, but temporary. They'd agreed to one week. Then she'd leave to focus on her career, in New York or Miami or whatever city offered the next career move. He'd . . . figure it out later.

That meant the clock was ticking on the amount of incredible sex they could have together.

Starting now.

Luis passed the light-stained hutch in the foyer where his car keys nestled in a white ceramic bowl shaped like a clamshell. At the bottom of the wooden staircase he paused.

"Here, put me down. I can walk up." Sara wiggled in his arms. Her crotch rubbed against his stomach and he ached to be inside her.

"What are you talking about?" Biceps flexing, he tightened his grip on her buns. "You're not even half the weight of our practice dummy. You questioning my abilities, woman?"

Without waiting for her to answer, he took the stairs by two. Piece of cake.

Sara craned her neck to look down at the empty foyer below. Sunlight shone through the rectangular windows framing the front door, painting golden streaks across the dark wood floor.

"My, my." She fanned herself with a hand. "Talk about hot stuff. Why have I never dated a firefighter before?"

"Because you've never met one who measures up to me."

Right brow quirked in an oh-really way, her windblown ponytail swinging behind her, she pursed her lips in a sexy pout he planned to take his time kissing away.

"Promises. Promises," she teased.

Never one to back down from a challenge (ask his older brother, who initiated and lost their jalapeño-eating contest in middle school), Luis continued down the short hall to the bedroom he and Sara shared.

He pushed the door shut with his foot, then spun to press her back against it. Her eyes flared, the color darkening to the rich blue of the open ocean when he took the *Fired Up* out for a little deep-sea fishing.

She jutted her chin, a come-and-get-me move that was like waving a red flag in front of his raging desire. He grazed his teeth gently on the tip of her chin, fighting the increasing urge to give in to the primal need to take her. Right here. Right now.

Her legs tightened around his waist, inviting him closer. "Show me what you got, stud."

He reared back, surprised yet totally turned on by her assertive bedroom talk.

Sara's brows furrowed. She scrubbed a knuckle at the tiny grooves between her brows, the first hint of insecurity he'd spotted since they'd gone into the water together.

"Um, that sounded sexier in my head," she mumbled. "Less corny-movie-line-ish."

The cutest blush spread from her chest, up her neck, and into her cheeks.

"I'm down for corny movie lines," he told her. "And I'm *really* down for this."

He ducked his head to drop a kiss on her collarbone. Another under her jawline. One more at the right corner of her mouth. Loving the way she melted in his arms.

"Yes," she murmured, turning her head to meet his kiss.

He didn't need to breathe. Didn't even need food to survive. He simply needed her. This.

Her mouth hot and wet on his. Her body ready and willing. Carnal lust blazing with its intensity.

Sara moaned with pleasure. Her fingers clawed at his shirt, struggling to lift it.

"Off," she demanded. "Now."

He grinned, sandwiching her lower body between his and the door so he could use both hands to shuck his black tank.

Dios, he could get used to her looking at him like this. As if he were a delicious meal she couldn't wait to devour. Knowing he made her feel that way stoked his ego. Filled the gaping hole he kept hidden deep in his heart with wonder and ecstasy.

He hadn't realized how alone he'd been until Sara. Until she bulldozed her way into his dull, predictable, solitary life with her bright smile, engaging personality, and determination.

Agreeing to her crazy idea had changed him. He didn't stop to consider why or precisely how. He couldn't. Not when she gazed at his torso with those gorgeous, desire-filled eyes. The pink tip of her tongue slowly drawing across her bottom lip as if savoring what was to come.

Reaching behind his back, Luis unhooked her legs, then grasped her toned thighs and oh, so slowly slid her down the front of his body until her feet touched the hardwood floor.

He grasped the hem of her top, pausing for her assent. She lifted her arms over her head for him. Luis tugged the orange Lycra material up her torso, stretching it carefully over her face, then her ponytail, stopping when he reached her forearms to leave the stretchy material cinched around her. Lightly clasping her slender wrists with one hand, he held them in place above her as he cupped her jaw with the other and ducked down to cover her mouth with his.

She grazed his lower lip with her teeth. Sucked it into her

mouth. Laved it with her tongue, then surprised him by taking control of the kiss. Driving him wild with each thrust of her tongue as her lithe body mimicked the motion against his.

His erection pulsed, begging for release.

As if she too were nearing her limit of foreplay, they broke apart, chests heaving. Eyes locked. In the quiet of the house, a rush of emotions fueled by the intensity of their pent-up desire built to a frenzy, sweeping over them with hurricane-force winds.

Suddenly they were scrambling to remove their beach clothes. Her bathing suit top flung across the room to land on the shelf next to the flat-screen TV. His board shorts and her bottoms were kicked aside. Together Luis and Sara moved to the bed, its ocean reef comforter apropos for the culmination of the titillating foreplay that had begun back at South Beach.

Sara pivoted into the bathroom, where Luis heard the rasp of a zipper.

Arms behind her back, his sexy mermaid returned to the foot of the bed where he waited. She whipped out a condom packet, her face lighting up like she'd found the key to paradise and was willing to share.

Unfortunately, it was only one. As in. One. Single. Packet.

Torn between laughing out loud or groaning his disappointment, Luis looped his arms around Sara's slender waist as he shook his head. "*Ay, sirena*, one isn't going to be nearly enough. But it's a start."

They tumbled onto the bed together in a tangle of arms and legs and shared laughter.

"Would you rather . . ."

Sara popped a green grape in her mouth and pondered what options to throw at Luis in their back-and-forth getting-to-know-you game.

In the past, she'd played for fun. Challenging friends with surface-level, purposefully difficult-to-choose-between, often meaningless options.

With him, she had an ulterior motive—find out what made this strong, moral, generous man to whom she was in danger of losing her heart tick.

They sat on the bed facing each other. He, leaning against the padded headboard. She, cross-legged in the center of the mattress. The sheets, a rumpled mess after their delectable lovemaking. And yes, making love with Luis could most certainly be described as beyond delectable.

The man had an uncanny, toe-curling way of finding her body's sensitive spots. Like the juncture between her ear and jawbone, the hollow at her inner elbow, the base of her spine, her inner thigh as he trailed his tongue higher.

Sara shivered as desire unfurled inside her in warm, heady waves.

Good god, they'd already used two condoms from the box she'd packed in her toiletry bag, having modestly left the container in the bathroom at first. No need to appear greedy. Although frankly, when it came down to it, there was no denying her eagerness. The mere thought of Luis's lips kissing her, licking her, driving her wild again set her body on fire.

Sex with Luis had been the most intense, sensual experience. Absolutely incredible. And scary.

Scary because she couldn't stop herself from wanting more with him. More of everything. But as much as she might want to broach the topic of life, a relationship, after this week, she couldn't squelch the unease that he might not be interested.

That maybe the reason he hadn't been able to forgive his brother's betrayal stemmed from Luis's deep love for his fiancée. A love that had been twisted and taken advantage of by a woman whose deathbed confession and bid for absolution meant Luis hadn't been given a chance to express his own hurt and humiliation over having been used and deceived in such a despicable way.

Instead, he'd listened, comforted his beloved in her last days. Bestowed the forgiveness she sought as she died, leaving him to take out his pain and anger on his brother. Without achieving his own sense of closure.

Years later, Luis remained unable to trust. Or move on.

No wonder he wasn't keen about lying to Sara's family and had been adamant about keeping her away from his.

Mamá Alicia's caution whispered in Sara's ear: *Cuidado con lo que pides.*

Sara had wished for a way out of the mess Ric's no-show had spawned. Now she found herself facing an even bigger, potentially heartbreaking fiasco if she wasn't careful.

Stretching out her arm, she snagged her water off the nightstand. She took a swig, but the metallic taste of unease lingered.

"Quit stalling or you lose your turn." Luis nudged her knee with the back of his hand.

He adjusted the fluffy pillow lodged between him and the white upholstered headboard, then snagged a raw carrot from the platter on the mattress between them.

Earlier, after disposing of the second condom, he'd grabbed a pair of boxers, then run downstairs for snacks while she peed and cleaned up in their bathroom. Sara hadn't bothered digging out clothes, choosing instead to slip on Luis's black tank.

If she had buried her nose in the material and inhaled his earthy scent before putting it on . . . well, he didn't have to know. By the time she heard the wooden steps creaking his ascent, Sara had scrambled back on the bed in his shirt and a pair of panties.

He'd returned balancing a serving platter overflowing with green grapes, baby carrots, and a hunk of Gouda cheese with one hand. In the other, he'd clutched a resealable bag of baked pita chips and two water bottles.

Let her go on record as stating what an absolute turn-on it was to see a man with a body that looked like it'd been sculpted by Rodin's talented hands, and a mischievous smile that made her pulse blip stroll into her bedroom. Especially when he came bearing food meant to silence her growling stomach.

Would you rather stay in this bed with me all week or are you still hung up on the ex who clearly didn't deserve you?

Sara took another healthy swig of water, stalling. He nudged her knee again, and she glowered at his impatience.

She swallowed, tried to work up the nerve to ask a more personal question, then chickened out and went for another generic one.

"Okay, would you rather bungee-jump or skydive?"

"Easy. Bungee-jump." He snagged another carrot. "I already went skydiving on a weekend trip to Orlando with Carlos a few years ago. You?"

"Skydived with some sorority sisters at a place outside Tempe when we were in college. Might bungee-jump." She hitched a shoulder in a not-sure shrug. "I'm on the fence."

"How come?"

She picked up a slice of Gouda and nibbled on a corner, considering. When she looked up, she caught Luis staring at her mouth. Self-conscious, she licked her lips, catching a crumble of the nutty, smoky cheese with her tongue.

Heat flared in Luis's dark eyes, the deep mahogany deepening to a rich reddish-brown.

Sara's breath hitched. Lust throbbed in secret places that should have been sated after their spine-melting romps. Should have been, but far from it.

Which left her with two options for how to answer his question: keeping things simple and focusing on the great sex or digging deeper and pressing for a different kind of intimacy.

"I'm on the fence because the thought of some big rubber band keeping me from certain death doesn't compute all that well in my brain. Sure, taking risks has helped me get ahead in my career. But I'm not too keen on situations with a high probability of me getting hurt."

Like falling for a guy who couldn't, wouldn't, resolve his past.

Luis bit into a baby carrot, the crunch loud in the quiet room. He chewed. Swallowed. All the while his inscrutable gaze remained on her.

"I can respect that," he finally said.

Sara released the breath she hadn't realized she'd been holding. Uncrossing her legs, she kept her left knee bent to avoid knocking their food platter and extended her right leg to prop her foot on the pillow. All the while wondering if he understood the subtext of her answer or if his thoughts remained on thrill-seeking vacation adventures.

"My turn," he said, and she swore she heard a challenge in his words.

Head tilted pensively, he scratched his jaw. The motion had her recalling the feel of his scruff rubbing against her sensitive skin, rough and tantalizing.

Maybe she should stop reading into their situation. Enjoy it for what it was . . . an island fling that her inability to stand up for herself with her family had put into motion. Her therapist would have a field day with this if—no, when—Sara revealed the details. She knew the danger of hiding from the truth.

"Would you rather . . . ?" He paused, and damn if the calculating look in his eyes didn't have her wondering what he might be up to.

"Would you rather maintain the undercurrent of tension with your sister or have a heart-to-heart while you're on neutral turf here?"

Bam!

Talk about not wasting time with subtext and just tossing a grenade in the middle of their game!

Annoyed, with herself for tiptoeing and with him for barging right into the morass of her family drama, Sara pushed herself toward the foot of the bed. Away from a discussion she wasn't particularly interested in having.

"Stop." Luis grabbed her right ankle, holding her in place. "Don't run from this. From me."

The loose grip he held on her leg let her know she was free to go if she really wanted to; he wouldn't force her to stay. The sincerity and conviction mingling in his expression. The truth hidden in the corner of her soul.

They all intertwined, weaving into a rope that tied her in place like one of those beautiful yachts they'd seen at the dock behind the Custom House yesterday.

She stilled. Her breaths coming shallow and fast. She stood at a crossroads, moving in infinitesimal increments in the right direction. One she wanted to go.

But old doubts peered from the shadows. Armed and ready to trigger unhealthy behaviors she'd fought hard to curb. There'd been a time when she would have weakened, gorged herself on junk food or laced up her running shoes desperate to leave those doubt-fueled fears in the dust.

Not anymore.

And yet, while her therapist regularly stressed the importance of open communication, Sara continued to shy away from her sister's challenging personality and the inexplicable grudge Robin held against her.

Luis gently caressed her shin and calf. Not pushing, not backing off either. She eyed him warily, contemplating her options. Two could play this game.

"Would you rather stay angry and distant with your brother," she asked him, "or do your part to try mending your fractured relationship?"

His fingers tightened around her calf for a second. Two. Three.

Then he released her leg and clasped his hands on his lap. His serious, tough-guy expression slid into place, blanketing his rugged features and dulling his dark eyes.

Sara stared back, feigning a confidence level her quivering insides belied. They had danced around their family problems. Pushing each other on different occasions. Never head-to-head like this.

Would he wash his hands of the discussion? Of her? Because she'd gone too far?

If so, then he wasn't the man she thought . . . hoped . . . he really was.

Outside on the street a car honked. A warning that soon their private interlude would be over and her family would return.

But she and Luis had crossed a line in their previously platonic, ignore-the-simmering-attraction relationship. She wasn't sure if they could go back to their charade as friends. Honestly, it wasn't what she wanted.

Luis pressed the butt of his palms against his eye sockets as if they pained him. His muscular chest rose and fell on a heavy sigh. "*Coño*, we really suck at this game."

A sputter-laugh burst from Sara's mouth, expelling her pent-up anxiety. Charmed by his ability to find humor in their tenuous situation, she plucked a green grape and threw it at him. The piece of fruit hit his washboard stomach, then bounced onto his lap.

"Hey?!" he complained.

An amused, self-deprecating smirk pulled at his lips as Luis plucked her lame ammunition from the bunched material of his navy boxers and stuck it in his mouth. He picked up the food platter, moving it to the nightstand on his side of the bed.

Then, with a rakish black brow quirked, he grasped her ankle again and tugged her closer. A rush of pleasure filled her as her butt slid across the peach-colored cotton sheets.

"*Ven pa'ca*," he bid, his deep voice encouraging her to come to him. Hands at her waist, he lifted her up so she could straddle his lap.

Sara laid her hands on his bare chest, marveling at her paler skin against his. Different, yet they shared so many similarities when it came to their family lives.

Luis's hands slid slowly up her back, splaying over her shoulder blades, stopping when they came to rest at her nape. She melted under his tender ministrations. Marveled at how utterly beautiful and wanton she felt in his arms.

Overwhelmed by the swirl of lust and genuine affection coalescing inside her, Sara pressed her forehead to his. Her lids fluttered closed. The scent of ocean water, sweat, and sex surrounded her, a perfume she longed to bottle up and savor later.

"What a pair we are, huh?" Luis whispered.

Sara opened her eyes and met his gaze. Desperate to know what he was thinking. If he was as torn and conflicted about where they stood, about their pasts and the problems they had yet to face.

"What are we doing here?" she asked, unable to keep her doubts silent any longer.

Luis combed his fingers through her hair, tucking the loose tresses behind her ears. Tenderness blossomed in her chest when she noticed he still wore her ponytail holder on his wrist where he'd slipped it on after gently removing it from her hair earlier.

"I'm not sure," he admitted. "You challenge me in ways I normally resist. But somehow, with you it's different."

He ran the pad of his thumb along her jaw, an awed expression in his eyes as they tracked the caress.

"You make me want to try. Make me want . . . things I haven't allowed myself to want in a really long time."

Humbled by his admission, Sara tucked her head in the crook of his neck. His strong arms wrapped around her and she nestled in his protective embrace.

"It's probably just the great sex fogging your brain," she teased, relying on humor to mask the intensity of her emotions.

His chuckle rumbled in her ear. "Could be. But I'd be lying if I said that was all."

His honesty sobered her.

"How about if we take this"—she traced her palm lightly over his pec, awed by the combination of his soft skin over the hard muscle—"one day at a time? See where it leads."

Not quite the Would You Rather question pitting her against his ex that Sara had kept to herself earlier, but she wasn't courageous enough to put that out there. Yet.

"And on Friday we'll decide?" Luis trailed off at the mention of the end date of their original agreement.

Sara waited for him to continue.

When he didn't say anything, she interpreted it as a silent, mutual decision to deal with that when the time came.

Her cell trilled an incoming text message alert. Sara bit back a resigned sigh at the interruption. It trilled a second time, and she reached over to grab the phone off her nightstand.

A message from her mother popped up on the screen: *Finished golfing. Ordered clubhouse drinks. Home in 45.*

Sara imagined her mom typing the message like she rattled off orders in the OR. Direct. No-nonsense. No emotion, or emoticons, involved.

"It's my mom," she told Luis. "Looks like they'll be here in less than an hour."

"Okay." The uncertainty in his single-word response mimicked Sara's sentiments.

Dejected, she set her phone on the bed, then snuggled back in his arms.

Her gaze cut to her cell, her message app still open. Three little dots hovered underneath her mother's first message. Seconds later, another text appeared: *Love you.*

Like the Florida sun peeking through the clouds to cast its rays through the bedroom skylight, clarity brightened Sara's perspective. Her mom was trying. Making a true effort to change their relationship. So were her dad and Jonathan.

Maybe, instead of stressing about what-ifs, she should simply accept the situation that was before her and make the most of it.

Grab ahold of what she had, instead of worrying what she may not down the road. Therapy had taught her to take it one day at a time. Today had been a marvelous day. Her decisions, her actions, could help it stay that way. Or not. She preferred the former.

Sara sat up abruptly.

Luis frowned. "You okay?"

"Would you rather conserve water and shower with me or save time and shower with me?"

Luis's face lit up at her question. His lips spread in a wicked smile that had her entire body humming with tantalizing anticipation.

He let out a victorious, "Yes!" then swung his legs off the bed and scooped her up in his arms. "Now there's a question that requires some research and exploration before answering."

Oh, she knew they couldn't avoid the issues that awaited them outside these four walls. But that didn't mean they couldn't enjoy discovering all the exquisite ways they worked well together. That's exactly what she planned to do.

Chapter 17

Luis stepped out of the bathroom to find Sara, dressed in red running shorts and a black sports bra, perched on the foot of their bed. Running sneakers already laced up and her blond hair pulled back in a sleek ponytail, she was ready to head out for a four-mile run together.

"Here you go. One black, no-fluff coffee." She rose to hand him a supersize mug with the green and white zero mile marker sign plastered on the side.

"Thank you." Taking the mug, he inhaled the rich, bitter aroma. After the busy night they'd spent getting far too little sleep but engaged in much more pleasurable activities, he'd need a second cup to fuel his day when they got back from their run.

"So, your mom and Robin ultimately decided today's schedule is the Audubon House, the Mel Fisher *Atocha* museum, and browsing the shops around the Custom House, right? With a day on my boat tomorrow, right?"

He eyed Sara over the rim of his cup as he took a sip of the hot liquid.

"Are you sure you're up for that? I mean, if Robin gets on a roll, our only option would be to throw her overboard." Sara's face scrunched in a cute grimace. "My parents and Edward probably won't go for that idea. Now Jonathan, I might be able to convince him."

Her blue-green eyes squinted as she gazed up at the ceiling like the answer to her dilemma might be found in the creamy paint swirls.

"Or," Luis bent to drop a kiss on her pouted lips. "There's no avoiding each other out there. So, you two take a walk or sit on the beach and try clearing the air after I drop anchor at Snipes Point."

He swatted her butt playfully and eased around her to grab a tee from one of his drawers.

"You gotta admit, she was in a good mood last night when they returned," Luis reminded her. Setting his coffee next to a photo book on life in the Keys, he hunkered down to rummage through his clothes.

"Because she beat everyone in golf, duh."

Luis grinned at Sara's aggrieved tone.

In his *familia*, Robin's competitive nature would fit right in with his siblings. But he understood there were different dynamics between Sara and her sister. Unspoken disappointments, no doubt differing interpretations of the slights they'd each felt as children growing up with two highly successful, driven parents who expected the same from their children and may not have given them all the attention and love they wanted. Though Ruth and Charles were doing their best to make up for it now.

Another gray KWFD T-shirt in hand, Luis pushed the drawer closed and rose. "I think it's pretty sweet your parents want to take all of you on a Mediterranean cruise."

When he stuck his head through the neck hole in his shirt, he found Sara watching him. He took his time lowering the shirt over his torso, enjoying her reaction. Appreciation glittered in her eyes turning them the color of stormy Gulf of Mexico waters. The same color that had gazed back at him in the throes of passion last night.

"Ahem." He cleared his throat and pointed two fingers back and forth between his eyes and hers. "Keep looking at me like that and we're gonna wind up indulging in a different type of exercise."

The blush seeping into her cheeks had him nearly reaching out to wrap her up in a fierce hug.

"Oh, that's definitely happening," she assured him, her brows waggling to emphasize her promise. "You can count on it."

That easily, his body responded to her husky words, his mind jumping from hugs to moves that were far more carnal.

Luis cradled his coffee mug tighter, more to keep his hands busy and his thoughts off the two of them diving back into bed together.

"Anyway, back to the topic. Thank you for deftly sidestepping my parents' questions last night!" Sara pressed her fingertips to her temples, as if she were channeling a stressful memory. "When they asked about your availability to come with us on the cruise, poking for info about your commercial real estate business and our long-term plans, I froze."

Shit, he had, too.

Mostly because the idea of spending more time with the Vances, even prickly Robin, held unbelievable appeal. Even if that time didn't involve the bonus of a Mediterranean cruise.

International travel, any travel, had always been his sister's dream, not necessarily his. Anamaría had curtailed those aspirations after their dad's heart attack the summer after her high school graduation, staying home instead of jetting off to conquer the world alongside her boyfriend like they'd planned. Alejandro had gone off and made a name for himself as a photojournalist. Anamaría had stepped in to help care for their *papi* while he convalesced. Then she eventually joined the family business, becoming a firefighter paramedic like the rest of them.

Since then, her travel consisted of a few meet ups with her training clients at their various races across the United States.

As for him, sure, he wouldn't mind seeing a little more of the world, but he was also fine sticking close to home on his island. Enjoying game nights like they'd done the past few evenings here. Taking the *Fired Up* out on the water. Spending quality time together, whether that meant doing the mundane or the adventurous, like convincing Sara to tandem bungee-jump with him.

If, somehow, come Friday, they decided to keep taking it one day at a time with each other.

"I think we did okay throwing them off course," he told Sara. He hoped so anyway. With Charles and Robin, both discerning in a manner different from the others, it was difficult for Luis to get a true read. "It was easy to redirect the question and get your mom talking about the cruise options she's researched."

"That was a good move." Sara tugged her ponytail tighter as she nodded.

Luis slid his running pouch onto his arm, secured the Velcro strap around his biceps, then stuck his cell phone, ID, and some cash inside the pocket. "You ready? It's almost eight thirty. That sun's going to start getting brutal."

"Let's go." Sara spun on her red and white sneakers and headed for the door.

As they neared the bottom of the staircase, voices drifted to them from the back of the house.

"Oh! I forgot." Sara paused by the hutch in the foyer. "My mom hired a yoga instructor for a private class here today and Thursday. She invited us to join if you'd rather do that instead."

"God, no!" He shuddered, imagining himself twisted like a pretzel and pretending to enjoy it for Sara and her mother's sake. "Anamaría would kill me, after torturing me first, if she found out I took a yoga class from someone other than her. She's been nagging me to try her sunrise yoga-on-the-beach class for ages. I usually tell her I'll wave as I run by."

Sara chuckled and moved down the hallway passed the framed tropical prints. "Let me go tell my mom we'll take a pass on the yoga."

"I'll come say good morning."

Luis followed Sara into the kitchen where they found the large pass-through window to the outside patio dining area opened. Out back, the morning sun bathed the dewy foliage in its swath of light and glinted off the pool's surface.

He spotted Ruth standing near the steps leading to the oasis pool area. She was talking to someone he couldn't see, gesturing toward the back lawn area, near the waterfall. Still recovering from the ravages of chemo, her skinny frame looked even tinier in black leggings and a slim-fitting tank. The results of her double mastectomy and decision to forgo reconstructive surgery were evidenced by her tank's fit. Something she adamantly refused to let define her.

They're battle scars from a war I intend to keep winning!

This proclamation had been given while the two of them were

seated on the patio late yesterday, enjoying a post-dinner drink. His, beer. Hers, another putrid purple vitamin-and-mineral-infused smoothie.

"Oh, hi, honey! Are you two joining us?" Ruth waved for them to come outside.

"We're going to stick with a run," Sara answered.

Ruth's expectant smile faltered, and Luis felt like a first-class heel for disappointing her.

"I'm worse than a yoga novice and would hate to slow down your private class," he told her.

"Nonsense, it'll be fine. Here, come tell them, dear." Ruth motioned to the person she'd been speaking with, probably the private instructor off scoping out the grassy area outside the master bedroom.

"Mom, that's his nice way of saying yoga's not his thing," Sara insisted.

Luis gave her a don't-blame-me frown as he downed his coffee.

"Dr. Vance, I don't mind making this a group class if you'd prefer. Whatever you'd like works for me."

At the sound of his sister's voice coming from somewhere outside, Luis sucked in a shocked breath. Unfortunately, he already had a mouthful of hot coffee. It slid down his windpipe and he choked like a drowning man. Black liquid spewed across the sink, making an abstract splatter across the white tile counter on the patio side of the large pass-through window.

Sara threw him a bewildered look and smacked him on the center of his back. Hard!

He endured another painful whack, his eyes watering as he stared out at the back yard. His worst nightmare in this whole charade he and Sara were playing came to life when Anamaría climbed the three steps leading up to the porch.

Ruth spread her arms as if welcoming them all to her yoga-themed fiasco about which she remained, thankfully, clueless.

"Anamaría, this is my youngest daughter, Sara, and her partner, Luis Montez. Maybe you'll have better luck convincing them to stick around for your class."

Gracias a Dios, his sister was not only a world-class athletic trainer and firefighter paramedic but also the best damn poker player who possessed the absolute best damn poker face. Luis had learned from experience to avoid playing against her unless he wanted to lose his shirt or, when they were kids, extra free time because he was stuck doing her chores.

Anamaría crossed the wooden deck, her long dark hair caught in a high ponytail, the length hanging in a braid to her shoulder blades. Her hyperfit body sported formfitting black shorts and a sports bra under a white tank with "AM Fitness" scrawled across her chest. Her hazel gaze pinned him to the spot like a spear running through a king mackerel.

"My pleasure," she said. The flash of you-are-so-busted triumph in her hazel eyes alerted him that she might play along now, but he'd owe her for it later. In spades.

Anamaría squeezed his hand in a death grip the likes of which would impress their brothers. "You know, what many bulky men have in strength and endurance they often lack in flexibility. The third, equally important element of a truly healthy, balanced workout routine."

Yeah, he knew that. She'd harped on him about it ad nauseam over the years as she'd taken classes and workshops, earning her personal trainer and nutritionist certifications.

"I'll keep that in mind," he muttered.

"Um, hi, nice to meet you." Sara held out her hand, interrupting Luis and his sister's infantile handshake to the death routine. "I didn't get your last name. What was it?"

"Navarro. Anamaría Navarro." Strangely, as his sister turned to address Sara, Anamaría's poker face slipped away, a wide-eyed, awed expression taking its place. Her mouth spread in a huge grin, the dimple in her left cheek making its appearance. "*Ay Dios mío*, I am going to try my best not to fangirl, Ms. Vance, but I'm a *huge* follower of your blog and Instagram account. The way you've managed your career and business is a true inspiration. I'm a fledgling small-business owner myself, determined to do things the right way."

It was almost comical. The juxtaposition of horror and surprise on Sara's face at his sister's gushing speech.

"Please, uh, call me Sara." She stuck out her hand to shake, wincing when Anamaría clasped it in both of hers and gave an exaggerated pump. "I appreciate you saying that. If there's some way

I could be of help, maybe we could, um, chat about your business later?"

Sara's confused gaze swung to Luis. Unfortunately, he was right there with her. Confused, unsure how or even if he wanted to involve Anamaría in their mess.

What the hell were the odds Ruth would hire his sister, potentially sabotaging Sara's ruse?

Even more strange, who knew his sister would have the social media hots for the same woman he couldn't wait to get alone again, so they could continue where they'd left off earlier this morning?

Coño, this situation couldn't get any more screwed up.

"Thanks, I really appreciate the offer," Anamaría told Sara, then she turned to him with that smug, saccharine sweet smile she flashed when she knew she had the upper hand. "You know, I could use a little help bringing in some equipment. Mr. Montez, would you mind assisting me?"

"Who the hell is Luis Montez?" Anamaría started in on him as soon as the front door closed behind them.

"Keep your voice down," he hissed. He leaned over to peer through the rectangular windows lining the door's perimeter to make sure he and Anamaría hadn't been followed.

Once he knew the coast was clear, he grabbed her by the elbow, rushed them down the stairs and front walk, through the white picket gate, to her blue Honda Pilot parked across the street.

"Don't shush me! *¿Quién carajo es Luis Montez?*" she repeated, jerking her arm out of his grasp.

"No one."

"Uh, apparently not, since that's the name Dr. Vance used when she introduced you as her famous daughter's *partner.*"

"It's complicated." Luis paced a few steps away. He spun to pace back, then repeated the same loop, mind-boggled. "You're not involved, so don't worry about it."

"News flash!" Fingers spread wide, Anamaría crossed her hands in the air, moving them apart as if she highlighted her words on a marquee. "I *am* involved! I'm about to go back in there and lie to a client."

She jabbed a hand toward the rental house. *Coño*, the girl was on a roll. And when his baby sister got worked up, forget injecting a word in edgewise

"A well-paying, influential client, based on what my contact at the Casa Marina's Spa al Mare indicated when I booked this gig. So, sorry, *hermano*, but this *is* my business now. Like, actually, my business. *AM Fitness.*" Anamaría stressed her company name, pounding her flat palm over her company logo on her chest. "Now, what the hell am I walking into when I go back in there?"

His sister's words hit him like a barrage of pellets, stinging with truth. Shit, she was right. Even worse, for someone who despised lies and liars, he was going to have to ask Anamaría to join him and Sara in this tangled knot of deception. One that, if they weren't careful, would wind up turning into a noose.

Frustration mounting, Luis speared a hand through his hair, sliding it down to squeeze at the headache forming at the base of his skull.

"Okay, I'll level with you," he said, giving in because it was the right thing to do. His sister deserved the truth if he was going to ask her to lie. "But you have to promise me this is between us. Not Carlos. Not Mami. Only us."

Anamaría narrowed her eyes suspiciously.

"*¡Prométeme!*" he growled.

She held up her hands in surrender. "Fine! I promise."

"Here, open your trunk so it looks like I'm helping and not arguing with you."

Anamaría hoisted a brow as if she were surprised by his knowledge of subterfuge. Still, she followed him to the back of her SUV and lifted the hatch.

"I ran into Sara on Friday around lunch, at the airport when I dropped some food off for Carlos. She was in a bind, some jerk stood her up, and she needed someone to step in to help, as her..."

He paused, embarrassed to actually admit this next part. He knew what his sister, his entire family, would think: Who are you and what have you done with my brother?

Saying yes to something like this was completely out of character. And yet he'd had the best damn three days of his life so far, thanks to Sara.

"Her *partner*, are you serious?" Hands on her hips, Anamaría gaped at him.

He gestured for her to grab something from her car, and she leaned in, reaching for the basket of rolled yoga mats and foam blocks she provided for her clients.

"Uh, yeah," he answered lamely.

The basket plunked down onto the gray trunk carpet. "No way. It's like in one of those rom-coms I love watching."

Luis winced, already seeing the hearts in his sister's hazel eyes. The last thing he needed was Anamaría playing matchmaker when he had no idea how or even if anything could come of this alternate reality he and Sara had conceived.

"Not exactly," he cautioned. "Sara's mom has been sick and this vacation was supposed to be stress-free for her. Then Sara's idiot boyfriend ditched her, but she didn't want her mom worrying about it. She was in a tight spot and I had the time off. It seemed natural for me—"

Anamaría's trill of laughter rudely interrupted his explanation.

"Let me get this straight. Saint Navarro stepping in to save the day for one of this generation's most sought-after social media in-fluencers. That seems natural to you?"

He shrugged, his annoyance mushrooming when she threw back her head and laughed again. Her ponytail braid swished along her back when she shook her head, eyeing him with bemusement.

"How the hell was I supposed to know who she was?" he com-plained. "You know me; I'm not into all that social media stuff."

"Un-freaking-believable." Anamaría sank onto her vehicle's bumper with a huff.

Eyes squeezed shut, she tucked her chin to her chest and pinched the bridge of her nose. A perfect imitation of their *mami* when they'd been out of control as kids and her patience thinned.

"I have been practically cyberstalking Sara Vance for over a year." His sister squinted up at him in disbelief. "Reading her blogs and posts, combing through articles about her, following her ad-vice. Ever since I decided to try growing my AM Fitness brand and client list. I would kill—*kill, me oíste?*"

"Yes, I hear you. Half the damn block hears you!" He craned

his neck to peer at the Vances' rental home, praying Sara or, *por favor no*, her mother hadn't stepped outside.

"I would kill for half an hour of her time as a professional, so I could pick her brain. And you! You randomly run into her and wind up—Wait a minute, *ay Dios mío!*" Anamaría slapped a hand to her forehead. A stricken expression tightened her high cheekbones and widened her big eyes like an actress in one of their *mami*'s and *abuela*'s telenovelas. "Sara is the blonde everyone's seen you with all weekend?"

Luis stumbled back as if his sister had slapped him with her accusation. "What do you mean, *everyone?*"

"Oh, you are so screwed, *hermano.*"

"What? Why?"

Hands on her slim hips, Anamaría scrunched her face in commiserating dismay. "Mami's on to you."

"No way?" He shook his head. At his sister's commiserating grimace, the knot of doom in his stomach expanded like a dry sea sponge dipped in water. "How?"

"Freddie Lugo told his mom that he saw you with a blonde at Mallory Square Friday night. Señora Lugo asked Mami about it. Then, Señora Lopez called Mami to talk about some church function and she mentioned seeing you and a blonde riding bikes on Duval yesterday. And, apparently, after you ran into Franco Peréz grabbing lunch at Sandy's on Friday, he said something to Carlos at the boys' T-ball practice. Carlos let that cat out of the bag in a group text Mami sent this morning."

"What group text? I wasn't on any group text today." Luis reached for his cell in the runner's pouch strapped to his arm.

"You think Mami's gonna include you in a thread trying to dig up info on you? *Por favor*, even you, San Navarro, know better than that. How many group texts have we been on without Enrique?"

She had a point.

Perturbed, Luis shoved his cell back down in the pouch and zipped it closed.

"I gotta say, you sure are putting a dull on that halo's shine, in a big way, aren't you?" Anamaría punched him gamely in the stomach, an impressed smirk curving her lips.

"I liked you better pissed off or fangirling. Not smug," he grumbled.

"Aw, come on. It's not often you're involved in some kind of *chisme*. The only gossip I remember was when—" She broke off, lunging forward to grab him when Luis spun away. "I'm sorry I brought that up. I know you don't like to talk about her, or what went down."

"It's fine; forget it." Luis stared down at his sister's smaller hand clasped around his wrist.

"Look, I know what it's like to feel betrayed by someone who claims to love you." Anamaría's voice trembled. The shadow of depressing memories darkened her face. "Not that what Alejandro did after he left town compares to what you went through. I get that. But, you were there for me. You always are." Her grip tightened on his wrist, her words scratchy with hurt. "I'm just sorry you can't let me do the same for you."

The fact that his inability to deal with Mirna's deception and death pushed his sister from teasing laughter to the stark pain lacing her words so quickly shamed him.

Maybe Sara was right. Maybe it was time he figure out how to put his past to rest. For himself and those who'd been forced to tiptoe through the minefield he had laid around him for protection.

"Look, whatever you're doing here, you know I got your back." Anamaría stood up and pulled the basket of supplies to the edge of the trunk. "I'm simply warning you. Mami knows that you've been spending time with someone new. She's going to want to meet her. Soon. I wouldn't be surprised if she twists your arm to bring Sara to *familia* dinner tonight."

The mere idea of Sara sitting at his *mami*'s table, confronted with the inevitable Navarro Cuban Inquisition, made Luis's blood run cold with dread.

He sure as hell hoped his sister was wrong. No way would he put Sara through that.

At noon, while the Vance family and Luis waited for a table at Bistro 245 overlooking the harbor teeming with sailboats and catamarans bobbing on the water, Luis received the forewarned text from his *mami*.

I cannot wait to visit with your new amiga at familia dinner tonight. 6 PM. No falles.

Don't miss.

Coño, her edict had been laid down. And no matter how badly he may want to, Luis knew better than to defy his well-meaning, henpecking, *chancla*-throwing *mami*.

Chapter 18

Sara drummed her fingers on the center console in Luis's truck, the sound echoing the ominous beat pounding in her head. She peered in the passenger side rearview mirror at the "Welcome to Key West Paradise USA" sign with its brightly colored tropical sunset scene growing smaller in the distance behind them. Ahead, US 1 was a gray ribbon leading them toward his parents' house in Big Coppitt Key.

"How far did you say the drive was?" she asked, not quite hiding the trepidation chipping at her self-confidence like a woodpecker high on an energy drink.

Luis cut a worried glance her way, then went back to watching the road when a car signaled into their lane.

"We'll make a left onto Diamond Drive around Mile Marker Ten. It's roughly twenty minutes from downtown, without traffic."

That meant she had about ten more minutes to pull herself together. To center her thinking on positivity and stop the spiral of doubt that could trigger unhealthy urges.

Her fingers thrummed the console again, telegraphing her agitation. Out of the corner of her eye, she watched Luis.

Hands clenched on the black leather steering wheel, he drove with his body rigidly straight in his seat, his expression schooled in his infamous, calm game face. From the moment they had said good-bye to her family and closed the front door behind them, Luis had slipped into the tough-guy, man-of-few-words Vin Diesel role that had drawn her to him on Friday.

A role she now knew he often played as a way of protecting himself from deep emotional wounds he tried to deny.

Ones he hid well behind that serious game face, along with the fun-loving, the honest, and especially the tender lover sides she'd come to care for.

But, once again, they were about to break the one cardinal rule from the very beginning he had asked her to respect. Don't involve his *familia*.

Guilt pressed down on her like a two-ton whale. Sara closed her eyes, blocking out the peach, orange, and purple early evening sun streaks smearing the sky.

"I am so sorry about this," she offered, knowing the words were little compensation for what lay ahead when they arrived at his childhood home.

A deep groove cut in between Luis's brows at his frown. "For what? I'm the one dragging you out here. Away from fine dining at a five-star restaurant with your family to a buffet-style madhouse with mine. Where, as much as I'll try to fend her off of you, I'm fairly certain my mom will be in prime Cuban Inquisition mode."

The exasperation tinging his voice coupled with his over-exaggeration assuaged Sara's fears and tickled her funny bone.

His frown deepened at her chuckle. "What's so funny?"

"The Cuban Inquisition? Really?"

His eyes bugged out, his brows rising high. "Uh, yeah! Just wait."

She sighed, oddly comforted by the fact that, despite the potential trouble her meeting his family could cause, Luis seemed mostly worried about her. His kind streak no longer surprised her really. It simply confirmed one of the multiple reasons why she was falling so hard and so fast for this generous giant of a man.

"At least, we can count on Anamaría for help deflecting," he continued. "Mostly for your sake, not mine. She'd love to see me squirm. But for you, the biggest name in social media influencer circles and her absolute idol, she'll take heat from Mami."

"I am not the biggest name," Sara deferred, slightly embarrassed by Anamaría's effusive admiration this morning. Though also proud that her career trajectory would inspire his sister. "But I was serious when I said I'd sit down to go over her business plans, answer any questions."

Luis waved away her offer. "You don't have to do that. You're on vacation."

"I know I don't *have* to; I *want* to. She's got a lot of drive and energy. Important traits in this business. Her website and Insta accounts are pretty good. She could use a little tweaking with her branding. Some help networking within her target markets. Maybe—"

"How do you know all that?" Luis interrupted.

"I looked her up this afternoon. I'm serious; if I can offer some guidance, I'd like to."

Releasing the steering wheel, he grasped her hand where it rested between their seats. He raised it to his lips and pressed a kiss on her knuckles. Warmth spread down her arm, oozing across her chest to wrap around her heart.

"You're pretty amazing, you know that?"

Sara hitched a shoulder, secretly pleased by his praise. "I try."

He winked, and she found herself grinning back at him like a lovesick fool.

They reached another key and soon passed a military base. The truck continued traveling north on an overpass, but her gaze followed the exit road heading toward a black and white structure, its support beams and a small guardroom straddling the roads in and out of the base. The words *U.S. Naval Air Station Key West* were emblazoned across the front.

Silently, she stared at the dense vegetation outside her window. Palm trees and flowering bushes peppered the land. Thick mangroves with their green leaves and twisting brown roots filled the areas where land and ocean water met.

Too soon they neared a green and white road sign indicating "Big Coppitt Key."

Luis laid their joined hands on his jeans-clad thigh, his face sobering.

Sara's heartbeat slowed. Dread reared its nefarious head to whisper destructive thoughts in her ear.

"You're sure I'm not underdressed?" She smoothed a palm down the skirt of her Lilly Pulitzer floral print swing dress. The navy and multi-blue-hued patterned material was a new favorite, the dress a gift from a recent photo shoot. But the halter neck and cutaway shoulders weren't exactly meet-the-parents conservative. She'd grabbed a thin cover-up sweater just in case.

"You look beautiful." Luis squeezed her hand reassuringly. "I wasn't kidding; our *familia* dinner is the opposite of formal. Carlos's kids often show up in their baseball clothes after practice."

"Thank you. You clean up pretty good yourself."

Her gaze slid from his deep green polo to his dark jeans and tan court sneakers. Pretty good didn't nearly begin to describe him. In almost anything he wore ... and didn't wear ... Luis Navarro was the epitome of hot. With a capital *H*.

The flash of the blinker on his truck's instrument panel had her breath hitching.

Luis shot her a you-okay frown as he slowed the vehicle, waiting for a break in the southbound traffic so he could make the left turn.

"Same stick close to the truth game plan," he reminded her. "We recently met here. Struck up a friendship, and I'm simply playing tour guide for the week." He patted her hand on his thigh, then released her to maneuver the steering wheel as he pulled onto Diamond Drive.

The street was lined with a hodgepodge of older houses low to the ground and new ones up high, built after regulations stipulated homes be raised to prevent flooding during hurricane season. Palm, poinciana, and other flowering trees she couldn't name provided shade. Bicycles and boats decorated several yards, and she caught sight of the canal that ran behind the homes on each side of the road, allowing them easy access to the ocean at the end of each street.

A mixture of stately two-story stucco beauties and smaller, more modest homes, the neighborhood spoke of the varying demographics of Keys dwellers. Those who had lived here for generations, hardworking and determined to stay despite the rising cost of living, and snowbirds from up north who retired and made the long-awaited move to the warmer climate.

"We'll be fine," Luis said as his truck slow-poked down the

road. "At least neither one of us is pretending to be someone different. That makes it easier. And divert the conversation if needed."

She nodded, repeating the simple instructions to herself with each breath in and out. Stick with the truth. Divert. Stick with the truth. Divert. Stick with the truth. Divert.

"And when my *mami* asks about our wedding date you—"

"Wait! What?!"

She slapped a hand to her chest afraid her heart might jump out onto the dashboard it pounded so hard. Marriage questions? His mother would freak if she found out that Sara and her son's relationship was an arranged, fake, potentially short-term relationship. The, um, opposite of marriage material.

Even if it felt like more than that now.

"I figured that would get your attention," Luis teased. "You were starting to hyperventilate on me."

"You!" She swatted his arm in protest.

He grinned, but Sara quickly ducked down to peer out the windshield as he pulled his truck into a wide driveway running under the left half of a raised modest siding house with cream paint and dark brown shutters.

Wooden steps started at the edge of the driveway and went half a flight up before hooking left to end in a small porch at the front door. Lush bougainvillea vines trailed around the support beams and latticework along the bottom half of the stairs adding an explosion of bright magenta color in a warm welcome.

Instantly Sara's doubts swelled, billowing in a cloud of uncertainty.

She fell back against her seat, rubbing at the center of her forehead as if it would erase the negative thoughts spiraling.

"Hey, come on, what's going on?" Luis slid his hand behind her shoulders, his strong fingers kneading at the tension in her neck. "We got this."

"Truth?" she whispered, remembering their conversation minutes before he'd met her parents Friday afternoon.

"Always."

Sara peeked at him from under her lashes. "Even though this wasn't supposed to happen. Me meeting your family. Us getting . . . you know, intimate."

"Very intimate," he teased, his eyes flaring with lust.

Desire sparked in her belly but wasn't strong enough to dispel her misgivings.

"What is it?" Luis asked, as if he sensed her disquiet.

"I want them, your *familia*, to like me. Really badly want them to like me. And I'm trying not to go there." There being the root cause of her OSFED. The fear she continuously fought to dig out of her psyche. "But what if they don't? What if I'm not enough?"

"Aw, babe."

Luis swiftly unbuckled his seat belt and twisted to face her. Gently he cupped her jaw with one hand, tucked her loose hair behind her ear with the other. His handsome, rugged face softened with sincerity, Luis leaned closer to press a chaste kiss to her lips.

"*Cariño*, there's no doubt they're going to like everything about you. Hell, Anamaría already loves you more than she loves me. You're too loveable to resist."

How did he do that? How did he know exactly the right thing to say and do to calm her?

Grateful for his words, his calming presence, Sara hooked a finger in his open collar and drew him closer. Her lips sought his for another butterfly soft kiss. Luis nuzzled her nose with his, then pulled back, his smile brimming with confidence.

"You're going to wow them," he whispered. "No doubt about it."

"So, do you see yourself married with children in the near future?"

Heads swiveled sharply. Luis choked on his water. Anamaría's gasped "Mami!" was punctuated by a fork clattering onto a stoneware dinner plate.

Sara cringed in surprise at Señora Navarro's blunt question. Goodness, Robin had nothing on Luis's mom when it came to speaking her mind.

"Mami, *por favor*," Luis warned.

"*¿Pero qué pasa?*" the older woman complained.

"What's wrong is, that's a very personal question and Sara just met you. Everyone."

Sara figured there was no need to get into a discussion about how long they'd all known her. That wouldn't end well for her and Luis.

"Papi, help me out here," Luis implored his dad, who sat at the head of the table, the family patriarch and, similar to Sara's dad it seemed, also the unofficial umpire.

Tall and broad-shouldered like all three of his sons, José Ramón Navarro made an imposing figure. His salt-and-pepper hair was parted and combed to the side in a classic, debonair style that had nothing to do with hiding a bald spot. The lines bracketing his eyes and mouth told the story of a man who worked hard and loved deeply and laughed often, while the seriousness in his dark eyes reminded her of Luis's quiet strength.

Señor Navarro looked past Luis on his right to meet Sara's gaze. She smiled and forced herself to maintain eye contact, no matter how unnerving the older man's perusal might feel. He dipped his head politely, then reached for the platter of sweet plantains Carlos had set between them on the other side of the long rectangular table.

"Lydia, at least let us fill our plates before the Inquisition begins," Luis's father said, his sober expression softening as he gazed down the length of the table at his wife of nearly forty years.

Luis had not been kidding earlier when he apologized ahead of time for his *mami*'s interrogation. Even Señor Navarro called the barrage of questions by name.

Lydia Navarro humphed at her husband's request but silently set the cream stoneware serving bowl filled with white rice in front of her older grandson, José.

"Sorry about that," Anamaría whispered, angling toward Sara, who sat in between Luis and his sister.

Sara hoped her tentative half smile didn't look as forced as it felt. She slid the salad bowl toward Anamaría, chanting Truth. Divert in her head.

Her gaze collided with Enrique's on the other side of Anamaría. His lips quirked in a sly smirk. Apparently, he was enjoying having someone else in the hot seat for a change. Based on what Luis had shared, his younger brother had typically been the cause of dinner table uproars growing up.

As adults, Enrique was still wreaking havoc, at least where Luis was concerned.

Sara quirked a brow at Luis's younger brother, happy to have already one-upped him when she first arrived.

Enrique had greeted her in the living room with a smug, "Still searching for the perfect souvenir? Or have you realized you can't leave without one of my wood paintings?"

Señora Navarro had smacked him on the back of the head and delivered a warning to be polite.

The smart aleck switched to Spanish, bemoaning the need to be on his best behavior in his own home just because they had a semi-celebrity visiting.

When Sara chimed in with her thanks for the compliment, in flawless Spanish, Luis's mother had practically beamed, patting Sara's cheeks with glee when she learned Sara was fluent in their native language.

Enrique had the grace to mutter a chagrined, "You're welcome," and ignore Luis's grumbled, "Smartass." Anamaría had high-fived Sara on her way into the kitchen to help with final dinner preparations.

"Would you like some picadillo?" Luis asked, drawing Sara's attention. He held up another round ceramic bakeware dish, this one filled with a delicious smelling ground beef concoction with green olives, raisins, and bell peppers. Lowering his voice, he added, "No pressure to eat anything you're not up for."

Under the tan linen tablecloth, she put a hand on his thigh, expressing her thanks for his understanding. Certain he was remembering the embarrassing fiasco over dinner with her family at El Meson de Pepe Friday night.

"I'd love to try it, please."

"Picadillo is Lydia's specialty," Señor Navarro told her. "You won't find better anywhere in the Keys."

"Not even at Miranda's, and that's saying something," Carlos added.

Nods from the others around the table and a "the bestest" from little Ramón, whose Captain America shirt already sported a drizzle of honey mustard salad dressing, had Luis's mom preening at the same time she waved off the compliment.

"Miranda's?" Sara asked everyone in general.

"*Ay, mijo*, you haven't taken her to eat at Miranda's yet?" Señora Navarro chided Luis. She shook her head at him with parental dismay, before addressing Sara. "Our close family friends, Victor *y* Elena Miranda, own a Cuban restaurant in Midtown. Anamaría used to work there in high school. At one point, we thought she might be running the place alongside their oldest, Alejandro. *Pero—*"

"But nothing," Anamaría jumped in. "That's old news, Mami. Anyway, Sara, my brother should take you before you leave. The food's delicious, and the owners are good people. If you enjoy your meal, I know they'd really appreciate you mentioning Miranda's when you blog about your vacation."

"I had planned for us to stop by for lunch yesterday," Luis said. "But we got a little sidetracked at the beach and wound up not making it."

Sidetracked. Sara wiped her mouth with her napkin, covering her smile. That was one way of putting how they had spent their afternoon alone at the rental home.

Resting his left arm on the back of Sara's chair, Luis reached across her to hand his sister the picadillo dish. "Excuse me," he murmured, the words a whisper near her ear. His chest pressed against Sara's shoulder. His left hand splayed on her upper back, heavy and warm.

For a time-warp moment she was in their room, wrapped in his embrace, indulging in the pleasure-filled activities that had "sidetracked" them from lunch at the Navarros' friends' restaurant. She ducked her head to glance at Luis under her lashes. The satisfied curve of his lips told her he knew exactly what his touch had her remembering.

Across the table from them Carlos cleared his throat. Sara straightened in her seat and found Luis's older brother and his wife studying her and Luis.

Her cheeks flushed and she reached for her water glass.

Luis rubbed a slow circle on her back, his touch lingering before he turned to start eating.

Carlos nudged Gina with his elbow, but then one of their boys asked for help serving himself and their attention turned to their son.

The rest of the meal passed in a blur of family updates from the week past and the ones ahead, a plea from the two boys for their *Tío* Luis or *abuelo* to take them fishing on one of their boats soon, and a battery of questions about Sara's family, career, and personal life.

Sara found herself caught up in the easy banter, and Señora Navarro's scrumptious authentic Cuban food had Sara cleaning her plate. The boisterous *familia* atmosphere reminded her of dinners at Mamá Alicia's house when Sara was a kid. Another loud, entertaining, loving family coming together to nourish their bellies and their hearts.

As a child, then a teen, and later a college coed, Sara had wished and prayed for a similar dynamic with her own family. Now it seemed that her parents, Jonathan, and Carolyn were trying to include her in their lives. Only, she was the one who had to stop keeping them at arm's length in the guise of protecting herself from rejection.

Doing so she only wound up hurting herself.

Oddly, while she and her family might be finding their way to healing their rifts, based on what she'd seen tonight, Luis's family was either used to the rift between him and Enrique or they believed there was little they could do to resolve it. The brothers participated in conversation at the table, but each barely spoke directly to the other. Everyone else talked around them, jumping in to fill awkward moments.

Knowing the caring, kindhearted man Luis was, Sara felt certain the fracture in his relationship had to eat away at him. Much like hers with Robin.

Luis had pushed her to reach out to Robin, attempt to find some semblance of understanding between them. For his own sake, she wished he could do the same with his younger brother.

With school the next day, as soon as dinner finished, Carlos and Gina readied the boys to leave. A flurry of good-bye hugs and kisses and knucklehead rubbing with the kids ensued.

Carlos wrapped Sara in a tight hug, whispering something about fate and shaking up Luis. Before Sara could ask what he meant, little Ramón tackled her legs and begged for his adios kiss on the cheek.

Moments later, her hands full of dirty plates, Sara followed Anamaría to the kitchen, where Luis's mother had already started tackling the dishes by the sink.

"If you're free on Thursday morning after you finish your yoga session with my mom, how about we plan on connecting to review your business plan?" Sara told Anamaría.

Luis entered with the last of the serving dishes in time to catch his sister's squeal of glee.

"What did I miss?" he asked.

"Your girlfriend helping your baby sister," Señora Navarro answered, her rubber-gloved hands deep in the soapy dishwater. "They're already bonding like two sisters-in-law; isn't it wonderful?"

Luis heaved an exasperated huff, mouthing, *I'm sorry*, at Sara behind his mom's back.

"*No me faltes el respeto*, Luis," his mother chided.

"How could you possibly know I'm disrespecting you, Mami? Your back is to me," Luis complained, setting the dirty dishes on the counter by the sink.

"A *mami*'s intuition. Here, *dame un beso*." She tilted her head for Luis to kiss her cheek as she had requested. "You too, Sara."

Delightfully surprised to be included, Sara hurried over to give Luis's mom a farewell kiss.

"Anamaría, go get your younger brother to come say good-bye so you can all head back to Key West. It's late and you know I worry about my babies driving the highway at night."

"Thank you so much for your hospitality," Sara told Señora Navarro in Spanish.

"It is good to have you here, *mija*. I look forward to many more *familia* dinners with you at our table."

Sara's stomach hitched with uncertainty. Neither she nor Luis responded.

Stick with the truth. So far, they'd done well executing their plan. That didn't make her guilt weigh any less heavily on her heart.

As they drove home in the dark, Sara couldn't stop thinking, yearning, for their truth to include more Navarro *familia* dinners like tonight.

She only had three days to find out if Luis might want the same.

Chapter 19

Life couldn't get much better than this if you asked Luis.

Bueno, it could, but he wasn't much for gluttony. Unless it came to the sexy woman currently sprawled in his arms while the *Fired Up* floated in the shallow waters off Snipes Point on a sunny, wispy-clouds day.

A Wednesday with local schools still in session meant they had the sandbar and surrounding area to themselves. Come the weekend, the clear water would be teeming with sunbathers and beach lovers old and young. People grilling on their boats, floating in tubes and on crazy blow-up rafts. Footballs flying in the air, sometimes even from boat to boat.

The weekend could keep its crowds. Luis preferred the quiet peacefulness of right now.

Feeling keenly satisfied, he adjusted the ball cap shielding his face from the intense midday sun, then went back to lazily dragging his fingertips up and down Sara's bare arm. They lounged on a seat cushion in the bow, Sara resting spoon-fashion between Luis's bent knees, her back against his chest. She shifted slightly, her shapely legs stretched out in front of them, their smooth skin a soft golden glow from the sun's kiss.

"I think they're having a good time." He pointed to her family standing waist-deep in the water closer to the shore.

Used to the intense Phoenix heat, they'd slathered on sunscreen, with Ruth and a couple others opting for long-sleeve swim shirts for extra protection. Sara, bless her thoughtfulness, had foregone her shirt and enlisted his assistance applying another layer of sunscreen a few minutes ago.

Luis had taken his job seriously. Tube of SPF 50 lotion in one hand, he'd rubbed the white substance over every gorgeous inch not covered by her sexy black bikini. And wound up trying to hide the hard-on tenting his suit. Sara's promise to help him take care of it back in their room hadn't helped his predicament. The little minx.

"Yeah, they're definitely enjoying this," Sara mused. "My mother looks so happy. Thank you for this."

Craning her neck to gaze up at him, she smiled her pleasure. Of course, it felt only natural for him to dip his head for a kiss.

She opened her mouth for him, her tongue brushing against his. A hint of the lime seltzer water she preferred teased him, along with the heady sweetness that was hers alone.

Her slender fingers clung to his nape, urging their kiss deeper. Lust flamed through him. Blood surged low in his body, swift and ready. He ached to cup her breasts in his palms, dip his hand into her bathing suit bottom, and bring her the delicious satisfaction he knew he could give her.

Over the past three nights they'd each wantonly discovered the erogenous zones that drove the other wild. He loved the way her eyes dilated, his name on her lips as she reached the pinnacle and dived over the cliff, her hands and mouth and tongue luring him over the edge with her.

"Hey, are you two gonna sit there and make out all day or come join us?"

Luis chuckled against Sara's lips. His eyes drifted open in time to catch her giving her brother the finger.

"Geez, the guy's taking this bratty older brother routine to the extreme," Sara grumbled, collapsing back against Luis's chest.

"Ah, I'd venture to guess that you actually like his attention." Luis gave her right temple a chaste peck before whispering in her ear. "I'll let you in on a little secret. Brothers needle the ones they love the most."

"That's because you're obviously warped."

He threw back his head and laughed, enjoying the feel of Sara's body shaking as she joined him. He patted her right hip, a signal for her to stand up so he could, too.

"But you love my warped, depraved mind, don't you?"

For the smallest fraction of time Sara's hands stilled in the act of adjusting her bathing suit bottom. Long enough for him to catch it and regret his slip-of-the-tongue use of the *l* word.

"Oh, your depraved mind is only one of the many facets I find attractive, but I won't list them." She padded to the seat in front of the boat helm where she snagged her wide-brimmed straw beach hat. "No need for your head to get any bigger than it already is."

With a saucy wink, she blew him a kiss and flounced toward the dive door on the port side of the boat's deck.

"Smartass," he called.

The cheeky woman reached back to give herself a pat on the butt.

Amusement laced with an emotion he wasn't prepared to name spread through his chest. Ever since Monday evening when he'd taken her home for *familia* dinner, something inside him had changed.

Seeing her at ease with his loud, meddling family.

Receiving the *me encanta* text from his *mami*—to which he truthfully responded: *Sí, I like her, too.*

Reading Carlos's: *Hermano, you lucked out with this one. Gina and I approve.*

They were consecutive one-two-three sledgehammer blows to the foundation of the guarded reserve protecting his heart. A foundation Sara's charm, fun-loving spirit, and vulnerability rattled the longer he spent in her company.

Yesterday, the rain had them all lazing around the house. Luis and Sara spending a good chunk of the afternoon in their room. Him, reading a biography of Jacques Cousteau from the rental's living room bookshelf. Her, answering emails, talking to her agent, and reading over a contract that, if it worked out, would see Sara spending more time in Miami working on her clothing line.

They hadn't done anything extraordinary, but to him it had felt like an extraordinary day. Because of her.

With her family waiting for them, Luis followed Sara to the boat's deck where she turned to climb down the removable ladder. Halfway into the water, she paused, squinting up at him.

"I'm going to head to the beach." She turned toward the large sandbar's shore.

Luis did the same and found Robin, sitting by herself, the calm ocean lapping at her pale legs. Her parents and Edward strolled along the shore about thirty feet away. Behind them, the sandbar's dense vegetation awaited those willing to brave a hike through the mass of mangroves teeming with tiny ecosystems.

"Wish me luck." Sara let go of the handrail and sank up to her shoulders in the crystal green water.

He watched her swim away, marveling at her inner strength. A trait she questioned about herself at times. Yet here she was, taking that uncomfortable first step toward her sister.

While, had the situation been reversed and his prickly brother been waiting on the sand, the timing and situation ripe for a frank conversation . . . Luis would probably still be where he was right now. Standing on his boat. Alone.

Sara swam toward the shore, lamely batting away a stiff-arm-induced wave of water from her brother as she neared him.

"Leave her alone," Carolyn chided. The couple stooped shoulder deep in the warm water, Carolyn's arms around Jonathan's neck. "We're trying to have adult time here, remember?"

"Yeah, try acting like an adult, you big lug," Sara teased her brother.

He made a silly face, their banter fueling her strokes toward the beach and the other sibling she hoped to eventually find some common ground with.

Off to the right, her parents and Edward bent over, peering at something on the sand. A shell or crab or maybe a washed-up sand dollar. Fond of beachcombing, the three of them and Robin attended a yearly medical conference in Tampa. Last year they'd flown down a day early to enjoy a day on the beach.

The pang of jealousy Sara typically felt when thinking of the trips Robin, and often Jonathan, shared with their parents for one medical conference or another failed to materialize.

Progress, her therapist would say.

Yes, it was.

Her mom straightened, putting her hand above her eyes to shield them from the sun as she stared in Sara's direction.

Sara waved but continued swimming toward her sister.

Robin frowned as Sara neared, a fistful of wet sand drizzling through her open fingers. Behind her a piece of driftwood several feet long, battered and worn by the sun, saltwater, and sand, shifted under the tide's pull. Wavering between staying on the shore and being swept out to sea again.

Kind of how Sara had spent the past twenty minutes since Luis dropped anchor and everyone else jumped overboard.

"What are you doing?" Robin asked.

Reminding herself that her sister's brusque tone was the same with everyone, no need to read any slight into it, Sara slowed her swim stroke.

"Nothing. Just figured I'd join you." She reached shallower water, where she squatted, bobbing in the light waves.

"Suit yourself." Robin grabbed another fistful of sand, then let it slip away, aided by the lapping ocean.

"It's been a good trip, don't you think?" Sara tiptoed into the conversation. No use dive-bombing her sister right away with the hard questions, like *why are you always annoyed with me?*

"Yeah. It's good to see Mom getting stronger." Robin shifted to watch her husband and their parents, slowly strolling farther away, heads bent in search of the perfect shell.

"I agree. Honestly, I was pretty scared there for a while. Afraid we'd lose her. That I might not ever get a chance to—" Memories laced with fear rose to choke her and Sara rolled off the balls of her feet to plop onto her hip, cushioned by the soft sand. "Never get a chance to make her proud."

So much for tiptoeing into emotional territory.

Robin's face scrunched in a disbelieving scowl. "What are you talking about?" With an irritated scoff, she threw a handful of sand that landed in a series of tiny splashes across the water's surface. "Of course she's proud of you."

A gray seagull squawked overhead, mimicking the screech of denial howling in Sara's ears. The pain of rejection, the agony of how she had mistreated her body, the twisted thinking she was steadfastly working to untwist . . . they tumbled in on her like yesterday's steel gray storm clouds, thunder rolling, lightning flashing through her.

"That's ridiculous. You don't know what you're talking about," Sara argued.

"Excuse you?"

Rather than deter Sara like it usually did, Robin's condescending glare lit a fuse inside Sara. It hissed and flared and blew a powder keg on agonizing truths she had kept hidden all these years. All at once they came pouring out.

"My whole life I've tried so hard to live up to you and Jonathan. Knowing, because I've heard them say it a thousand times, how proud mom and dad are of you two. But me?"

She huffed a harsh breath and swatted away a mass of mossy green seaweed floating nearby. If only she could push away the hateful memories as easily.

"I've never been as academically gifted or just plain book smart or even musically-inclined. God those early piano recitals of mine were horrific, and Mom kept reminding me of how easily you had picked it up. Even Jonathan, until he switched to the guitar. Basically, I've always been all-around not as good as you at anything. I actually heard Mom say that to Mamá Alicia once. 'Sometimes you have to lower your expectations for your child.' " Sara pitched her voice to sound more authoritative, copying their mother's speech pattern. "Do you know what hearing that does to a teenager?"

The question ripped from her heart with gut-wrenching sorrow. Dully, Sara rubbed at the ache in her chest.

For the first time in Sara's life, her sister appeared to be at a loss for words. Slack-jawed, Robin plunked her hand on her lap. Sand spread across the top of her thighs, dribbling onto her navy bathing suit bottom.

The geyser of self-revelation waned, having depleted the fight out of Sara. Spent, she slumped lower under the water. A school of tiny clear and gray fish zigzagged around her knees blissfully unaware of the monsoon of emotions and recriminations rumbling above the surface.

Robin blinked a couple times, visibly pulling herself out of her shocked stupor after Sara's revelation.

"And yet I'm the daughter whose birth made our mother set aside a promising career," Robin said, her astringent voice softened with self-recrimination. "Did you know she actually turned down a fellowship on the East Coast because she and Dad didn't think it wise for one of them to single parent while they were separated?"

Robin's shoulders sagged, ill-fitting dejection settling over them. Her brow creased as she shook her head. Then, as quickly as her mood dipped, she shook it off.

Abruptly straightening, she splashed water onto her lap to rinse away the sand. "So, I pushed myself. In high school, undergrad, med school, residency. It got worse when I started working at the hospital with Dad." Her gaze lifted to Sara's, empathy shone in her stormy gray eyes. "Because I used to believe I had to prove to her, and to myself, that giving up that fellowship and staying home until Jonathan and I started school wasn't for naught."

Used to believe.

Past tense.

"And now?" Sara asked.

"Now the only person I have to prove anything to is me. And my patients. They need to know they're in the best hands when they come into my OR. I know for a fact that they are."

Chin high, Robin stared at the open ocean, confidence bordering on cockiness in her tight jaw. A smattering of freckles chased each other across the bridge of her nose, trailing into her cheeks. They reminded Sara of the picture of their mom and a young Robin on her first day of kindergarten. Posture straight and stiff, their mom smiled for the camera, one hand on her eldest's shoulder. Robin's tiny face wore the same determined expression she normally wore.

Sara used to think that stone-faced look was a foreshadow of her sister's surliness. Now she knew a child's desperate desire to make her mother proud lay behind it.

"What helped you turn that corner? Relieve that pressure?"

Sara asked, wondering how her sister had succeeded where Sara had failed. Horribly. Until Mamá Alicia intervened.

"Not what. Who."

Robin tilted her head toward Edward.

"He doesn't mind that I like working long hours, but he knows when I've pushed myself too far, and I need to unwind, even before I do. He gets me. The same way Luis seems to get you. And Carolyn with Jonathan."

"Oh, I don't know about Luis and me."

"Well, I do. And I'm seldom wrong."

Sara snorted a laugh. Even in the midst of their first heart-to-heart, her sister managed to insert her ego. And though Robin might be off base grouping Sara and Luis in with her siblings and their spouses, Sara had to admit Luis did have a knack for calming her when her thoughts threatened to spiral. Like he had Monday evening when they arrived at his parents' house.

Still, who knew what would happen come Friday when she boarded her flight back to New York. They had yet to talk about anything past this week.

Over near the *Fired Up*, Luis and Jonathan tossed a football. Carolyn watched, her arms looped around a bright orange float noodle. Their laughter carried on the humid breeze. A wistful smile tickled Sara's lips. She wanted more days like this. Family time with them all together, including Luis.

Especially with Luis.

A pontoon boat motored slowly by. The passengers and boat captain waved hello. Luis called out a warning about shallow water in some of the nearby channels. The Captain tipped his ball cap before revving the engine's throttle.

"Look, we both have issues stemming from our childhood." Robin shrugged a shoulder, as if the troubles of their past were that easily brushed off. "I'll admit, it bugged me to think that here I was, busting my ass to prove myself while they were coddling you. Plus, you had Mamá Alicia showering you with attention, while I'd been stuck with a bunch of college kids who were more worried about their social schedules and making an easy dollar. But I didn't realize what you were dealing with, and that's on me. I was an adult; you were a kid. I should have made the effort. But let's be real. When it comes to touchy-feely crap like this"—Robin motioned between the two of them, frightening off another school of tiny fish—"I'm the first to back away."

"I hadn't noticed," Sara deadpanned.

Robin rolled her eyes.

Leaning forward onto her hands, Sara floated her legs behind her to alligator walk the few paces that brought her to Robin's side. She sat next to her older sister, bumping their shoulders together.

"I appreciate you being honest with me," Sara said. Bending her knees, she hugged them to her chest and rested her chin on top.

"Same here. It pieces things together better in my mind. Your ED. How and why it manifested. Why you moved to New York after signing with that agent, even though Mom had just been diagnosed. God, that pissed me off. It seemed so selfish. Leaving when she needed us the most."

Guilt soured Sara's stomach as she recalled the fight she and Robin had in the kitchen at their parents' Scottsdale home the night before Sara left for New York. The palpable fear she'd lived with 24-7 back then. The seesaw between recovery and falling back on bad habits. The pressure to sign the sponsorship contract, thereby elevating her social media influencer status and increasing the odds of professional success.

The maelstrom of fears and pressures had driven Sara to yell hateful barbs in response to Robin's snide, disparaging digs.

In the end, Sara had stormed up to her room, then left in the morning without telling Robin good-bye.

Sara buried her face on her raised knees, ashamed.

"I was so scared," she murmured. "It felt like I was on borrowed time with Mom." Swiveling her head, she stared at her sister, desperate for her understanding. "That need to prove myself before she was gone drove me insane. Sometimes it still does. But I'm working to lessen the pressure."

And yet here she was with a fake boyfriend. Oh, the irony.

"Believe me, I get it." Robin laid a comforting hand on Sara's shoulder. "I've been there. The key to remember is where you are now. You're in a better place, physically and mentally. Sounds like you're kicking ass with your business. And you have time to make peace with Mom. Who is really wigging me out with her whole *kumbaya* movement."

"So, I guess I shouldn't ask if you want to hug it out then?" Sara teased.

"Oh my god, you too?!" Mock horror widened Robin's eyes before she surprised Sara by throwing her arms around her.

The hug was tight and tender and over quickly.

Robin pushed to her feet, wiping sand from the back of her bathing suit bottom. "Now don't get used to these heart-to-hearts. I think I've met my quota for at least the first half of the year. Deal?"

Sara grinned. "That's what you think. Mom might have other ideas."

"Ugh, don't remind me." Together they turned toward their parents. The beachcombers were headed back in their direction.

Edward held something in his palm, and Sara's dad peered down at it, their dark heads dipped close.

As if she sensed her daughters talking about her, Sara's mom lifted her gaze from the sandy shore to them. She raised one of her talented, highly trained hands, the ones that had saved and improved the lives of countless children in her OR for decades, in a tentative wave. The hopeful smile trembling on her lips belied the concern creasing her thin face.

"What class of mollusk did you find?" Robin asked, raising her voice to be heard over a boat approaching their slice of paradise. "Any luck spotting a cephalopod?"

"No. But I discovered a few intact bivalves," Edward called back. He held out his hand for her to investigate.

Robin traipsed through the shallow water toward her husband, their scientific identification of the shells Sara would have identified as peachy or creamy or simply pretty proving the veracity of Robin's earlier claim—she and Edward "got" each other.

The right partner could do that for a person.

Robin assumed Luis might be the one for Sara. There'd been plenty of times over the past five days that made her believe perhaps it could be true. But . . .

But as giving and passionate as he was when they made love, despite their private, intimate conversations, she couldn't squelch the niggling sensation that he still held part of himself back.

It was there when he deflected her question about what Carlos meant the other night when he whispered about fate and shaking things up. And the serendipitous timing of her visit coinciding with Luis's mandated time off.

Mandated?

According to her and Luis's game plan this entire week, they were supposed to deflect questions they didn't want to lie about. To others. Not between them.

What was he keeping from her?

Had all they shared only been a simple distraction to Luis?

Had she set herself up for disappointment by jumping into something too fast, aga—

Stop!

The command screamed inside her head. Halting the negative thought spiral. Don't go looking for bad, focus on the good, she repeated her therapist's advice.

Eyes closed, Sara tipped her face to the hot sun. She listened to the singsong call of birds from the sandbar's lush vegetation melding with a boat engine's rumble and Luis's excited, "I got it," as her brother tossed him the football. Underneath her feet, the sand shifted with the tide's pull. Warm water lapped at her legs, wrapping a piece of seaweed around her shin.

She soaked in all the details like a thirsty sea sponge. Snapped a mental picture memory she would carry with her, always.

Focus on the positive.

Today had been a *great* day, and there was more to come.

Chapter 20

"Today was a good one, huh?" Luis paused at the top of the steps leading to the rental home's front porch.

Wanting one last moment with Sara before meeting back up with her family, he guided her away from the thin rectangular windows outlining the front door, toward the rattan rockers where he could steal a kiss or two without being seen from inside.

"Yeah, it was," she said. Her smile brimmed with a joy that brightened his day like the morning sun peeking over the Atlantic's horizon.

"I'm proud of you," he told her, his hands on her shoulders drawing her closer.

"Me too. My talk with Robin went better than I thought. Should have done it sooner. Which I'm sure my therapist will tell me."

But she'd done it. Faced her fear of being honest and baring her pain with her sister. Shame slithered in Luis's chest.

Doggedly he ignored it, concentrating on Sara and the amazing progress she'd made with her family this week.

"You're incredible, you know that?" He dipped his head to brush his lips against hers. Craving more.

The straw beach bag hanging from her left wrist knocked against his hip when she wrapped her arms around his waist, going up on her toes to meet him stroke for stroke. Her moan of pleasure encouraged him. Hungry for all she offered, he cupped her butt, brought her lower body flush with his. Showing her exactly how quickly she aroused him.

If only her family weren't waiting for them inside.

Reluctantly Luis pulled back to nip at her chin. Take a couple love bites of her jawline. Sara lolled her head to the side, giving him easy access to her slender neck and the sensitive spot behind her ear. She smelled of sun, surf, and sweat . . . a heady combination that had him addicted to her. For her.

"If we keep this up," he murmured against her warm skin, "I won't be able to walk in there without making a spectacle of myself."

"Mmmm, but it feels so good."

It sure as hell did.

Everything about this entire week did. Almost too good.

Which was why his doom and gloom radar had been blipping ever since her family had driven away from the boat ramp near his house in Big Coppitt, heading home to wash up and start preparing the fish they'd caught for dinner while he and Sara cleaned and stored his boat.

The whole time she toiled beside him—scrubbing the deck, cleaning the workstation behind the boat helm where he'd cut their bait and cleaned the snapper, rinsing and storing the life vests—he couldn't stop thinking that she was the absolute perfect first mate. On the *Fired Up* and in his life.

He needed to tell her that. Get it out in the open.

But old insecurities refused to completely release their grip on him.

So, he had remained quiet. Waiting for the other shoe to drop. Hoping it wasn't a steel-toed boot that wound up kicking him in the balls.

"We should head inside," Sara said on a sigh.

Her hands explored his back, teased the waistband on his board shorts, driving him crazy because their foreplay couldn't lead to the satisfaction both of them wanted.

"Mom already texted. Everything's ready. They're just waiting on us before putting the fish on the grill." Sara stepped backward toward the door. Linking her fingers with his, she gave a little tug. Like he wouldn't follow her anywhere.

As soon as they entered the home's cool interior, Luis heard a loud clamor of voices coming from the living room.

"I don't understand?" Ruth's distressed cry meshed with Robin's worried, "Mother, calm down," and Jonathan's firm, "You should leave!"

"Enough!" Charles's deep baritone, stiff with authority, cut through the bedlam, silencing everyone. "I am sure Sara has a valid explanation for all of this."

Sara sent Luis a confused frown.

Before he could say anything, she hurried down the hall. The slap-slap-slap of her black flip-flops against the hardwood floor galvanized him into action. Tossing his truck keys in the shell-shaped bowl on the hutch, he followed quickly behind her.

"An explanation for what?" she asked seconds before they reached the living room. "Oh!"

She gasped, rearing back and bumping into Luis. Her arms went slack at her sides, the big beach bag dropping onto the floor at her feet.

Luis grabbed her hips to steady her, peering down with concern when she went slack in his arms, her complexion suddenly pale. He ran his gaze from her parents and Robin seated on the sand-colored chenille sofa. To Edward, propped on the sofa arm near his wife. To Jonathan and Carolyn, squashed together on the matching over-sized ottoman. And finally, to a clean-shaven, slick-looking pretty boy wearing a pinstriped suit and a polished, whitened-teeth smile.

The stranger rose from his seat in the overstuffed chair angled to the left of the sofa. He tugged the bottom of his suit coat sharply, his too-large smile confident. It reminded Luis of a smarmy salesman ready to sweet-talk you into a deal on a piece of swampy, mosquito-infested property in the Everglades.

Luis's hands tightened on Sara's hips. Dread oozed through him, thick and suffocating.

"Hello, Sara, it's good to see you," the stranger said.

"Ric, what the hell are you doing here?"

Sara's harsh, horrified question confirmed Luis's worst nightmare.

And just like that, the steel-toed boot he'd been anticipating swung hard and fast. With dead-on accuracy.

Ric's schmoozy smile, the fake one that had grated on her nerves once she learned to spot its insincerity, slipped the tiniest bit at Sara's blunt question. Good, she hoped the jerk was sweating underneath his sports coat.

"You invited me, remember?" he had the audacity to say. He spread his arms as if expecting her to give him a welcome hug. "I thought you'd be happy to see me."

She actually laughed, surprised by his narcissism. "I'm not sure why. The last thing I said to you was, 'Go to hell.'"

"Sara?" Her father rose from the sofa, his impervious Chief Cardiothoracic Surgeon regal bearing firmly in place. Even in khaki shorts and a tropical print shirt rather than his white lab coat and stethoscope.

"It's okay, Dad. I've got this." She held up a hand to stop her father and anyone else from stepping in. Although, based on Ruth's shocked expression and the splayed hand on her chest, Sara's mother was incapable of speaking at the moment. The rest of her family ran the gamut from pissed off: Jonathan, glaring at Ric, to haughty superiority juxtaposed with concern: Robin, her gaze skittering between Ric and their mom.

Ric had the gall to open his arms wider, still awaiting her welcome hug. "Come on, you didn't really mean it, did you?"

"You should go, Ric," Sara said firmly.

"Don't you—"

"Please don't make this any more awkward than it already is," she interrupted, trying to remember what about him had appealed to her in the first place. "We were finished before you bailed on me. We've both known it."

"But we're good together," he reasoned.

"On paper, maybe." Sara shook her head, resigned to a truth she had ignored far too long. "But the reality is, no, we're not. And I deserve better. We both do."

It had taken her this week, the difficult steps paired with the amazing highs, to reach this important milestone in her recovery.

Having the first heart-to-heart with her sister.

Joking with her brother and sharing tight hugs with her parents. Meeting and falling in love with Luis.

Her heart stuttered at the truth she hadn't fully admitted to herself, and she pressed a hand to her chest, scared, but certain.

"Sara, I drove all the—"

"She asked you to leave, buddy." Luis stepped close behind her.

Sara didn't need to look over her shoulder to picture his tight-jawed, don't-mess-with-me glare. The steel in his gruff voice warned her.

Ric's gaze moved between her and Luis for several tense seconds.

Sara eyed him dispassionately.

"Fine, I'm out." Ric held his hands up, as if he was doing them a favor by acquiescing.

"Thank you." She tipped her head, determined to remain polite.

"So much for nice gestures like surprising your girlfriend," Ric muttered as he strode toward her.

Luis swiftly moved forward, angling his large body to shield Sara from her ex. "Nice would have been not standing her up in the first place."

"Whatever."

Ric's inane response to Luis's truth exemplified the degree to which fortune had smiled on her last Friday. First with Ric's no-show and then with Luis stepping up in his amazing way.

Moments later, the front door slammed behind Ric. Sara flinched. Framed artwork rattled on the shaking walls and a tense silence settled over the living room.

Sara faced her parents. Dread and, strangely, relief clashed inside her. She hated admitting the insecurity behind her foolish plan, but she was so very tired of the little pretenses negatively coloring her relationship with Luis when they were around her family.

She was ready for the truth to be set free.

"Mom, Dad, this is Luis Navarro." She gestured at Luis. "Driver Engineer and master diver with the Key West Fire Department."

It felt awkward, introducing him when they had all spent so much time together already, but he deserved to be shown that respect.

Luis gave a polite nod. "Sir, ma'am."

His dark gaze cut to Sara, and she realized he was waiting to take his cue from her, the mastermind behind their charade. Even though it had all blown up, he gave her the power to decide how they would proceed.

"What's going on here, Sar-bear?" Her father's confused frown made her stomach churn.

Uncertain, Sara slid her gaze around the living room. Her mother and Jonathan stared at her with dismay. Edward's pity and Carolyn's compassion stung. But Robin's stone-faced cynicism and Luis's tight-jawed apprehension cut the deepest.

"I, uh . . . the thing is . . . well, it's, it's kinda funny . . ."

She trailed off, unsure where to start. But funny was definitely not it.

Pressing a hand to her temple and her whirling thoughts, she paced toward the sliding glass door that opened to the backyard oasis. The serenity of the waterfall pool called to her. Around the left side of the yard, the gate on the eight-foot-high privacy fence promised freedom, the potential to outrun the pain of her loved ones' disillusion with her. That unhealthy escape had almost worked in the past. But she refused to go that route again.

Desperation clawed at her chest. She wanted so badly to not undo the progress she had made with her family. Certain any explanation she gave would only confirm her ineptitude in their minds.

And yet lies would only tarnish and destroy. Doubts pushed her to spit out the truth and lay claim to her foolishness.

"Ric Montez. The real one." She jabbed a hand toward the front of the house. "Is, as I'm sure you have already noted, a self-centered jerk I should have dumped months ago. A fact that was confirmed when he decided not to show up last Friday. A decision he didn't share until I had already arrived. I knew Mom was excited to meet my boyfriend, and Dad—"

Sara took a tentative step toward her father, pleading with every cell in her body for him to understand. Instead she was met by the disappointment she had always feared from them. She spun away, shattered, to pace her agitation.

"We wanted this week to be a special celebration for Mom. No stress." She wrung her hands, fear and shame driving her, dogging her steps back and forth in front of the sliding glass door. "The last thing I wanted was Mom worrying, thinking I can't get my life together. I can. I *am*. It's just—anyway. Rather than admit I'd been stood up and . . . and put a damper on Mom's excitement . . . I hired Luis as my pretend boyfriend."

"What?!"

"No shit!"

"Unbelievable."

The cacophony of responses from her mother and siblings halted Sara's pacing. But when Luis reared back as if she had slapped him, Sara immediately realized her blunder.

"Luis, I didn't mean—"

He gave a brusque shake of his head and she broke off. His nostrils flared. Pain flashed in his eyes, followed quickly by disdain. A mask of stoicism slipped into place, hardening his chiseled features.

Hands fisted at his sides, back and shoulders erect as if he were facing his captain, Luis addressed her parents. "Ruth, Charles, my sincere apologies for the part I played in this fiasco. I hope you can believe me when I say that it has been a true pleasure meeting you, and the rest of your family." He dipped his head toward the others.

"Son, it's not clear why—"

"Excuse the interruption, sir," Luis told her father. "The why of all this is not mine to tell. Since it doesn't appear that my *services* are needed here anymore, I will grab my things and head out." Laying a hand on his chest, he gave her mom a slight bow. "Ruth, I sincerely admire your tenacity and new outlook on life. I wish you well."

Then, as she murmured a forlorn, "Thank you," Luis left the room. Without sparing Sara a single glance.

He rounded the banister in the foyer, where he stopped, head bowed, his large hand squeezing the curving balustrade.

Sara waited, breath trapped in her lungs. Praying he would look at her. Give her a sliver of hope that there was a chance to make things right between them.

Instead, he disappeared up the steps.

Eyes burning with unshed tears, she buried her face in her hands.

"Oh, sweetheart," her mother crooned. Moments later, her skinny arms were around Sara, offering comfort. "Honey, this doesn't make any sense."

Ashamed at how badly she had bungled her explanation, cheapening what she and Luis had shared, Sara welcomed her mother's embrace.

"I know it doesn't!" Tears threatening, she scrubbed at her eyes, desperate to make things right. Afraid she couldn't.

"Why, sweetie?"

"I just, I thought—" Sara broke off on a shuddering sob. "Because—"

"Because she made a poor decision."

Sara cringed at her sister's blunt truth.

"Based on the fact that many of us—myself included," Robin continued. "Have not taken her or her career seriously."

Shocked by her sister's support, Sara swiped at her tears, then tentatively met Robin's gaze. Her smug, you-know-I'm-right expression had never made Sara feel particularly loved. Until now.

"Frankly," Robin continued in her usual brusque delivery. "I don't know why you're still down here. You should be upstairs, working things out with the guy who spent the last five days helping all of us"—she held up her pointer finger, circling it to indicate the entire room—"feel more like a family and less like an institution. Am I right? Or am I right?"

"I don't kno—"

"That was a rhetorical question," Robin interrupted Sara, her lips curved in a smug grin. "We all know the answer."

An hysterical giggle bubbled up Sara's throat.

Her mom squeezed her arm around Sara's shoulders with an encouraging smile. Jonathan jerked his thumb toward the front of the house. And her dad, her dad gave the wink he'd greeted her with every time he peeked into her room to say good night when she was a kid.

Relief, sweet and pure, rained over her.

"I could totally kiss you right now," she told her sister, hands pressed over her racing heart.

"Yeah, wrong person," Robin complained. "Now get out of here."

Jonathan's laughter chased Sara down the hall and up the stairs where she stopped in front of her closed bedroom door.

Her pulse pounding, she wiped her clammy palms on her beach cover-up. She sucked in a shaky breath, then counted down from ten as she slowly released it.

The technique did absolutely nothing to calm her racing pulse.

Positives. She had to focus on the positives.

The truth was out. No more subterfuge. No more pretense.

They could be open and honest with everyone. With each other. That was a good thing.

Buoyed by her reasoning, Sara opened the door and stepped inside, closing it quietly behind her.

Luis stormed out of the bathroom, his shaving cream and black toiletry bag in his hands. He gaze cut to hers, but he didn't say anything as he continued to the bed where his duffel sat open, his clothes thrown haphazardly inside.

His drawer under the long plank desk sat open, empty. His running shoes and tan dress sneakers no longer sat in their spots next to the wardrobe. He wasn't wasting any time getting out of here. Away from her.

"Can we please talk for a moment?" she asked, choosing to stay by the wardrobe, giving him some space.

"I don't know what there is to say."

He jammed the shaving cream canister into his duffel with a harsh shove. Muscles flexed and bunched in his arms and torso, on full display through the supersize armholes ripped nearly to the hem of his tank. Barely concealed anger warred with his usual self-control. It pulsed off him as if he were Bruce Banner mid-transformation into the Hulk.

Confusion bled into her remorse. Yes, she could have, should have, explained the situation better. Did that warrant this degree of reproach?

"Don't leave like this," she pleaded.

"I was hired to do something that's no longer necessary."

"Look, that came out wrong downstairs."

"No worries. Now I know where we stand."

Scared by his implacable demeanor, she lifted her arms in supplication. "I was freaking out and described things poorly. I'm sorry. But is that really reason enough to blow things up between us?"

"Things. Things," he muttered under his breath. Grabbing one side of the open flap on his bag, he jerked it wider as he rummaged inside. "What *things* are you talking about? We had fun together. Achieved what we set out to do last Friday. I killed some time. You made progress with your family like you wanted. Missions accomplished. I mean, I'm assuming they'll forgive you for the lie; that's what families usually do."

"Except for you with Enrique, right?"

"No. Nu-uh." He backed away from the bed, shaking his finger at her as if she were one of his nephews in need of scolding. "I told you from the beginning, we're not bringing my family into this."

"But they already are."

"Don't go there." Luis continued backing up until his hamstrings hit the shelf desk behind him. A framed photograph of the rental home's owners standing on a sunset beach tipped over, clattering onto the desk. He ignored it.

Sara stepped toward him, gut instinct driving her to press. Make him confront the problems he brought to the table but ignored. "Your issues with the past, they've been in this room. On the beach, in your truck. Wherever we've been together, those issues have been there, too. Doing their part to hamper our chances of getting close. Truly close."

He blew out a harsh laugh. "You don't know what you're talking about."

A derisive grimace twisted his lips, but she saw it . . . the flash of recognition in his dark eyes before he turned away.

Sara prayed, harder than she'd ever prayed for anything, that he'd open up to her now. Instead, when he deigned to look back at her, it was gone. Pushed down, buried where he didn't have to deal with the past.

Anguish knifed deep into her chest with a poison-tipped blade.

"Tell me, what did Carlos mean about you having forced time off?" she asked.

Luis glared at her with his don't-mess-with-me scowl. He should know by now that it didn't work on her. She wasn't afraid of him. Only of his inability to let go of whatever kept him chained to the past.

"What did he mean?" she repeated, refusing to back down. This was too important. *They* were too important.

"Nothing. He's always talking without thinking." Luis crossed his arms, nudging a shoulder forward in an annoying *whatever* shrug. "Joking around. Gina complains that he—"

"Stop it!"

Luis's mouth thinned, his jaw muscle ticcing.

Hands on her hips, she tilted her head to stare through the skylight in the angled wall above him, seeking wisdom, guidance, anything that would help her break through this wall he had suddenly erected between them.

All she found was another gorgeous Key West sunset. The ball of fire had already begun its descent, leaving its breathtaking watercolor display across the sky in its wake. Right now, tourists and locals were gathered at Mallory Square, marveling at nature's artistic ability. Like she and Luis had done together not even a week ago.

Their relationship had skyrocketed into something amazing since then, only to dip in a nosedive set to end with a fiery crash and burn.

Sorrow clogged her throat as she stared back at his imposing figure. Legs spread in a wide stance. Impressive arms still crossed defiantly in front of his broad chest. Rugged face set in a stern mask marred by the disillusion in his dark eyes.

She swallowed, fighting the prick of hot tears.

"Please, don't do that," she pleaded, her voice raw with regret.

"Do what?"

"Deflect. That's what you're doing, right? It was our game plan. Deflect when someone asks a question we want to avoid or don't want to lie about."

He rolled his lips in as if holding back a response.

Sara spread her hands in front of her as if laying out all her cards. She had no Ace up her sleeve here. She only had her belief that when it came down to it, this kind, compassionate, goodhearted man would be honest with her. Because he valued honesty.

Luis sank down onto the shelf desk, anguish hollowing his dark eyes. "What do you want from me?" he rasped.

"The truth."

"The truth is that I'm not capable of going all in with something that is, or has been, based on lies. Not again."

"This situation is completely different. What you and I have shared, especially in here, in this room, has never been based on lies."

He shook his head, denying her claim, and Sara drew back, wounded by his rejection.

Horrified, she sank onto the edge of the bed as something new occurred to her. What if she was wrong? What if for him this *had* just been about killing time while he was off work? And he was fine ending things when she left on Friday. Which meant, unlike for her, it was no big deal to him if they ended things early.

"Maybe, maybe not," he said, neither confirming nor denying the terrible thoughts attaching to her brain like a nefarious vine. "But I can't risk it. I've done that once already. Taken a chance on a woman I thought I could help. Only, I got too involved, in too deep to see the truth. And nearly drowned in the end."

Each phrase he uttered was like a supersize sledgehammer pounding her hopes for their future into a fine dust the ocean breeze easily carried away. She wanted to rail at him to wake up. See what was right in front of him. Recognize the damage he was doing to his family, to himself, to the two of them because of his inability to move on from the past.

But years of therapy had taught her that an individual needed to possess the desire to achieve positive change in their own life. There was nothing she could say or do that would make any difference if Luis didn't want to let go of his fear.

And that's what this all boiled down to. Fear.

This strong, compassionate man who willingly ran into burning buildings to save others was too afraid to save himself. Too afraid to let the past go and live fully in the present. Even if, as much as it hurt, that meant without her.

"I'm not Mirna. I don't need saving," Sara told him, pressing a hand to her chest and the ache building there. "And I'm not your brother. In fact, I've been more than honest with you. I've trusted you with my biggest fears and secrets. Luis, I want to be with you, for more than just this week."

She rose off the bed, chin high. Defiant, in spite of the pain engulfing her. "But I need someone who's capable of being my true partner. If you can't forgive whoever or whatever it is you need to forgive so you're no longer living with one foot in the past and one in the present, then by all means, finish your packing and go. Leave." Her voice cracked as she gestured toward the door, certain if he walked through it he'd be taking her heart with him. "Because just like I said downstairs, I deserve better."

Luis stared at her intently, his expression a battle between misery and stoicism.

Every moment together . . . running into him at the airport, their first question and answer game, dancing at Mallory Square, late night talks in bed, playing dominoes and cards with her family, taking that first intimate step at South Beach, making passionate and tender and wild and sweet love, their silly Would You Rather game, *familia* dinner dodging marriage questions from his *mami*, titillating caresses on his boat today . . . they all tumbled through her mind like images in a video stuck on fast forward mode, speed racing to the end.

Only, she wanted them to keep replaying it. Reliving it all over again, together.

Her heart ached. Her insides clenched with fear and need. Every part of her tensed with anticipation and she prayed he would find it in him to trust her. Trust himself.

Luis pushed up off the shelf desk and snagged his duffel off the bed. Not even bothering to zip it closed, he hooked the bag's strap over his shoulder.

"You're absolutely right; you deserve better."

Sara's heart shattered, the sharp pieces ricocheting in her chest, leaving her wounded and bleeding.

"Take care of yourself, Sara," he said, his deep voice low, earnest. Sad.

The door clicked closed behind him and Sara slumped onto the bed.

She had done the right thing. Put herself out there. Asked him to meet her halfway. He simply didn't want to.

The pain of Luis's rejection consumed her. Tears burned her throat and eyes, falling in hot trails down her cheeks. She gave in to them. Deep, gut-wrenching sobs that came from a soul weary of not being enough for those she loved.

A tiny voice insisted that she *was* enough. She told herself that she would listen to it. Tomorrow. Tonight, the pain was too strong. Her tears fell faster.

Sometime later, her bedroom door creaked open and Sara peeked through her swollen eyes to find her mother tiptoeing inside. She crawled on the bed beside Sara and hugged her spoon-fashion.

"You cry all you want, sweetie. Mom's here for you."

Fresh tears soaked Sara's pillow and she hugged her mother's arms tighter.

Chapter 21

Luis turned down Eaton Street and sped away from the Vances' rental home, his head in a tailspin. His chest felt like an aluminum can that had been run over and crushed by a ladder truck. Twice.

What the hell had just happened?

In the blink of his fucking eyes, the day had gone from "best ever list" potential to total shit show.

Reeling from the reality that his entire world had bottomed out, he crooked his elbow on the driver's side windowpane and cradled his head in his hand.

As if he were walking through a call to file his report in the aftermath of a fire, he repeated the sequence of actions and dialogue that had led to his current situation. Him, alone in his truck; Sara, back at the house a devastated expression on her beautiful face.

One minute they were kissing on the front porch with him marveling at her strength of character, her ability to make that first move with her sister. The payoff it brought her.

The next, they were up in their room . . . her room . . . him feeling like a caged animal, agitated, uneasy. Scared.

His gaze cut to his black duffel, one of his running shoes teetering at the opening. About to fall onto the passenger seat where he'd tossed the bag in his haste to leave.

Shit, he'd done it. Left. Walked out. Turned his back on her. On the best thing that had happened to him in his life.

What the hell had he done?

Drowning in his own stupidity, he nearly blew through the red light at Duval. At the last second, he slammed on the brakes. The truck tires screeched to a halt on the hot asphalt. An older gentleman waiting to cross at the corner with his wife glared at Luis and wagged his finger, a reprimand for driving too fast in a heavily pedestrian part of town.

Rightfully chastened, Luis dipped his head in apology.

Sheesh. This was a new low for the infamous San Navarro. Pissing off old people he didn't even know.

Hurting the one person who had made him finally start to feel whole.

Frustration and disbelief swarmed like bees, stingers aimed and ready to do their damage. He smacked the steering wheel with the butt of his hand, pissed at the situation and himself.

The light changed and by sheer force of will Luis carefully eased his foot onto the gas pedal. He drove without thinking about a destination. Unsure of where or with whom he belonged if not with Sara.

He crossed intersections Sara and he had biked through, passed couples walking hand in hand like the two of them had done, cruised past the zero mile marker where he had snapped her smiling picture after she had taken a selfie. Eventually he wound up at the Southernmost Point and even in the waning early evening light he imagined her standing there with her family, the sun's rays glinting off her blond waves turning them to burnished gold.

Following the curving road, he realized where his subconscious had guided him.

South Beach.

The place where Sara had given him the safety net he needed to take that first step onto the high wire talking about what his past represented.

A baby step start to him dealing with the pain and betrayal and humiliation that had knocked him to his knees all those years ago. Burying it certainly hadn't helped. It was still there. Rearing its vicious head like a zombie, seemingly impossible to kill. Injuring relationships with his loved ones, causing problems on the job. Keeping him staunchly in that rut Carlos had complained about.

Case in point, the way he had rebuffed Anamaría the morning she showed up for yoga with Ruth. The times he'd been short with Mami when she tried to offer comforting advice. Barking brusque orders and second-guessing his crew during calls. Distancing himself from others at the station instead of shooting hoops or hitting the weights alongside his team. Refusing to consider that Enrique's explanations might hold up and, instead, virtually cutting off his younger brother.

Was that how he wanted to spend his life?

Walking away from emotional attachment. Beating up himself and those around him.

The Southernmost House, its peach and pastel Victorian architecture the subject of countless postcards and prints purchased by millions of the island's tourists, loomed on his right. Luis instinctively turned down the dead end of Duval. Lured by a siren's call he might never get out of his head. Somehow, he lucked into the last spot in front of the House.

A few people stood out on the dock extending into the Atlantic, their attention on nature's nightly artistic swirl of purple, peach, and reds across the sky. At this end of the island, sunset watching was a more quiet, subdued affair. That suited his current mood.

Hell, who was he kidding. It suited his usual mood. Until Sara.

The beach area and café on the left were less crowded than during the day but still fairly busy. A smattering of beachgoers lingered on the blue loungers, relaxing before going out for the night or sleeping off afternoon drinks, or maybe both. Others sat at the outside café tables, enjoying the kaleidoscope of colors drizzling across the horizon and into the ocean water.

Head bowed, his thoughts heavy with self-recrimination, Luis trudged toward the dock. He tried, but probably failed, to smile a return greeting to a young couple huddled in each other's arms where the sidewalk ended and the concrete dock began.

About halfway down, he turned his back to the setting sun's handiwork, choosing instead the shadowy shallow water where he and Sara had progressed their relationship from friends intent on ignoring their simmering attraction to sensual, intimate lovers. Where he'd held her in his arms, her long legs wrapped around his waist, keeping him safe from the demons he hadn't been able to slay. Where Sara had commiserated with him when he'd first told her about Mirna's treachery and his brother's presumed betrayal.

Presumed because, when it came down to it, Enrique had warned Mirna she needed to come clean. Sure, his guilty conscience had come a little too late, but it *had* come.

Luis had given Mirna a pass because comforting a dying woman had been the right thing to do. But her death had left him with no one to blame for her betrayal. Except his brother.

If Luis were truly honest, like Sara had asked him to be, it wasn't Enrique he was angry with. It was himself. For not seeing the signs. For getting so swept up in his saving-the-world mentality, he didn't realize that Mirna didn't really love him. And what he felt for her had been more a sense of obligation and compassion.

Nothing like the love he felt for Sara.

Because he did love her. *Dios mío*, how he loved her.

The admission knocked his legs out from under him, as if one of his siblings had snuck up behind him to swipe behind his knees. Luis crumbled to the concrete dock, catching himself with a hand and wincing when several sharp pebbles gouged his palm.

His elbow buckled and he landed on his ass, his feet dangling off the edge.

He stayed there, long after the sunset had faded. The dock and beach area emptied and a purply gray night brightened by fluorescent streetlights descended. The full moon illuminated a wavery silver path across the water's surface. And still, Luis couldn't bring himself to leave.

His phone buzzed in his shorts pocket and he dug it out. Carlos's name scrolled across the screen.

For a second, Luis thought about not answering it. Staying in his desolate world, apart from everyone.

Whether due to fate or God or a nerve tic, his thumb tapped the green icon to accept the call.

"Hey, *'mano*, what's going on?" Carlos's cheerful voice sounded loud in the quiet of the empty dock.

"Catching sunset."

"You mean you were; it's nine thirty. My bad, am I interrupting romantic time with Sara?"

Luis watched a fish jump in the water. The splash sent concentric circles across the surface, growing bigger, then disappearing as if they had never been. Would Sara, after creating such a huge splash in his life, disappear now that he had screwed things up?

"Hello, you still there? Need me to let you get back to Sara?" Carlos asked.

"No. It's just me."

"At Mallory Square?"

"No, I'm at South Beach. Look, did you need something?" he barked, frustrated with the who's-on-first routine with his brother.

"*Coño*, what crawled up your shirt? Gina and I finally got the boys in bed and I figured I'd see how it went out on the *Fired Up* with her *familia*. But I can see you're in butthead mode. Frankly, I'd hoped being with someone as cool as Sara would knock some sense into your sorry ass."

"My sorry ass messed things up. It's over."

The admission slipped out before Luis could stop it.

Several beats of silence passed; then he heard Carlos tell Gina, "I'll be right back, babe."

The heavy scraping sound of a sliding glass door in need of WD-40 opening, then closing, carried through the phone. He figured Carlos had moved outside by their pool for some privacy.

"What the hell's going on?" his brother asked, concern weaving through his tough-love act.

Luis heaved a sigh, part of him wanting to stick with his regular *nothing, I'm fine*. But that way led to more of this. Him sitting alone. Pining for the woman he loved.

"I'm hanging out here on the dock at South Beach asking myself the same damn question," he admitted.

"You want me to come meet you? Maybe grab a beer at Waterfront Brewery?"

Luis dug two fingers in the space between his brows, massaging at the headache throbbing behind his eyes. "You're probably not the brother I need to talk to."

"Wait a second, *qué dijiste?*"

"Don't be a jerk; you heard what I said."

Luis didn't have to be with Carlos to guess that the jokester probably had a finger stuck in his ear, pretending to clear out the cobwebs, certain he was hearing things.

"It's the same damn thing Sara insisted. Before I told her to mind her own business and walked out."

Picturing her anguish, the tears he had caused, gutted him.

"Look, you know me," Carlos finally said, all trace of humor gone from his voice. "I don't do that woo-woo, let's talk about our feelings crap. I've never pushed you to see a shrink who's gonna ask what you see when you look at a blob of ink that's like something one of my boys painted in art. Like I said before, you gotta find a way to get over what happened. Especially if it's screwing up what you've got going with Sara now."

Luis hung his head. Like an anchor tied around his neck, the weight of past hurts dragged him under the murky water of regret and recriminations.

"If you won't listen to me," Carlos continued. "Or Mami and Papi. Or your damn captain. Listen to Sara. Don't mess that up. The way you were looking at her the other night, the way she was looking at you. That's how Gina and I feel about each other. That shit's golden, *'mano*. Don't let her get away."

"What if I'm too late?" Luis's question came out in a rough whisper, born of fear and despair.

"Do whatever you have to do," Carlos advised. "Make peace with Enrique. Make peace with yourself. Then go get Sara back. Whip out some of your San Navarro magic that used to make you Mami's favorite. Till I gave her the first grandkids."

Luis barked out a laugh, the sound loud along the darkened pier. "I'll always be her favorite."

"Whatever. Now, I got a fine woman waiting inside for me, so I'm hanging up. No need to send me any money for my therapy fee, just know you'll be watching the boys the first weekend Gina and I can get away."

A tiny spark of hope ignited in Luis's chest as he slid his phone into his pocket. His mind whirred, plans taking shape, tightening his chest with determination and, *coño*, a measure of fear.

He needed to find Enrique, apologize for the self-blame Luis had put on his baby brother's shoulders. Follow Sara's example and take that first step to make amends.

Once he'd proven himself worthy of her, there was an incredible, amazing, inspiring, and sexy-as-hell woman he intended to win back.

Chapter 22

Luis pulled up to his parents' house early the next morning and parked next to Enrique's black SUV. Peering at the backyard, he was relieved to see their dad's pale green and white Everglades 253cc still tied to the canal dock.

Papi had mentioned plans to go fishing today once Enrique got off shift. Luis needed to talk to his brother before they left.

Now that his mind was made up, Luis didn't want to waste any more time.

He hopped from his truck just as Enrique strode out of the storage room they'd helped Papi build between the pillars elevating the older house. Several fishing rods in one hand and a beat-up gray tackle box in the other, Enrique headed toward the boat. Luis followed.

The moment Luis's footsteps hit the wooden deck at the foot of the back stairs, his brother called out, "*Oye,* Papi, I don't see—"

Enrique broke off when he glanced back to find Luis, not their dad, behind him. He frowned at Luis's chin jut of a hello.

"Mami and Papi are finishing breakfast." Enrique gestured toward the house with the fishing poles, then continued moving to Papi's pride and joy.

The *Salvación*, Papi's older-model Everglades fishing boat, had witnessed countless significant Navarro *familia* moments over the years. Luis and his brothers learning to navigate the channels in search of the best fishing and dive spots. José and Ramón reeling in their first fish. Carlos proposing to Gina at sunset the day after high school graduation.

Like its name implied, the 24-footer had also offered many of them salvation in the form of time spent soaking up the serenity of the water after a tough shift at the station. Now Luis hoped the old fishing boat could help him salvage his relationship with his brother.

"I'm not looking for Mami or Papi. I came to talk to you."

Enrique's boat shoes squeaked on the fiberglass deck as he climbed aboard the *Salvación* and stepped to set the gear by the center console. "I'm a little busy. We want to get out on the water before an afternoon storm rolls in."

"This won't take long."

"Look, I had a crappy shift." Enrique spun to face him. Tired lines bracketed his mouth. Dark shadows half-mooned under his hollowed-out eyes. "We lost a fifteen-year-old. Kid overdosed on fentanyl after his girlfriend broke up with him."

Coño. Luis grimaced, empathy burning in his chest. It was never easy losing a victim. But when the call involved a kid, that stuck with you. Long after your shift was over.

"Lo siento." Condolences rarely helped, but Luis uttered the words out of respect for his brother's obvious distress.

Enrique shrugged off the sentiment.

Like every Navarro, Luis knew his brother prided himself on believing the invisible Teflon body armor they mentally strapped on at the station made them invincible. Without it, or the ability to compartmentalize when shit went bad, no firefighter lasted very long on the job.

Or they wound up getting put on forced time off.

Luis winced, reminded of his own culpability in his current predicament.

"It is what it is. I'm fine." Enrique's dull voice was drowned out by the grating noise as he slid a blue and white chest cooler into the far corner of the boat's stern. Then he bent to peer at the engine nearby.

Luis recognized his brother's game. After a tough shift, keeping busy, especially with mundane activities, helped dull the troubling images, sounds, and smells that were hard to forget.

"Did the chaplain stop by the station this morning?" Luis asked. Not that he had availed himself of those services too often over the years.

"I bugged out before he showed up. I'm good, just feel for the kid's parents. It was senseless. Avoidable. Same as that college girl texting while driving a couple weeks ago."

"Same as Mirna."

Busy inspecting the bait prep area, his brother froze at Luis's calm mention of his ex's seldom-spoken name. Chiseled jaw stiff, lips a thinly pressed line of stark anger, his brother straightened and faced him. A small shake of Enrique's head warned Luis that his brother edged closer to the fighting line. Luis knew exactly how that felt. He'd toed that line for years.

It drained a man. Made him lash out at the wrong people. Like the woman he loved.

One hand outstretched in entreaty, Luis stepped toward the *Salvación*. "I don't want to argue. Or rehash the past."

Enrique's body stiffened. His fists tightened at his sides, but he remained silent.

"Mistakes were made on all sides. Including mine," Luis admitted. He scraped a trembling hand over his head, gripping his nape as the truth finally broke free. "Mostly Mirna's. But I should have caught the signs. Part of me knew something was off."

Antsy and uncomfortable under his brother's sharp scrutiny, Luis paced along the edge of the concrete seawall, his gaze drawn to the Gulf at the end of the canal. He'd spent innumerable hours out there seeking solace. Sara had taught him he had to work for it. Peace of mind and heart wouldn't magically find him.

"I wanted to think I could save her from her messed-up life," Luis went on. "But ultimately, I couldn't save her from herself."

"Or my spiteful threats that day." Enrique's gravelly admission drew Luis back to the boat.

Regret battled pain in Enrique's dark eyes. "My bitterness, mostly aimed at another woman who wasn't even there that day, pushed Mirna too far. I'll live with that responsibility, that guilt, for the rest of my life."

"Mirna made her own decisions. Good or bad. That's on her."

Enrique's harsh scoff frightened the neighbor's tabby sunning itself on the ledge separating the two seawalls. "And yet you easily forgave her. But not me."

Shame soured Luis's stomach. "That's the problem. I didn't, couldn't, forgive any of us. Especially her, though I gave Mirna the words before she died. I couldn't forget her betrayal. And it was easier to be mad at you than admit my own shortcomings. That kept me rooted in the past. Until . . . until now."

"Until Sara." Enrique spoke the words Luis had kept to himself. Uncomfortable bringing Sara's beautiful spirit and tenacity into a conversation filled with regret and mistakes.

Luis nodded.

The sun moved behind a cloud, darkening the morning sky, but Luis's tired spirit brightened when his brother's stiff shoulders relaxed. Despite the tired lines marring what Anamaría called Enrique's infamous *GQ* looks, a semblance of his cocky grin curved his lips, hinting at his roguish charm.

"I'm happy for you." Enrique took the wide step from the boat onto the seawall with ease. The two brothers shook hands, then wound up in a one-armed hug.

"Gracias, *hermano*."

"I'll regret that day at Bahia Honda for the rest of my life," Enrique said, remorse still haunting his voice.

"Let it go. Regret. Anger. They're soul suckers."

"I'll keep that in mind." Enrique's smile twisted into a tormented grimace.

The screen door to the back porch screeched its protest as someone opened it. Seconds later, lumbering footsteps pounded down the stairs.

"But"—Enrique punched Luis playfully in the arm—"I'll also remember today, when you showed up at Mami and Papi's looking like a lovesick puppy."

Luis dodged his younger brother's second punch, then looped his arm around Enrique's neck in a chokehold.

"You should be so lucky," Luis grunted as they jostled, each struggling to get the upper hand in their roughhousing.

"*Oye*, you two going to horse around or get my boat ready so we can head out?" their father bellowed from the bottom of the steps.

Luis and his brother broke apart. Though not before Enrique took one last jab at Luis's abdomen.

"Cheap shot," Luis grumbled. He straightened his T-shirt, giving his brother the side-eye. "We okay?"

The weight of encumbered history slipped away with Enrique's brusque nod.

Luis elbowed his brother playfully in the ribs, two could play the cheap shot game, before greeting his dad with a love smack on the shoulder on his way toward the house. Then, he took the back stairs by two in search of his mom. He didn't have to go far.

Inside the screened-porch area, his *mami* waited. Dressed in a bright floral house *bata* that fell mid-shin on her plump figure, she clasped her hands as if in prayer. A tremulous smile wavered on her lips. Her beautiful hazel eyes brimmed with tears.

"*¿Todo está bien?*" she asked.

No, everything was not good. Not yet anyway. But he'd cleared the air with his brother. That was the first step.

Rather than answer her with words, Luis looped his arms around his mom for a hug. He dropped a kiss beside the *moño* of hair on top of her head. "I can't guarantee no more fighting. But the old argument is over."

His *mami* sank into his embrace with a muffled cry. Her tears wet the front of his T-shirt, but Luis welcomed their release. These tears were ones of relief and joy. They were a long time coming, and he was ashamed of his part in causing them.

He tightened his arms around her, murmuring, "*Está bien*," over and over until she quieted. When she beamed a teary smile up at him and asked if he'd already eaten breakfast, he followed her inside. Cooking for her *familia* comforted her, and he could use a little of his *mami*'s comforting himself.

Memories of Sara's first *familia* dinner swarmed him as soon as he entered the house. There she was, laughing with his sister in the living room. Blushing at his *mami*'s blunt interrogation tactics during dinner but taking them in stride.

Sara belonged here. She belonged with him.

Luis prayed he would figure out how to make amends. It couldn't be too late for them.

No amount of forced time off would help him get his head on straight if he'd lost her.

Sara sat next to her sister-in-law crammed in the tiny third-row seat of her parents' rental SUV as they headed to the airport Friday morning.

Her father slowed at the curve in the road that brought them to the long stretch of Smathers Beach. Sara gazed out at the light sandy shore, the wide palm trees providing shade, and the hardy bushes planted near the sidewalk edge. The shallow shoreline, with its varying shades of blue, invited sunbathers to cool off in the warm, salty water and linger on the sandbars.

She sighed, wistful for what might have been, yet refusing to cry anymore when she thought of Luis and their time together.

It seemed like just yesterday, and at the same time much longer, that she'd first seen this two-mile stretch of public beach. Its food trucks and gear rental stands parked along the wide sidewalk still beckoned. Same as a week ago when she and Luis had driven away from the airport in his truck as strangers.

The day he'd said yes to her crazy idea. The day he had answered her SOS wearing his KWFD tee and scruffy workbooks, driving his behemoth of a truck. Her very own big-screen hero come to life like many a schoolgirl's fantasy.

But then, reality and his inability to live in the here and now had stepped in to blow up the slice of paradise she'd been living in for the past week.

Her cell phone vibrated in her hands. Another text message from Anamaría popped up on the screen. *Safe travels.*

Thanks! I'll be in touch next week, Sara answered.

The thumbs-up emoji appeared under her last message.

Unable to resist temptation, Sara scrolled up to read yesterday's part of their text thread. Anamaría had reached out, letting Sara know she understood if it was better that they change their scheduled lunch date to a video chat in the coming weeks. If Sara remained willing to offer Anamaría some business advice.

Luis's name appeared in their thread, and Sara stopped scrolling.

Anamaría: I don't know the details, but I'm sure my idiot brother messed up. Luis is a good guy. But let's face it, men can be dumbasses. At least in my experience.

Sara: "Dumbass" is an apt description. :-) Please know, my offer to help you still stands. If you're good with it, I'd rather not let my breakup with Luis get in the way.

Anamaría: I'm in. Let's compare schedules next week and see what works. Thanks!

Working with Anamaría, helping her learn how to grow her business and brand, was an exciting prospect for both of them. Sara and her agent had been discussing the idea of her teaching an online seminar for budding social media influencers. Mentoring Anamaría would give Sara useful experience for that project making it a win-win for them both.

Of course, the idea was back-burnered now that the contract for Sara's clothing line partnership with the investors had been electronically signed. Tomorrow afternoon, she and her agent planned to celebrate.

At least something had gone right this week.

The sorrow she hadn't been able to ditch since Luis had walked out Wednesday evening squeezed her chest. With a heavy sigh, she leaned her temple against the passenger window's cool glass and eyed a catamaran floating aimlessly on the water.

"You doing okay back there, sweetie?" her mom called from the front seat.

Carolyn patted Sara's thigh. Her mother hen mode remained in high gear, as it had since Sara came down for breakfast yesterday morning. Her face puffy thanks to her crying jag.

Sara shared a sad smile with her sister-in-law, then peeked in between Robin's and Edward's heads to give her mom a thumbs-up.

Actually, more than finalizing the contract had gone right over their family vacation. Sara's heart-to-heart with Robin. The beginnings of a plan to meet Jonathan and his family for a trip to Disney World later this summer. And Sara's blossoming relationship with her mother.

Ironically, crying your eyes out in the dark while your mom strokes your hair and lists all the things about you that are amazing had a cathartic, bonding effect on people. At least for the two of them it did.

The Vance family weren't the Brady Bunch, that's for sure. But Robin had said it best—not that anyone would admit it to her. Over the course of their time in Key West, in part thanks to Luis's calming disposition, they had all grown closer. Become more like a family than an institution. For that, Sara would always be grateful to him.

The airport's green and white sign appeared ahead on the left and her dad slowed to make the turn.

"The website said there's no curbside flight check-in," her dad announced. "We can return the rental, then head to check in. I think, Sara, you're United, and the rest of us are American, correct?"

"Yes, but it's a small airport. I'm sure our gates are close." Her mom twisted in the front passenger seat to address the rest of them.

The SUV drove between the terminal and the parking structure at a snail's pace with Sara's dad stopping to allow a family with two young kids to cross. As they neared the rental car return at the far end of the terminal, Sara stared up at the large mural of the cornflower blue, yellow, and white Key West Conch Republic flag painted over an entire section of the two-story building's facade.

Inevitably her gaze strayed farther down to where Monroe County Fire Rescue Station 7 was housed. Carlos's station. A pang of sorrow pierced her heart when she saw the parking spot where Luis's truck was now parked—

"Stop!"

The cry burst from her and Sara's dad stomped on the brakes. The rest of her family jerked forward in their seats.

"What the hell!" Robin scowled at Sara over her shoulder.

"He's here. Luis is here. That's his truck." Sara pointed at the supersize F-150 that, second to the *Fired Up*, was his most prized possession.

A car honked behind them before swerving to go around. An older uniformed security guard approached, no doubt to tell them they needed to keep moving.

The driver's side door of Luis's truck opened. He stepped down the running board, shut the door, and moved to the front of his truck. Hands wedged deep in the front pockets of his dark jeans, the muscles in his gorgeous arms straining at the short sleeves of his red polo, he stepped toward their vehicle.

The security guard drew closer. Luis called out and waved to the guy, who smiled a greeting at him. They exchanged words; then the guard ambled back toward the arrivals area of the terminal.

"Let me out!" Sara cried.

She tapped nervously on the back of the middle seat, urging Robin, Jonathan, and Edward to hurry up, so she could climb out.

Luis stopped walking as soon as the SUV's passenger door opened. He stood on the gravel area where they'd first met, waiting.

Heart in her throat, Sara clambered over the middle seat's slanted backrest, hiking her floral maxi dress out of the way to avoid tripping. She landed awkwardly on the asphalt, her dress catching on the bottom seat cushion.

Jonathan and Edward had moved around back to grab her suitcase. Robin stood between the side of the car and the open door, blocking Sara in. Her sister grasped her shoulders, gray eyes serious, her game face firmly in place.

"Promise me you're going to make him grovel," she demanded.

"Robin!" their parents chided in unison.

"I say grovel!" Grinning, Carolyn leaned out from the backseat to hand Sara her Goyard tote.

"You are corrupting my wife," Jonathan complained to their older sister, wheeling Sara's hard-sided silver carry-on behind him.

Robin ignored them all. She gave Sara's shoulders a tiny shake. "Promise me. You're worth it."

Sara gave her sister a quick hug and whispered, "I promise."

"Go get him," Carolyn said softly.

Robin stepped aside for Sara to pass.

When she reached the sidewalk, Sara turned back to her family. "I love you."

A smattering of "we love you, too," "back at ya," and Robin's "of course you do" brought a huge grin to Sara's face. Her siblings and Edward climbed back in the SUV. With everyone waving good-bye, her father drove off to circle the airport and try not to miss the left turn into the rental return area again.

Sara kept her gaze trained on their vehicle until it disappeared behind the redbrick ruins of the museum on the main road. She stared at the calm ocean across the street, the lone Jet Ski speeding by, skimming the water's surface. Suddenly nervous to face Luis.

Now that her family was gone and she stood on the hot sidewalk alone, she couldn't help wondering if maybe she had jumped the gun.

Just because he was here, the same time that she would need to arrive to make her direct fight to Newark, didn't necessarily mean he had come looking for her. Maybe he was visiting Carlos at work again.

"Sara, will you please come talk to me?" Luis's soft entreaty called to the lonely part of her soul that ached for him.

Grasping the carry-on bag's hard plastic handle, she swiveled in his direction, determinedly keeping her expression bland.

"The other day you seemed to think there was nothing left to say," she answered.

"The other day I acted like an idiot."

Surprised by his unexpected admission, she drew up short. Her suitcase kept rolling, clipping her sharply on the ankle as it smacked into her.

"Ow!" She bent down to grab the sore spot.

Gravel crunched as Luis moved to kneel at her feet. Blood oozed from an inch-long gash along her ankle. He wiped it with his thumb. Fresh blood oozed out again, dripping down to her heel.

He rose, sweeping her up in his arms.

"Luis!" she gasped. "What are you doing?"

"You need to elevate this and get a bandage on it to stop the bleeding." He strode to the driver's side of his truck, where he opened the door and set her on the high seat.

She watched, nonplussed by his overly protective behavior, as he retrieved her suitcase and returned to her.

"I can take care of this after I check in," she told him. "I'm sure it'll be fine."

"I have a first-aid kit in the backseat. Let me—"

"Luis, stop."

He paused, his hand on the driver's side passenger door handle. He closed his eyes and the air seemed to whoosh out of him. Now that she was closer, she noticed the pain-filled stress pinching his rugged features.

Like her, it didn't look like he had spent the last day and a half living it up in Key West.

"What are you doing?" she asked softly.

"I'm trying to apologize to you." The dejected frown creasing his brows and clouding his dark eyes made her heart ache.

"By bandaging my ankle?"

"Yes. No!" He rubbed a hand along the back of his head, clearly frustrated. At what remained to be seen though.

Sara dug in her purse for a pack of tissues and pulled one out. Luis took the tissue from her and applied pressure to the gash.

His large hand wrapped around her ankle, and she shivered at his touch. He glanced at her from under his lashes. The tenderness in his expression had tears stinging her eyes, but she blinked them away.

A moment of tenderness would not erase what had been said between them on Wednesday. Before she could let him in again, she had to know if anything had changed with him.

"I drove to the rental house at ten, but you were already gone," Luis said.

"We checked out and had a late breakfast at Camille's. Ana-maría recommended it."

He nodded, a strange hesitancy replacing his normally confident demeanor. Ducking his head, he checked her gash to find it continued bleeding, so he applied pressure again with his left hand. His right gently stroked the inside of her lower leg as if in comfort.

Desire flared, racing up her leg, tingling in her core.

She longed to drag him closer, feel his strong arms around her, and lose herself in his kiss. It would be good. Oh, so good.

But desire wasn't enough.

"What are you doing here?" she prodded when he didn't say anything.

"I remembered you were on the Newark flight. And I figured . . .

well, hoped, I guess . . . I might catch you. That maybe you'd stop here. At our spot, before you left."

"Our spot?"

He straightened, filling the doorway with his broad shoulders. "Yeah. One of many on the island, actually. It's like you've left your mark. Everywhere I look, everywhere I go, I see you."

"Interesting." Exhilarating, actually, but she couldn't let herself get excited. She'd spent the last part of her family's vacation crying her eyes out because of his inability to be honest with her. Now wariness ruled. "My mark, huh? Kinda makes me sound like a dog peeing my way around Old Town."

He laughed, the worried shadow blanketing his handsome face shifting a little.

She smiled at him, loving the tiny laugh lines that fanned out from his eyes. The curves that bracketed his mouth. Signs of happiness.

Softly, he tucked her hair behind her ear, caressed her jawline, then reached for her hand, holding it gently between both of his.

"I'm sorry I hurt you," he said, his expression filled with regret. "You were right: I was scared. It was easier to blame Enrique for everything when I didn't get to blame the one person who deserved most of it. Mirna. And myself. I felt foolish for not recognizing her duplicity. For mistaking my desire to help her for love. And again, I made Enrique take the brunt of that. But you . . ."

He raised their joined hands to press a kiss to hers. "Your bravery showed me that I could put myself out there. Admit my mistakes to Enrique. Start making amends with him. And most important, admit my feelings for you."

Luis peered at her intently as he kissed her knuckles again. Love . . . god, she hoped that was love . . . blazed in his dark eyes.

Sara bit her lip, afraid to move, afraid to breathe. Afraid if she blinked, she'd wake up and find this was all a dream.

"I love you, Sara Vance. My life was dull and lonely and stuck in a rut until you walked into it. All sunshine and smiles and strength and vulnerability and *everything* good. The other day you said you wanted to be with me, for more than a week. I hope my hardheadedness hasn't scared you away. Because I'm here now. I'm all in. If you can forgive—"

Sara cupped his strong jaw with her palms and kissed him.

For a second, Luis didn't move; then his arms encircled her, tugging her tightly against his chest. She slid to the edge of the seat and wrapped her legs around his waist.

He groaned and deepened their kiss, his mouth insistent and sweet. Heat filled her as their tongues danced, mated. She moaned with pleasure and his mouth moved to trail little nips at her jaw, her neck, the secret spot behind her ear.

"Please tell me this means yes," he whispered, sucking her sensitive earlobe into his warm mouth.

"You had me at 'I love you,'" she answered, her soul singing with elation. "And in case it wasn't clear, I love you, too."

Luis drew back, his intense gaze meeting hers. His big hands slid from her upper arms to the side of her neck, his thumbs softly caressing her collarbone.

"Total honesty here. I don't want a pretend seven-day island affair. I want it all, with you." He ducked down to press a chaste kiss on her forehead. "Only you."

Sara laid a hand over his heart. "Only you."

Luis flashed that sexy half smirk that never failed to make her giddy with awareness. Sara grinned back as she gathered his shirt in her fist and pulled him toward her.

He covered her mouth with his, their kiss hot, intense, breathtakingly beautiful. Just like the Key West sunset that colored the skies above this magical island that had brought them together, this week and for always.

Acknowledgments

I've always wanted to bring readers along for a visit to Key West, my adolescent home. The idea for the Navarros—a hardworking, faithful *familia* devoted to each other despite disagreements, dedicated to their jobs, and the island they call home—has been flitting through my imagination, Luis and Anamaría and Enrique's voices whispering in my ear for several years. But I couldn't have brought them all to life without the help and support of some incredible people.

First, to the Seller boys . . . well, men now, dear friends since high school . . . Eric, Keith, Mark, and John, my sincerest thanks for sharing your stories and answering my never-ending questions about life as a firefighter in the Keys. And special thanks to the firefighters at Monroe County Stations 7 & 8 who let me hang out for a day, put on some gear and work out, and tag along on a few calls . . . you're all heroes in my eyes. Any errors here or in the Navarro *familia* books to follow are all mine.

To the authors who talk me off the ledge when the words don't feel right and the pressure is on . . . my Fiction from the Heart sisters, my 4 Chicas Chat *hermanas*, and the ladies of the #Thermostat crew . . . this author life we love isn't always easy, but it's worthwhile in large part because of your friendship.

To the small but growing number of #LatinxRom authors . . . our stories, those of our *gente*, deserve to be shared and cherished, so we keep writing and calling for more! *¡Mil gracias por su apoyo y amistad!*

To Martin, Esi, and Norma, first-class editors and key members of my Kensington *familia* . . . my thanks for believing in me.

To Rebecca, my ah-mazing agent, thank you for taking this wild ride with me and for giving such fabulous pep talks.

I am nothing without *mi familia* . . . Mami, Papi, Jackie and JD, your faith and love are true blessings. And my girls . . . Alexa,

Gabby, and Belle, all I do is with the hopes of making you as proud of me as I am of you. You're my true inspiration!

And finally, to you, readers . . . heartfelt thanks for spending time with my Navarro *familia* and all the characters that I hold in my heart. I hope you come to love them as much as I do, and that you enjoy visiting my home town.

Abrazos/hugs,
Priscilla

There's more to come for the Navarro family
in the second book in the Keys to Love series,
available soon.

Love Priscilla Oliveras?
Keep reading for a sneak peek at
HIS PERFECT PARTNER,
the first book in the
Matched to Perfection series.

And be sure to get the whole series

HIS PERFECT PARTNER
HER PERFECT AFFAIR
THEIR PERFECT MELODY

Available now
wherever books are sold.

Chapter 1

The hottest guy to ever hit Oakton, Illinois, lingered outside her dance studio doorway, bringing Yazmine Fernandez to a stutter-step stop.

Seriously, the guy was like manna-from-heaven Latino *GQ*—from the top of his closely cropped jet-black hair, down his six-foot muscular frame, to the soles of his shiny wing-tip shoes.

Behind her, seven pairs of dancers scrambled to remember the next step in the preschool father-daughter Christmas dance. But Yazmine couldn't look away.

"Hey, a little help here?" One of the dads waved at her from the back row.

"Sorry." Yaz listened to the music for several beats, then fell back into step with their "I Saw Mommy Kissing Santa Claus" routine.

In the studio's mirror-lined wall she caught the stranger's flustered scowl. Even frowning, he still made her heart hop-skip in her chest.

Dios mío, she'd obviously neglected her social life for too long. Sure, her dance card had been pretty full with other obligations for nearly eighteen months now, but her lack of partner-dance practice shouldn't account for the heat prickling her insides. In her line of work, hunky guys were always on the cast list.

Then again, drop an attention-grabbing, well-built man into a room full of suburban soccer dads, and a woman's thoughts naturally wandered down a road better left untraveled.

Untraveled by her, anyway.

The newcomer's gaze skimmed across the people in her studio.

Yaz brightened her smile, but he turned away without even noticing her. Disappointed, and strangely self-conscious, she tugged at the bodice of her camisole leotard as she led the group into a jazz square.

The song's second verse transitioned to the chorus repetition, and Yaz wove through the front line to get a better look at the back row. "Left hand, Mr. Johnson—your other left."

The dad groaned, his daughter giggling at his exaggerated grimace.

"Don't worry, you'll get it." Yaz peeked over the child's shoulder to the studio doorway again.

The hunk glared down at his phone, flicking through something on the screen. His mouth thinned as he slid the cell into the pocket of his suit jacket. Yaz's stomach executed a jittery little sashay.

This guy had to be in the wrong place. No way she'd forget meeting him before at the dance studio.

Yaz dropped her gaze to his left ring finger. Bare.

Not that it should matter to her. She'd learned the hard way it was much better to look than to touch. Especially if a girl didn't want to get her fingers singed, or her heart flambéed.

Besides, as soon as Papi's oncologist gave him the all-clear, she'd be on the first direct flight out of Chicago, headed back to New York and Broadway. Nothing would stand in her way this time.

The holiday song drew to a close. Fathers bowed. Daughters curtsied. GQ stepped into her studio.

Anticipation fluttered a million, spastic butterfly wings in her chest. He probably needed directions to another business close by.

Yaz hurried toward him. "Excuse me, do you need some help?"

Or, better yet, a no-strings-attached date for a night out in nearby Chicago?

"Papá!"

Maria Garcia jumped up from her seat on the floor along the back wall, running to fling her arms around the man's thighs. Everyone else in the class turned at the commotion.

Increíble. Apparently the hunk *did* belong here. To the usually subdued, adorable five-year-old who'd joined the class in mid-September.

At his daughter's screech of delight, the worried scowl vanished from the man's features. Relief and joy surged in. For a moment Yaz bought into his pleasure, savoring the smile that softened his chiseled face with boyish charm.

Then, with the stinging slap of a bitter Chicago wind, Yaz recalled the number of practices Maria's father had skipped over the past two months—the number of classes when the child had sat alone in the back and the number of times she'd had to partner with Mrs. Buckley, her grandmotherly nanny, because her father had failed to show up as promised. Again.

The attraction searing through Yaz's body cooled as fast as if she'd dunked herself into an ice bath after a marathon day of rehearsal.

Bendito sea Dios, the prodigal father, more focused on his advertising career than his child, had finally arrived—tardy, of course. Blessed be God, indeed.

"You made it!" Surprise heightened Maria's high-pitched cry.

"I sure did, *chiquita*." Mr. Garcia scooped up his daughter and spun her around, the picture of familial bliss.

Maria grinned with pleasure.

Still, Yaz couldn't stop remembering the hurt in the little girl's eyes over the past weeks because of her father's absences. Legs shaking, she strode to the corner table at the front of the room and jabbed the stop button on her iPod speakers. "Everyone, let's take a five-minute water break."

Mr. Garcia and Maria stepped to the side of the room so the other class members could head to the lobby area.

Anger over the weeks of disappointment he'd brought on his daughter pulsed a heavy, deep bass beat in Yaz's chest. She sucked in what was supposed to be a calming breath and counted to ten. Then twenty.

So much for her brief fantasy of a friendly night out with a hunky stranger. Her first since long before she'd left New York to come home. That definitely wasn't going to happen. Not with this man.

* * *

"M'ija, I'm sorry I'm late."

The trite words burned Tomás's lips with their insignificance. No matter how many times he apologized, he knew he'd never forget the dejection crumpling Maria's shoulders when he'd finally spotted her sitting in the back of the room. Knowing he'd put the sadness there was like a swift punch to his gut.

He tried so damn hard to be a good father. Still, more and more often it felt like he was falling short.

"It's okay." Maria gave him a sad version of her normally sunny smile. "At least you made it for a little while this time."

This time.

Guilt latched onto him, sinking its claws into his shoulders. Talk about feeling like a loser single parent. Lately, his drive to be the best at work had him short-changing his daughter. Sure, he'd landed a prize client today, but the extended negotiations had made him leave the office late, remorse riding shotgun on his mad dash out of the city.

"Come on, Papá." Maria linked their fingers together. "I want you to meet Ms. Yazmine. 'Member, I told you about her."

Ha, it was impossible to forget. All Maria talked about was her new dance instructor. Apparently the lady walked on water.

Maria pointed to a tall, slender woman standing at a corner table up front. The previously crowded room and his anxiety over not being able to find Maria when he'd first arrived had to be the only explanation for his not noticing the beautiful instructor earlier.

Now, there was no missing her.

Ms. Yazmine's black hair was pulled back in a sleek bun low on her nape. On someone else the style might have looked severe. On her, it accentuated her smooth forehead, high cheekbones, elegant neck, and sun-kissed olive skin. She wore a black, figure-hugging spaghetti-strap leotard with tights, and a short, filmy skirt fluttered over the thighs of her long, toned legs.

Hands clasped, feet set in a dance position he couldn't name, Ms. Yazmine had him picturing a different kind of position altogether. One not quite appropriate for their current surroundings.

Heat pooled low in his body. *Ay, ay, ay,* this woman could sell sand in a desert. She was an ad-man's dream.

Hell, any man's dream.

A guy could probably get used to having a woman like her dancing around in his life.

Tomás sucked in a surprised breath, wondering where *that* thought had come from.

"*Vente.*" Maria paired her command for him to come with a tug of his hand, dragging him across the floor. "Ms. Yazmine, I want you to meet my *papá.*"

Tomás could have sworn he saw her flinch, but the instructor set her iPod down and slowly turned away from the desk. She gave him a stiff, yet polite, smile.

"My apologies for being late. It's nice to meet you." Tomás held out his hand, noting Ms. Yazmine's hesitation before she placed her cool hand in his.

"I'm glad you could finally join us, Mr. Garcia." She might appear delicate, but her grip was as firm as her voice. "I was beginning to wonder if you'd make it."

There was no missing the reproach. Clearly they were starting off on the wrong note.

"Longer than anticipated meetings, shifting schedules. Sometimes they can't be avoided, no matter how hard I try. But I'm here now, ready to give this a shot." He swung an arm out to encompass the room, tamping down his irritation at having to explain himself. After all, he *was* twenty minutes late.

Experience, and his *mamá*'s advice, reminded him that he'd catch more flies with *leche quemada* than vinegar. Something she'd often said as she spread the sweet caramel confection on his morning toast.

"Maria and Mrs. Buckley have been trying to teach me at home, but I've been told you're the expert."

Yazmine arched a brow. Probably letting him know she wouldn't buy his compliment so easily. Strangely, he found that appealing.

"I appreciate the thought," she said. "My students make my job easy though. They work hard both in and out of class."

"Well, I've got a mean salsa. I can handle a merengue, or a Mexican polka, but ballet . . . ?" He shook his head with a grimace. "Not really one of my strong suits."

"I can probably help with that." The edges of her generous mouth curved up, smoothing the censure from her voice.

Aha! A crack in her prima donna shell.

"*Sí,* Papá can't really get the grapevine." Maria's dark brown curls bounced as she crisscrossed her feet to demonstrate the step. "But I said you could help him. 'Cuz you helped me. You're the bestest dancer in the whole world."

Yazmine knelt down to Maria's eye level, flashing her a genuine smile brimming with warmth. An uncomfortable pang rippled through him as he wondered what it would be like to have Yazmine smile at him in the same welcoming way.

He cut the thought off before it went any further, his sense of self-preservation sharpened in the years since his divorce.

"Thanks for your vote of confidence," Ms. Yazmine told Maria. "Even better, I love seeing you so excited about dancing." She tapped Maria's nose gently, eliciting a giggle Tomás hadn't heard often enough in the two months since he'd moved them out of Chicago and into the more family-friendly suburbs forty-five minutes northwest of the city.

Right now, he didn't quite know what to make of Yazmine Fernandez. Her engaging smile and lithe body captivated him. Her subtle reprimand rankled. But he'd kiss the ground she walked on if she helped his daughter shake off her recently acquired reticence. He missed Maria's spunkiness.

Nothing he'd tried, not an impromptu trip to the zoo or an afternoon picnic in Grant Park, had helped. She'd been outgoing and talkative in her old kindergarten class. Here in Oakton, she'd withdrawn and still wasn't quite comfortable with others.

"I'm gonna be a famous dancer just like you." Maria's brown eyes lit up like Christmas morning.

"Sounds like a good plan. Why don't you go grab a quick drink from the fountain while I chat with your *papá*?"

"Okay!" Maria skipped off and Yazmine rose with a grace she'd undoubtedly acquired from a million or so dance classes.

"You're great with her," Tomás said.

"She's a pleasure to have in class. All my students are."

Alluring *and* comfortable with kids.

Stepping closer to the desk, Yazmine picked up a white binder. "Actually, I've found that any problems I encounter teaching are few and far between." She flicked a quick glance his way. "And rarely involve the children themselves."

There it was again, the hint of admonition from her. It pricked his conscience, making him feel like a front-runner for Worst Father of the Year.

Damn. He tightened his jaw, uncertain whom he was annoyed with more. Her for making the assumption or himself for having to admit that she might have a point.

"I take it you see me as one of those problems."

"I don't mean it to sound that way." Yazmine's chest rose and fell on a sigh. "Maria really wants to perform this routine in the Christmas show. Honestly, I'd love for the two of you to share that experience. But if you check the attendance sheet, I'm not sure it's going to be possible."

Yazmine leaned toward him so he could peer at the open binder with her. The scent of violets wafted in the air, tickling his nose. Unable to resist, he dragged in a deep breath, filling his lungs with her tantalizing perfume.

"Even though this is a special performance, the Hanson Academy of Dance attendance policy still applies. If a dancer had this many absences in a class for another number, we'd pull him from the show." Yazmine tapped the page in front of them.

He followed her pink-tipped finger from his neatly printed name across the row of spaces that should have been checked off to indicate his attendance. The blank spaces were glaring proof of his parental short-comings.

The violets enveloping him withered, choked by the remorse settling around him like a toxic mushroom cloud.

"I'm doing my best." The words were more of a muttered curse, pushed through his gritted teeth.

"Please, you don't have to defend yourself to me." Yazmine pressed the open binder to her chest, concern blanketing her face. "Maria's the one who needs to know that this is important to you."

He gave her a curt nod, not trusting his voice to betray his growing frustration. Maybe he wasn't doing such a class-act job at parenting, but with his nanny's help he'd learn. Get better. He and Maria would be fine. Failure was not an option.

"Look, I shouldn't have—" Yazmine broke off. Her lips pulled down with resignation. "I simply want you to be aware of the situation. That's all."

Tomás was tempted to walk away, but he kept his feet firmly planted. He hadn't run from anything in his entire life. Now was not the time to start. No way would a simple father-daughter dance or an appealing yet prickly instructor get the best of him. Maria depended on him.

"Why don't we see how it goes today, and then we'll take it from there," Yazmine offered as the students returned.

Maria skip-hopped into the room. With a sweet grin that instantly relaxed his shoulders, she waved him over to join her in the back line of dancers. The breath-stealing tightness in his chest instantly eased. At the same time, his resolve to do his best for her hardened like quick-drying cement.

"Deal."

Yazmine blinked at his brusque tone.

"Don't worry. I can do this," he assured her, softening his words with a smile. "I won't let my daughter, or you, down." He made a silly face at Maria and she giggled and, that easily, wrapped him around her finger a little tighter.

From the moment he'd held her tiny squirming body in his arms, he'd vowed to do whatever it took to make his baby girl happy. Nothing would change that.

Tomás slipped off his suit jacket and tossed it over the barre. Then he pocketed his cufflinks and deftly rolled up the sleeves of his white dress shirt as he moved next to Maria. The opening strains of "I Saw Mommy Kissing Santa Claus" filled the studio once more.

"Here we go, everyone! Five, six, seven, eight." Yazmine clapped as she counted out the beats.

Beside him, Maria counted aloud as well, the same way they'd practiced at home. He tried following along, but with his thoughts lingering on the intriguing instructor, he fumbled the opening steps.

"*Ay*, Papá, the other way." Maria nudged him with her elbow when he nearly collided with the dad next to them.

"Yeah, I know," he grumbled.

Great. It probably looked like he'd never practiced at home at all. Maybe Ms. Yazmine hadn't noticed.

He peeked up at her to check.

Her lips quirked with the hint of a teasing smirk he should have found annoying rather than enticing, she exaggerated her steps for him to catch on.

Before long, Tomás understood why Maria was so enamored with her teacher. Why Maria brimmed with excitement when she spoke of her dance class.

Yazmine Fernandez was great at what she did, full of a vibrant, intoxicating energy. Whether calling out the next move with encouragement, or waving her left hand at a dad reaching out to twist his daughter toward him with the wrong arm, she showed absolutely no sign of impatience. Her pride and delight in her job were palpable forces.

He could relate to that.

In spite of the negative tone of their earlier conversation, her charisma and charm beckoned him like a front porch light welcoming a weary traveler too long on the road. Too long on his own.

His mind lost in the idea of Yazmine waiting at home for him, Tomás bumped into Maria, knocking her off balance.

"Oof ! Not that foot, Papá."

"*¡Perdón!* Sorry, I got it." Damn, between his minimal practice and his mind's unwelcome meanderings, he was doing a spot-on impersonation of someone with two left feet.

Halfway through the dance his frustration level rose again when he and Maria were forced to stand off to the side because he didn't know the rest of the steps.

"You'll learn it, Papá," Maria assured him. "We'll keep practicing together."

Together.

The word spread warmth through him as if he'd taken a sip of prime Mexican tequila. It had been Maria and him, the two of them together, since the day Kristine had chosen an overseas promotion over their marriage and child. It hadn't been easy, but he would figure things out. Even if it meant learning ballet to make Maria happy.

The strains of the song drew to a close and the rest of the dancers applauded everyone's efforts.

"That's it for this week." Yazmine glided over to pause the music.

Sighs of relief along with a muttered, "Thank goodness" rippled through the crowd of fathers.

"You're all doing a great job." Sincerity colored Yazmine's words, shone in the reassuring expression she shared with her students. "Remember to practice over the Thanksgiving holiday next week. We'll see you the following Wednesday. Same time, same place, same go-get-'em attitudes from everyone. Right?"

Across the room she sent Tomás a telling glance. Message received. No more absences. No tardiness.

She didn't think too highly of him. While normally he'd shrug that off as none of his concern, for some inexplicable reason it really bugged him.

He should smooth things over—for Maria's sake. Ms. Yazmine *was* her favorite dance teacher after all.

While everyone else headed for the coatrack by the school's front door, Yazmine stayed near the desk, thumbing through her iPod display screen. She didn't appear to be in a hurry to leave. Perfect.

"Hey, *m'ija*," Tomás told Maria, "grab your coat and I'll be right there."

"Okay." Curls bouncing, Maria danced out of the studio.

Relief at seeing her acting more like her old self tempered his unease over the potentially uncomfortable conversation in store for him.

Yazmine gathered her belongings as he approached her, steeling himself to play nicely with the sexy taskmaster. She glanced up, her brow furrowing when she saw him. "Is there something you needed?"

Loaded question.

Somehow in the course of half a dance lesson this woman had his mind considering ideas he hadn't allowed himself in years.

"We didn't really start off on the right foot tonight. I wanted to apolo—"

"No, don't." She held up a hand, her mouth set in a firm, no-arguing-with-me line.

"Excuse me?"

"I'm the one who should apologize. It's not—" She broke off, rubbing a hand across the worry lines marking her forehead, then smoothing it over her already slick bun before releasing a heavy sigh. "I've had a lot going on today. I probably came on a little too strong with you earlier."

Sincere words, but spoken with a mouth quirked in the opposite direction of a smile. The kind of apology his *mamá* would have made him try again.

For some bizarre reason Yazmine's half-baked apology charmed him. Made him want to change the negative vibe arcing between them, without looking too closely at why he felt compelled to do so.

"Apology accepted. And appreciated." He flashed her a reassuring smile. The one he used to sweet-talk his staunchest opponents in the boardroom.

Her frown deepened. Man, she was a tough cookie.

He didn't move, didn't change his expression. Allowed his smile to work its magic.

Then, like a soldier reporting for duty, she straightened her shoulders and gave him the barest hint of a nod. "Okay, then. You held your own fairly well today in class, up to a point. I can get you ready in time for the Christmas recital, *if* you don't ditch any more of our practices."

There it was again, the hint of a challenge. As if she still questioned his ability to hold up his end of the bargain.

Crossing his arms, Tomás gave Yazmine the once-over, intrigued, if slightly exasperated, by her conflicting signals.

Stern disciplinarian ruling her studio.

Affable teacher who charmed his daughter.

Sexy siren luring him with a single glance.

Megawatt smile on a mouth that didn't mince words.

Why should it matter whether or not she liked him? He was long past caring what others thought. Long past high school where, as the "wetback" from the wrong side of town on scholarship at Deburg Prep, he'd felt desperate for acceptance.

Maria's sing-song voice carried in from the lobby.

That's why he was still here trying to charm Yazmine Fernandez. Maria's happiness made this matter.

"Look, we don't have to be friends. Hell, we can settle for acquaintances."

"Mr. Garcia, I think we—"

"I'm not finished."

Yazmine blinked at his interruption.

"Maria's the most important person in my life. From the way you handled the class tonight, I can see why she admires you. I'm doing the best I can right now. Yeah, I'm aggravated when it's not good enough. But I'll do anything for my daughter, even get up on a stage and make a fool of myself. As long as she's happy. That's what counts. I'm pretty certain that's one thing you and I can both agree on. Right?"

His words hung in the air, an olive branch if she chose to accept it.

After several tension-filled moments, he watched as Yazmine's shoulders visibly relaxed. The worry lines marring her beautiful face smoothed and the tightness around her mouth eased.

Tomás waited, uncertain whether he'd get another swipe of her sharp tongue or one of her infectious smiles, calling himself all kinds of crazy for wanting the latter.

Ay Dios mío. Yazmine's heart skipped. Tomás Garcia in protective Papa Bear mode, his impassioned words gruff with sincerity, presented quite a persuasive package.

Arms crossed, she eyed him, trying to gauge how much of what he said was true. How much was a good spin from a man who made his living convincing people to buy what he was selling.

She'd played the workaholic game before, gotten hurt and hurt others. It was a dangerous pastime.

"Honestly, it's nice to hear how much you care about your daughter," she said.

"I'm glad you approve."

She narrowed her gaze at him, not sure whether he was teasing or patronizing her. "Look, I enjoy having Maria in my class, and I do my best to be a good teacher."

"Like I said, based on today I'd say you're quite successful. My daughter certainly thinks you can do no wrong." Tomás hitched a broad shoulder in a half shrug. "How about we try this again. I can make a better first impression."

"There's no need. It's fine. I respect someone who's dedicated to his work."

Hands on his hips, Tomás's eyes flashed with skepticism. "I sense a 'but' you're leaving out."

Ay, the man was the epitome of hardheaded. When it came down to it, she could be too. "You really want to know?"

"I wouldn't ask if I didn't."

"Fine. *But*," she stressed the word, "you should make sure it doesn't leave your loved ones feeling second-rate."

His jaw muscles tightened and Yaz swallowed back a curse. Great, she'd crossed the line. Yeah, he'd pushed, but he was also a student's parent. She should have remembered that and thought twice before challenging him.

"Maria's a wonderful addition to my class," Yaz continued, a pale attempt at making amends, but she had to try. "Granted, she's usually a lot more reserved than today, but she's coming along fine."

"She hasn't dealt with our move here as well as I'd hoped." Tomás turned to glance back toward the lobby. Yazmine followed the direction of his gaze and saw Maria sitting with another student on one of the sofas. "I'm beginning to wonder if the move was a mistake."

Tomás Garcia as the confident ad-man she could easily deal with. His concerned-father side strummed a softer chord within her. A chord she struggled to silence. "It's only been a few months since you arrived in Oakton. Change can be hard on a kid, no matter her age or the situation. Give it time."

"You speaking from experience?"

She shrugged off the question. No need to spill her guts to him. To anyone.

Tomás dipped his head in a slight nod. "Time. That's what Mrs. B keeps telling me."

"Listen to her. Your nanny's a wise woman."

His mouth curved up and his dimple made another sexy appearance. A spark of awareness sizzled low in her belly.

Dios mío, she should have walked away after she'd pissed him off. She had no business feeling any sort of attraction to him. She had no room for distractions.

Scooping up her binder, Yaz eased around Tomás, heading for the door. He fell into step alongside her, brushing up against her. The hair on his forearm tickled her skin, sending pinpoints of awareness peppering up her arm.

Yaz took a deep, steadying breath only to find herself appreciating his musky scent. *Basta*, she chided herself. Enough already.

"So you think it's too soon for me to worry about her?" Tomás asked.

"Uh, yeah." Yaz tried to focus on his question rather than her unpredictable hormones. "I'll admit at first I figured Maria was simply a shy child. But every once in a while I'd see a flash of her spunk. Then, when I mentioned the Christmas show, her hand shot up to volunteer. It actually took me by surprise."

"You and me both," Tomás grumbled, his chuckle softening his dry tone. "I thought she was kidding when she told me."

His humble words and easygoing charm were at odds with the man Yaz had envisioned during the weeks of his no-show routine.

"This dance class stuff isn't really my forte," Tomás muttered.

"Don't worry about the recital. If you're serious about practicing, you'll catch on. You did a decent job today."

"But there's room for improvement?"

"Yeah."

He threw back his head and laughed, a rich sound that swirled around her, enticing her to join in.

"You don't pull any punches, do you?" he asked.

"I get the impression you can take it. Though, I guess, I probably overstepped my bounds earlier . . ."

"Man, that apology is killing you. Isn't it?" He moved quickly, stepping in front of her to block her path.

Keep walking, she warned herself, unnerved that he seemed to read her so easily. That didn't bode well for a girl with secrets she didn't want to share.

"You just can't bring yourself to say the words if you don't mean them, can you?" The note of respect in his voice intrigued her.

"No, not really."

"Good. I'd rather hear the truth than some candy-coated lie. I'm a big boy."

It was like a hand-delivered invitation, but she stopped herself, barely, from letting her gaze travel the length of him.

What she would give for this man's level of self-confidence. But she was great at pretending. "I take every aspect of dance seriously. Even the father-daughter Christmas routine."

"And it's important to Maria, so that makes it important to me. Maybe we have more in common than we realized."

His naughty grin widened and Yaz gulped. Between his cleft chin, hide-and-seek dimple, and smiling eyes, she could get in some serious trouble with this guy.

The truth was, after her farce of an engagement to Victor had ended, she knew her life had no room for personal relationships. She understood well the sacrifices needed for her to be successful in New York. Papi had given up his dreams of stardom for their family. She owed it to him to see his dream for her come true.

Her heart heavy with the fear of disappointing her loved ones, Yaz edged away from Tomás Garcia's distraction. "Like I said, as long as you keep practicing and make it to class, you'll catch on, Mr. Garcia."

"Tomás." He placed a hand on her arm to stop her. Heat surged through her at his touch. "My name is Tomás. *Encantado de conocerte.*"

Dios mío, he was pleased to meet her?

The man stood less than a foot away, close enough that she could see his five o'clock shadow. Tempting enough to make her wonder if she pressed a hand to his starched, white shirt, would she find his heart pounding as fast as hers?

Ay bendito, she was undeniably losing it.

"Well, uh, Tomás, we'll see you after the Thanksgiving break." That gave her plenty of time to get her head screwed back on straight.

"Oh, you will certainly see me after the holiday. You can count on it." He gave her a cheeky wink, then strode out of the studio.

Her knees wobbled. Those words coming from any other parent wouldn't have made her think twice. Coming from Tomás Garcia, they made her think about a lot more than what should have been a harmless dance class.